TOO SOON

A Novel

Betty Shamieh

AVID READER PRESS

NEW YORK AMSTERDAM/ANTWERP LONDON TORONTO SYDNEY NEW DELHI

AVID READER PRESS
An Imprint of Simon & Schuster, LLC
1230 Avenue of the Americas
New York, NY 10020

First Avid Reader Press hardcover edition January 2025

AVID READER PRESS and colophon are trademarks of Simon & Schuster, LLC

For information about special discounts for bulk purchases, please contact Simon & Schuster Special Sales at 1-866-506-1949 or business@simonandschuster.com.

The Simon & Schuster Speakers Bureau can bring authors to your live event. For more information or to book an event contact the Simon & Schuster Speakers Bureau at 1-866-248-3049 or visit our website at www.simonspeakers.com.

Interior design by Ruth Lee-Mui

Manufactured in the United States of America

1   3   5   7   9   10   8   6   4   2

Library of Congress Cataloging-in-Publication Data

Names: Shamieh, Betty, author.
Title: Too soon : a novel / Betty Shamieh.
Description: First Avid Reader Press hardcover edition. | New York : Avid Reader Press, 2025.
Identifiers: LCCN 2024030545 (print) | LCCN 2024030546 (ebook) |
ISBN 9781668046548 (hardcover) | ISBN 9781668046555 (paperback) |
ISBN 9781668046562 (ebook)
Subjects: LCSH: Palestinian American women—Fiction. | LCGFT: Novels.
Classification: LCC PS3619.H35426 T66 2025 (print) | LCC PS3619.H35426 (ebook) |
DDC 813/.6—dc23/eng/20240729
LC record available at https://lccn.loc.gov/2024030545
LC ebook record available at https://lccn.loc.gov/2024030546

ISBN 978-1-6680-4654-8
ISBN 978-1-6680-4656-2 (ebook)

For Hany and Alexander

PART I

1

ARABELLA

New York City
2012

It was not that September 11 felt like just another day in New York to me. It's that I had to pretend it wasn't. I was only traumatized by how little I was traumatized. If you were thinking about hating me already, don't worry. You're in great company. Also, try as you might, you can't hate me as much as I hate myself.

I had more skin in the game on that day than most New Yorkers who wound up with intact skin. In short, I had almost been killed. I was tunneling my way under the Cortland Street subway station minutes before it imploded under the weight of the Towers, fuel, and human hatred.

So, I had been closer to death than my artsy New York intellectual and theatre friends, who stared out at the world with eyes bleary with horror, at the first public gathering I attended on September 17. It was at New Dramatists. I was a month into my yearlong gig as a director-in-residence there. In a circle, we sat in that unconsecrated church in the heart of Hell's Kitchen to "come together" as a community. They all looked fearful, anguished, dazed. Childlike and innocent, but in that *Lord of the Flies* kind of way. If anyone was gonna be Piggy, and wind up with their head smashed in, it was clearly yours truly. I was waiting for someone to slip up and exclaim, "What kind of animals could do such a thing?!" and then watch all the eyes in the room turn to me.

And, if that happened, I knew I would snap and spew vitriol of a rather intense nature. Say some regrettable things. In other words, tell the truth.

"Not feeling particularly safe? Surprise, surprise! The world's a fucking terrible place! Innocent people die horrible deaths every fucking minute of every fucking day. I'm always painfully aware how easily I could have been one of them. I'm a Palestinian. Yeah, yeah, I was born in America. But my parents never really left and neither can I. When the country you are from no longer exists, you can't ever truly emigrate from it. Give my people a homeland, so I can finally ditch it! Give it the big middle finger and pledge allegiance to another flag! Until then, I was born there, I live there, and I can't leave there. Not a day goes by where I don't feel haunted and hunted. Every day is like September 11 for me. Welcome to how I feel all the time."

But thankfully, that liberal crowd was careful. Measured. They even outdid themselves in their estimations of how much Arab blood was on American hands, spouting facts and figures I was not politically astute enough to keep in my head. Or rather did not have the inclination to do so. I—of course—didn't say a damn word. For fuck's sake, I'm a theatre director, specializing in postmodern interpretations of Shakespeare. I could recite every major monologue in *Hamlet* before I could tell you one solid fact about what year which administration gave what order to bomb what Arab country. But I could probably give you a strong opinion about why.

While they debated whether it was safe to use the subways again (conclusion: it was unsafe, but we had no choice), I wondered if, had I died in the attacks, it might be assumed that I had been a part of planning them. That happened to a few 9/11 victims, who were Americans of Middle Eastern descent. They were investigated and posthumously cleared of all charges. That would be some shit, wouldn't it? To never feel truly accepted as an American, but to be killed because you represented America. Then, to have it assumed you were complicit in the attack that robbed you of your life. Good times.

My British shrink at the time pronounced that I was repressing my feelings, insisting I had been impacted by the violence of the attacks on my beloved city, despite my sense of alienation. A pert blonde who bore a resemblance to a young Camilla Parker Bowles, she said I was turning my feelings of sorrow into anger. Because, of course, my sorrow might overwhelm me. So, according to her, I wasn't actually angry.

I didn't have the heart to argue. I had a policy of studiously avoiding extensive discussions of Middle Eastern politics, even in therapy. It would tax me too much to dwell on my family history, where we are from and why we're not allowed to return. I couldn't afford to let myself fall into a funk. It was hard enough for me to get out of bed in the morning. Also, rarely necessary until at least noon on most days. My *Yaba* made a lot of bread. Literally. My dad bought a bread factory within a few years of leaving the Christian quarter of Jerusalem to study Engineering at San Francisco State. His Palestinian ass is now the number one manufacturer of sourdough in the world (God Bless America!). Hence, I was no starving artist. And I probably wouldn't have lasted a year working in theatre in New York if I had been. But that's beside the point. I was savvy enough to get the memo that it wasn't worth the physiological toll it took on my body to engage in such conversations, which would turn contentious more often than not. Let some other motherlover start a war of words. This ensured I was less likely to be triggered. My heart need not flutter like a butterfly with its ass on fire, the juices of my stomach could remain in their lining. No thank you! I come in peace and—in peace—I intend to motherfuckin' stay. Just trying to direct some good productions of Shakespeare. Life is hard enough trying to stay relevant in an increasingly culturally irrelevant art form.

Since men who looked like my brothers were now crashing planes into buildings, I wondered if I needed to look for an Arab shrink. So, if she said weird shit—like I was feeling sorrow when I was damn sure I was feeling anger—I could take it for what it was worth rather than wonder if her analysis of me was colored by her own discomfort with facing an angry Palestinian. We're much more manageable when we are sad.

The shrink had basically said I was numb and hadn't been able to process my reaction to September 11. You, Arabella Hajjar, are in for some fun. A meltdown is on its way. You're going to swim in a tsunami of grief. Wait for it.

I didn't think she was right until I entered my apartment on an unusually dark early evening in May over a decade after September 11. To be fair, that day was doomed from the start. I had been dreading it since I got the invitation to the opening night performance of the latest play at the Public Theater five weeks earlier. "What does one wear to an off-Broadway opening of a play one hates at a theatre that one abhors?" I wondered (possibly aloud) as I put my key in my door and stepped inside. To my horror, without warning, my window into the world had changed.

The glowing tip of the Empire State Building was warped! Some demonic hand had tugged at the tip, making it longer and now shaped like a menacingly sharp needle. For my thirty-fifth birthday, a few months before that fateful night, my parents had bought me a one-bedroom apartment on the thirty-fourth floor of a high-rise in the Village with an unobstructed view of the crown jewel of the New York skyline, the Empire State Building. Not a bad birthday gift, right? Unless you understand why they did it. My parents had given up on my finding a husband. They didn't want me to ever be forced to live with my three spoiled brothers and the insipid Palestinian American princesses who had married them. For them, securing housing for their single daughter was an act of love. The saddest of the many tragic tales that I heard of the early days of Ramallah, which my Christian tribe, known as Al-Haddadin, founded in the 1500s, involved old maids being abused (always psychologically but sometimes even physically) in the homes of their brothers by their sisters-in-law. "A sister had no chance against a wily wife" is a sentiment I often heard murmured among the women of my family, which always struck me as a polite way of saying men couldn't be trusted to side with women they couldn't sleep with against those they could. Moving into a one-bedroom alone in your midthirties does not portend particularly well for one's romantic future. You can't help but wonder if the super is going to find you, fifty years later, because the smell of your lonely death has spread and someone has to do something. First world problems, I know. Yet, problems just the same.

Might I have reacted differently to this change in the New York skyline on a different night, if I had not been both heartbroken and enraged about having to attend the opening of *that* show at *that* theatre? Perhaps. It had even started out as an especially hard morning. My grandmother had called, waking me up at the ungodly hour of eight a.m. Twelve full hours before showtime! I picked up the phone and Teta Zoya was midshout. My grandmother thought the connection was made when she dialed, not when the other person picked up.

"*Bint!*" It was usual for my grandmother to address me as "girl." I guess, when you have twenty granddaughters, names can be hard to keep straight. Over the line, I could hear the clicking of her gas stove as she turned it on. She was clearly making coffee, probably in the doll-like silver pot designed to make one espresso cup at a time. After she was widowed, she excavated the miniature pot from a box she brought to Detroit from Ramallah, probably as a reproach to her only son, my Khalo Ghassan. He had not invited her to come live with his family in their McMansion in Bloomfield Hills, which, as a dutiful only son, he had been expected to do after my grandfather was gone.

"*Sabah El-Kheir!*" I greeted her, trying not to sound sarcastic as I wished her good morning. I stumbled to my kitchenette and popped in a pod to start my own coffee. But what she said next froze me in my tracks.

"*Akeed intey bitla ma wahid yahoudi!*" Teta Zoya murmured softly. Where had she gotten the idea I was dating a Jew? And why did she sound so casual about it? Nothing about my grandmother was casual. Or straightforward. She had been raised by, from all accounts, an SOB of a father and a mother who was famous for her meekness. I couldn't help but think that if my great-grandmother was considered meeker than average among illiterate Palestinian peasant women born in the mid-nineteenth century, that chick must have been so unassuming she barely spoke.

I could hear Teta Zoya softly breathing on the phone. Imagined her standing in her pristine kitchen in the heart of the most Arab of American cities, Detroit. Waiting for her coffee to brew and for me to fall into some kind of trap.

Thankfully, I realized in time that Teta was using one of her infamous ninja-like conversation tactics. Designed to bring secrets to light. In Arabic, this strategy was known as *irmee el-kilma*. "Throw a word." She'd accuse you of a random transgression and observe your reaction, gathering information that might come out inadvertently. In this case, by announcing she had knowledge I was currently doing a Jew, she might be able to get me to confirm her suspicion. Or to blurt out something like, "Not at all. Stephen is Chinese!" as another cousin had done when accused of dating a Greek boy. That cousin was promptly talked into marrying a very personable (but rather short) Palestinian orthopedic surgeon whose main drawback was that he (and therefore eventually she) was destined to move to Mississippi. My Teta couldn't understand how I was still single past thirty-four. At that age, my great-aunt went to Kuwait to be a nurse and married herself a mighty wealthy and stout Texas oil man. Basically, it was the oldest age any woman in our family (who managed to get married) had ever married. There was no way I wasn't living it up as a single girl in New York. Teta could hardly keep her eight daughters in line back when she had left Ramallah for Detroit in the sixties. But she did. Talked (read: forced) them into marriages before any of them turned eighteen. My Teta was no joke. You could play tic-tac-toe on the long bruises that traversed my mother's belly, dark rivers on her sandy skin, the remnants of brutal beatings Teta Zoya had meted out to all her brood back in the day.

I flipped the switch on my own single-serve coffeemaker. Together we listened to it grind. I was the granddaughter who everyone agreed took after Teta Zoya the most. That meant I—of all people—had the tools to deflect her.

"*Ya rayt!*" I told her. I wish! With those words, I confirmed her worst fear. Not that I would marry a Jew, but that I wouldn't marry at all. Born in an era when indigenous Muslims, Jews, and Christians lived together throughout Palestine, she had known a number of mixed marriages in our hometown of Ramallah in her younger years. What a failure her granddaughter would be if she couldn't catch anybody! Not fricking anybody?

I could hear her spoon striking against the walls of her coffeepot as she mixed in the grinds. *"Hada darab aleyki?"* she asked. I took my first sip, burning my tongue, before answering. No, no one had called. She had given my phone number to a woman who had wanted to set me up with her grandson, a doctor.

"The boy be traveling every country, *Bint*. He go, go, go. Like you. He working. Borders Without Doctors. Big shot!" she told me in her halting, haiku-like English. She spoke English to me when she wanted to make sure I understood her every word. She didn't trust my comprehension of Arabic, the language that had been my first one but that I seemed to be steadily losing.

"Hilew," I told her. That's nice. I meant it, too. Always good to hear some of us were becoming big shots.

"Only *hilew* if he calls you. His grandfather, Aziz, was first doctor in Ramallah. Aziz find me on refugee boat to America. The one your grandfather no go. Me alone with children. Against my wanting. But Aziz care for me. *Zay hu kan jowzi,"* she told me, and she fell silent.

Like a husband? Interesting. Had she dug him? This was the umpteenth time Teta Zoya had tried to set me up. My grandmother was part of a vast network of displaced Palestinian matriarchs across the world whose sole purpose was to ensure their children married other Palestinians. To make families in the diaspora that resembled the ones we might have made if they'd never left. The men I met through them were generally spoken for. Taken. Usually wildly in love and living with an American woman or—in a more interesting case—a man. Their mothers hoped my sexual charms might magically alchemize their dross-for-brains offspring into golden boys who thought marrying full-blooded Palestinians and making more of us mattered. These cats would wearily drive up from Paterson or Long Island or even as far as Philadelphia to prove a point to their mothers, not to really meet me. Few ever called me again. This disappointed me more than I cared to admit. I hadn't had a relationship that lasted longer than two months with either my artsy rainbow of boy toys or respectable Palestinian American professionals. Thus, I was an epic failure at dating American-style and equally sucky at catching a husband the old-fashioned way. It's not that I was dying to be a doctor's wife, but I wanted to be wanted. By someone.

This grandson of the first doctor in Ramallah hadn't thought I was worth his time. Embarrassing, especially because Teta informed me that his mother had cut out a motherloving picture of me from a feature on my theatre work in the *Detroit Free Press* and forwarded it to him wherever he was doctoring without borders.

Teta and I were both quiet on the phone, contemplating the fact that if Aziz the Younger was reaching out to touch someone, it wasn't me. Why did I feel dejected that a boy I had never met didn't call? It was like being stung by a bee you didn't swat at. (What? Wait! Ouch!)

"I saw show on Al-Jazeera. Doctors can cut inside your *bouton*. Freezer it. So you have babies later, *Bint*. Do it! Me old. I live more than two of you. No one ever wants to be the mother. But you should have child! More than one! So you no die alone."

"Got to go, Teta. *Ma Al Salama*," I said.

My grandmother and I both hung up the phone feeling sorrier than before we spoke. I had many hours to kill before the show. In those days, television was terrible and held no charms for me. I knew I had to get inside a theatre, lose myself in a story. Find a way to forget I had to attend that play later that night. I remembered I had promised one of my favorite students, Ava, that I would someday stop by and sit in on a rehearsal for her thesis project at Marymount Manhattan College, where I was an adjunct professor.

I wandered my way to the cathedral that is the Grand Central Terminal, pausing to take in its design of constellations and vast vaulted ceilings, before I descended via crowded escalator to the entrance of the subway: the Hades of New York. Grand Central Terminal is to its adjoining subway station what my mother's *salon* is to the rest of our house in Atherton. A fancy place designed for guests to enter and exit. Its neatness amplified the wildness of the rest of my family house. My mother rebelled from Teta Zoya's fastidiousness by refusing to be a good homemaker. My father had known hunger as a boy living in Jerusalem after the *Nakba*, and was too parsimonious to pay for a maid. Not a winning combination in that regard. But they otherwise got along swimmingly. The fact that they had more money than they knew what to do with (and were admired in American and Palestinian circles alike) helped. I pulled out a dollar for the man with no legs who sat on the floor—which only further emphasized his lack of limbs—at the bottom of the escalator. I put the money in his cup without being able to look him in the eyes. Then, I tunneled up to 72nd and made my way to the Marymount campus, essentially a building on the Upper East Side that was indistinguishable from the outdated-looking coops that surrounded it. I silently slipped in the back of the rehearsal room, a classroom with the chairs pushed in a corner, but a site for magic nonetheless.

My mood lifted, as it usually does when I'm in a theatrical space. I could feel my body relax as I watched Ava, a petite alabaster girl from Ohio whose dyed blue-black hair and piercings did little to make her seem older than her nineteen years, shape the actors into a decent retelling of *A Streetcar Named Desire*. They were working on a scene where our tragic heroine, Blanche, sings her heart out in a bathtub. "Sing louder!" my student coaxed her actor. "Show us what unbridled joy looks like so we understand what is about to be crushed." Like an incantation, those words transformed the gangly teenager playing Blanche into a majestic figure, an embodiment of every woman who would ever be destroyed for daring to want too much or be too free. I slipped out of the rehearsal room at four, giving Ava a thumbs-up that made her blush at first and then beam. The sight of her smile brought tears to my eyes for reasons I didn't quite understand. Something to do with how I handled my power and her vulnerability. I knew I got that moment right. It was not a feeling I had often.

Still hours left to kill before the curtain would rise at eight and I would be trapped, forced to watch *that* play. Miraculously, it didn't seem so bad anymore. It was live theatre. Something unexpected might happen. I practically skipped the sixty blocks back to my place, watching the sky turn from blue to black. The whole way home I did not glance backward. Let it be known I was Lot, not his wife. So, I had no clue what was in store for me.

During the first few months in my apartment, the changing colors on the Empire State Building were for me what I imagined a pet would be for other people. I would open the door and look for it. It greeted me. Made me feel I was sharing my space with an evolving, alive thing. It reminded me of a Lite-Brite creation, something childish hands had lovingly pieced together with sticks of light. Now, with its new sharp point, it looked like ambition unleashed. I'll get higher than I deserve to be with the building blocks I can afford! I will pierce through everything!

"They're fixing something on the tip. Those are temporary work lights. The skyline isn't going to be permanently changed," I tried to convince myself. "Tried" is the operative word. Clearly, no one would go through the expense of putting that monstrosity of a sharpened glowing needle on the tip of the Empire State Building unless they thought it was a bright idea. Unless it was here to stay. How many more changes to New York could I endure? All at once, an image of a man who had jumped from a tower flashed in my head, a picture that seemed to be printed everywhere after September 11. He was upside down, had one leg bent, and was wearing a white uniform. A worker. Part of the waitstaff at Windows on the World. On that day, he was up earlier than the rest of the city, probably prepping himself emotionally for serving douchebag customers. Not trying to be a big shot. Or run the world. Or kill the competition, in whatever form that competition might have come. That man was trying to make a living. What does he get for his efforts? Fire. Smoke. Heat. Suddenly, the burnt smell that was in New York for days after the attacks was in my nose again, the first Tower to fall imploding over and over on replay in my head. The meltdown my shrink had predicted had arrived, a decade late. Full force. I ended up facedown, alternately sobbing, screaming, and pounding on my floor with my fists.

"This is my home! My home! Leave my fucking home alone!"

"Shut up!" a man from another apartment yelled.

"You shut up!" I yelled back. But, having a neighbor to tell you to shut up proved to be useful actually. Who knows how long I would have been screaming and banging my fists if I had been as alone as I felt? I had a theatre opening to attend and had to get ready, now with the added challenge of trying to look like I had not been crying.

That was hard to do on good days, since walking into the Public Theater always made me want to cry. Or spit. Guess the shrink had been worth $175 per hour. My pendulum indeed always appeared to swing between grief and rage. The founder of the Public, Joe Papp, had been arguably the most powerful and radically leftist artistic director in American theatre history. Truly a visionary artist. A pioneer. An advocate for so many voiceless people. That's what made what he did to mine so particularly painful.

In 1989, Papp had invited a group of Palestinian artists from the famed El-Hakawati Theatre to perform at the Public. The show was announced. Plans were made. At the time, I was in high school and believed I was destined to be the next Meryl Streep (note: rewind the story of every adult working in theatre and you'll find an aspiring child actor). I heard about this Palestinian show by happenstance at the annual crab feed of the San Francisco chapter of the AFRP, the American Federation of Ramallah, Palestine. It was a social club for the descendants of the founding families of Ramallah that became one of the largest Arab-American organizations. If it sounds very specific and exclusive, it was by design. My grandparents' generation, who founded chapters in cities across America, wanted us to stick together. Even fellow Palestinians from neighboring Christian towns who married into our clans were made to feel like they never entirely belonged. Over the din of three hundred of my people cracking crab, my mom's uncle's wife's sister bragged that her nephew by marriage was performing in a show by a Palestinian troupe in New York. I sensed a chance to finally visit the city I knew had to be my home. I asked my parents to take me to see it.

To my delight, they said yes. My parents were exceedingly indulgent of my whims. Was it because they were poor as children and couldn't bear to deny me anything? They never truly assimilated into American culture, so it was easy for me to play it off that in America, it was expected you'd take your daughter across the country because she wanted to see a show. They turned to our travel agent, a cousin sitting at the next table, and asked her to book our flights that night.

Then, Papp rescinded his offer to El-Hakawati Theatre and canceled their performance at his theatre. We found out while in New York when we called my mom's uncle's wife's sister to find out how to buy tickets. She said the Palestinian theatre company was looking for a different New York theatre to showcase the play, but it wasn't happening exactly as scheduled. She seemed miffed about it, but not angry, so we found no reason to be. We didn't understand that once a show was canceled at the famed Public Theater, you would be hard-pressed to find another venue with the same cachet. There was no way to go but down.

Instead of *The Story of Kufur Shamma* at the Public Theater, we saw *The Phantom of the Opera* on Broadway. We were in New York only twenty hours in total. But it was long enough for me to stand fixed like an island in the center of the atomic glow of Times Square, forcing the rivers of mere tourists to make their way around me, and vow I would be back someday to stay.

Later, when I stumbled on a dissertation in the Yale library about economic censorship in the American theatre, I would learn that there were conflicting stories from Jews and Arabs (no surprise there!) about what happened at the Public. Some claim Papp personally told them he feared his board would shut him down, that it would jeopardize funding for his entire theatre if he presented a show by Palestinian artists. Later, he would say publicly that wasn't the case, that it was his personal decision to revoke the invitation, and to suggest otherwise was anti-Semitic. Whatever the real reason, the show did not go on for my people at the Public. Not then. And not since. Not one story by a Palestinian writer on that illustrious stage ever.

Footprints in the Promised Land, whose opening performance that night I felt compelled to attend, was the closest we seemed able to come. A famous (but not particularly interesting) white British playwright had written a monologue about his trip to Israel/Palestine. Some folks bored their grandkids with travel stories. Not this dude, who was recently knighted. Apparently, Sir Famous Playwright/Blowhard's travel story to the Holy Land was interesting enough to command the stage of the most important American theatre company. The turning point in the piece arrives when our man, who presents himself as having no connection to either side, reveals the truth. He has skin

in the game. He is married to a Jewish woman, which he realizes af-
fects how the Israelis and Palestinians feel about him. This is somehow
surprising to him. Then, he makes the incredible conclusion that the
situation is quite complicated and he has no clue how Palestinians and
Israelis can move forward together.

Six months earlier, I had refused a job to work on *Footprints in the
Promised Land*. Rather sharply. Not because I hated the insipid script,
which I obviously did. It was truly a waste of an audience's evening,
thousands of hours of hundreds of people, time that they would never
get back. When you work in a dying industry like theatre, you feel struck
in the gut every time someone farts away the resources that could be
used to make innovative, ambitious, or (at least) fun work. People will
watch shitloads of bad TV and come back for more, because it's cheap.
You're not captive to a story. It's easy to change your mind. Not so
when it comes to theatre. But that wasn't why I said no.

I had been led to believe (or wanted to believe) that I was going
to be asked to direct the play. To lend it some cultural legitimacy by
having a Palestinian director attached to this vanity project of an En-
glishman. When I was called into a meeting with Tiffany, an artistic
associate at the Public, I was prepared to talk about how we might
improve on the script, possibly by interviewing and including impressions of the playwright from the Palestinians and Israelis he had
met. So, it wouldn't be just a show about how he perceived them, but
also how he was perceived. I was going to right the wrong that the
founder of the Public Theater had done to my people when he didn't
give them a stage. A Palestinian story might never stand alone on
that platform. But our voices would be part of a chorus. Included. I
would no longer need to walk long blocks to avoid the weirdly askew
streets of Astor Place, which was around the corner from my apartment, so I could avoid passing by the Public. Or feel my heart race,
my jaw lock, and my fists clench when a bus with an advertisement
for its latest (not Palestinian!) show sailed by me. I could stop feeling
outraged that we had been silenced once and terrified that we would
stay silenced forever.

I still cringe when I remember how I strutted into the lobby of the

Public and greeted the artistic associate, Tiffany, with her limpid blue eyes and blond hair she wore without layers. Never the liveliest of ladies, Tiffany seemed especially lethargic that day. She acted as if it took too much effort to raise her hand and pat me on the shoulder after I went in for a bear hug. We sat down at a table in the lobby.

The song goes, if you can make it in New York, you can make it anywhere. But no one tells you that you have to keep making it. I established a name for myself for my reinterpretations of Shakespeare, since I staged comedies as if they were tragedies and vice versa. I had graduated from Yale Drama in June of 2001, having enjoyed the distinction of being the first woman to claim the title of Artistic Director of the student-run Yale Cabaret. Had a hit show at the New York International Fringe Festival six weeks later. It was an adaptation of *Twelfth Night*, which traditionally is presented as a comedy centered on a woman who finds herself shipwrecked and alone in a strange land. In my version, our heroine is violently gang-raped in a dance sequence at the start of the show. She disguises herself as a man not as a lark, but in order to survive in a way a woman cannot as easily do. It was a hit. I was twenty-five. The offers to direct shows started coming in. My second show was *Othello: A Post-Racial Farce*. In it, Othello was clearly a madman with a tick, constantly swatting at flies that weren't there. Setting it in Belfast, I cast an actor who was Black Irish as Othello. So, to the New York audience, it appeared he was white and didn't seem to know it. The Black theatre critic for the *Times* got that I was commenting on how arbitrary and absurd it is to distinguish people by the color of their skin, in a way we don't do by the color of their hair. Another hit. A job at the Public would catapult my career to the next level. I was determined to get there. Even if I had to direct something as buttfuckingly banal as *Footprints in the Promised Land* to do it.

"You know how much we admire your work," Tiffany told me. I smiled, tight-lipped, hoping to force my face into looking calm. Humble. Patient. Was she speaking as if in slow motion? Or was I just manic? Put your money on me being manic. I folded my hands in an attempt to contain them from making "Come on! Come on!" gestures. Then, she added, "We think you would be a great addition to the team of *Footprints in the Promised Land*. Because of your background."

Did this cuntologist have to make it crystal that there was no way I would get a job offer if it weren't on a show about the Middle East? Apparently so. Was she clueless when it came to how her words would land on artists of color? Or did she mean to be demeaning? Her washed-denim eyes stared out at me vapidly. I decided to vote for clueless.

"You were the first person John Brock asked us to hire as his assistant director!" she announced.

Assistant? To John Brock? If anything was designed to show me the gap between who I was and who I wanted to be, it was this job offer.

The kid had graduated two years behind me from the Yale School of Drama, though his career catapulted ahead of mine, as was expected when a tall, white man actually had chops and a modicum of emotional intelligence. Given the pressure to hire a Palestinian on this particular show as opposed to the latest Young White Dude du Jour, how much did they not think I was a contender? I'd thought I was a few more acclaimed downtown hits away from directing in their Shakespeare in the Park series, the most prestigious venue for classical work in the country. From there, of course, it was only a matter of time before my work would be on Broadway!

A curtain had been torn open, and I couldn't unsee what I'd seen. I felt that particular panic you get when you just miss your exit on a freeway and are frantically trying to jump to the lane where you need to be. Willing to risk life and limb rather than accept you made a mistake and turn around. I understood intellectually my career was far from over. I was not old. I knew that if I could power through this ungodly painful passage of being a midcareer artist, I might one day become a master. But I was clearly far, far, far away from it then. The knowledge knocked the wind out of me.

"I'm not at a stage in my career where I still assist. Gotta go. Late for my next meeting!" I stammered to Tiffany, and literally ran out of the lobby.

I said yes to the invitation to the opening performance of *Footprints in the Promised Land* that Tiffany emailed me because I didn't want to look like I was angry. Though I dropped my British shrink a couple of months after September 11 and never did the work of finding an Arab one to replace her, I had paid for enough therapy by that point to know that, unsurprisingly, anger was my default mode. So, if my instincts were to stay the fuck away from that insipid show out of rage, my intellect told me it would be a good thing to lend my support, be seen, and schmooze in the hope I might be hired for another show. Or maybe I just liked to torture myself.

I dressed in a simple little black dress, forcing myself not to look at the monstrous new tip of the Empire State Building as I walked toward the packed lobby of the Public. I opted to stay by the door, but the crush of the crowd kept pushing me forward. "Just love the Empire State Building's new look. They installed LED lights!" I heard a chipper young voice say behind me. But when I turned around, I only found older faces, the usual patrons of the theatre. I prayed the lights would flicker, signaling it was time for the show to begin and closer to when the night could finally end. I had mentally rehearsed how I would congratulate John Brock in a way that did not reveal I wanted to shove my foot up his ass.

I dreaded encountering Tiffany, but the chick I should have been worried about was Lisa-Turned-Layla. She was the perennial Palestinian American playwright-activist who was always invited to these kinds of openings at the Public. Just like me. Could they do a show about the Palestinian-Israeli conflict with no Palestinian artists involved? Yes, of course. But could they do it and have an all-white audience on opening night? *Ce n'est pas possible! Nyet!* Never! That would be racially insensitive and no one in American theatre would want to be (accused of) that.

Lisa-Turned-Layla and I kind of hated each other. She—like me—had gone to Harvard for undergrad and went straight to graduate school at the Yale School of Drama. But, in the summer in between, she had changed her American name to an Arabic one to exoticize herself. I snarkily introduced the idea of calling her Lisa-Turned-Layla to our mutual friends to "distinguish" her from the other Laylas we knew (Eric Clapton single-handedly made it the most popular Arab American girl name of our generation). I had not opened several emails from her, including ones with the subjects such as "EVEN SEVERAL JEWS ARE SIGNING THIS PETITION! RESPOND ASAP!!!" and "THIS IS NOT ABOUT THE PETITION—ACTION REQUIRED!!! RESPOND ASAP!!!"

There she was. Flanked by none other than John Brock and Sir Famous British Playwright/Blowhard. Eyes darting everywhere, looking feverishly giddy with her plump lips parted. It was as if there were an invisible gnome licking her clit under her low-cut sequin red ballroom gown, a miniskirt in the front with a long train in the back, which she paired with camel-colored cowboy boots. (Really, Bitch? A ballroom gown for a downtown opening? Really?)

Even I had to acknowledge we looked like sisters. Same prodigious curves, cream coloring, almond-shaped black eyes, and round faces framed by the same springy curls we both tamed straight. Our similarities were only on the surface. She hailed from a rich Jerusalemite clan who ran in the social circle of the upper-crust families of Edward Said and Rashid Khalidi, the moneyed Palestinian immigrants who became shining stars of the American intelligentsia. Women of my clan had been bused in (via donkey cart) from our village of Ramallah to work as maids for pampered women from clans like hers.

Either she was doing funky Bohemian girl correctly in her ball gown and cowboy boots or I was nailing it in my flattering little black dress. I got the feeling as I saw men in the room looking at her as she waved at me that, in that instance, she had gotten something right. She was, it must be admitted, thinner than me. I turned away and grabbed a free glass of wine from a low table, which I downed in one gulp. I hadn't eaten all day. I had been too upset.

Yoav, my favorite sound designer, motioned me over from across the packed lobby. He was so tall he loomed over the crowd. I grabbed two glasses of wine for us and headed in his direction. An Israeli American kid, he, too, had been my classmate at Harvard College and Yale Drama School. In that moment, I realized Yoav—with his dark eyes and curls—also resembled me. The other parallels between him and me were obvious. His folks immigrated to the United States from the same land—which we called by different names—before we were born. Both of us were young for our class, having skipped a grade and arriving at college at seventeen. Since we both recently turned thirty-five, at that point, we had known each other for eighteen years. That meant Yoav had been in my life longer than he had not. We kept it professional, even talked with each other about the people we dated. But, at random times that spanned over the many years I'd known him, I was almost sure he was imagining when he looked into my eyes what it would feel like to be inside me.

Entirely possible I was projecting. Yoav was the person I trusted more than anyone else in a room when I was directing. And when I was directing was the only time I truly trusted myself.

I was halfway to Yoav when I saw Lisa-Turned-Layla point at me from across the room. The little huddle of folks around her, including John Brock and Sir Famous Playwright/Blowhard (the star of our show, who should have been backstage prepping his voice since he was supposed to perform his monologue for us in a matter of minutes), all seemed to turn together in my direction, slowly and eerily, as sunflowers follow the light.

Clearly, Lisa-Turned-Layla was telling them I was a coward. Years ago, she had outed me as a Palestinian. I had been rather successfully passing as white until she was interviewed about my work in a feature about me in *American Theatre* magazine. Lisa-Turned-Layla said, "Arabella's work is essentially Palestinian at its core, even if the text she uses is Shakespeare. She melds the concepts of tragedy and comedy in a way that is clearly in the tradition of all our best modern Palestinian art, like our classic tragicomic novel *The Pessoptomist*." And when the interviewer quoted her and asked me if I agreed, I got flustered. Lied. Pretended I hadn't heard of the only book my father, who was not bookish, gave me when I was in high school. Were any of my ideas original? Or was everything I made derivative? (Yes? No? Both?) Then, I proceeded to babble, apparently blurting out some exceedingly unsavvy shit, including (but not limited to), "Talent always wins out in the end. My career is proof of that. I don't ride on the fact that my parents were immigrants. Very few of the many artists who are obsessed with race in American theatre actually have the chops to make truly innovative work." The interviewer cut off the rest of my statement, which was that so few of *any* of us—of *any* race—have the chops to do that. Still not a clever or important or interesting point, but the one I had been trying to make. It was my way to signal to white readers that I was no product of affirmative action. Never spoke of my background. Made it my mission to pass as white. No one could accuse me of using being Palestinian to get theatre work because I was, in fact, terrified that it would mean I'd never work. Thank heavens that this article came out in a time before Facebook existed. People read it and called me an asshole but had no platform to allow hundreds of people to concur.

Lisa-Turned-Layla began waving wildly to me and exaggeratedly mouthed the words "we need to talk." No, we don't, though. We really don't. I had thought it best to ignore a petition that called for a Broadway theatre to honor the boycotting of shows that were funded by Brand Israel, an Israeli governmental program designed to use culture to showcase aspects of Israel that had nothing to do with the unfortunate fate of the Palestinians. Not all Israeli art or artists, mind you. Just the projects that had been funded by that wing of their government. Signing it felt like declaring oneself a Red just at the exact moment McCarthy was getting his schlong sucked deep enough by America to start orchestrating the executions (!) of Americans. No thank you! I wanted to work! I was going to direct Shakespeare's entire canon. In America! But it turned out most of the hottest young theatre artists, including several Jewish American rock stars like Yoav, had added their names. The petition actually became the "it" thing to sign, complete with the most famous of the it-sters publishing a letter put out by Human Rights Watch in support of the boycott in an ad in the *Times*. Lisa-Turned-Layla was absolutely going to berate me, in front of this entire lobby, for not signing it. I could feel it as she made her way in her boots (clop! clop! clop!) over to me.

"Have you gotten my emails?" she panted. I'm not exaggerating when I say the girl was breathless with excitement.

"What emails?" That was the lie I was going to stick to. I was that girl who climbed every mountain, swam every sea, and signed every human rights petition, no matter how controversial and potentially devastating to my career. Yep, that was me. Emails? Never got 'em.

"Check your spam. I emailed you several times. We got the grant!"

Vaguely, I remembered saying "Sure, kiddo!" to Lisa-Turned-Layla a million years ago at a party when she asked if she could put my name down as a director on a grant application for funding for a theatre production in Palestine. It was part of my "say yes to everything" life reboot I was attempting after my career nosedived. For longer than was reasonable, I didn't get the memo that I had been a flash in the pan that had lost its sizzle and was now corroding. I kept turning down off-off-Broadway gigs long after my off-Broadway offers dried up, feeling like if I took a step backward, I'd get stuck there and never move forward. Would never direct on the big B-way. Soon, I wasn't being asked to dance anymore. By anyone. By the time I went back to the off-off-Broadway venues looking for a job, I had so thoroughly turned off everyone with my 'tude that I couldn't get hired anywhere. Or maybe ageism and sexism made it so women directors heading into middle age hardly ever get work?

I was not taking this job! But how to let the poor girl down easy? Schedule, schedule, schedule! That's what I claimed as an excuse the last time she had asked me to work in Palestine on a production with children from refugee camps. I hated other people's children in direct proportion to how much I wanted one of my own. The perfection of their beauty was the scourge the world used to torture me for my childlessness now that I had turned thirty-five and had to start cracking that nut soon if it was going to be cracked.

"It's going to cover the entire cost of a production of *Hamlet*," she said. Ah, now I remembered. She had applied for a grant to do a production of her Arabic translation of *Hamlet* with a professional Palestinian theatre company. I had agreed to direct it.

Her eyes gleamed. The eyes of true believers in revolution are always brighter than most people's. Always. I know because my eyes never shine like that.

"We're going to tour our show all over Palestine!" she continued. Touring a conflict zone full of armed settlers and soldiers? Not for me. Good night and good luck, y'all.

"As lovely as that sounds, I can't—" I began to say, but she interrupted me.

"The top staff at the Royal Court Theatre are coming for opening night!"

Wait, what now?

"Royal Court Theatre of England?" I said, incredulous. I had seen a production of *Equus* there when I was in high school that made my panties wet and not just because a dude was naked in it and I saw my first adult wee-wee (although that helped). When the lights go up on a show that good, I forget myself. I forget how condemned I feel being just an "I"—experiencing only what I can know and no more—until the moment my lights go out.

"Yes," Lisa-Turned-Layla said slowly. Clearly, she was only now registering I didn't remember all the details of what exactly I had said yes to during my phase where I had made saying no a no-no. "The Royal Court Theatre is cosponsoring the project. They've heard a lot about your work."

The folks at the biggity big RCT had heard of my work? Hell, yes, they did! Perhaps the disparity between who I was and who I wanted to be was no Grand Canyon. Was it a gulf I could traverse in this lifetime? Not unless I made work that people in power would see, people like the top staff at the Royal Court Theatre.

"They're very excited you're on board to direct."

"And I'm very excited to be on board, Layla," I said, forcing a smile and trying to make my eyes shine the way hers did.

But even though I said yes again in that moment, I told myself I didn't have to go back there. Didn't have to face what my life would have looked like if my parents hadn't said "peace out" and left. I could call my agent first thing tomorrow and beg him to try to drum up another gig anywhere first. I imagined my apology email to the Royal Court Theatre, feigning I was in demand and already had another show

I was committed to directing during that time frame, but making it clear I was available if they had other projects at other times in other places like, I don't know, *England!*

The lights flickered at last, indicating the show was about to begin. Lisa-Turned-Layla and I melted into the herd, shuffling toward our seats. Yoav stood by the entrance to the theatre, letting people pass until I reached him.

"Is the melody working for you?" he asked me as I handed him one of the cups I was still holding. That question was our shorthand in the rehearsal room for whether we were on the same page. But it became the way we checked in with each other.

"It's a melody," I said. That was our signal something was wrong. Our way to sound an alarm. His dark eyes widened with worry as he watched me down my glass of wine.

"Where are you sitting?" he asked me.

"Front row, baby!" I announced. Too loudly. As he frowned and reached out his hand to take my empty cup, it struck me again that Yoav had aged and that meant so had I. But I knew the wrinkles creeping on the edges of his dark eyes and carved into his otherwise smooth young tawny skin did nothing to diminish his charm. I wasn't so sure if I could say the same for me. He definitely was no longer the boy who worked with me on *The Tempest* our first year of college, when we instinctively understood we both were way more intense and devoted to theatre than not only the other kids in our class but also anyone else we had ever met.

The lights flickered again. Time to find our seats. I left Yoav standing with my empty cup and his full one. Feeling his eyes on me long after I left him. Why had he never made moves on me or I on him? How many drunken opening nights—celebrations of shows made by our friends and ones we made together—in the past eighteen years had we hung out together? Countless. How many Jewish men had I had during the "I'm officially whoring around as much as possible" phase that seemed to recur every three years? Also countless. Why never him? Perhaps I purposely stayed away from the men I actually liked, whom I might fall in love with, because some part of me preferred to be alone.

I wanted to tell Yoav about the gig in Palestine. I could ask him if he'd be my sound designer. If he'd come with me. Should I?

No. I wasn't taking the job. I saw there was an empty chair between two men in the front row. My seat. When I recognized the famous face of one of the men whom Providence had placed next to me, I began to hatch a plan so I might not have to. I gave myself permission to hope.

2

ZOYA

Jaffa
1948

Mothers who don't fantasize about abandoning their children turn to thoughts of suicide, which is—to some—the ultimate form of abandonment. How was it possible I gave birth to seven daughters in twelve years? And why had they insisted on testing me on that day of all days? By nightfall, the eyes of my beloved were going to behold me. He had not found me wanting when I was a girl.

"*Yema!*" one of my seven cried out, startling me. My corker sliced its way through the soft skin of the squash in my hand, rendering it unusable. I squelched the urge to smash it underfoot. I was making the most sensual of dishes for my beloved. *Mahshey.* Literal meaning is "the stuffed," and—of course—it is often used as a euphemism for other kinds of sustenance. You present your guest a cornucopia of round tomatoes, pointed carrot, and cylinders of squash. It looks simple. Ordinary. It looks how vegetables grow out of the ground. Bite in and find your mouth full of minced roasted lamb, tender rice, and cinnamon. Hollowing it properly was the trick. If you punctured through the skin, it would leak. The whole pot would be mottled with grisly flecks of meat.

"Food is always first tasted with the eyes. As is almost every kind of pleasure. Am I wrong?" my father had once asked a cousin of my mother's, leaning a bit too far in her direction with a twinkle in his eye.

This woman had been sent back to her parents' home in disgrace the morning after her wedding night. The virginal blood her husband expected to find on the sheets was not there. So, men of my father's ilk felt she was fair game, made improper innuendos in her company. Innuendos that I, as a girl, had to pretend not to understand. That cousin never visited our house again, which was a shame. I did not yet understand why she was called *Ikhsara*. What turned a woman into waste?

"*Yema! Yema!*"

Earlier than I needed to know it, I did glean that women were the insatiable ones when it came to love. As young as six, I would hide under the table, ignored, whenever my most audacious aunt, Miriam, would visit for a cup of coffee. When other women visited, they would try to read the patterns in the coffee grinds of their cups, believing they could glimpse their fates if they looked hard enough. Miriam allowed no one to do that in her presence. Put a dirty cup in my aunt's face and she'd strike it out of your hand. "I know the future. We're all going to die. In the meantime, give me some gossip." Give me a story worth hearing. Show me a cautionary tale. Point out who is richer and how he cheated to get that way. Tell me who is fighting in what family and why. The present is so interesting. I have no time for the future.

"Is it not surprising how quickly a man is so completely satisfied? And for so long?!" Aunty Miriam asked one day as they were baking bread. Thus, I knew to expect a disparity in the time it took for the different sexes to be sated. My childhood home had been a one-room cave-like dwelling in Ramallah, where the kitchen was the bedroom and the bathroom was outside.

It was a far cry from our three-story stone villa in Jaffa with enough rooms for my daughters to be able to be separated at night. From each other and from my husband and me. A house with a view of the sea never lost its charm. Having a spectacular view was the only difference between being desperately poor and unexpectedly rich that truly mattered to me. It made me understand my father's hungers. Wealth was almost worth what my father was willing to do to get it. Almost. From my bedroom window, I could catch the reflection of the sun as it set on the water. It lent each day's departure a touch of grandeur, even magic, as the brightness of the heavens were mirrored below for a breath before darkness descended. I was forever thankful that I could look back on my life and know I spent part of it in a house by the sea where, at any moment, I could tune into the movement of water against earth that always felt like the world was whispering "Yes! Yes! Yes!" Even after we lost that house and the country it belonged to with it.

Needless to say, I never allowed my children near when my women-folk were visiting. They were instructed to stay out of the kitchen, my domain. I knew more than I should have as a child and, more important, I remember how I learned it.

"Yema! Yema!"

"Ma hada kalimney!" I screamed. They heeded my words and were silent. "And don't call me *Yema* in front of the guests!"

I had tried to train them to call me Mama, like the children who had always attended British-run private schools in Jaffa, to drop our *falahi* accent in front of the city dwellers who now populated our world. But to no avail. My kids had grown up in Ramallah. They were going to sound country no matter what. They couldn't help it. Should I have tried to bribe all seven into going to bed before dinner? Children, can you go to sleep right now? Perhaps not wake up until you've turned eighteen? I'll give you baklava.

"Yema! Yema!"

"Ye'nan oumkun. Ye'nan oumkun!" I muttered. Let your mother be damned! It was the only curse against them I ever allowed my lips to utter. So, if my words had power, I alone would bear the consequences of them. I pulled out the innards of the next squash with precision. Too thick and the taste of the vegetable would overpower the richness of the meat. Too thin and it would burst.

That night, I was to sit between two very different men, the one I was married to and the one I had wanted to marry. My husband, Kamal, had long ago gotten used to our maid's cooking. But all the food I offered Aziz, I would make myself. I wanted to touch everything he would consume. I put down the corker, to rest.

The thought of Aziz always made me feel languorous, unsteady on my feet. I first felt that heaviness, that desire to be on my back, when Aziz turned to look at me at the Midnight Easter Mass in the Church of the Holy Sepulchre. I was twelve and so was he. Everyone in Ramallah knew he was going places. A French monk had said he was brilliant and arranged for him to attend a Catholic school in Jerusalem. But the joke among us was that the French had low standards for our children. The yardstick they used to judge a Palestinian boy's intelligence was whether he had an aptitude for their language, which Aziz apparently did. It was said he taught himself French. He must have known it was his ticket out. Aziz was as tall as I was petite. His floppy black hair was the smoothest I had ever seen while my tight chestnut curls had a sauciness that nothing could straighten. He was a boy built of sinewy muscle and I was already all curves. Dark-skinned as I was light, which I knew meant—if I had no other features to recommend me—I would forever be considered pretty.

As I crossed his row on my way to take communion, he looked at me. I have to thank the glow of the candles for turning my skin luminous. Our chanting stirred currents through the air between us. The same rhythms vibrated in our bellies and bones. Our eyes met. He winked. Your first adult pang of lust is often the sharpest, because you don't recognize the feeling. It felt fated that mine took place in a church, the site where a sacrament could sanctify the joining of a woman and a man, where you utter magic words and it suddenly stopped being sinful to act on your desires. His mother slapped his face in the direction away from me. It's uncouth to ogle a girl. It's also dangerous, if she has hot-blooded brothers. By Aziz's age, most boys knew you could only safely sneak a glance at a girl if you could manage to do so without turning your head. You only got to see what you could glimpse out of the corners of your eyes. It was in those glimpses at the souk, street, and church that I watched Aziz transform from a gangly bumpkin boy into a dapper city man when he returned to our village to visit his parents, before he left our country altogether to attend medical school in Beirut. I had heard he started a practice in Jaffa. It was one of the reasons I was thrilled when Kamal told me that he was moving our family here.

Seventeen years had passed since that night in the church. Would Aziz, now an esteemed doctor, have accepted an invitation from my husband five years earlier? Before we were rich? Or did his saying yes have something to do with me? Did he remember my name? Had he ever known it in the first place? I picked up the corker and hollowed out another squash. Aziz was inundated with invitations from every Ramallah clan. It was an honor to have him at your table, and a burden to poor families who would slaughter a chicken they needed for eggs to feed him well. It was known he was polite, but rarely accepted. Now everyone from Ramallah wanted to hobnob with us, to see the house by the sea Kamal had built.

Kamal had been lucky on his last trip to America. Unfathomably lucky. Every few years, he and several men from our village went for yearlong stints to Detroit to make money working in factories and then return to Palestine. On that last trip, he came back earlier than expected, dragging two large brown leather suitcases with him. He opened one in front of me. It was packed with American dollars, more money than I had ever seen. I was sure he had committed a crime. But, what?

Kamal was afraid of the evil eye. For protection from it, he always wore a blue amulet, an ugly misshapen eyeball that looked like it had been wrenched from the head of a sea monster, around his neck. That particular superstition, the belief that your blessings could be destroyed by the power of other people's jealousy, made little sense to me. If the evil eye worked, Ingrid Bergman would surely have already gotten leprosy. We women of Palestine, who could afford a movie ticket to see *Casablanca*, all envied her with venom. When Kamal took me to see it, he watched her and whispered to me, "Your skin is as light as hers." It was an observation I had already made myself. My whiteness was the only thing anyone ever seemed to notice about me, so I mentally compared my coloring with every woman I encountered. Ever watchful, always looking for confirmation I remained the fairest of them all. Kamal made love to me that night and every night after for a week. I gave up trying to make him wait until his mother, who slept with us in the only room we had, was asleep. Perhaps I even enjoyed it a bit, subjecting a woman who seemed bent on humiliating me to the sound of her son loving me. Cruel? Perhaps. Blame it on Ingrid. We Arab women, who watched that doomed love story set in the Arab world, aspired to be her, not the dowdy figures in the background who were supposedly Moroccans that were the backdrop—the foil—to her perfect loveliness, which our resentment never managed to mar. I should add, when Kamal affixed an enormous evil eye amulet over the entrance of our new villa, I did not object. But I never imagined Aziz would visit. Would he think it was I who wanted that monstrous angry eye to glare at every guest who entered our home?

For the man who had studied in French, I would wear my black-and-white Chanel dress, a gift from my husband. Kamal had provided me with more luxuries than even a man like Aziz, if he ever married, could give to a wife. Kamal was good-looking, too, with his short but stout commanding body and wide, dark eyes with lashes longer than mine. What did it matter that Kamal, unlike Aziz, didn't have the distinction of being the first doctor in our village? Who cared that Aziz had a stature in our community that Kamal never would? The power of academic prestige is mostly an illusion, like a guard dog without teeth.

Money can purchase several forms of status, like the renown of being the woman in my clan who had the largest villa any of us had seen. It dwarfed the two-story old Jerusalem homes that had once seemed like palaces to me, where my bastard father tried to force me to work as a maid, turning a blind eye to what often happened to country girls who worked in the homes of city folk. This house, Kamal bought me.

It still made me sheepish when I remembered how furious I had been with him for leaving me with his bitter widowed mother and boarding a boat to America so soon after the birth of our first daughter. Kamal stayed with his uncle Raghib, whom I never met, in Detroit. This uncle, who had never married, was called a loner—a polite way of saying he was effeminate. They were working in the same factory on the day his uncle was crushed to death in an accident. Kamal was the only relative whom Ford could find to pay the accident settlement. He returned on the next boat back to Palestine. He arrived before his letter telling me he was on his way reached me.

"Zoya, should I share the money with my cousins? They are Raghib's nephews, too," he asked, holding our daughter in his arms.

I did not want to be responsible for influencing him to do wrong.

When men falter, a woman is often blamed. So, I used my trick of playing people like flutes, making my words come from their lips.

"Ask your mother," I said.

Let her tell him what I wanted to say, which was let's keep it all for us. She did but, unfortunately for her, never had the chance to enjoy it. She unexpectedly died within a week and I found myself living among the city people my father had once wanted me to serve. A son with many brothers, he had inherited only one acre of his father's olive orchard. He was obsessed with owning more land. My older sisters would beam when he called them *binat quayseen* as they handed over their dinars to him at the end of each week. Don't expect me to clean excrement happily in the hope that you'd call me a good girl and take all my earnings. I knew all the land my father bought with our wages was eventually going to my brothers. I also knew where his compliments led me.

I grew up in the shadow of the British occupation. I had recurring nightmares about their soldiers entering our village. But, during the day, I could handle the British Empire. At recess at the Ramallah all-girls school, where I was always first in my class, I invented an elaborate game, "Palestinian Women Versus British Soldiers," in which we usually convinced them that our climate was too hot for them or stole their guns. Either way, we managed to get them to leave. Al-Sitt Elaine, my favorite teacher who doubled as our principal, used to sit outside while we played at recess and watch our game, a look of joy in her eyes. She was my mother's age but never dyed her hair, so she appeared old and dowdy. In a large notebook, she wrote down the lines we said that she thought were especially delightful, which—it must be admitted—were usually mine.

Our game grew more elaborate. We started repeating our favorite storylines, the seeds of a ritual we began to remember and reenact, as other kids would gather to watch us. The middles we improvised, but the ending was always the same. The colonizers were overwhelmed by our cunning and went home. Or stayed and faced the consequences. Either way, in the end, we were free.

I was twelve when I discovered Aziz, and he planted in me the seed of a dream that I might grow to marry an educated man. It was also the year our olive trees betrayed us. They didn't yield their usual treasures. My father couldn't afford to pay the mortgage of a new acre he had bought on the surrounding rocky hills of Ramallah. He would stomp around the house, screaming and striking at us at the slightest provocation. One morning, as I was readying myself for school, he approached me with a smile.

"Can you read a newspaper, Zoya?" he asked me, holding the latest issue of *Falastin*.

I looked to my mother, whom everyone called Imdelalah the Second. I sometimes even called her that, too. My father had been married to a fiery eagle-eyed lady by the same name for seven years, our neighbor. Tall and shapely, Imdelalah the First was a widow with three sons by her first husband. She remained the object of my father's lust even after he left her to marry my mother. The Orthodox Church wouldn't grant him a divorce, so he changed denominations, converting from Jerusalemite Orthodox Christian to Roman Catholic, in order to marry my mother in a different church. People jokingly said he had chosen her, a slight motherless thirteen-year-old girl, as his wife chiefly so he wouldn't have to remember not to call out the wrong name.

"We have been Orthodox Christians since the time of Christ!" my grandfather—who died before I was born—was said to have lamented. But my father didn't care. Every denomination of Christianity had a foothold among us Christians of the Holy Land. In Ramallah alone, we had Anglicans, Baptists, Quakers, Coptic, and Greek Orthodox Christians. Christian missionaries of various stripes would come to the Holy Land dreaming of converting Muslims. They had little luck there. So, they only ended up converting the indigenous Christians to their particular sects, usually by bribing them with the promise of work visas abroad or better education for the children in the schools they built in our midst.

Imdelalah the First was ten years older than my father. It was said that he had loved her ever since he was a child. Why else would he have married an older widow and taken in her three sons? But, for seven years, she bore him no children. *Yaba* expected to have many sons to work the fields he was sure were destined to be his. Nothing would keep him from his destiny.

"Leave me for another woman? Have you lost your mind? I bore three boys from my first husband. They are all the sons you'll ever have," Imdelalah the First allegedly told him. "Face it. You're infertile, *ya ihmar*."

It was easy to imagine Imdelalah the First calling my father a donkey. It was clear he was still in love with her. My father's eyes would look to her door every time he stepped out of ours. He sent her gifts, clearly trying to worm his way back into her affection. He bottled the first press of his olive oil every season and presented it to Imdelalah the First. I know because he would send us children, offspring of the second and very different Imdelalah, to carry it to her. She would take it wordlessly, hating us children as much as we hated her. Did he still visit her? I half feared I would see him sneak out of her home and the shame would kill me. My mother wouldn't know how to put a stop to it. Just like she didn't know how to put a stop to what he eventually would do to me, what she must have known he was planning when he handed me that newspaper.

"Please read me an article," he said. Had he just said "please"? To me?

"Where do I start, *Yaba*?" I asked.

"Anywhere, *Bint*. Show us how smart you are."

Why was he asking me to read to him? And in the morning? My brothers took turns reading the newspaper to him by candlelight at night. Whatever the reason, I was going to show him how excellent I was. I scanned the front page and found articles full of the usual railing against British colonialism and the occupation. Nothing new. Nothing worthy of beginning the first words I was asked to read for my father. Religion and politics did not matter to him. Money did. The British soldiers had no intention of buying up land he wanted for his olive orchard. It was the European Jews with their French francs and English pounds and German deutsche marks who were likely to drive up our land prices. The hike in land prices was all that concerned him. He had no idea of what was in store for us. He could never have imagined that every square foot of new land he bought by overworking his children and squeezing our household dry would be taken from him.

I opened the newspaper. An insert fell out, a reprint of a letter to the editors. The letter had been written by a scientist, whose name I did not know. I began to read aloud. I imagined it was Aziz who was listening to me read. For Aziz, I made my voice steady. Clear. For him, I did not stumble.

"I believe that the two great Semitic peoples, each of which has in its way contributed something of lasting value to the civilization of the West, may have a great future in common, and that instead of facing each other with barren enmity and mutual distrust . . ." I read.

I stole a glance at my father. His head was cocked to the side, like a cat trying to decipher whether the footsteps he heard belonged to a predator or prey. Our eyes met. "Go on," his gaze seemed to beckon. I did.

". . . they should support each other's national and cultural endeavors, and should seek the possibility of sympathetic cooperation. I think that those who are not actively engaged in politics should above all contribute to the creation of this atmosphere of confidence."

I slowly sounded out the European name of the writer. Albert Einstein. Who was he?

"He might be a genius in science, but he's clearly a simpleton when it comes to real life. Who talks of sympathetic cooperation between any two peoples? Only the stupid, which you clearly are not. You read better than me, *Bint*. You might even read better than your older brothers."

I beamed.

"You're so smart that you don't need to go to school anymore."

I could feel my face grow hot. Getting me to read had been a trap to justify denying me the education my sisters had. I thought I would have one more year at least. They had been allowed to go to school until they were fourteen before he sent them into strange houses to serve as maids, which *Yaba* now apparently wanted to do with me. No more school. No more Al-Sitt Elaine. No more games where Palestinian peasant girls would best armed soldiers, day after day, in newly ingenious ways. I clenched my jaw to keep myself from screaming. Why make me read for him? Why didn't he just order me to start working? He could have. But to make me confirm I was too advanced for my schoolwork was clever on his part. He could make me work younger than his other daughters had and not feel a twinge of guilt about it. But I learned a lesson that day. Never show how smart you are. It will be used against you.

Yaba turned to my mother and asked her the question that was never a question. Because she always gave the same answer.

"*Anjud, ya Mara?*"

"*Anjud.*"

Isn't that right, O Woman?

It is right.

My mother kept her eyes down, refusing to meet my angry glare. I wanted her at least to acknowledge she knew she was failing me. I knew, when I had daughters, I would fail them. There is no way for mothers not to in our world, perhaps in any world. You have to be free yourself to free someone else. I, too, might take them out of school or marry them against their will. But I vowed I would look them in the eye when I did.

"I want to stay in school, *Yaba*! I have to continue to learn, so I can teach my younger brothers. Ziyad is very smart. With my help, he could become a doctor. Like Aziz."

I felt a blush rise to my cheeks. Why would I bring up a strange boy's name? To my father? If he noticed, he didn't care.

"You'll work to help feed your fat mouth. Or I'll marry you off to Nadeem!"

The elderly widower, Nadeem, was a bogeyman to girls in our village. We were told if we were bad, we'd be married off to him. Old and senile, he would wander the village streets crying out "Where are my chickens?" The strange thing is his family never owned chickens. They were that poor. Didn't stop his sons from trying to find him a wife to take care of him so they wouldn't have to. They eventually got a girl from an orphanage. The truth about men was, no matter how little they had to offer, it seemed there was always a woman who was poorer and could be forced by circumstances into marrying him. But the threat of being married to a senile man didn't touch me. Not then. I had a card to play that my elder sisters didn't.

"You can't marry me off. I haven't bled yet!"

His eyes widened. That's when the discussion was over. No talk of women's blood in our house. Now my mother looked me in the eye, a gleam of life suddenly in her. She was glad she could find a reason to be angry with me, not him. I had been vulgar. I had transgressed. Whatever happened next didn't matter. I would get what I deserved.

He punched me in the belly. When I bent over in pain, he lifted my chin almost tenderly only to strike me in the stomach again. Not the face. Never the face. He needed that pristine. He would eventually have to marry me off, after all. I don't remember the pain of childbirth. I will remember what his fists felt like for the rest of my life.

"Tomorrow, be up and ready to work."

It was then that I got my idea. I would best him yet. Yes, I would work, but not the job he intended for me.

"I will, *Yaba*," I said.

I was being forced out of school, but that wouldn't be the end of my story. In my mind, I had already decided I was destined to be the wife of the brilliant Aziz. That belief made me bold. I would not be loaded into my father's cart and driven like my sisters to Jerusalem, where they dispersed themselves among the Palestinian houses that seemed like palaces to us, to slave away for dog-faced women and their wolfish husbands. More than once, I had heard Zakiya, my elder sister, complain of a silver bearded man at one house filled with French furniture and walls of mirrors who sat in the middle of their living room. With his legs wide open. So, she had to bend before him, clean under and around him, while catching reflections of his hungry eyes watching her as she worked.

Though *Yaba* thought it was fine to deposit my sisters in the households of strange men, they still weren't allowed out of the house except for church on Sunday. No strolling in the garden of Al-Muntazah or trips to the souk without a male relative accompanying them, usually one of my five brothers, who liked to pace the streets, looking for excitement. They could be induced to bring one of us sisters along in the vague hope we'd stop to greet a friend and they could sneak a good look at the girl.

My brothers, even the youngest, Ziyad, got up at the crack of dawn to harvest our olives. Any later and the sun made it too hot to work. I arose with them.

"You can't pick olives and be in the sun all day. No one wants a dark wife," my second-eldest brother, Mounir, told me when I joined them at breakfast. He didn't want trouble with *Yaba*.

"I have white skin. I don't tan. I burn," I told him.

Yaba wordlessly watched me leave to join my brothers in the field. He must have understood a willing field hand was worth more than a surly maid. He undoubtedly realized I would never totally bend to him. He would have to kill me first.

But my mother took me aside, giving me a flask of water.

"Zoya, keep Ziyad close to you."

I was annoyed that she felt I needed to take care of him. At eight, he was better at climbing trees than I was. But then it dawned on me. She wanted him close to protect me.

"Don't wander off alone in the fields. Always be careful. Men get to a point when they can't stop themselves from doing what they want to do. Stop them before they get to that point."

"How do I do that, *Yema*?"

Her eyes got the glazed look she often wore. It made it so you could look at her eyes but not see into them. Then, she dropped her gaze altogether as she answered my question with an urgency I had never seen in her before.

"Be impolite! Overstep! Fight! Defend yourself before you are attacked! A man looks at you, yell! He touches you, strike him. If he forces his mouth on yours, bite off his face! Don't freeze! Fight! Promise me that you'll fight. *Itemneesh hada!*"

Don't trust anyone. Did she mean what she said? Not my father? Not my brothers?

My mother responded to questions I couldn't ask by repeating, "Anyone."

What had happened to her? And why did she seem so sure that

it might happen to me? I kept my youngest brother close as we harvested our trees. My four elder teenage brothers ignored me as usual.
But, day after day working alongside them, I watched them. I got to
know their rhythms. At some point, each of them got agitated, moved
about like a restless panther, full of complaints. The sun was too hot,
the food tasted off, the hours too long. One by one, they would excuse
themselves to relieve themselves, and not come back for a long time.
When they did, they would seem calmer and did their work wordlessly.
What had happened in the time they were alone that could cause such
a change?

I picked olives and dreamed of Aziz. I married Kamal, a man I met
on our wedding day, and dreamed of Aziz. I bore Kamal children, made
a life with him among city folks, and dreamed of Aziz. But I loved an
illusion. I knew nothing about Aziz, the actual man, whom my husband
had run into in the town square and invited to dine at our villa on a
whim.

Even if Aziz had no memory of that night in the church, I felt confident I could charm him. I had been a pretty child and I had grown into a
pretty woman. I was young yet. My daughters were often mistaken for
my sisters, a feat even considering I had my first one at fifteen.

Kamal, in the other room, turned on the radio. Umm Kulthūm's
voice blasted so loud I could feel the rhythm vibrate in my belly and my
bones. *"Inta amri!"* she belted. You're my life. If only this song could be
playing when he arrived!

Aziz was finally coming to me. And who had invited him in? My
husband—that gruff man I married whose only advantage was that he
was not cruel.

Our telephone rang. Who could be calling? No one ever did. We
were the only people in our circle of family and friends who could afford a phone.

"Bonjour," my husband answered. Being colonized by the English,
we—at the time—felt that using French to answer the phone was a
form of resistance. None of us thought to answer this European inven-
tion, a marker of our newfound wealth, in Arabic.

"Ahlan, Aziz," Kamal said. My body went rigid.

"Of course! It would be an honor to have her. Any friend of yours is welcome here."

Her? A friend? Oh, no. Kamal came to inform me of what I already knew.

"The sly dog apparently wants to bring a date."

"Who is she? Where is she from?" I asked, my mouth dry.

"He didn't say."

"What's her name?"

"Golda."

I nodded to Kamal and he left the kitchen. Golda is a Jewish name. Was she a local girl, a Palestinian Jew whose family had been here for generations? Or one of the light-skinned European ladies who seemed to be arriving by the boatloads into Jaffa? This Golda was surely educated. Only the educated thought that rules didn't apply to them, fancying themselves free enough to court people of different religions. She probably would make me look like a *falaha*, a country bumpkin, part of a world Aziz had gladly left behind. She might even be, terror of all terrors, a blonde. My skin might be egg-white, but in no way could I compete with a natural blonde.

"*Yema!*" my youngest daughter cried out.

My corker again sliced through the skin of another squash.

She and my middle daughter burst into the kitchen, accusing each other of something I had no space in my brain to understand.

"I said stay out of the kitchen!" I hollered, and flew at them. I caught the littlest one by a braid I had woven and struck her belly with the flat side of the corker over and over. Her cries enraged me. They were volleys of demands I couldn't fill, vortexes of need pulling at me in opposite directions. I had to fight, fight, fight to not be torn apart.

Kamal rushed inside and grabbed my wrists. I let go of my daughter and the corker at the same time. She fled as it clattered to the ground.

"What's wrong with you, Zoya?" His eyes were wild with rage, his grip on my wrists tightening. Please, God! Just let him not strike me in the face. Anywhere but my face!

"I told her to stay out of the kitchen."

"Hit my child like that and I'll kill you," he said.

"When I do, I want you to," I told him.

His angry eyes went defeated when he understood what I was try-ing to tell him. I had not been in control. A demon possessed me. Be-cause it had no other home, that demon wanted me to live. Nay, to thrive. It struck my child with my hands. It used my mouth to hiss in her ear, "Scream! Scream louder!" I couldn't clamp down the elements of my soul that turned murderous when pushed too hard. Save them from me. Save me from myself.

3

ARABELLA

New York
2012

I had an inkling I might wind up in bed with Woke Movie Star when I saw I would be sitting next to him during the show. The other guy we brought along with us to my place was rather a surprise.

Woke Movie Star stood and bowed ceremoniously as I made my way past him to get to my seat. The world deemed him "woke" because he was that guy who imagined himself alive to the injustices of the world, awakened to the politics that gave him—a white male movie star—such unfathomable power, unlike anything that has ever been glimpsed in the animal kingdom. Did I mention he attended political rallies? Not in support of Palestinians, mind you. He was not batshit crazy. But who was I to judge? Neither did I.

Ten years ago, his manager had reached out to my agent after the reviews for my production of *Twelfth Night* came out. Famous actresses in their forties were hunting me down at the time. Inviting me to their enormous lofts in Chelsea and Tribeca. Legitimate ladies, Oscar and Emmy winners who took their trophies and fled Los Angeles to New York at the first sign of crow's-feet. Pretending they really wanted to work with me on my small off-Broadway shows in New York because they were intellectuals. Not mentioning that they weren't getting hired to be in movies at the same rate as before. It's very weird to be that young and to have movie stars wanting to work with you for basically no money. I noted the hunger, the intensity of their need to work to stay alive, in these aging actresses. But it was only now that I was in my midthirties that I actually understood it. Woke Movie Star was the only man who reached out to me in all that time, those heady early years when it felt like everything was possible.

Ten years in New York will do a lot to a girl. Did Woke Movie Star even remember me? Implausible.

"Here we go," Woke Movie Star whispered in my ear as the lights went down. The hot, unexpected breath made me jolt upright in place.

As Sir Famous Playwright/Blowhard stepped onstage and sat down in a pool of light, I promptly forgot Woke Movie Star. When a show begins, my mind enters a tunnel. Nothing exists, save the story that's about to unfold. Even when theatre is bad, it engages all my senses. Perhaps even more so. My mind grinds away harder, spinning with thoughts of how we could have made everything work. I feel in my bones this playwright/performer's entrance is wrong, wrong, wrong. There's no way a director should force a person to step into a spotlight unless they possess stage presence, which our playwright unfortunately does not. What does it mean to have presence? It means you'll listen to a performer speak with the pleasure normally reserved for hearing the opening chords of your favorite song. You observe him or her standing still with the wonder with which you watch an acrobat.

How to stage this show better? How to make it work? Axe the stage lights altogether. The playwright should be seated onstage as we the audience walk in and find our seats. Let us get used to the idea of him being in the space, as opposed to suddenly appearing. Then there is no letdown, no thwarted expectation that a transformation is about to occur. He's just a man, telling a story. Give us the feeling that any one of us could easily hop onstage next and tell our own. That will make an audience generous. Forgiving. Only people who are in a generous and forgiving state of mind know how to listen. Suddenly, for a moment, he's not a sir or a blowhard or a playwright. He's just a man who has a right to tell his story. Not even a man but an overgrown child, which is what we all are in the end. Floppy blond hair with salt mixed in and innocent eyes. Within the first few minutes of the show, I realized the script was better than I initially thought.

Should I have swallowed my pride? Taken the assistant job to the not-untalented white boy who graduated from drama school after me? There's a saying among theatre people that we live by: Work begets work. Say yes to every opportunity.

"Maybe only doing Shakespeare is limiting me," I considered. "Is it time for me to take on Marlowe? Should I ask this famous motherfucker sitting next to me to do a public reading of *Doctor Faustus*? I could convince some producers to come. I don't have to go to Palestine to get a gig!"

Woke Movie Star shifted in his seat toward me. I noticed he was observing my reaction to the show out of the corner of his eye. He smelled expensive and clean. Ten years ago, when I met him in the office connected to his palatial penthouse in Soho, it was clear he hadn't showered. His manicured hand now found its way to my knee. I let him touch me. Ten years earlier, I had not.

"Read about you in *American Theatre* magazine," Woke Movie Star had purred as he settled down by my side on his couch. "What are you up to now? What's your dream project?"

"I want to stage *Macbeth*," I told him. I had directed a student production of it with Yoav when we were undergrads. Yoav and I had talked about revisiting the play, possibly presenting it as a comedy. I was advocating for that idea with a potential producer, even though the concept didn't feel quite fully formed. Something about the death of Banquo's children that I couldn't make funny.

"You mean the Scottish play, don't you?" Woke Movie Star said. Most theatre folks believe it is bad luck to say "Macbeth" aloud. People who took superstitions seriously, whether Arabs or Americans, got on my nerves.

When he tried to kiss me, I reared my head back and left.

Back then, I hadn't felt attracted to him in the least. His face had been seen on screens across the world, but so what? He was two decades older than I was. I didn't find him to be particularly clever, and cleverness was what I valued most in a man. I considered myself to be as worthy of the title of artist as he was, if not more. I didn't need him to validate me in any way.

Yes, ten years in New York will do a lot to a girl. Now, when Woke Movie Star started stroking my knee in that darkened theatre, I felt how he had obviously expected me to feel when, a decade earlier, he hadn't bothered to bathe before trying to bed me in his office. Full of incredulous joy. Flattered beyond belief. Men see me. I exist. I attract, therefore I am. When the person seated on the other side of me also leaned my way, I turned in surprise. So discombobulated was I by Woke Movie Star being placed to my right—and what it might mean for my career if I could get him to act in my next show—that I hadn't recognized the man at my left. This young gun was a thirty-year-old version of Woke Movie Star. He was a series regular on a zombie show. I think he played the main zombie. I recalled reading something about these two men. They had been in a war movie together and were friends.

Main Zombie put his hand on my other knee. Cold and calculating is the opposite of hot and bothered. And there was no cucumber cooler than I was right then as the war buddies polished my kneecaps. All I could think was that I should consider reviving the idea of *Macbeth the Comedy*, especially if I could convince either of these fuckers to play the murderous fool in my production.

The lights brightened, turning my attention back to the performance onstage. Sir Famous Playwright/Blowhard was now awash in the color of dawn. Not natural light, as I would have suggested, but not a bad choice, either. A mournful Middle Eastern lute played. Now, that was a bad choice. Too obvious, it's like playing "Yankee Doodle" to signal a change in locale to America.

Their hands became more insistent, searching. I kept my legs slammed together. I was sober enough to do that. We three stared forward politely, good theatre patrons that we were. And we hustled out at intermission, passing Yoav in the doorway.

"Arabella!" Yoav called, and I stopped in my tracks. He clocked the two men who were holding me up. Was not impressed.

"Are you okay?" Yoav asked evenly. A wave of sobriety struck me. Yoav and I didn't ask one another if we were okay. We were never straightforward with each other like that. What might we reveal if we were? I know what I'd say. "You're a shit for making me say it first, but I love you." And I'd mean it. Both things.

Wave of sobriety over.

"Yes! I love the melody, Yoav! Love, love, love it!" I told him too loudly, and towed my escorts out the door. We left Yoav standing there.

Somehow, we made it to the entrance of my apartment, past the doorman, whose eyes I could not meet, and into the elevator.

Before the doors could close, the men sandwiched me between them. Grinned at each other while rubbing their erections against me as the elevator shot up flight after flight. After tonight, no one would be able to say I hadn't lived it up as a single woman in New York. If things didn't get out of hand, meaning I made it out alive. What if one of them was into choking girls out? Was I really worried about that? Should I be?

I had been taught to be wary of men. I was the first girl in my family to go to college. Possibly the only woman in my line who had ever lived alone. "*Itemneesh hada!*" was the parting advice my mom gave me when she deposited me in my freshman dorm. Don't trust anyone. I watched as she suspiciously eyed a pack of spry elderly male professors as they stood in a circle on top of the steps to the library, as well as the puppy-eyed graduate student advisors we met who would live with us in our dormitories. My mother assumed every straight man would try to bed me and that didn't make them unredeemable. It made them just, well, men. Creatures, not fully in control of their body parts. When they're not penned in, stay out of their path.

How her word of advice rattled me! Don't trust anyone means anyone. Including yourself.

I couldn't go back to Palestine. I needed another job. If I could convince one of these motherlovers to work with me, I might get one.

The doors of the elevator opened. The men pulled apart to give me space to fish for my key and open my door. Before we could step inside, my phone rang.

It was an international number. Could it be from France? Was it the Comédie-Française calling? I pitched a project to them two years ago. Oh, bountiful world! Had you sent me a reprieve from despair, aka a real directing gig, perchance at a theatre that isn't in a conflict zone?

"Got to take this. It's work," I announced. "They want to talk casting."

Their four blue eyes widened. Talk of casting in front of any actor anywhere, no matter how famous, and it's like a dog with a bone. They'd come to their senses and realize their stature vis-à-vis mine eventually, but—in the moment—instinct takes over. Their eyes go blind with hunger. They can't help it. They're so used to asking, begging, "Can I star? Let me star!"

"Go inside. I'll be right in," I commanded. They nodded solemnly, followed my instructions, and closed the door behind them.

I answered the call. A warm masculine voice spoke my name as if it were a question.

"Arabella?"

"Speaking," I said. Who was this man?

"Hi! I'm Baby Aziz. I mean, Aziz. Sorry. My family calls me that. To distinguish me from my grandfather. I got your number from my grandma, who got it from your grandma. Wow, this is not awkward at all."

I stepped away from my door and into the stairwell.

"Not a bit," I told him. If he registered the ice in my voice, he didn't show it.

"I heard you're a theatre director. That's so cool. I acted in high school. Nowadays, I just act like I know how to dodge bullets."

Okay, that was weird.

"My grandmother mentioned you work overseas," I said, and winced. I'd revealed we had discussed him in detail.

"I don't work. I mean, I'm a medic right now, but not for money. I volunteer. Finished my residency in emergency medicine a while back, but I'm not quite ready to settle into a practice. I went to Ethiopia, Mexico, and Yemen first. They were really just places for me to cut my teeth before I was ready to come here."

"Where is 'here'?"

"Gaza. I'm trying to, you know, save my soul. Got to make up for our parents leaving Palestine, don't we?"

"They had no choice," I said. He went quiet on the line for a moment.

"Everyone has a choice. They could have ended up as second-class citizens in Israel or noncitizens living under military occupation in the Palestinian territories."

"Or dead," I told him, stating the obvious.

"Yes, they could have ended up dead. Like many of our people who had the courage to stay did."

Cute. Actually, really uncute. Aziz was a true believer in revolution, in steadfastness, and in the idea of an honorable death for a noble cause. We were clearly a mismatch of epic proportions. That knowledge was a relief. I could be myself.

"I'm glad my parents left. I have zero desire to return to Palestine. War zones aren't my thing. But get this! Tonight I got offered a chance to direct a production of *Hamlet* in Ramallah. If I take the gig, it's only in the hope that my skills and/or my sex appeal might get noticed by the big British theatre company sponsoring the project. I guess you could say, if there is an Artists Without Borders, I'm not joining it. I should probably get off the phone now. I have two men in my room waiting to have a threesome with me."

"Two, huh? That sounds fun."

Well, that wasn't the reaction I was expecting. I remembered the profile picture of him I spied on Facebook. Dude was a dead ringer for a young Omar Sharif.

"Ever partake in a threesome?" I blurted out.

"Um, maybe?"

"There's no 'maybe' when it comes to threesomes, Baby Aziz."

"You're right. Okay. I was offered the opportunity to engage in an act involving two women while I was doing rounds in med school. Nurses. They're a wild bunch. Who knew?"

"Probably every straight dude who goes to med school. It's probably why most go in the first place. So, did you refuse their offer?"

"No, but I extracted myself. Mid-process. I didn't want to disappoint either lady, and male anatomy makes disappointment highly probable. Women are, well, built to last. You're lucky in that regard."

"Probably only in that regard."

"If I was a girl and I liked the two guys, I'd give it a go."

"Well, that settles that."

We were both silent. I found I wasn't ready to get off the phone.

"Besides the need to dodge bullets, how is life in Gaza?" I asked.

"Can I not answer that right now? I'm trying to keep you on the phone. If I start talking about what I saw in Gaza today, you'll start asking yourself, 'Why am I listening to this guy instead of getting serviced by two men at once?' And I wouldn't blame you. Let me play the good listener. Tell me, Arabella. Aside from getting a really cool job offer, how was your day so far?"

"Shitty. They added LED lights to the Empire State Building and it pissed me off. Worse. It freaked me out. Probably has something to do with the trauma of September 11 being imprinted on my sensitive soul. Also, I'm scared as fuck to go to Palestine."

Palestine. It wasn't a word that rolled off my tongue except with other Arabs, whom I rarely hung out with. I knew so few in theatre, and fellow theatre rats were really the only folks I knew how to befriend. The rest of the world was not weird enough to understand us. So, I called my parents' homeland the Holy Land, Palestinian Territories, or the West Bank. Names that made no one uncomfortable. Any and every name except the one my family for centuries used to mean home.

"You should be. Come anyway."

"My grandmother would flip if she knew I was working with a British theatre company. Sometimes I think she blames them for what happened to us more than the Zionists. That, and she's sure the Royal Family put a hit on Diana and Dodi because they couldn't stand that Her Royal Privates were being invaded by an Arab."

"I'm with your Teta. Not about Diana and Dodi. I have no opinion about that. But the British did colonize us for decades, promising us independence if we allied with them against the Ottoman Empire. Then, they proceed to split our country into two very unequal halves, setting the stage for endless conflict between us and the Zionists."

"Yeah, yeah. No one's perfect. They gave us Shakespeare. And the funds for a new Arabic production of *Hamlet*! Directed by one of our nation in exile's very own lost daughters, no less."

"You don't seem lost, Arabella."

"You don't know me."

"I want to see your production of *Hamlet*," he said. I had a flash of inspiration. An image, actually. That's how my best ideas for interpretations of Shakespeare come to me. I imagined a dark-eyed girl smiling wryly before she asks the question of all questions, "To be or not to be?" while being undeniably female.

If I was going to direct *Hamlet* in Palestine, I was going to put a girl in the title role. In that moment, "if" transformed into "when." In other words, I decided I was going to take the gig. I would do an avant-garde cross-dressing take on the classic and call it *Hamleta*.

Cradling the phone to my ear, I began descending the thirty-five floors of stairs, leaving the two randy stars alone together in my apartment. Walked through the lobby and onto the dark city streets, where I would retrace my steps around the Village and talk with a man, whom my grandmother conjured for me, until the streetlights were replaced by the sun.

4

ZOYA

Jaffa
1948

Kamal switched off the radio when Aziz knocked at our door. Had he left it on, we would have heard the broadcast of the terrible news along with the rest of the world. My night with Aziz would not have lasted as long as it did.

I rushed out of the kitchen, unsteady on my uncomfortable white heels that I regretted not breaking in. Kamal opened the door and boomed his greeting.

"Ahlan!"

"Ahlan!" Aziz boomed back. I stepped forward. There he was, a pillar in my doorway. I had never before stared into the face of this creature, who as a boy once glanced my way and changed my life. It had been seven years since the last time I had spied him on the streets of Ramallah. He'd been in line to order at Rukab's ice cream parlor. I hid from sight, pregnant at the time with my third daughter. Or was it my fourth? I thankfully was not pregnant now. My love looked older, a touch of gray at his temples. By his side stood a woman.

"This is Golda," Aziz said, and stepped aside with a gallant flourish so she could enter first.

"Ahlan. Thank you for having me," she told us in perfect Arabic. Clearly, Golda was a local girl.

I drank her in, looked at her as a man might. As he must. She wore a green silk suit with a pencil skirt that was short enough to threaten to show her knees. The curve of her breasts against the jacket revealed they were no bigger than a man's mouthful. Raven hair and olive skin. Pert and petite. Nothing unduly voluptuous about her, except her black eyes that seemed too big for her otherwise delicate, gazelle-like face. Not wholly unattractive. Okay, she was exquisite. But I knew, in my own way, so was I. I could compete.

"Golda and I met in medical school in Beirut," Aziz told us. "She was first in our class and I was second."

Okay, I could not.

"*Bonsoir*," I managed to whisper, determined to use the little French I knew. They stepped deeper into our salon, the formal entertaining room full of imported Versailles furniture and walls of mirrors that I didn't allow my children to enter. A pang of guilt engulfed me. How could I have beaten my own child so mercilessly today? And for what? To impress this man who brings me this woman? Good luck if they married. They'd need it. There were more and more skirmishes between the European Jewish arrivals and the local Palestinians. Some were even speaking as if the widespread feuding were the rumblings of a war on its way. Impossible. The British would clamp it down. Rule us from afar as always, no doubt. Still, did Aziz not desire Golda madly? There must be such fire between them. The world treats such couples, who defy the religion of their forefathers to be together, as if they are uncouth. Why? Is it the depth of their passion, or their weakness in the face of it, that makes them unseemly to the rest of us? Do we resent the freedom they exhibit to choose their own way, unfettered and unafraid? Or what it says about we who do not?

I could see the reflection of Golda's slender but shapely back in the mirrored walls. She had the Katharine Hepburn haircut that was all the rage. As did I.

"You have a lovely home," she said.

"*Merci*," I told her.

In that reflection, I noticed that her pressed curls were frizzing, threatening to come undone. Suddenly I understood why I must have insisted to Kamal we install those walls of mirrors when we were furnishing our home. The mansion where my sister had worked as a maid had mirrors like that. Though I had never seen it nor, thankfully, served the lascivious master of that house, I had replicated my idea of its design. To me, those mirrors represented absolute power. It signaled that in this space, I could watch you from almost every angle.

"Sit," Kamal commanded. We sat. Aziz waited for Golda to choose a love seat among our gilded couch collection and then he settled by her side. The first time I sat next to Kamal had been on my wedding day. Golda seemed completely at ease among us strangers. Was this pretty doctor ill at ease anywhere? I sat opposite them. Kamal stayed standing, smiling wryly at Aziz. I could almost hear Kamal informing his friends later that night as he went to relax and smoke hookah with them at *al-cuhwa*, as he did almost every night, that the doctor was surely getting sex from this woman.

"Where are you from?" I asked Golda. Let her be a bumpkin! Let her be a daughter of farmers who grew up with no shoes in a poor Jewish village like Bat Yam or Hartuv!

"Jaffa," she said, and smiled. No luck there.

"Her family lives just around the corner," Aziz said, and took her hand. Their eyes met. Some message that I could not read passed between them.

Kamal and I exchanged glances, too. Not even married couples held hands in public.

"How about a drink? Arak or whiskey?" Kamal asked Aziz. Now that my husband finally spoke in more than monosyllables, it was clear he still had the *falahi* accent of our village. Did he not realize these people had studied in Beirut? Beirut, the Paris of the Middle East?!

"I never say no to arak," Aziz responded, using the *falahi* accent as well. To be polite, I'm sure. Showing us he wasn't too uppity to remember where he came from. No wonder he was beloved, revered even, in Ramallah. There's no way he used that accent in Beirut. Not if his life depended on it.

Kamal stepped to the bar to make Aziz's drink. I had laid out five different kinds of freshly roasted nuts in crystal bowls. Aziz grabbed a handful of salted pistachios. He caught me watching his hands, his long, elegant fingers curled around a fistful of nuts in the way I so often longed he might grasp my flesh. Our eyes met. Could he read I desired him? He looked away, embarrassed. I got my answer.

"You were not so polite when you were young, ogling me in a church," I wanted to hiss. I heard the crack of ice hitting glass as Kamal prepared his cocktail, making me aware I was slacking on my hostess duties. It was unseemly for a man to ask another man's woman if she wanted a drink. That was my job.

"*Voulez-vous boire quelque chose?*" I asked Golda in what must have sounded like ungodly bad French.

"Arak as well," she answered in Arabic. I knew Kamal would mention to other men that Golda was a drinker, another indication this lady was loose. The women of Ramallah liked our arak, but only in the privacy of our own homes. Only in secret. I stood to get her a drink. But Kamal waved me away before I could, indicating he would handle it.

I sat back down. Stared at Golda and Aziz and they at me. There seemed to be nothing to say.

"Do you still make theatre?" Golda asked me.

"What?" I said.

"Aziz said people talked of the revolutionary plays you wrote," she said. Had he? I glanced at him. This proved Aziz not only knew my name, he knew more about me than my husband did.

"My wife is no writer," Kamal said firmly. It wasn't the idea of my writing that made him nervous. Plenty of our neighbors in Jaffa fancied themselves undiscovered Scheherazades and had a volume or two of poetry they wrote in their rooms. Newly rich and comfortable, Kamal didn't like talk of revolution. Let the British occupiers stay a bit longer. Let the European Jews buy up large swaths of land and drive up the prices. Yes, it took an uncle dying in an American auto factory accident and our hoarding the settlement money, but we now could afford to pay those prices. The world need not be dismantled just yet.

"Girlhood games. I never wrote anything down," I said.

"But Al-Sitt Elaine did. Al-Sitt Elaine was my great-aunt."

How had I not known that my favorite teacher was related to my great love?

"Al-Sitt Elaine transcribed your plays in one of her diaries. A book of them. She was so sorry that you left school so early."

I colored, looked away, wishing Aziz and this woman gone. How much easier to fantasize that Aziz and I were lovers than to have to see him! To discuss cheerful matters, like how little schooling I had.

Aziz seemed to sense he had touched a nerve.

"I owe my education to Al-Sitt Elaine. There's nothing wrong with being a farmer like our fathers. But that's all I'd be if it were not for her."

A flood of gratitude left me breathless. He still held Golda's hand, but he leaned toward me.

"People think I taught myself French, but it's not true. Al-Sitt Elaine taught me in secret. Told me to tell the French priests I had picked the language up all by myself. She said always make people believe you are smarter than you actually are."

"Is it not better to be underestimated?" I asked. To keep hidden the scope of your intelligence? The immensity of your capacity for love? He seemed to hear all the questions I couldn't ask and responded with a word.

"No," he said.

Had Aziz come here planning to tell me this? Had he manufactured a reason to run into my husband? Had he sought me out? He was a man who was famous for refusing dinner invitations.

"Golda, can I have the book?" he said. She smiled and pulled out a notebook with a soft white cover, the kind my teacher used to favor, from her elegant large black leather purse. She handed the notebook to him and he offered it to me.

"Zoya," he said. It was like I had never heard my name said aloud before that moment. "Al-Sitt Elaine would want you to have this."

I took the notebook and opened it. The first page read, in bold lettering, "These are the plays of my best student. Her name is Zoya but, in my mind, she should be called Nijmeh, because she is my brightest star."

"I've read your plays. They're delightful," Golda piped.

How I detested her in that moment! She had read my words. It was as if she admitted she had sniffed my undergarments. And who had given her my words, the keys to my mind, to carry in her purse for him? None other than the man to whom I had long ago given the only key to my heart.

"You were Al-Sitt Elaine's favorite student," he told me, realizing I seemed uncomfortable, and I instantly forgave him. Was there anything he could do that I would not forgive? I found myself overcome with emotion, to be told I had been favored by the one I favored.

"I loved her more than my own mother," I managed to say in a voice somewhere between a whisper and a moan. The truth of what I said, and how it seemed to threaten to unravel civilization itself, hung in the air.

I kept my eyes fixed on Aziz, willing them to express to him what I couldn't. I don't love whom I should. I love whom I love.

"Your mother is a good woman!" Kamal protested, still standing at the bar. He was very particular about the arak, ice, and water combination of his cocktails. Of course Kamal would think that of Imdelalah the Second. It made me more marriageable that my mother had a reputation for being subservient and meek. What a shock it had been to Kamal and his mother when they discovered I did not take after her.

Kamal stepped forward and placed down three drinks. One for each of our guests and himself. So keen was he on observing this loose woman who held hands with men and drank in public, he was oblivious to the fact that I couldn't stop staring at the man who brought her.

"Thank you again," Aziz said to Kamal.

"For what?" Kamal muttered as he plopped himself down next to me, looking like a bull more suited for pacing in a pen than sitting on a gilded love seat.

"For having us."

"I invite everyone from Ramallah who now lives in Jaffa to my house. It's only proper," Kamal bristled. My husband had a wonderful knack for never knowing how to say "my pleasure" when you thanked him. Kamal downed his drink in a few gulps. I could tell he was nervous.

"It's kind of you to remember your friends," Golda said. "When I came back from medical school, all of my old classmates were already married. Every single one of them. They rarely make time to see me anymore, especially the mothers."

And why should they, Golda? You have traveled. You have studied. You have lived. All they've done is create other creatures who might one day travel, study, and live.

"Shame on them!" Kamal told her. The outrage in his voice annoyed me. This is a man who ignored me if I spoke of my friends or tried to confide in him. On my first trip to Ramallah after I had moved to Jaffa, my oldest friends were surly with me. These were the former classmates I had cast in my skits when I was still allowed to attend school. Now they seemed to only laugh at jokes when I was somehow the butt of them. Was the hostility I was feeling my imagination? I wondered.

No. Rima—whom I always cast as the star—actually applauded when I tripped over a rock and fell in the souk. As I made my way to my feet, instead of offering me a hand, she snarled, "Guess becoming rich hasn't taught you how to walk better than the rest of us, has it?"

When I tried to tell this story to Kamal, he had literally walked out of the room. But he was all ears when it came to listening to Golda. And all eyes, too.

Aziz turned to me.

"How many children do you have?" Aziz asked. Ask me something better, Aziz. How many children would I abandon to run away with you? A million.

We were a childless house at the moment. I had banished our seven daughters to the house of my neighbor, a wealthy and miserly widow named Rashida. I was paying her off in ridiculously expensive European chocolates, which she never ate but saved to give to her relatives who expected gifts during Ramadan. On a whim, I disabled the telephone so she could not call me and disturb our dinner. Revealing the number of children I had would be reminding Aziz how many times I had been mauled, at the very least, by my husband, hence not part of my plan. But Aziz kept staring at me, waiting for an answer I had no intention of giving him.

"Our share," I said as I delicately slid an empty mother-of-pearl ashtray closer to Aziz so he could discard his pistachio shells. He smiled his thanks and I felt myself grow hot.

"Seven!" crowed Kamal as he dumped a handful of his empty shells in the ashtray I had placed before Aziz.

"*Ism Allah!*" Aziz said politely. "In the name of God" is what you were supposed to say when someone mentioned their blessings. To indicate that they recognized it was God's will that you had your good fortune. But one look at Aziz in his bespoke gray wool suit and his carefully shaved face made one doubtful that he desired a houseful of chaotic children of his own.

Golda's perpetual smile slipped momentarily from her face and she eyed me anew. I could tell what she was thinking. This woman seemed too young to have seven children. The reality is no woman of any age should have seven children.

"What kind of doctor are you?" Kamal asked her, continuing to play quite the journalist again. Despite all his staring, I knew he wasn't sexually interested in Golda. He literally only had eyes for me. I used to wish he would chase after the maids or visit the occasional prostitute, if only so he would leave me in peace instead of so often pregnant.

"We're both ophthalmologists," she said. Kamal nodded. From his expression, I knew he, like me, had no idea what that meant. Their drinks were now drained.

"*Itfudal!*" Kamal said, gesturing for us to move to the glass dining room table where my silver platters were still steaming. I eyed the feast critically and was pleased. The cornucopia of vegetables that are not what they seem, stuffed as they were with meat, spice, and rice, looked flawless. The tabouleh was so carefully chopped that every tomato square was the same size. The smooth hummus and chunky baba ghanoush were arranged in alternating stripes of equal size, adorned with flashes of orange-red paprika, and enveloped by layers of pita bread cut into precise quarters. Skewers of scallops shimmered like opals. The rice was laced with fried pine nuts and roasted lamb. Aziz pulled out the chair for Golda and she sat.

Kamal, never one to be outdone, pulled out my chair for me

opposite her. But he shoved me into it so far forward that my breasts were almost touching the table and I had to adjust. Why could it not be Aziz who was seated in front of me?

"The food looks amazing," Golda said.

"Zoya is—" Kamal started to say.

"Very adept at finding good help," I interrupted, realizing then that I didn't want Aziz to believe I cooked. I wanted him to instead imagine me reading poetry in a silky night-robe I ordered from Paris.

I would spend the evening watching Golda eat. Could she possibly chew every bite with her mouth closed? Maintain perfect poise through an entire meal? No doubt if any woman could, it would be she. Again, I thought of the daughter I brutally beat as I stared at this woman. Did her mother ever strike her? I couldn't imagine it. No, Golda was coddled and allowed to be educated. How else do you become a doctor, a healer, a woman in a man's profession who was still blessed with the beauty to attract the most attractive of men?

Sharing a meal can be more intimate than sex. I was counting on holding on to that thought. I invested it with the power of truth. Because, as we four sat around the table, I knew Aziz and I were never going to make love. Or was it too soon to be absolutely sure of that?

"Itfudal," Kamal said, gesturing with his hand for Aziz to eat.

"Itfudal," I repeated, my eyes on Aziz. Help yourself to everything. Everything.

Aziz smiled, took a skewer of scallops, and put it on Golda's plate. We began to pass around the platters. Golda seemed unwilling to take her share.

"She only eats seafood," Aziz explained.

"You should have told me," I said flatly. Who cares what she eats?

"I don't like to be a bother," she said to me.

"But I love meat," Aziz told me. He speared a chunk of lamb and put it to his mouth. For the first time, Golda caught that I was staring at Aziz. Probably because, in the moment, Aziz finally seemed to relax in the knowledge, rather than be embarrassed, that I looked at him with bold unapologetic lust, that I would devour him if I could.

"So delicious. *Selim adeyke*," Aziz said after he swallowed. God bless your hands. I feel a thrill of triumph. He was speaking of my hands and our God! Ours.

He lifted his fork again.

The doorbell rang. Again and again. The person outside pressed the button over and over, not waiting to give us time to answer. Kamal beat me to the door.

It was Rashida. My seven daughters spilled into the house. Loud and boisterous.

"Have you heard the news? I've been calling and calling!" Rashida cried.

"What news?" I said with not a little exasperation. After I counted their seven heads, I wondered why she was bothering us.

"We're all going to die. It's war now! It's war!" she said.

"Tell us your news, but calm down first," Kamal told her.

"The Zionist forces are coming! They intend to massacre every-one who isn't Jewish! Every one of us!" she ranted. "They went into Deir Yassin, a village with no soldiers. Not one! The villagers had even signed a nonaggressive pact with their Jewish neighbors! Did it matter? No. They killed everyone. Men, women, children. They tied a young boy to a tree and burned him alive, so people would hear him scream-ing and run out of their homes. And, as they ran, the Zionists shot them in the back. None of us are safe!"

Our daughters stood staring at us. Listening. Big-eyed. Frightened. This was a world where children were being burned alive. Nothing makes a man feel more impotent than a child's fear.

"Go upstairs!" Kamal hollered at them, and they ran.

"Can I go to your father's house in Ramallah for a while?" Rashida asked. "I can pay. If it's already full, just let me sleep on the roof." I was trying to wrap my mind around what she was saying, but all I could do was respond to her immediate request.

"Of course! You're welcome to go there as our guest. We would never accept payment from you."

That would turn out to be untrue. There would be so many refu-gees clamoring for a place to stay that my father eventually would charge

Rashida, along with a score of elegant city folks who found themselves penniless and on the run, to sleep in tents they set up in our olive orchard. Because it was my father in charge, it would be only those who could pay who'd be allowed to stay. Ramallah was considered safer. The Zionists had no designs on it like they did on Jaffa. Not yet.

"They're going to kill us all! There is no stopping them. We need to save ourselves. We need to run."

More neighbors appeared at our door, crowding in. The proud Fatima and her four sons who always liked to remind me women from Ramallah made the best maids. The sickly Mannal, whom fortune never smiled upon because she could only bear one daughter but who felt more blessed than me because at least she only had to feed, house, and marry off one. These women, who had always disdained me, and their children shouted questions at us.

Can we go with you to Ramallah? Will your relatives take us in? If we stay here, they're going to kill us all. Their words came at me like music punctuated by the same refrain.

We will pay! We will pay!

"That's not necessary," I said over and over to our fancy Europeanized "friends" in Jaffa. The women were wearing their gold under their grandmothers' handwoven *thobes*, so they would look poor and less likely to be robbed while on the run. Most would never see their homes in Jaffa again. When the first war was over, those homes would be razed or simply given to Jewish families who came from different corners of the world. Those families would then bar the door to the handful of our people who got foreign passports and returned to exclaim, "You took my house. My grandfather planted that tree. That very tree. I have the deed to this house. I have pictures!"

Those who could cry outside the doors of their houses were the lucky ones. The majority ended up in refugee camps in Gaza, the West Bank, Jordan, and Lebanon. They were never able to leave those camps and return. Not they. Nor their children. Nor their children's children. Why? Because, on another continent, a genocide took place that we had nothing to do with and the survivors of that genocide decided the only way they'd ever be safe was to drive us out.

"We have to run!" Rashida cried.

"Zoya, we need to get out of the city until things calm down," Kamal announced.

It was a turning point in my life. And, like most turning points, I didn't recognize it. My family would begin a journey that night, one that had no end in sight. We would leave our home in Jaffa. The skirmishes between recently immigrated European Jews and local Palestinians had metastasized into all-out war. We would lose. I would never again see that home or the book of my words written in my favorite teacher's hand that—in my haste—I'd left on my gilded couch. I would learn my home was deemed too beautiful to destroy, which meant it was instead given to a Jewish family. Most of the country now called Palestine would be renamed Israel.

Women would play a role in every aspect of the war. A leader among those Zionist women was named Golda; very different from the woman Aziz brought to our house that night. This Golda would say that there was no such thing as Palestinians. She would literally say we did not exist, therefore what the Zionists would have to do and did do to remove us from our homes could never have happened. What little land Palestinians would be allowed to have to make a country, or at the very least a reservation, the Zionists eventually would conquer and control within a few decades, claiming God Himself wanted them to have it all.

But, at that moment, my attention was still on the couple sitting at my table. I walked back to my dining room and saw I didn't have to tell them the news. The light had gone out of Aziz's eyes and Golda was crying. They clearly had heard everything.

"We should get you home," Aziz told Golda softly. She nodded. I realized with more than some satisfaction then that it wasn't likely they'd manage to stay together. It might have worked for couples like them to have bucked tradition, to have lived happily ever after together, in the past. But it wasn't going to work for them now.

5

ARABELLA

New York

2012

I was fast asleep when my phone rang at nine in the morning. Less so when it rang again a half an hour later. I finally dragged myself out of bed to look for it. I was exhausted, having stayed out circling the Village until five in the morning, talking on the phone to Aziz. I only returned to my apartment when I felt sure the two famous actors must have gone. Still, I knocked gingerly at my own door before letting myself in, half afraid they might jump out at me. Intellectually, I knew I didn't owe them sex. But did I owe them an explanation for why I had left them alone in my apartment and didn't return?

After some searching, I found my phone on the floor by the door. I saw several missed calls from Yoav.

"Where's the fire?" I said when Yoav answered on the first ring.

"Are you okay, Arabella?" he asked. "You seemed out of it last night."

"Just last night?" I joked. "I'm doing better than I thought."

"Yes. Just last night," he said slowly. "Are you okay?"

Being on the phone with Yoav so soon after I had hung up with Aziz thrilled me. In my groggy hungover state, I had a sense their disembodied spirits were both in the same room with me. A different kind of threesome.

"Keep your knickers on, Arabella," I thought.

Aziz had made promises to me on our call. If I took the gig in

Palestine, he was going to pick me up from the airport in Tel Aviv. Make sure I got settled. I felt the hand of fate was pushing me toward him. If it worked out between us, our relationship would move fast. We were from the same clan, descendants of the patriarch and matriarch who founded our village. There was nothing casual about the way we met. We were set up by our grandmothers. He wouldn't have called and I wouldn't have answered if we weren't looking for something serious. I could be a mother within a year. A year! Less. I felt half-married to Aziz already.

It imbued me with what I imagined was a married woman's boldness when it came to flirting with other men. With the security that I had someone else to fall back on, I decided to finally investigate whether Yoav had any feelings for me with a directness I'd never before dared. In other words, I didn't feel like answering Yoav's question. In fact, I had a question of my own.

"Why does it matter to you if I'm okay or not, Yoav?"

"What?" he asked.

I repeated the question.

"Because I care about you," he stammered.

"Why?" I asked.

"Because we're friends," he said.

Friends? Just friends. There I had it. The answer I did not want.

I wanted to be locked into some torturous Romeo and Juliet story. Also, I thought being with a Jewish man might somewhat protect me. Fewer people would be able to entirely dismiss me as an anti-Semitic bloodthirsty raving terrorist bitch if I, in a candid (read: drunk) moment, ever let down my guard. If I talked about how much my mind, body, and spirit abhorred the idea of theocracies, any society explicitly designed so that a crackpot who happened to be born a certain race or creed had more power, privilege, and fun than the rest. Or if I expressed a touch of the immense impatience I had with those who not only thought nothing of trying to explain to me that expelling or subjugating my people forever was the only way to secure the safety of their own, but also considered me to be the unreasonably crass one if I begged to differ. I wanted an excuse to not talk to the conservative shitheads in my extended family who would make it a point to shun me if I got together with a man from a different tribe, a tribe that hadn't been so friendly with ours as of late. I loved the idea of living in a way that was unquestionably modern! Iconoclastic! Scandalous!

All that was true. But I would have fallen for a guy like Yoav no matter what his background. I dug him from the moment we met in our Introduction to Theatre seminar our freshman year. The teacher had paired us up to write out the subtext in the opening scene of *All My Sons*. We soon found out we liked the same kinds of stories told in the same kinds of ways. When I decided to stage a student production of *The Tempest*, I asked him if he wanted to be involved.

"Sure."

"What do you want to do? Act? Or do lights? Sets?"

"Anything you need, Arabella."

"But what do you want to do?"

Young Yoav thought for a moment.

"I used to compose. Been thinking about trying my hand at sound design."

"I'm sure you'll be brilliant at it."

And he was. Thus we began an artistic collaboration that had lasted for the past eighteen years. I was lucky to have found him. Yoav was always underplaying his intelligence, which made him a rare bird at Harvard. It seemed as if he had read every book or play that had been written. Or at least every one that I could name. When a guy is that smart, he doesn't have to be hot, but he was! He was! How could I not have developed some feelings for him? But I was looking to be a mother, and everything I knew about Yoav made me doubt that he would be dependable in the fatherhood department. He didn't seem to give a shit about money or to mind that he lived with two roommates in a basement apartment in Williamsburg. He relished out-of-town gigs. He'd work for free just to hang out in a different country. Though I knew him for close to two decades, Yoav always retained an air of mystery about him. He rarely spoke of his family. That's hard to do in theatre, where oversharing is the norm. I knew his dad was dead and he was estranged from his mother, who had not remarried. The few facts he'd let slip about her were that she was an Egyptian Jew whose first language was Arabic, and that she had left Egypt in the 1950s. I learned all that when we grabbed a meal at Ruzana in Brooklyn and he ordered *molokhia* soup. Though delicious, this green soup looks like the Loch Ness monster threw up in a bowl. Not something just anyone might randomly pick off a menu. When I expressed surprise at his culinary choice, he told me his mother used to make it for him.

To my knowledge, she never once visited him in college, not for a Harvard parents' weekend nor to see any of the shows we made together. The only other detail I knew about Yoav's mother was that, instead of lunch, she ate frozen yogurt at the Forty Carrots café in Bloomingdale's every day, which I learned after suggesting we grab a bite there when we were rehearsing *Twelfth Night* nearby at the 59E59 Theaters' rehearsal space.

"That's the one place in New York I don't go," he said.

"Why not?" I asked.

"My mom goes there every day at noon and has a small cup of yogurt. Every day."

"Really? Why?" I asked.

"She's fucking nuts. I don't know. Her family was rich in Egypt before they immigrated. Being served at Bloomingdale's reminds her of a place back in Cairo where she ate pastries as a kid," Yoav said. "But she doesn't eat pastries anymore. She hardly eats anything."

His harsh tone took me by surprise. I had a habit of defending the parentals of other people, trying to give them the benefit of the doubt. It used to annoy kids in high school that I wouldn't let them talk shit about their own parents in peace. It was a knee-jerk reaction on my part, a fear that the stone slabs of the original Ten Commandments would fly from heaven and bitch-slap you upside the head if you didn't honor your mother and father. Or at least refrain from bad-mouthing them.

This was particularly strange, because it wasn't like I was Daughter of the Century. My mother's incessant phone calls drove me mad. She had always been really anxious, which I was beginning to understand was a result of profound insecurity. On some level, she remained the immigrant child who felt lost and unable to understand the rules everyone else did. Decisions as mundane as what food to serve when it was her turn to host her book group flabbergasted her. She expected me to stop everything I was doing whenever she called and instruct her on what to do. I found the three annual pilgrimages to San Francisco I felt obligated to make for Easter, Thanksgiving, and Christmas onerous as hell. But I never missed a holiday. Never.

What kind of man could ice out his own mother? Clearly, Yoav was a guy who could cut out anyone who pissed him off badly enough. And the reality was—and would probably forever remain—that I was prone to pissing people off.

"Yes, we are friends, Yoav," I told him bitterly. "That we are. Unfortunately."

I let that hang in the air for as long as I could. Then I remembered I was being a dick about something.

"Congrats on the Tony nomination, by the way," I told him. "It's well-deserved."

"Thanks. And it'll be well-deserved when you get your Tony nod, too."

"That's never happening, Yoav."

"Exactly what you said when I told you that you'd someday get an Obie. And you got one, didn't you? What's the lesson here?"

"No one knows shit about shit?"

"Exactly. And Arabella Hajjar wins more than she expects to."

Classic Yoav. He could always manage to make me feel okay. Better than okay. Hopeful. I'd be forever glad he was in my life, even if only as an infernal motherfucking goddamn friend.

"I've been offered a gig to direct a production of *Hamlet* in Ramallah."

"Wow! Isn't that where your parents are from?"

"Yeah. It's being sponsored by the Royal Court."

"Fuck yeah it is! That's amazing, Arabella. I'm planning to hit Asia soon. I'll be close enough to pop over. When is the opening?"

I did not want to tell him. Yoav was the type of guy who would "pop" anywhere to see a show, especially when a friend was involved.

Sometimes, he'd even sojourn to faraway places just because he had read an article about a performance and thought it sounded cool.

I didn't need Yoav mucking up my shot at dating Aziz, a man who was (lo and motherfucking behold!) actually interested in me. On opening night, I wanted to sit beside someone who saw me as more than a friend as the lights went down. If Yoav was there, I'd spend that time looking for a sign that he wanted to be that guy. I knew myself. I'd be trying to use Aziz to make him jealous. I wouldn't be able to help it. One thing I learned from the women in my family was that the greatest (sometimes only?) power you have as a person is the power of refusal. You don't need to respond to a question just because someone else wants an answer. No one can make you.

"Gotta go!" I said. "I'm late for a lunch appointment."

I hung up the phone before he could ask me again about the opening. Or make me explain how I could be late for lunch when it wasn't even ten a.m. Why had I mentioned lunch? Because lunch was on my mind and I knew where I intended to go. Bloomingdale's.

6

ZOYA

Jaffa, Ramallah, and the Atlantic Ocean
1948–1963

Your body can be hurtled through space faster than your mind can catch up with it. You can arrive in a place before it hits you that you've left another one. I would have that experience first when I fled Jaffa, then again when I found myself aboard a boat to New York.

On the night of the Deir Yassin massacre, Aziz hurried Golda out our door, his arm tight around her as he passed our panicked neighbors.

I watched them until they disappeared around a corner as Kamal told our neighbors they could follow us to Ramallah if they could make their own way. We had enough on our hands trying to find out how we would get our daughters to our village. We owned a car, a silver Pontiac Streamliner, but Kamal never kept the tank full. He preferred keeping extra money in his pocket to gas in his car. So, we did not have enough fuel to make it to Ramallah. Kamal said he dared not risk being stranded on the road. He bought the car as a symbol of his wealth, not as a vehicle intended to transport his entire family when massacres were occurring around us. Kamal, who moments before had seemed so certain we had to flee immediately for our lives, began to waver.

"We can hide in the house. Is it safer to stay put?" Kamal asked me.

As if to answer his question, a barrage of mortar fire sounded in the distance.

"We need to leave tonight," I said, and he nodded.

Kamal made phone call after phone call, looking for a driver. No one seemed to be answering. Finally, he found us a ride back to Ramallah with a man who delivered oranges in a donkey cart.

"It's better that we look poor. If the Zionists catch us, they may take pity on us."

"The poverty of the villagers of Deir Yassin didn't protect them," I said.

It was the first time I invoked the name of the massacred village, but it wouldn't be the last. Over the decades of my life, after the bewilderment of dispossession dissipated and made room for doubt about our decisions as a family and a people to settle in its place, I would tell myself we'd had no choice but to abandon our home and run. We couldn't have stayed. Always remember what happened to the people of Deir Yassin! Those villagers signed a non-aggression pact with their Jewish neighbors, for heaven's sake. They were still killed. What would the Zionist forces do with us if we stayed after Jaffa fell? We had to leave, we told ourselves. We believed it. Most of the time.

Even the way we used words changed. *Al-Nakba* means "the Catastrophe." But forevermore, we'd never say it again to reference any other catastrophe except the One in which we lost our country and our home.

"Our driver will take us by the way of Wadi El-Nar," Kamal told me, the steep, precarious road known as the Valley of Fire. No tank can follow you through the Valley of Fire. No jeep would want to. If we didn't fall off a mountain cliff, we'd be safe. Donkeys know how not to fall. But the rickety wooden cart our driver brought with him was unenclosed. As it rounded the curves, it was possible a person might be thrown from it.

I stared at the painfully skinny teenage driver with shifty eyes and an Adam's apple that seemed too big for his body.

Another round of mortar fire erupted. Was it my imagination or was it getting closer? Maybe it wasn't Zionist fire. Maybe it was the sound of our forces coming to liberate us?

The front of the cart next to the driver was the safest spot.

"Sit next to him. You might be pregnant," Kamal said. "It might be a boy this time."

I shook my head.

"Our daughters are the only sons I can give you," I said.

"Then they're all the sons I want," he said, and kissed my cheek. He took my hand and walked me to the front of the cart. I sat next to the driver and took my youngest girl in my lap. She was the one I had beaten earlier that day. Behind us, Kamal and my six other girls settled among canvas bags of oranges.

Whenever I glanced back, I caught the silhouette of Kamal, somehow encircling all six girls as they sat in the wagon. It was as if his arms had grown longer by the sheer force of his will. In a world where men cursed the birth of daughters, he loved ours. He was going to hold on to the family we had created together. My heart had been absent from my marriage until that moment. No man existed right then but him, the person who had always been present for our children. He had tried to protect them, even from me, which often is what—of all things—is hardest and most necessary to do. Unless, of course, you find yourselves in the midst of war.

The driver began to whistle as we started on the steep road. I resisted an urge to push him out of his own carriage. To take the reins. I sat as far away from him as I could on the hard wood bench we shared. We had paid him to help us to flee armed marauding murderous gangs. It felt as if his whistling was alerting unseen forces in the night.

"I am so sorry for hitting you earlier today. Do you forgive me?" I whispered to my girl. Tears streamed down my face.

"I'm sorry I came in the kitchen when you said not to, *Yema*," she answered.

Poor children. If the source of their pain is their parent, that parent is often also their only source of salvation. I do not remember the experience of carrying this particular girl in my belly. Her birth felt like a blur of torture. They all did, after the shock of my first. But I would always remember how it felt to have her asleep in my arms, the bodily comfort bringing relief, even in my terror for her. It was that feeling I would long for decades later, as I lay withering away alone in Detroit. Not to be held, but to hold a child who forgave me everything, who gave me absolution I did not deserve.

The road through the Valley of Fire would be busy that night. Streams of city folks and villagers were toiling ahead and behind us, mostly on foot. We passed the seaside and saw families crowding into boats that rowed into the night. The mass flight of Palestinians had begun, though we didn't recognize it as such at the time.

Even the full moon did little to dispel the darkness once we started on our precarious route. I was glad I couldn't see the steep drop below; the edge looked only inches away from the wheels of our cart. Shadowy figures roved around us in the dark. There was a tumble behind me and the dull sound of a body hitting the bottom of the valley below made my blood run cold. I turned and, to my relief, saw Kamal had all six of our girls sitting with him still encompassed in his arms.

"It is just a bag of oranges that toppled over. Just oranges," Kamal said, seeing the panic in my eyes. Our tired girls had been resting their legs on the bags. One of them must have kicked in her sleep.

"A whole bag?!" the driver hissed.

"I'll pay for them," Kamal told our driver.

"Yes, you will," he muttered. How I hated him! Finally, we passed the most dangerous part of the Valley of Fire and I could breathe again as the road to Ramallah widened.

By dawn, I stood back in front of my father's door, remembering how I had left it on my wedding day with the sounds of the women of my family trilling with joy. I had felt the relief of escaping my father's house more intensely than the anxiety of marrying a stranger. Did that mean I had been—in my own way—happy? Maybe not, but I had been happier than I was now, when I had to return to that same house with a husband and seven daughters. We weren't the only ones who were waiting there.

Men surrounded my father's home, strangers crowding around our door. They wore stylish city clothes with pants and shoes dusty from walking. Their womenfolk waited a few paces down the hill, standing among suitcases and bags and their children. One woman had brought a sewing machine with her, an enormous green European contraption that she was leaning on. No doubt it was the source of her livelihood. Who else would lug a machine of that size around? Where had she carried it from? I suddenly remembered my book of stories Aziz brought to me. Had leaving it behind been a mistake?

My father was known to be one of the biggest landowners in Ramallah. The refugees—who didn't know enough yet to understand that's what they had become—seemed to be negotiating prices with him. For what? Apparently, anything they could get.

How much would you charge us to pitch a tent? Need a hand in your field? People need to eat, even during wartime, right? So, how about it? I'll work cheap. I'll work for food for my children. I'll do anything. Just until I can go back to Jaffa, to Haifa, to Acre. I'm a doctor. I'm an engineer. I'm a welder. I'm a professor of literature. I'm a very pretty boy whom men of a certain ilk like to keep around. Are you of that ilk?

I watched these men beg my father for help in their uppity city accents, never knowing how it annoyed us country people to listen to them mar our language.

When city folks spoke, they dropped the harder *c* sound. An entire letter of our alphabet they erased when they spoke. Their talk sounded feminine to my ears, especially as they appealed for help. How hard I had tried to adopt that accent! I was suddenly proud my children never could.

My father listened with a patient smile on his face. He never did a damn thing that wouldn't somehow benefit him, but he took a long view of things. I could see him calculating. These relationships might prove helpful when the British returned to stamp out the fighting. Or when the armies of other Arab countries came to liberate us. Or when the land itself revolted and rose in sandstorms to drive out those who dreamed they could erase us. Whatever the method, even my exceedingly practical father assumed that somehow the fighting with these Zionist madmen would end. We, who were the majority of the population, would go on living as we had always lived on our land. So we all believed. When our lives returned to normal, as my father was sure they would, it would be savvy to stay on the good side of the city people while offering them nothing. So, as they begged my father for help, he always responded in the worst way possible: *"In sha Allah."*

God willing. If He wills it, I'll help you. But I myself am not promising anything.

I knew he was enjoying their pleading, their naked displays of desperation, because I knew him.

"Bring your families here," he commanded.

The city men motioned the women and children over.

"You can stay in my orchard as long as I don't catch you or your children touching my trees. I count the olives on every branch every morning."

The Adams and Eves, newly expelled from Paradise, chorused, "Yes, of course! We promise we'll keep our hands to ourselves! Your trees are your trees."

When I approached him, my father seemed happy to see me. He didn't immediately throw me out nor tell me that my husband's clan should harbor me and my children, as he would do to several of my unfortunate sisters. My husband was wealthy. If my father allowed us to stay with him, he knew Kamal would be obligated to provide expensive gifts that covered the cost of our food and upkeep. My father had been hankering for a plow from Kamal's new hardware store, his latest business venture. None of us could imagine we'd never see that store again.

The loss of a home is bewildering, but how had we stayed bewildered for so long? Why didn't we take more seriously the Zionists' claims that this was to be a homeland for Jews alone, and that they believed we Palestinians had no place in Palestine? You have to be Palestinian to understand. Everyone wanted a foothold in the holiest place in the world, from the missionaries who came from America to the Turks who believed the Ottoman Empire would one day rise from the ashes. Having grown up in the shadow of British colonialism, I assumed someone would rule us. But I could not comprehend that they wanted to drive us out for good.

"Your mother needs you, Zoya," my father said, which surprised me. He rarely spoke of anyone's needs but his own. When I stepped inside his door and saw my mother, I understood why.

War doesn't stop people from dying in ordinary ways. It hastens it, though. Over the past year, I had begun to notice my mother seemed to suffer from strange tremors. She accommodated these physical changes, as she had done with everything else that was thrown her way, without complaint.

"Only fill my cup halfway," she told me one day as I poured her coffee. That was unlike her. She drank *cahway* by the buckets. We used to tease her and say it was her only vice.

"Why?" I asked.

"That's all I want," she told me. But when I saw how her hands shook like small brown leaves in the wind, it was clear she would have spilled had I poured her more.

"*Yema*, you should see a doctor," I said, but I was too distracted to pester her. I only visited Ramallah when I felt particularly forlorn about being continually slighted by the snobs of Jaffa, especially the mothers at the private schools my children attended. I had invited these women to dine at our villa and none had returned the favor. In our world, this was an insult of epic proportions. For some reason, making them accept Kamal and me—to include us in the parties they held for each other every Sunday where they waltzed to European music they played on horn gramophones—had felt like a matter of life and death. Absorbed by my own problems, I chose not to take my mother's tremors seriously. It was as if the maddening meekness of her nature, the perennial fright she felt in the face of my father, could no longer be contained within her mind. It was now manifesting itself physically. Perhaps it was easier to find a way to blame her for the symptoms of her illness than face the fact that she was undoubtedly ill.

I found my mother lying on a cot near the door of our one-room home. The stench in the room hit me in the face, a smell that could only come from human waste. She looked so frail, as if she were starving to death. How could that be? It had only been two months since I had last visited. If her staring eyes hadn't blinked at me, I would have taken her for already dead.

"*Yema!*" I cried out. Was I being punished for saying aloud that Al-Sitt Elaine was more precious to me than my own mother? I didn't believe there was a God who was keeping score. Who killed your parents to punish you for not loving them enough. To me, religion fell in the realm of silly superstitions. But ingratitude is an ugly thing nevertheless.

My mother had borne me into this world, suckled me, and soothed me when I was sick. Al-Sitt Elaine thought me clever but had done none of those things. How was it my mother's fault that she was illiterate or hadn't been able to defend me against my father? She couldn't defend even her own self.

I crouched down next to her. The left side of my mother's face was frozen, as if she was already half a corpse. Not knowing what to do, I poured a cup of water, lifted up her limp body, and put the cup to her lips. The water dribbled down her chin. If she could swallow, she didn't seem to want to.

Her lips formed into a weird misshapen half smile that unnerved me. It made her seem mad. She had trouble forming words.

"*Bukh* . . ." my mother started to say. "*Bukh* . . ."

"Yes, *Yema?*" I asked.

But she fell silent. Speaking was not worth the effort.

"We need a doctor!" I told her.

She shook her head weakly.

"*Bukheel!*" she managed to say. Cheapskate.

Her eyes had a glint of light in them. Was it glee?

"Are you talking about *Yaba?*"

She nodded. I had understood her meaning. It must have been a word that was on her lips for decades. A word she never dared utter until now. It would be decades later that I could enjoy the fact that, with whatever life energy she had left, my mother had managed to insult him. To name what he was. To finally fight back. In my agitated state, I tried to fill the room with words so she wouldn't have to.

"I'm going to take good care of you. You have been such a good wife and mother, *Yema.*" The glint in her eye was gone. Good wife, good mother. That was what people always said of her. It seemed she had no patience for it now.

"At least you outlived the bitch next door," I told her, and she brightened again. This was the kind of talk she wanted to hear. The discarded Imdelalah the First had recently succumbed to liver disease, rumored to be caused by drinking too much arak.

That first day back in Ramallah, I stayed indoors to tend to my mother. I was shocked when she didn't alert me and urinated on herself. I stepped outside. My father was sitting on the veranda.

"Has she seen a doctor?" I demanded to know.

"Of course. I paid for the charlatan from Bir Zeit to see her. The man charged me three dinars to tell me there is nothing he can do. Doctoring is nice work if you can get it. You are paid even when you fail."

"Why didn't you tell me she was so sick?"

"Your mother did not want me to. She's only started not being able to hold her water recently. The *kasiya* cleans her and I pay her a whole cup of olive oil per week," he said, clearly feeling he got the worse end of the deal.

"How often does she come, *Yaba?*"

"Once a day."

"Once a day!"

"If I make her come twice, she'll ask for more oil," my father said. I left him standing there and returned inside.

I had to wipe the mother who had wiped me. Though such work cannot be done gladly, it can be done gently. I was determined not to show my disgust. Smiling, I cleaned and wrapped my mother in a towel, then went outside to wash her soiled clothes and bedding. Behind the house, I found Kamal, standing alone and smoking. I told him how ill my mother was.

"Might she eventually be okay?" he asked. I shook my head.

His eyes shone with sympathy, something I had not seen in my father. Had I been a comfort to Kamal when his mother died? I hoped so. When our daughters emerged from my father's orchard, hot and tired from playing hide-and-seek, he decided to treat them to a trip to Rukab's ice cream parlor so I could tend to my mother uninterrupted.

Kamal took my father along. When they returned, it was clear they were already at odds. Had my father somehow hinted we were a burden? Probably. That night Kamal announced if he couldn't go back to Jaffa immediately, he might as well board a boat for America. Make some American dollars and come back, as he had done so many times before. I was against the idea.

"Why not?" Kamal said. "It'll be at least a few months before the fighting dies down and I can reopen the hardware store."

"Months? It won't be more than a week before we return to Jaffa."

"It might be longer," Kamal said. "Maybe as long as a whole year?"

"*Mustaheil!*" I insisted.

"Nothing is impossible, Zoya."

"You had workers in the hardware store, Kamal. Are you really ready to go to break your back in an America factory again?"

"I can still handle factory work. You don't think your husband is going soft, do you?"

I had always assumed he only had eyes for me, but maybe I was wrong. Why the sudden eagerness to return to America? Did he have a girlfriend he longed for back in Detroit? I was jealous for the first time in our marriage. Was love for my husband, a love everyone swore would blossom eventually in the hearts of girls forced to marry strangers, beginning to unfold within me?

"Never," I flirted. "I just think a man with your brains is above such work."

I shouldn't have said it, as he would repeat it over and over in the years to come. "A man with my brains is above such work."

There wasn't enough room for all of us to sleep in my father's house. So, Kamal and my seven girls slept in our chicken coop. I stayed to tend to my mother, who moaned in agony all night.

In the middle of the night, a bomb went off in the souk of Ramallah. It sounded like the earth itself had ruptured. For the first time, I allowed myself to give in totally to terror. The Zionists had followed my family to our village. Those who had slaughtered Palestinian men, women, and children in Deir Yassin called themselves the Stern Gang. The name itself inspired fear as did their bloody rhetoric. They vowed anyone who wasn't Jewish would not be allowed to stay, including the British. They had killed Lord Moyne, Churchill's minister in the Middle East, as well as a UN mediator, Count Bernadotte. What would they do to us?

Though no one died in the empty souk, the bomb rattled us. My father demanded we, too, go out and sleep in the open air of our orchards the next night.

"We evacuate the house. So we aren't killed in our homes while we sleep," my father announced.

I could tell Kamal didn't agree or particularly care for my father's authoritative tone.

"There could easily be an airstrike on your orchard," Kamal told him. "We are no safer there than we would be here."

"*Hakey habal*," my father said. Nonsense talk.

Kamal forced a smile. I knew Kamal would be booking his passage to Detroit sooner than later if these skirmishes went on much longer. Skirmishes, that's what I called them, even after waves upon waves of refugees passed through our village each day, bringing more stories of more massacres. The Zionists apparently didn't let our people hide in their houses. They'd round them up in the village squares and shoot one or two men as an example, usually someone who tried to negotiate with them, then watch as the rest stampeded their way out of their cities and villages in terror. Our entire orchard was dotted in makeshift tents, including the one my father pitched for our family to sleep in on our second night in Ramallah.

Though I dared not tell Kamal, I agreed with my father. No one was trying to eradicate the land of its trees, so we'd be safer if we slept among them.

My mother had to be carried in Kamal's arms like a bride to the fields. The sight of him, who had loved my daughters and me so fiercely, holding my mother brought me to tears. I wanted to let him do the thing he liked most to thank him but, of course, we could not find the privacy. As I lay down next to my mother, I stared at the outline of our trees, which stretched up toward the stars. They looked like the gnarled hands of giants who had been buried. Taken for dead, but reaching out of the ground, trying to break through.

It takes a lot of power to ingest anything. You must chew on it, over and over. Break it down. Whether my mother was capable of swallowing, I wasn't sure. But I did know she wasn't trying. She would make great effort to control the working side of her face when she tried to speak. But, if I put morsels to her mouth, she would keep it agape, so food and water would slide right out.

"I will kill a chicken tomorrow and make you a broth," I told my mother.

"*Laet*," she said with much effort. No.

"You need to see a specialist! When the fighting settles down, we can travel to Beirut to find one."

"*Laet.*"

"Why not? Maybe a specialist can help you?" I practically shouted. To my surprise, the little glint in her eyes seemed to grow, as if she found my display of rage amusing. Her eyes asked: Can you not pretend you have patience with me, *Bint*? Even now?

I fell silent, hollowed with despair, as her lips kept forming no, no, no. She was trying to say something.

"*Laet* Sameh," she managed to tell me.

"No Sameh?" I asked. She nodded with as much vigor as she could muster.

Amo Sameh was the uncle she had stayed with when her mother died. She had been mistreated by Sameh's wife, who both overworked and underfed her. But it wasn't her name on my mother's misshapen lips as she was dying. He had done something unspeakable to her. Unspeakable it would remain.

"You don't want Amo Sameh at your funeral? Is that what you're trying to tell me?"

She blinked hard and nodded again, a movement now so slight I thought I might have imagined it. I did not then know those would be the last words she spoke, but I sensed I understood her meaning correctly.

"He will not attend," I had promised my mother. It was a promise I would keep when we buried her within the week. It got me through my grief to know I had a duty to her. I was to keep that man away from her corpse. My other sisters, who were largely absent as she was dying, busied themselves with making her ready for viewing. Worrying over the cut of the dress she would wear and her hair.

I knew the real task had been entrusted to me. I was going to make sure that my mother's body, which we would allow people to view at our home one last time before the burial, was finally safe.

When the detested old man, stooped with age and eyes cloudy with cataracts, arrived at our door to pay his respects, I stood in the doorway.

"You are not welcome, Sameh," I hissed. "My mother did not want you here. Make an excuse and go home."

"Huh?" he said. My words, though spoken with great emotion, had been lost on him, as he had grown rather deaf in his old age. Since I could not loudly tell him to go, lest others hear me being rude to an elder and not understand why, I'd have to expel him a different way.

"You look *ayan*," I told him. Sick.

"I feel fine," he said.

"I have no doubt about that. Men like you always do. But you are *ayan* nevertheless. Go home. Rest."

In the way I said that last word, he knew I was telling him to drop dead. I saw it dawn on the old man that my mother must have spoken to me about him. I felt triumphant as I watched him hobble away. I had honored her wish. Jubilant, I walked to the church. It was only when they put her pine coffin in the ground of the Ramallah Christian Cemetery that I collapsed. Her body was safe now and my duty had been fulfilled, so there was nothing shielding me from despair. Kamal held me up as I wailed and clung to him, almost indecently. As he walked me home, I was so happy for his strong arms, his alive heart beating. I was glad to be his wife.

"I'm booking a flight to America. To work for a while. I will send for you and the girls as soon as I can," Kamal told me that night, giving me a new reason to mourn.

"My mother just died. How can you leave me right now?" I asked before realizing he had delayed his trip to say his final goodbyes to her. It had been a kindness to wait as long as he had.

I begged Kamal to take us with him, that we should travel as a family. But he shook his head. We didn't speak of our house in Jaffa or our hardware store anymore. How and when did the shift between "we have to return immediately" transform into "we must make a life until we can return" happen to us?

"It'll only be for a little while," he told me. "Maybe I'll buy a business and bring you and the girls over. Would you like to live in America for a few years?"

We never acknowledged the fact, which the Zionists seemed determined to drum into our heads and hearts, that neither we, nor our children, nor our children's children would be allowed to return. We kept telling ourselves we would. But we would have to make do in the meantime. It would be easier to make do in America.

It turned out to have been the wrong call to have hidden and hoarded the settlement money from the Ford factory. When we moved to Detroit, we found it a place full of hostile cousins, as they had learned how we made our windfall—through blood money that we had not shared with all who possessed that blood. Instead, we sank it into the villa and a hardware store we would never see again. His relatives, who had been dirt-poor and emigrated to America for economic reasons before the founding of Israel, turned out to be the winners in the end. And now they hated us.

For over a decade, I stayed in Ramallah while Kamal lived in America alone, working in the same Ford factory where his uncle had been killed. He went back and forth only twice, paying my father to house me and our children. Kamal impregnated me on both trips. I bore him another daughter, my eighth girl. Naya was the color of copper, the darkest of my brood.

"Good luck marrying her off," my father told me when he saw her. He would never have predicted that Naya would marry better than her light-skinned sisters and that her daughter would attend the best universities in the world.

I found a wet nurse among the refugees and paid her in scoops of lentils and rice to suckle Naya. I was too exhausted to love another child. She would find parental love in Kamal, when he came back four years later and met her on his second visit back to Ramallah.

Many of our men disdained their daughters, especially so if they hadn't been able to sire a son. But Kamal clearly adored little dark Naya, like he loved the seven girls I bore him before. He would not walk anywhere without carrying her on his shoulders, so eager was he to keep her near him, to make up for the four years he hadn't known her.

He was carrying Naya when an old woman approached him in the souk. Kamal was on his way to take all eight girls to Rukab's ice cream parlor. This old woman, a stranger, promised Kamal that God would reward him in the way He rewarded all good men who truly loved their daughters.

How does God recompense such men? Money? Health? No, He gives them sons, of course. Truly loving your daughters meant you would eventually stop being tortured by having too many of them and be blessed with a boy. But you couldn't fake that love. If you resented the birth of a girl even slightly, God would know it.

"You will have a son next," the one woman told him. According to Kamal, she then disappeared into the crowd.

Though I considered myself above such silly superstitious sentiments, I could not help but feel the old lady had been right somehow. Because nine months after Kamal's second visit, I bore our only son, Ghassan. That boy I nursed myself.

As the years passed, I lived for the day Kamal would write and tell me it was time I could join him in Detroit. In his absence, I began to believe what people said about growing into loving one's husband, because I felt I suddenly had. I craved Kamal's touch. Each night for years, I closed my eyes to sleep, trying to drown out my father's snores, and pretended Kamal was just outside and would be coming to me shortly. I couldn't wait to be back in his arms. He never caressed me. His big paws didn't know how. But there was something satisfying in the way he took me with animal passion.

When Kamal finally sent me the much-awaited letter, informing me it was time to bring the children and join him, my desire for him had welled up to an unbearable pitch. I packed our belongings. As Kamal instructed, I took the children with me when I applied for the travel funds from the refugee relief organizations that were springing up to help masses of Palestinians deal with the logistics of our new reality. In that reality, we were suspended in the state of never knowing if we would have a state of our own. Our perpetual homelessness was especially difficult to fathom, much less accept, because we were living within walking distance of our houses.

When I got those funds, I did exactly what Zionists dreamed every one of us Palestinians would eventually do. I left Palestine. Yes, I left my homeland cheerfully, shamelessly. With a song on my lips and love in my heart for my husband, I flew with our children from the Jerusalem International Airport to Beirut, where I boarded a boat crowded with Palestinians that would take us to Alexandria. At that port, I dared not get off like the rest of the passengers, afraid to leave my nine young ones alone on the boat and afraid to go with them into the famed Egyptian city to see it, as all other passengers seemed eager to do. From Alexandria, we sailed to Naples. In that Italian port, I and countless other Palestinian refugee families marched our children from our tiny, crowded boat to the deck of a huge liner set to sail to New York. At the helm of the ship that would take me to my husband's arms, I spotted a man standing alone. Erect as a statue, he seemed transfixed as he stared at the open sea into which we were about to be launched. It was Aziz.

7

ARABELLA

New York

2012

I never intended to speak to Yoav's mother. I had only wanted to catch a glimpse of her. If you're still curious about where a man comes from, you can't truly be over him. And over him I was desperate to be. Let me face the monstrosity who made him. The Bitch Goddess, the woman he had known first. I thought that might help me move on. But should I have believed such thoughts? Was I really trying to wrench myself free of my unwelcome desire for Yoav by seeking his mother out? Or was I—without her awareness or consent—auditioning her for the role of grandmother in the family I still desperately wanted to make with him?

Bloomingdale's was the ultimate Manhattan department store, with its mix of high fashion for the uberwealthy and semi-affordable fare for the aspirants. The merchandise lived on different floors, of course, yet it was housed in the same building and staffed by people whose relatively measly salaries meant they couldn't afford most of what they sold, yet were expected to look as if they might. In that way, it seemed designed to be a microcosm of New York.

When I arrived at the café, I spotted Yoav's mother immediately. Indji Cattaoui was her name. She had snagged one of the few tables and there was an empty seat in front of her. Was she waiting for someone? The most recent photos I had seen of her online were at a fundraiser for a synagogue in Bensonhurst, where Yoav grew up. She was an architect, according to a site that thanked her for volunteering her design work to the new Jewish community center for Levantine Jews.

In the pictures and in real life, she resembled Jackie O. Or rather a better-looking actress who might be cast as the former First Lady. Though Indji had larger doe eyes, a softer chin, and higher cheekbones, they shared the same slender build and dark good looks. The same ability to look regal even in all-white capri pants, a peach linen top that dared not wrinkle, and impeccable white sandals. I was overdressed for a day of shopping. Had weirdly put on the same black cocktail dress I had worn the night before, now with flats. Because the day felt like an extension of a night where so much had happened. I had scored a directing gig in my ancestral homeland and a date with an unreasonably handsome man upon arrival. Twenty-four hours earlier, I had none of those things.

Indji had a small plain white yogurt in front of her. It was untouched. I went up to the cashier and ordered a yogurt, too. Indji stared straight ahead, not eating. I approached her.

"Do you mind if I share your table?" I found myself asking.

She gave a "be my guest" gesture.

"I love this yogurt," I told her. "It's the only treat I allow myself."

I felt her take me in, clearly noting I was not slim.

"I make it a meal every day," she said. "Since I'm not long for this world, perhaps I should branch out. Apparently, I have breast cancer."

I felt my jaw drop.

"I'm so sorry," I told her, and meant it. Did Yoav know?

"Do you have family?" I asked her.

She looked at me as if she found my question strange. As she lifted her eyebrows, her expression quizzical, I suddenly saw her resemblance to Yoav. How many times had I caught him looking that way with his headphones on during rehearsals, trying to listen to the music and words together? To figure out if the sounds he had selected were underscoring or overpowering the story we were trying to tell.

"Why?" she asked me.

"I was just wondering if you had enough support."

"To have a family doesn't necessarily mean you have support. I have a son. But he doesn't speak to me. So, I'm not telling him about my diagnosis. My mother used to say the saddest thing in the world was a childless woman dying alone. But she was wrong. Do you know what is infinitely sadder than that? It's a woman dying alone with a child who doesn't bother to visit her."

"Tell your son that you're sick. Whatever happened between you, I'm sure he would want to know," I told her with a surety I only could muster because I knew Yoav. Or I thought I did. He was unfailingly kind to everyone. He would visit his dying mother and help to take care of her. Wouldn't he?

"As I mentioned, my son and I aren't on speaking terms right now."

She took a bite of yogurt but looked sorry she did. I realized she must be feeling nauseous.

"What's your story, Pretty Young Lady?"

"You think I'm pretty? Thank you. That's nice to hear from such a glamorous person."

She smiled in that way only a woman who was accustomed to hearing compliments can.

"Tell me your story. You're young. You must be in love. That's what young people do, don't they? They fall in love."

I felt an urge to bolt, to jump up and run away. I thought suddenly of Aziz, his teasing voice on the phone, and how it seemed to make my body go alive. The picture I saw of him on Facebook flashed in my head, his wiry body with muscular arms under his bulletproof vest with the word MEDIC written across on his chest. I wanted to lurch myself through space and time toward him. Toward safety. Toward the textbook appropriateness of mating with a man from my village, who was one of my kind. Toward womenfolk who would welcome me into their family fold, who had sought me out, hoping I would join their circle. Hoping I would make them grandmothers.

The greatest gift one can give oneself is to be where one is wanted.

Yes, I hadn't even met Aziz, but we had spoken for hours. I was open with him in a way I had never been before with any other man. All that was left was for us to meet, right? But the fact of the matter was Aziz was still a stranger. How could someone whom I only experienced as a disembodied voice suddenly be a counterbalance to my Yoav, who had been making shows with me for almost two decades? I probably shared more meals with Yoav than with anyone else outside my immediate family. We would haunt Veselka, downing their cheap drinks and meat pierogis, almost every night when we were working together. Hours that slipped into years that had turned into decades of creating side by side. Yoav had composed the sounds that underscored the best work I had ever made or might ever have the chance to make again. In that moment, I lived in the space—that stasis—between being pushed and being pulled. That push to be modern, radical, and free tugging against that pull to find comfort in a community and identity that mattered deeply to me, if only for no discernible reason other than it had mattered to the women who had come before me.

"Yes, I'm in love. But there's a problem."

"There always is."

"I'm Jewish and he's Palestinian," I found myself saying. I saw my words land on her. What had compelled me to tell such a lie?

I tried to will myself to find an excuse and disappear, but I couldn't bring myself to leave. This conversation would probably be the only time I ever spoke to Indji, the unseen evil mother and matriarch, deeply devoted to her religious community but estranged from her own son. I was taught women were the people you had your primary relationships with. Who your mother-in-law was might have equal importance to who might be your mate. You were paired up with a husband, each flawed in his own way and interchangeable, but your real connections were with other women.

"Do you think I should defy my family and try to be with him?" I asked.

"No," she said simply, and I could tell why Yoav hated her. Because I suddenly did. Even on the verge of death, had she no words of wisdom that rose above the din of this dismal world that she would soon be leaving behind? No insight into the importance of true love for we who still had time?

"If you loved this man enough, you wouldn't need to ask me. Or anyone. You would know you simply cannot live without him. Nor he without you."

She was right. I could live without Yoav. Unhappily, but I could. I had. And he certainly seemed perfectly capable of living without me.

"I want to be a mother," I told her. "More than I want to be a wife."

"You are so different from me. All I wanted was to be a wife. One particular man's wife."

As I listened to her story, I understood what she was sharing with me was the essence of her soul. More than simply hearing it, I breathed it in. Inviting a competing history into your worldview is disorienting. It flips a switch in your brain and your vision suddenly becomes kaleidoscopic. The shards of your people's history are true and clear, but they don't coalesce into a neat picture of saints and sinners. Because I was a stranger, Indji could be free with me. Unguarded. I was about to learn more about Yoav's mother than I would ever know about the interior life of my own.

8

ZOYA

The Atlantic Ocean
1963

Aziz stood at the mast of our ship and, as if he sensed my presence, turned to look straight at me. He was dressed in the same wool suit he had worn to my home and seemed steady on his feet. I, on the other hand, felt unmoored. The ocean beneath us was rocky, forcing me to stand wide on two legs to avoid falling.

Of the sea of young and old Palestinian faces on that deck, Aziz's was the only one I recognized. He approached me.

"*Salaam Aleyki*, Zoya," he said to me.

"*Aleyk Al-Salaam*, Aziz," I whispered.

He saw my children milling about me. I introduced each one by one. On the night he visited, I had tried to keep them out of his sight. It now seemed like a ridiculous thing to have done. Why? Did I fancy he was going to leave his elegant, educated girlfriend and run away with me? Or I with him?

We were riding in steerage, the bowels of the ship. My children were eager to explore the boat and meet the other children aboard. They would rather play marbles below than see us start to set sail.

"Can we go down to our cabin?" Ghassan asked me. I nodded.

Aziz and I watched them go.

"Where is Golda?" I could not help but ask. I wished I hadn't. He hadn't asked me where Kamal was.

"Home," he said. Of course. She was back in Jaffa, which was enclosed within the borders of the amputated land that was now firmly under Zionist rule. It was probably the only time I was glad a Jewish woman was allowed to remain where I was not. I had Aziz all to myself.

"Did you bring the book of your plays?" he asked me.

"No, I left it in our house."

"In Jaffa?" he asked. I nodded.

"I saved that book for you from my aunt. I brought it to you. Now it's lost for good! Like our country!" he practically shouted. *"Ghabiya!"*

Stupid. That's what we called ourselves when we remembered the things we left behind when we ran. Stupid. How could we have not believed the fiery rhetoric of Zionists, who called our country a land with no people, which meant they intended to do everything they could get away with to make it so? Stupid. How could we have not noticed the astounding asymmetry in power between us and not known what was coming?

It was one thing to call oneself stupid. I would not tolerate someone else naming the thing I knew I had been, not even Aziz.

"You think I'm stupid? Look in the mirror! Had I had half the chances you did, I wouldn't have been second in my class in medical school. I'd be first, *ya Ihmar.* I would never have gone around faking I magically taught myself French while I was being privately tutored. It only made the rest of the boys in the village despair when they couldn't manage to do the same. I would tell the truth about myself. Because the truth about me—how much I know with how little opportunity I had to learn it—would be enough to shame scholars everywhere."

Aziz burst out laughing suddenly. I found myself smiling sheepishly.

"Scholars everywhere, eh?"

This we found funny, too. The other Palestinians edged away from us, leaving us standing alone.

There were plenty of men and women snapping at each other on that boat, but our sudden mirth made us seem suspect, as if we were slightly mad.

"It would shame writers, too. You know that's what I aspire to be.

I want to try my hand at writing our people's story. In between shifts at the Ford factory, of course. My cousin already got me a job on the production line. Lucky me," he said bitterly.

"Can't you work as a doctor?" I asked.

"I'd have to learn English," he said.

"So learn it!" I told him.

"Easier said than done. I studied because I had Al-Sitt Elaine making me do so until I got into medical school. In medical school, I studied with Golda."

It was hard for him to say her name.

"Did you love her?" I asked.

"Does it matter now?" he said.

"It always matters who you love," I told him, and the look in my eye was unmistakable. There was no question he could see that I wanted him to make love to me. Was he amenable to the idea?

He stood up straighter but looked down.

"I could help you," he told me with averted eyes. "I read your plays many times. I remember their plots. We can reconstruct them together."

We could do that. Or we could find a quiet broom closet and plan to meet there to make love in the middle of the night.

"Why? They're irrelevant now that the Israelis are in charge. My plays are about British occupiers."

"No, they're not. Your plays are about justice! Justice that we will obtain!"

Hadn't he just said that all was lost for good? Does trauma make you unstable? Rewrite your DNA so optimism and pessimism are forever intertwined? Is that what our lives would be like now? Would we forever be swinging between hope and despair, sometimes within the space of a breath?

"Yes, we will get justice! Or die trying. That is what we must teach our children."

Our children? I blushed. He dropped his gaze again. It felt as if we were dancing around a fire that was suddenly extinguished. We realized who we were, and who surrounded us, and said our goodbyes. Each of us headed purposefully in different directions. But I would search for him. Seek him out throughout our journey. It would be a night of sudden storms when everyone was seasick below that we would catch each other alone for the first time. The motions of the sea had no effect on either of us. We had stomachs of steel.

9

ARABELLA

New York and Tel Aviv
2012

Breathless, I ran to my terminal. Rushed inside the plane and the flight attendant snapped the door shut behind me. I was locked in on a plane to Tel Aviv. There was no going back.

I had dawdled about my apartment too long, reluctant to leave my beloved New York. I would be staying in my great-grandfather's house in Ramallah, a one-room stone affair perched atop the ridge of the largest hill in our village. It was where my mother had been born after my grandparents fled Jaffa. Our house was surrounded by mansions built with money our neighbors had made abroad. But our family didn't visit enough to warrant that kind of investment. It had modern plumbing and fixtures now, but even getting my mother's several siblings to agree to pay the cost of that had been a fight. I remembered, as I was packing, our family home was no bigger than the one-bedroom I was leaving. My great-grandfather had been alive when I visited for the first and last time, a pleurisy old figure who lived alone. His eyes would beam with joy when anyone spoke to him. Your eyes only light up when someone talks to you when it's clear few ever do. Even as the time of my afternoon flight grew closer and closer, I couldn't pull myself away from my window, my view of the New York skyline, trying to memorize the shapes of the co-ops as well as the landmarks. Thankfully, during the day, the Empire State Building's new needle wasn't lit up, so it remained invisible from my vantage point.

My mother told me the view from my great-grandfather's house in Ramallah would be different than it was the last time we visited. There were now apartment buildings, parks, and homes of Israeli settlements in sight on the hilly orchard that my great-grandfather had bought long ago and was now lost to us. Confiscated.

Worse than having our land taken from us was that we Palestinians were never allowed to buy it back with the money we made abroad. The vast orchards, where a young Teta Zoya had picked olives, had been bulldozed. My mother, usually too busy shopping to impress her American friends and living the dream to get heated about politics, warned me of the "great fun" I had in store for me, which was watching Israeli families lounging around swimming pools in the pristine Jewish-only settlements, which was only especially irksome when the Israelis had decided we had enough for the day and cut off our water.

"There are always winners and losers. Most of us are both. My Manhattan apartment was built on Native American land," I intended to remind myself every time I got angry. To keep my cool. To see my job like it was a military mission. Get in, direct a play, get out. Yes, and figure out if I wanted to pursue a relationship with Aziz.

My cab had run into traffic on the way to the airport and I hadn't given myself enough wiggle room to account for it. I read once that being perpetually late means you're functioning but frightened at your core. Together enough to know you have to be somewhere but falling apart to the point that you can rarely do it within the appropriate time frame. Procrastination is a form of protection. The inevitable slights of the outside world are continual reminders of where you are in the pecking order. How likely you are to be expendable. Thrown out of your tribe, which—for so long—meant certain death.

As I made my way to my seat, I thought again of Indji's words. How the story of her Egyptian Jewish clan, who had shaped Egypt before they were forced out of it, felt like it was part of my collective memory, imprinted into my DNA. How was that possible? I had only met the woman once.

"I was promised to him. And he was the handsomest man in the world," said the dying mother of the boy I had closely watched grow into a man.

I was assigned to a middle seat in the middle of the plane. When I found it, I was horrified to see who was in the seat next to mine. Lisa-Turned-Layla was sporting a silk black eye pillow on the top of her head—the way a cool person might rest a pair of sunglasses—and that useless U-shaped travel pillow was snuggled around her neck. She had booked our tickets. Of course, she had taken the aisle seat for herself. We were about to spend a month working together. Did we have to sit next to each other on the long flight between New York and Tel Aviv, too? I was still livid with her about outing me as a Palestinian in *American Theatre* magazine. I knew I should get over it. That cat was out of the bag. Now I was one with the people, aligned with the revolution, making theatre designed to bring down the Man! And everybody in our relatively small world knew it. There was buzz about our show already. Our press release got picked up on several theatre blogs. Some were calling it an artistic reuniting of Palestinians living inside and outside our historic borders. As I suspected she would, Lisa-Turned-Layla ate up my idea of having a woman play the starring role and changing the title to *Hamleta*. Gender-blind casting of Shakespearean plays was all the rage in New York, but no one we knew of had done it in the Middle East yet. Lisa-Turned-Layla looked as pleased as I've ever seen anyone sitting in coach. Why shouldn't she be? She had convinced the artistic staff at the illustrious Royal Court to foot the bill for our entire production and had secured herself the job of translator of the text. This show was her baby.

"Hi, Arabella! I got us some snacks," she told me. I sidled my way into the middle seat next to her. There she was, skinnier than me and offering me Snickers. Fuck her forever.

"No thanks, Lisa," I told her.

"It's Layla," she corrected me.

"Of course," I said. I popped in my earplugs and closed my eyes, to signify I wasn't in the mood to talk. In that self-imposed darkness and relative silence, I found myself alone again with the words of Yoav's mother.

"I was named after Indji, a beautiful cousin of mine, the daughter of our family's scion who had died young and long before I was born," Yoav's mother had told me. "They named me that to endear me to the wealthier members of my family, no doubt. You see, I'm from the penniless branch of the Cattaoui family. That's like saying you are a Kennedy with no money." As she kept speaking, I noticed the reason she reminded me of Jackie O. was not entirely an accident. There was a physical resemblance, of course, but she had styled her short, thick, dark hair just like the former First Lady during her Camelot era. She had studied her. Emulated her. Probably never knowing she was prettier than the icon of style. Or knowing it too well and wanting you to make the comparison between them that I had and come to the same conclusion. She went on, "We are from Catta, a few miles north of Cairo, but we had moved to the city a few generations before mine. Cairo was the Paris of Africa. Cosmopolitan. Diverse. There were people of every corner of the world living and mixing there. Yes, we were Jews. But we felt as Egyptian as the pyramids. Until we weren't."

I opened my eyes. Caught a glance at the people who were sitting around me. Like most flights to Tel Aviv, ours was filled mainly with Israeli and Palestinian passengers, who were placed together in rows, trying to ignore each other's presence. A strikingly young-looking Orthodox Jewish couple with twin boy toddlers on their laps sat in front of us. She was sporting a dark wig and he a black suit and long beard. Lisa-Turned-Layla had taken the seat to my left while there was another Palestinian girl to my right. She was wearing a hot-pink hijab, tight jeans, and dark liquid eyeliner with Cleopatra tails. The chick was popping gum and playing Egyptian pop tunes so loudly on her headphones that I could make out the words. *Habibi, habibi, habibi!* My love, my love, my love! The refrain of every love song and, incidentally, an Arabic word that both Israelis and Palestinians alike used to mean the same thing.

One could spend a lifetime doing academic scholarship on the linguistic parallels between Hebrew and Arabic, both Semitic languages, which shared several of the same words. Or cite how, at weddings, we both lifted the couple on chairs and danced in circles. But I didn't have a lifetime to spend that way. There were those in both Israeli and Palestinian peace camps who tried to say coexistence was possible if we only focused on our similarities. How can we fight forever? Half the time we can't tell each other apart. But, nah. That didn't matter. That ideology posited we should see ourselves as part of a larger tribe that encompasses both our people but didn't dismantle the tribalism that was at the core of the conflict.

Who understood tribalism better than I did? For fuck's sake, I came from a village that disdained marriage and mixing with Christian Palestinians from the very next Christian Palestinian village. For centuries. Even among their descendants who were born in America. The allure of belonging is powerful. Its siren song's refrain calls out to you, "The world is not really full of strangers. You are never truly alone." But it necessitates having people on the outside. It finds a way to make people separate. And separate is never equal. It's the inferior parts of our humanity that hunger for group identification. The less proud you are of your personal achievements, the greater the need to celebrate the triumphs of your "team." An aggrandized and sanitized version of those achievements, no less.

There we were, assorted members of two warring tribes stuck on a plane in transit, that unique form of imprisonment. Each of us in our own way preparing to be tortured by time. Waiting for the moment in the journey when we make the mistake of checking the hour. Lose our shit when we realize how far we still have to go. Have to stop ourselves from exclaiming, "When, for God's sake, when will it ever be over?" We, the passengers from different worlds going to the same place and knowing we would be treated differently once we arrive, were quiet with each other. No one wanted to make this any harder than it had to be. Eager to be separated at the border, which we would be soon enough. The Israeli customs officers would be there to stop and take aside practically everyone with an Arabic name. But, while on this flight, we couldn't tell who was who just by looking at one another, especially those who weren't donning yarmulkes, hijabs, or crucifix pendants. Yoav's mother had believed me when I said I was Jewish.

I regretted that I'd sought her out right before I was returning to

Palestine, a place already full of so many of my own ghosts. Because it made me understand the psychology of most Israelis. I didn't want to have to do that. I didn't want to let her story enter mine.

"In my family, we were beys and pashas. That means we were noblemen. A cousin of mine, Alice, was a lady-in-waiting at the Egyptian royal court. She was believed to be the mistress of King Fuad. At any rate, she might as well have been. Alice wielded more power than his actual wives. It was Alice's daughter, who died tragically young, that I was named after. Another cousin of ours was a member of the Egyptian Parliament. In 1915, he negotiated the independence of Egypt from Britain. Our independence. Or so we Jews of Egypt thought at the time."

Lisa-Turned-Layla elbowed me hard as she bent down to reach under the seat in front of her, jolting me.

"Sorry," she told me. I forced a smile.

We were still taxiing on the runway. She produced a minuscule and very expensive-looking device from a sleek leather bag.

"I downloaded *Airplane!*" she announced.

"What?" I said.

"The movie! Want to watch it with me? It'll kill a couple of hours. I brought another pair of headphones that I could hook up for you. I thought it would be meta to watch *Airplane* on an airplane."

Could this chick get more annoying? When it came to that question, a flight attendant, stalking the rows for transgressors, and I were apparently on the same page.

"Keep your items under the seat until takeoff!" the flight attendant snarled at her, saving me the discomfort of having to decline her offer. I closed my eyes.

What you face—what I was soon to face—as a Palestinian in exile upon returning requires a hardness. Clarity. Steadfastness. Indji's words destabilized all those things in me.

"When Israel was created, some Jews thought we'd have to leave Egypt," Yoav's mother told me. "But the regime took great pains to make us feel welcome, even after Egypt had suffered defeat at the hands of the new Jewish state. My father refused to leave. He only spoke

Arabic. In that language, he explained to my mother that the Jews would always be welcome in our beloved Egypt. Why? Because we were their movie stars, lighting up the screens across the lands. No one could expel their own movie stars. My father was a gambler, a ne'er-do-well. And, among the many things he didn't do well was predict the future."

Indji's eyes clouded over with emotion I couldn't read. Nostalgia? Guilt? No, her eyes betrayed a trace of amusement. She was judging her father for his flaws and herself for not quite being able to forgive him for them.

Our airplane finally lifted for takeoff. I felt a rush of relief. The journey had begun. "Aziz!" I muttered. Since we had begun speaking every night, I weirdly found myself saying his name under my breath like some sort of mantra, an incantation I repeated, especially whenever I felt overwhelmed by my decision to go. In that moment, I needed to excise the words of Yoav's mother out of my head. To think only of Aziz, who had promised to be waiting for me once I got through "the Israeli welcome," an experience reserved for every Palestinian who tried to return, even for a visit. Stateless refugees living in camps or as "guests" in other Arab countries, the descendants of those who fled during the Catastrophe and the bulk of our people in exile, weren't ever allowed to return. But people like me, born to parents who held citizenship elsewhere, had a shot. You would have to enter with a foreign passport, though you were never treated as a citizen from the country. You were a Palestinian and taken aside at customs as soon as you landed. What happened there depended upon the mood of the customs officer. You could be released after a few minutes or forced to wait without explanation for hours at a stretch. Asked a question or two about why you wanted to visit Israel or interrogated relentlessly with the same questions about your family tree, which apparently their database had mapped out of every Palestinian family. Your luggage could be checked again quickly or you could be strip-searched. You could go on your merry way or be detained at the airport and returned "home" on the next flight out.

I had been separated from my parents the last time I visited—the customs officer took me aside and asked me about my grandfather's eldest brother. Apparently, he wrote a letter to the editor of the *Detroit Free Press* the Israelis didn't appreciate before he died *thirty years ago*. Did I know what he had written about? I hadn't. The customs officer saw my clueless face, betraying my ignorance about this apparently egregious letter to an editor, and let me join my family who were waiting in baggage claim. Was it any wonder I never signed petitions for Palestinian rights? Had I gotten a different customs officer that day, he would have denied my visa and forced me to leave on the next flight.

I once heard an Israeli official describe their erratic and inexplicable policies toward Palestinians as "the boss has gone crazy." You never know what to expect or what to brace yourself for. Or are able to forget who is boss.

Aziz had booked a dinner for us at Al-Muntazah, my favorite restaurant in Ramallah. But my thoughts weren't of Aziz. I was leaving Yoav behind in New York but carrying the story of his dying mother with me.

"In my family, we only married other Cairene Jews. In fact, we thought it preferable to marry our first cousins. That was normal at the time, even in Europe. Darwin did it." Yoav's mother seemed to be daring me to make a face. Say something. I kept my expression blank, not wanting to convey the wrong emotion, eager for her to go on.

Lisa-Turned-Layla pressed the button that asked for passenger assistance. The flight attendant appeared.

"Hi! I ordered a low sodium meal," Lisa-Turned-Layla began.

"We're not serving yet," the flight attendant snapped, and disappeared behind a curtain.

"We are going to hit some turbulence shortly but scheduled to arrive at Ben Gurion Airport on time," a pilot announced happily over the loudspeaker. Ben Gurion.

"When the prime minister of Israel, Ben Gurion, invaded Egypt to topple President Nasser and take the Suez Canal, the fate of the Egyptian Jews was sealed. But my fate had been sealed long before that," Yoav's mother had told me with a look in her wide brown eyes that made me feel she had not been sorry about that. "I had been promised to a rich Cattaoui cousin in marriage when I was six and he was thirteen. My father had saved one of the wealthier cousins from drowning while on holiday together in Alexandria. Asking for my hand in marriage, a poor but already pretty child, for his eldest son was recompense for my father's brave deed and a kindness to my mother. Everyone knew my father was a gambler. Even if he ever managed to earn enough for my dowry, he would never manage to keep it. The boy I was betrothed to was named Shalom and he had green eyes. Green eyes! Can you fall in love at age six? I did. Israel was created, but none of our family moved there. Why? We were the Cattaoui family of Egypt. We stayed, even after it got hard, and the police began harassing Jews and falsely charging them with espionage. Shalom went to America to go to college. I wasn't worried. He would return to Cairo when he was ready to marry. He would honor the promise his father had made. He would sow his wild oats and come back for me."

Lisa-Turned-Layla burst out laughing. A loud, unexpected gunfire sound that split the relatively silent shared space. She had managed to get her device out and was enjoying the shenanigans of *Airplane*. The Orthodox young woman in front of us turned to see what was so funny. The gum-popping veiled Palestinian girl to my right and I exchanged a smirk, which Lisa-Turned-Layla caught. She looked at me, confused. Hurt.

To avoid a conversation, I turned away. Everyone else seemed to be watching the in-flight movie on the tiny individual screens in front of them. It was an action film. Not *Rambo*, but it might as well have been. I closed my eyes.

"The Egyptian regime threw us out. Anyone with a foreign passport had to leave within a few days. My family had no foreign passports, but still they made it impossible for us to stay. We, who had lived in Egypt for at least five hundred years. Probably more, but that's as far back as anyone can count," Indji told me, seeming to gain in strength as she spoke. Why five hundred years? Why roughly the same number of centuries that my family could trace our roots to Ramallah? As I sat there listening to her in a café in a department store in New York, it wasn't her speaking anymore. It was the story of my grandmother, leaving Jaffa. It was the refrain of every woman who is told she must be erased from her place.

We left our homes. We brought only what we could carry. Everything else was lost.

"The man I was supposed to marry couldn't return to Egypt. I moved to Israel. He stayed in America. He married someone else instead and eventually so did I."

In that instant, I understood a truth about myself that I wish I never had to. It takes both extraordinary compassion and bravery to care about people who are unlike yourself. Neither were traits I possessed in a particularly great supply. I fretted over the plight of Palestinians only because I was one. Had I been born Jewish, I would have been a Zionist, perhaps a militant one. I would have insisted we had a homeland. I would have wanted it secure. By any means necessary. I would have said what Yoav's mother said to me to any young girl who asked.

"No, Young Lady. I don't think you should defy your family. Your history. Your people. There are plenty of men from your own kind."

That is what echoed in my head for the hours we were in flight, and I was glad there was a man of my kind waiting for me. I felt warmed by the idea that I did have my own tribe and I belonged to them.

When we finally touched down, Lisa-Turned-Layla, the veiled Palestinian girl with too much makeup (still popping gum), and I trudged off the plane in a row. As expected, we were separated from the Jewish and other American passengers as soon as we landed, which meant roughly half of those of us who had shared the flight were now being detained.

We watched the lucky ones sail on by. To begin their adventures. Rest. Recover. I felt the familiar soup of humiliation, rage, and despair that churned within me when I was singled out as a Palestinian.

I promptly forgot my empathy for Indji and the Jews of the Arab world who had suffered like my family did when Zionist forces hounded them out. I was glad her son was a continent away from me, especially because I got unlucky in more ways than one with the customs officer who took me aside. The officer eyed me coldly. Leered at me and dared me to say something about it. The first question the officer asked me was about my great-uncle who had written the fated letter to the editor.

"How are you related to Habeeb Harb?"

Jesus Christ on the Cross! That question could only mean one thing. I had been selected for an interrogation. That meant they might turn me around and not let me in. My great-uncle Amo Habeeb had been a portly bald man who owned a shoe repair shop in Dearborn before he succumbed to a heart attack. Hardly a revolutionary figure. He wrote one letter to the editor of the *Detroit Free Press* decades ago comparing Israeli treatment of Palestinians to apartheid in South Africa. One. It also didn't matter that my uncle was Christian. So was Sirhan Sirhan, who had assassinated Bobby Kennedy for pledging to supply arms to Israel. And Edward Said, a founder of the field of postcolonial studies whose book *Orientalism* articulated how the dehumanization of colonized people in literature and justifications for colonization were often inextricably intertwined. And Hanan Ashrawi, who could take down a bullshit argument on the world stage in perfect English, because she had a PhD in it. We Christian Palestinians were deemed just as dangerous, if not more so, because our support for our rights as indigenous people showed it wasn't a religious war. I was considered worthy of an interrogation. God damn this world and everything in it! If they didn't deny my entry altogether, at the minimum, it would be hours before I could see Aziz.

"Are you finally coming to me, Arabella?" he asked me on the night before my flight. Yes! Yes! I was!

And what stood in the way? This fool. Thinking himself a hero by detaining and harassing a theatre director, who was so spooked she didn't so much as sign a petition stating she believed in all nonviolent means of supporting Palestinian human rights, because she wanted to avoid being subjected to precisely this kind of bullshit.

"He's my great-uncle. And he's dead," I said, trying to keep the edge out of my voice. Clearly, by the glare of the customs officer or secret agent man or whatever the fuck he fancied himself, I hadn't tried hard enough. We were adversaries already.

The one piece of advice Lisa-Turned-Layla told me was that under no circumstances should I mention that I was an artist. Artists were targeted and turned away more readily than most. It's not that we had more stories to tell, just better tools to tell them. I had to get on this man's good side. I had to get him to let me through. But, how?

I took him in. Dark eyes, olive skin. Mid-thirties. He was clearly a Sephardic Jew. We believed the Sephardic Jews serving in the Israeli army tended to be especially harsh—more readily violent—toward the Palestinians living under military occupation in the West Bank and Gaza. Cruder to those Palestinians who somehow had stayed on their lands within Israel's borders and managed to get Israeli citizenship. Some of us thought it was because, among the Jews of Israel, they themselves were discriminated against, and were considered lower on the totem pole than their Ashkenazi compatriots. But I think it had more to do with a memory of how their parents or grandparents might have been treated in the Arab lands they once called home. Just my luck that this customs officer looked strikingly similar to Yoav. If you saw them side by side, you'd swear they were brothers.

10

ZOYA

The Atlantic Ocean
1963

Aziz and I would have fifteen days on that boat together and I had already wasted ten of them. Of course, there were eyes everywhere. I caught glimpses of him at mealtime, but the single men would eat together on a plank far from the families. I felt like the only woman without her husband aboard. It wasn't true, of course. But the widows and wives whose men had gone before were traveling with brothers or fathers.

We, the Palestinian passengers with refugee status, were in steerage. We slept in bunk beds in the cramped quarters belowdecks. I had scrambled to secure us five sets of bunks against the wall, thinking myself clever. Hugging a wall meant one fewer set of neighbors. But it also meant we were farthest from the hatch, where the air was stifling. I took a top bunk and kept my youngest nestled in between me and the wall. Every night the rough seas knocked one of my eight other children off their nearby bunk onto the floor. The terrifying sound of a small body slamming against the floor and the howl that came after woke me almost every night. Each scream was like the first cry of a newborn, the shriek of affronted outrage as they discovered they had been thrown out of one realm into another. A frightening but welcome sound. That shriek meant they could shriek. It meant they hadn't fallen on their heads.

At mealtimes, we sat in long rows at wooden tables in the middle of the ship and were served by waiters. Bright-faced American boys who talked loudly in a language I had never tried hard to learn, preferring French. These waiters did a little dance, a shuffle, to balance themselves every time the boat rocked back and forth as they plunked food down before us. Most seemed as unwilling to talk to us as we were unable to talk to them.

My children took turns being seasick, except for Naya. She and I were strangely immune. I was desperate to get my other children to hold down as much food and water as they could. The best way to keep them settled down at meals was to tell a story, a tale from the *One Thousand and One Nights*, which my beloved teacher Al-Sitt Elaine had introduced to me. Each time I began recounting for them a tale she had first taught me, I remembered how, since she knew more stories than anyone else in our village, it was jokingly said of her that she knew 1,002 of the 1,001 stories by heart.

"What do you want, Children? 'Alia Baba and the Forty Thieves'?" I asked. "'Sinbada'? 'Aladdina'?"

My eldest, Myrna, rolled her eyes. She was old enough to know that I added my own twists to most of the 1,001 stories that I knew. In my retellings, I often changed the genders and names of the most famous characters. I told the stories as if the heroes were women rather than men.

"Alia Baba was a poor girl," I began. "Until she discovered a cave of treasures."

"May I sit here?" Aziz asked, startling me. He was standing before me in his elegant gray wool suit, which I noticed looked a touch threadbare, worn-out at the knees.

I had my children around me. We were being served risotto. The cook was Italian and it seemed we had risotto every night. We would get accustomed to it, the different texture, but we'd never like it. To us, lumpy rice that stuck together meant the cook had failed.

"Yes, of course," I said. He sat down on an empty chair on the other side of Ghassan. I was glad. It was less likely to make us the subject of gossip. There would be a male relative of mine between us, even if he was only five years old. I was glad I had managed to eke out a son after the many, many daughters. How much weight we make our male children carry! Even in his youth, and unbeknownst to him, my son was a form of protection for me, if only from vicious tongues.

Ghassan's face lit up as he looked at Aziz. It occurred to me that, since he hadn't yet met his father, he might in his youth somehow expect each strange man he encountered to be him.

"Who are you?" Ghassan asked. Aziz glanced at me before answering.

"I'm a fellow Ramallahite," he told him.

"Which clan?" my son asked. Aziz smiled at the adult question from a serious-looking young child. Ghassan did not smile back as he waited for his answer. He had absorbed this question as being the most important one.

"Yours," Aziz answered. Aziz and I had both descended from the same founding father of Ramallah, Yousef.

"So you're a shit-disturber," my son said.

That was our clan's reputation in Ramallah. Instigators. Igniters of new feuds and exasperators of existing ones. We relished being called troublemakers. We called ourselves that. We, who had descended from Yousef of the House of Rashid, liked making those around us feel they had to stay on their toes.

"This is Dr. Aziz," I said.

"I remember you. You once came to our house," Myrna said.

It hadn't occurred to me that my daughter would recognize him. It felt dangerous that she did. Better that Kamal never knew Aziz and I had ended up on the same ship.

"That's true. I wish I had the chance to have eaten more of the feast your mother made on that night," he said.

"I wish you had, too," I said. We all took another hopeful bite of risotto.

"*Yema* was just telling us a story," Myrna said.

"No, I was not!" I hissed, and immediately regretted it. How ugly is the voice of a mother snapping at a child! We have all been subjected to that sound, been targeted by a parent for speaking the truth when the truth somehow causes shame.

Aziz watched my children looking down, cowed into silence. They knew better than to contradict me, even if I was lying. Especially if I was lying.

"Eat up now, Children," I said.

They all picked up their forks obediently, including Aziz, who made a face when he tasted a bite of overcooked pumpkin that had been mixed in with the risotto. I took the breadbasket and handed it to him. His fingers brushed mine. I blushed and pulled my hand away. The realness of his body suddenly became apparent to me. As did the eyes everywhere in that crowded room. He was no longer an illusionary figure, a trick of light like a matinee idol on a screen. The sanctuary of my fantasies about Aziz had been invaded by the actuality of him.

"Your mother is an excellent storyteller," Aziz said to my children, but he kept his eyes fixed on mine. And his eyes were smiling. He leaned his long body back in his chair and I felt a flash of the same urge to crawl into his lap that I had that first time in church.

I gave him my most impervious glare.

He didn't seem to understand my look, that it was meant to signify that I was done with the conversation about my storytelling and he should drop it. Kamal would have understood. I felt the vastness of the valley between a man who knew how to read my expressions and a man who did not. I found myself longing for Kamal. I missed the security of being with the man whom the world had sanctioned I be with. To whom I belonged. Why? Because my father had given me to him. And was it not infinitely easier that way? To never have to signal to a man that you wanted him? Or to try to decode the mystery of whether he wanted you and risk being wrong?

"Your mother's skill at telling tales would shame our best storytellers. Both the living and the dead."

"You exaggerate," I told him. In Arabic, there is no word for foreplay. But there are many, many words for flirting. Was I fluttering my eyelashes? They seemed to do that on their own. To not belong to me.

Myrna, who was fourteen, narrowed her eyes at him as if she could sense what was transpiring between us. She had been taught to be vigilant about never exhibiting signs of being loose with men. By me.

"How do you know my mother's stories?" she asked. Accusation was in her eyes.

He leaned in, looked around, and spoke in a low voice that hinted of secrets. Spies. Conspiracies. Illicit love affairs.

"I read a book of them," Aziz told her.

"My mother wrote no books," she sparred.

"Doesn't mean one with her stories does not exist," he said.

Did he desire my daughter, who was a copy of my younger self? She was approaching a marriageable age. Aziz was a doctor. With the right support, he could learn English and practice medicine in Detroit, no doubt. Would that not be a brilliant match for my daughter? Is that not what I should be hoping for?

Myrna's face flushed. I could not read her expression.

"'Disarmament.' That's the title of your mother's story that is my favorite," he said, and my children leaned in to listen. Except Myrna, who picked at her nails, studiously ignoring him.

"We Palestinians had been occupied by the British Empire for many long years. The men of Palestine thought that meant the British were more powerful. But they were wrong."

Myrna looked up. She was old enough to recognize that whenever you had a chance to hear of how our men were mistaken—in a world that seemed to like to pretend they never were—you took that chance.

"The girls of Palestine knew differently," I found myself saying. "They were no smarter than us, nor more cultured. Our Scheherazade rivals their Shakespeare. Our colonizers are superior to us in only one way."

In that moment, I was no longer a bewildered young mother of nine children aboard a boat taking me to a foreign shore. I was back in my Ramallah schoolyard. I was a child again, who possessed the joy of being crowned the popular girl, the one who always knew how to make up the best games.

Aziz paused, allowing me to continue.

"They make better weapons," I said. "To defeat them, we must disarm them. One by one. But how?"

I glanced at my son, waiting for the answer, his eyes shining. Was he old enough to understand that what happened to us—the loss of our home—did not happen to all children? It did not happen to children whose people were stronger than we were.

I found myself unable to speak. Aziz sensed it and took over. We fell into taking turns telling the story. Together.

"We'll create jokes," Aziz said. "The greatest jokes in the world!"

"We'll spend all day thinking up jokes," I whispered.

"And every night dreaming up jokes," Aziz said. "And right before their soldiers are about to execute us—"

"Why would they execute us?" Naya interrupted. Aziz gestured with his hand. I'll let you answer that one.

"Not all of us, Daughter. Just a few. Just enough to scare the ones who survive into submission. Anyway, as we face their firing squad, they'll let us have a few last words. We will use that opportunity to tell a joke. An incredible joke."

"A joke of epic proportions!" Aziz hooted.

"A joke to end all jokes! Their soldiers will be overcome. Double over with laughter."

"They will be disarmed!" Aziz and I said together. Triumphant. As if we had truly found a tool to defeat every soldier of every empire. One by one. But, we hadn't. And my eldest daughter knew it. Just as she seemed to sense there was something untoward between Aziz and me.

"But what if their soldiers don't let us have a few last words?" Myrna asked. "What if they just send war planes and bomb us from above, never giving us a chance to speak with them at all?"

Clearly, my child was cleverer than my schoolmates. We had re-enacted my game of Disarmament for hours, taking turns playing comic revolutionaries and soldiers with senses of humor. Not one had ever stopped to ask that question.

"Then we die!" I told her, not sorry when I saw the shock in Myrna's eyes. If you don't want fairy tales, enjoy your dose of reality, Daughter. I saw Aziz was taken aback by my words. I felt a pang of shame, which morphed into rage. I told no lies. I am not a sweet woman, Aziz. If that's what you want, look elsewhere. I mirrored his appalled expression, to show him how he looked to me, and he smiled.

"I like the stories in *One Thousand and One Nights* better than that one," Ghassan said in a blunt voice that reminded me of how his father spoke. Aziz laughed.

"That's because you are young," Aziz told him.

"I agree," I said.

"You are young, too," he said. I felt myself grow flush. The dinner was over soon after and we were herded en masse out of the dining hall. Aziz waved to me as the crush of bodies making their way out took us in different directions. Aware of the eyes around us, I did not dare wave back.

"Why would that boring old man sit with us?" Myrna asked me when we were back in our cabin in steerage. I knew I had to put a stop to such questions immediately if I did not want them asked in front of Kamal.

"Perhaps he likes you. You're going to have a lot of men circling you soon. Wanting you to be their bride."

She made a face and went silent.

That night, the sea was rockier than ever. I stayed below in our cabin. One by one, except for Naya, my children all suffered bouts of seasickness. Naya helped me care for and clean her siblings, running to fetch water and discard bags full of filth. I felt guilty in the particularly gut-wrenching way only a mother with ill children can be. I had heard stories of torture, the strategies of the British Empire's policy of "pacification" by means of whips and hangings. It was said that the pain was so intense "it would make a mother beg God to inflict it on her own child in the place of herself." I stared at my children, whom I tried to love and protect. I believed I would never turn on them under torture. Physical pain didn't scare me. The thing I feared most in the world was shame.

As the boat relentlessly lurched from side to side, I cleaned up the messes that inevitably came. Volley after volley. The winds were not through with our little boat. They would not calm down.

Dehydration was a real fear. A child had already died aboard the boat before we had even made our way through the Straits of Gibraltar. I shuddered every time I remembered the shrouded little body, the thud it made when it was dumped lovingly by his two sobbing parents—but dumped nevertheless—into the sea. Eventually, our cabin was so heavy with the smell of sick that I had to flee from it, if only to catch my breath, at the first moment I got all my children to finally succumb to sleep.

By the light of flickering lanterns, I found my way to the stairwell, passing cabins where I heard people heaving and retching. I climbed the stairs carefully. The boat veered wildly to and fro. I stepped out onto the deck. The salt air whistled through me and I felt renewed. A moment of calm to savor as the boat seemed to right itself, as if we had slipped into the eye of a storm.

I was alone. Hanging close to the door, I stayed far from the edge; the brass railing that separated me from an oblivion seemed to beckon. I stared up at the half-moon, wishing I could take in this experience of solitude fully, crystallize it. How rarely had I ever had a moment to myself to contemplate the moon! It began to drizzle, that wetness so soft, it didn't strike against your skin as much as envelop you. When I felt the first drops of rain and heard them hit the deck, noisy as wet kisses, I still couldn't bring myself to go back inside.

Of all the human achievements, the earliest ones seemed to be the most astounding. People had figured out a way to cross an ocean! And, more incredibly, to find their way back home again! Glorious. Could we not also figure out how to live together better?

Would these wars between peoples ever cease? It seemed unlikely. Crazy. But so must have been navigating uncharted waters for the first time. All exploration begins in the same way. Undertaken by gambling men, who prefer to risk everything they have to venture out into the unknown rather than pay the cost they know is invariably coming if they remain forever standing still.

I took in a deep breath of the salty air. Before I could breathe out again, the ground beneath me shifted violently, knocking me to my knees. I cried out. A pair of strong hands reached down and grabbed mine.

11

ARABELLA

Tel Aviv and Jerusalem

2012

When I finally got released by the Israeli customs control officer, I found Aziz standing next to the sliding doors to the outside world. Wearing the hell out of a pair of white jeans and a black tee. His gleaming dark curls, a tad too long, only added to his Omar Sharif–like masculine charm. He greeted me with a ready smile.

"There you are!" he said. I found myself shy and had a hard time meeting his gaze.

"Hi," I said. As if my awkwardness was catching, the sparkle in his big chocolate eyes dimmed slightly. But still, his gaze sought mine. It asked, "Do you like me?" And my refusing to meet his eyes answered, "I don't know." Not in a coquettish way. In a petrified way. I don't know about anything, Aziz. Not about life and how to live it on my own terms. Or what might make me happy and how I would know it if it did. No wonder I had never had a real boyfriend. No wonder I had built a fantasy world around a guy I had only spoken to on the phone. Had I even asked Aziz about his past girlfriends or whether he'd been in love? No. I knew nothing about him.

He reached to take the one suitcase I was holding.

"Is this all you have?" he asked me.

I wanted to joke and say I was able to pack light because I opted to bring only one of my dildos. To ignite the easy banter that had been between us when we were oceans apart. Talk of sex was easier to do on the phone than in person, which could lead to actual sex and all the feelings that it might or—just as devastatingly—might not ignite in oneself.

"Yes. That's all," I said instead. I followed him outside to the parking lot. The heat hit me like a fist to the face. Joyful reunions seemed to erupt around us. Several generations of a Palestinian family crowded around a young man, a student abroad who was given a hero's welcome, complete with an elderly man who banged out a tune of welcome on a drum and a screaming baby. A young blond couple, both wearing hot pants, were making out with abandon a few steps away from them, lost in their own world and each other. Aziz led me to an old Mercedes, clearly a rental. We pulled out into the highway that cut through the desert landscape, which looked like a sea of skin on every side.

"Are you hungry?"

"No," I said.

"Where should we go first?" he asked. He turned to me and his eyes searched mine again. A beat too long. Not noticing the compact car in front of us was slowing.

"Watch out!" I yelled.

He slammed on the brakes just in time to avoid hitting it.

"Sorry," he told me.

"No problem," I said, and suddenly felt exhausted. The long flight and the interrogation at customs caught up with me. I could smell my sweat and the perfume I'd put on to cover its scent.

"Can you take me to Ramallah? I'd like to get settled."

"The checkpoint at Qalandia is closed right now. A kid skidded and lost control of a car. He was getting ready to attend his sister's wedding. The Israelis thought it was an attack on the checkpoint. They shot him."

"So, what should I do?"

"Wait," he told me. Stating the obvious. "I asked a friend to call me when they open the checkpoint. We've got a bit of time to kill. How about we go to the Old City?"

I nodded and forced a smile. The Old City meant Jerusalem. It was my favorite place in Palestine.

"Did you have a rough go of it at customs?"

I thought of the first hour of the interrogation with Yoav's double. The unmasked boredom on his face as he asked me the same questions over and over. How many brothers did your maternal grandmother have? What are their names? How many sisters? The half-hidden irritation in my voice as I answered the same answers. I told myself to pretend it was a banal play. We were both acting out the assigned little roles that someone else had cast us in. But I kept thinking there were better roles for us to play. Better places to be. Better things to do with that hour, time we would never get back. At least it wasn't just me who was wasting my time. We were in it together. It gave me a sense of peace to know that. Until he sent me out of the room.

"I was asked to name everyone in my extended family several times. Every great-uncle and every great-aunt on both sides. And all their children."

"Did you know the names?"

"Yes. I hung out a lot with my grandmother when I was young. She spoke about all those people." My extended family, including those who died long before I was born, were alive and real to me through the stories my grandmother told me. I knew all the names of the clans of Ramallah. All the feuds, too, and how they were resolved. I learned them in the way that I learned the stories of Jesus, Mary, and Joseph from my grandmother. Though she lived in Detroit and I in San Francisco, I saw her at the annual Ramallah convention, which we held at a different American city. Our convention was once featured on CNN as America's largest family reunion. Every year, to the horror of other guests and the staff, a thousand loud and unruly Ramallahites living across America overtook a hotel. Masses of us from every generation would gather to rent every available room and all the banquet halls, where we blasted the latest Arabic pop hits. Together, we'd sway to sounds of chirpy Arabic voices, fast-paced flutes, and electronic drumbeats so loud you could feel them vibrate in your belly and your bones. When the hotel forced us to shut down the banquet party, we'd gather in a lobby. Someone would bring a drum and we'd dance and sing folk songs. When we were shooed from there, we'd gather in the hallway.

Anywhere you'd look, you'd find dancing Arabs. I had never seen Aziz at any of the conventions. It was created to make sure we American-born children met and married from our clans. As if the descendants of the original founders of Ramallah never left our village. As if we still spoke Arabic. As if history had never happened.

"My grandmother mentioned she knew your grandfather," I told him.

"I never met my Sido Aziz. He died before I was born."

He changed lanes, following the signs to Jerusalem.

"Do you know why the Israeli official kept quizzing you on the names of your extended family?"

"No," I said.

"They're hoping you'll make a mistake. So they can say you lied to them. Have an excuse to deny you an entry visa. Did they question you the whole time?"

I thought how the customs officer, Yoav's double, suddenly stopped grilling me about my extended family tree and told me we were done. I thought that meant I was free. I smiled at him, the way I would if I had been helped by a clerk at a post office, but I wiped it off my face when I remembered that smiling was not part of our assigned roles. I thought I'd get my entry visa stamp and be on my way. I certainly wouldn't have smiled if I knew what was in store for me, which was being made to wait before I'd be allowed to pick up my luggage and go. For seven hours.

"No. They mostly made me wait. Why?"

"Does your family still own property?"

"My grandfather's olive orchards were taken. There apparently are new Israeli settlements on them now. But we still have his house."

"That'll do it. When they make you wait for no apparent reason, you're clearly tagged as no real threat. They want to make it unpleasant for you to return so you do it less often. So, little by little, we lose our connection to our land."

I realized, while I had been waiting to be released, Aziz had also been waiting. For me. For eight hours.

"It was nice of you to wait all that time for me," I said.

"You are worth waiting for," he said. He looked to see how his words landed and I again couldn't meet his gaze. I could feel myself blushing.

"Well, that's cheesy," I said. I was trying to drum up the spirit of fun we had on the phone, but my tone was off. Flat. Dead.

"But in a nice way," I added. He pushed the long bangs that were falling in his face out of his eyes and shifted in his seat.

It had been a mistake to have him meet me at the airport. I would have felt more alive after I had rested and showered. I wanted to be cheerful enough to give us a real shot. I both dreaded and desired him at that same time. I equally longed to rest against his strong chest and let him do what I could feel he wanted to do with me, and to open the speeding car's door and jump out. Was this what an arranged marriage felt like? That sense of a siren's call you couldn't ignore, dragging you to your destiny? Making you hurl yourself headlong toward another person. Slam the door on other lovers. Snuff out the kind of life you can only live if you stay single.

If it was an arranged marriage of sorts, was there anything so wrong in that? Why did the fact that our grandmothers set us up make me feel worse than if I had met him on the internet?

On paper, we were perfect for each other, even by American standards. He was Stanford all the way through med school and I had climbed to the top of the Ivy Leagues. The American couples I knew in New York were unions of flair and substance, meaning very few theatre artists married other artists. Most of my artsy friends, gay and straight, who had managed to stay in theatre had found themselves coupled with doctors or lawyers. Their matches weren't marriages of convenience. Or were they? Most couples had met on dating sites on the internet, which took the place of traditional matchmakers. Some people know how to pair themselves off without significant effort and outside help, but not many. I was one of that many, who simply was so self-conscious and self-absorbed that I could neither sense nor send the right signals to find a mate on my own.

Did I like Aziz or was I forcing myself to like him? He was handsome. He was smart. He was considerate. He was trying. So few men bothered. Was that what was turning me off to him, the fact that he seemed to like me? Was it because I didn't like myself?

"Did that girl annoy you on the flight?" he asked me.

"Which girl?"

"The playwright?" I had forgotten I had spent hours mocking Lisa-Turned-Layla on the phone to Aziz. I realized they would make a really great couple. If you asked either to describe themselves in a word they would have the same answer. Palestinian.

Mine would be director.

"She's not that bad."

"You said you hated her."

"Yeah, well, I'm not always a great judge of character."

Aziz glanced at me with questions in his eyes. What did I mean by that? Was I referring to him? If there were gods in heaven taking bets on whether I'd always manage to say the wrong thing and end up alone, the one betting against me would have scored a point.

I took out my phone to call Lisa-Turned-Layla. She picked up on the first ring.

"Arabella! I'm in Paris," her voice boomed over the line.

Clearly having overheard, Aziz nodded knowingly.

"What? Why?"

"The Israelis denied me entry. Because I signed the BDS petition," she said. That was the petition she had kept sending me. It was a peaceful and nonviolent movement that most Palestinian Americans (including yours truly) were too terrified of being smeared as anti-Semitic to sign on to publicly. Ironically, the argument that we, too, are technically Semites, since Arabic and Hebrew were both Semitic languages, seemed to hold no water nor provide any cover from the targeting, blacklisting, and harassment that would follow anyone who dared to support this seemingly benign petition. From my understanding, the petition didn't say Israel shouldn't exist. It assumed Israel did exist and called for a boycott to encourage its leadership to comply with international law, respect its original borders, and not annex more land.

"The customs officer told me to 'go home and sign more petitions.' They put me on the first flight back to New York, but I've got an overnight connection in Paris. Apparently, instead of baklava, I'm eating crepes tonight."

"Layla!" I interrupted, feeling overwhelmed. "What am I going to do? I don't know anyone at the theatre! I don't even know where it is."

"Everyone knows where it is."

"Dar Al-Masrah, right?" Aziz asked me. I nodded.

"I can take you there," Aziz said. Though I knew he was trying to be reassuring, I found myself nonplussed that he inserted himself into our conversation.

"You'll be fine. My job was to work on the translation of the text and that part is done. We're supposed to meet Ramez at the theatre at eleven tomorrow, and I've emailed him to explain it'll be just you," she told me. Ramez was the artistic director of the theatre company.

"I can't do this without you!"

"Of course you can. It's not like you even really like me, Arabella."

I glanced at Aziz. He kept his eyes fixed on the road, but I knew he could hear what she was saying.

"What do you mean?"

"You know exactly what I mean. You smirk when I speak. I admire your work, Arabella. I admire you. There aren't that many Palestinians working in American theatre and I don't know why you have it in for me."

Why? Was it because I knew she was brave in ways I wasn't? Or because she was bombastic, sending and resending me petitions I obviously had no desire to sign? As fucked-up and flawed as I was, I would never dream of inserting myself into anyone's life in the way she had mine. To demand that they express their politics and identity in the way I expected. Everyone had a right to privacy. A right to peace. If she wanted a come-to-Jesus moment, she was going to get it.

"You really want to know? I get my first cover-story profile in *American Theatre* and they interviewed you so you could talk about my work, which are adaptations of Shakespeare. Instead of talking about what I actually do, the contribution to theatre I make, you use it as an opportunity to show off about how much you know about Palestinian high culture."

"You're mad because I compared you to Palestine's greatest artists?"

"I'm mad because you took an article that was supposed to be about my work and turned it into a story about my race."

"Why do you think *American Theatre* did that cover story on you, Arabella? Yes, your shows did okay off-Broadway. But how many covers do they do of artists who haven't made it on Broadway? Hardly any. The editor, Ted Thompson, is my friend. We do activist work together."

Oh, no. Oh, no. Oh, no.

"He actually cares about our people, Arabella. He studied with Edward Said at Columbia. Ted saw the death threats, the firebombing of his office on campus, and the McCarthyite committees that the university put in place to intimidate him and other Arab professors. Ted wanted to do a cover story about a Palestinian American artist as a way of honoring Said's legacy. And I recommended you."

All this time I had been furious with her for "ruining" my cover story. She was the reason I had a cover story in the first place. How could I have been such a fool? I was chosen not for the art I made but for the art I made while being Palestinian. I had done everything in my life to never feel I got a leg up because magnanimous liberal white people felt sorry for me. I wanted to be angry. At her. At Ted. At humanity. But all I could muster was overwhelming shame.

"Well, if I had known that's the reason why Ted wanted to do a story on me, I would have turned it down," I stammered.

"So you could go on pretending to be white?"

"So I could be in control of my own brand!"

"Brand?! When artists of color use that word, it always makes me shudder. But, of course, you're not an artist of color, are you?"

I felt my face go hot. How dare she?! If I had to answer to anyone, it wouldn't be the likes of her. She, who self-produced her bullshit agitprop plays because no one else would. Amateur. Loser. Ah, there was the anger I had been reaching for! Hello, Rage, my old friend! You've come to save me from introspection again!

"What I'm not is a hypocrite. You think you're above having a brand? Lisa, you changed your name to Layla to exoticize yourself. Because if you didn't, no one would pay any attention to you at all."

Aziz let out a low whistle. I knew I had gone too far.

"I'm sorry," I said. "I didn't mean that."

"I gotta go."

She hung up the phone.

"Everything okay?" Aziz asked me.

"I'm an asshole, but otherwise, everything's peachy."

"You're not an—"

"Please. I'm not up for a conversation about what I am or am not right now. You think they'll open the checkpoint into Ramallah today?"

"No way to know, Arabella."

"Well, how am I supposed to get there? I have a meeting tomorrow at eleven."

"I can take you the long way through Wadi Al-Nar," he said. The Valley of Fire.

"Why is it called that?"

"It's through steep mountains. The road is pretty narrow."

No thank you.

"Why have a military checkpoint if Palestinians can get into Ramallah through a different road?" I whined.

"Why make Palestinians who have property here wait eight hours in Israeli customs every time they visit? To make us suffer. So we leave our land and don't return."

I wasn't going down that rabbit hole.

"What do you recommend I do?"

"You could come back to Gaza with me," he said. "There is a beautiful new beachfront resort with a seaside café where they serve the most incredible mango juice you've ever tasted."

"Really?" I asked.

"No," he said. "But there will be one day. We will build it."

Okey-dokey. His eternal optimism was cute on the phone. Now it seemed delusional.

"Are you sure you aren't hungry, Arabella?"

"Yes, I'm sure."

How else could we kill the time? I remembered I had an errand in Jerusalem, a favor for Teta Zoya. She had called me while I was in a cab to the airport. She made me promise to light a candle for her in Jerusalem's Church of the Holy Sepulchre, where she and her family had attended Midnight Mass every Easter and Christmas, until the day she left Palestine.

"You'll light a candle, right? You won't forget?" she asked me. I was distracted, willing my cab to move faster, sure I'd miss my flight. That cab ride in New York seemed like a lifetime ago. Her demeanor had seemed different than usual. My grandmother wasn't one to ask hesitantly for favors, especially among her progeny. She demanded them. I had a strange feeling something might happen to her before I could fulfill my promise.

I had a handle on the serpentine streets of the walled Old City of Jerusalem the last time I was here, but that had been over a decade ago. I'd probably have to ask around to get exactly where I needed to go if I went alone. Or I could make Aziz take me.

"Can I ask you a favor?"

"Anything," Aziz said, and flashed a smile at me.

"Great! Can you take me to the Church of the Holy Sepulchre? I kinda know where it is, but it's been a while. Made a promise to light a candle for my grandmother there. Since I can't get into Ramallah yet, I might as well get something out of the way."

"Sure. But you don't want to grab a quick bite first? Zalatimo makes the best pastries in the world."

"I know. I've been there. Another time," I told him. It would only occur to me later the reason he kept asking me if I was hungry was because he was.

It was the hour of morning when the orange of dawn still fights to remain in the sky. That is my favorite time of day to visit the Old City, as the souk awakens and shopkeepers begin unlocking their gates. Each opening of a door is like a sudden bloom of a flower in a field, surprising and beckoning one's eyes to peek at the once hidden colors within. Would it be earthy rows of spices arranged in perfect pyramids, glinting gold, bolts of cloth begging to be unfurled, or electronics with sleek buttons shining like the silver unblinking eyes of fish? The rhythm of the clatter of carts within the city's walls mixes with roaring engines, the beeping of cars, from the world outside. If you wander through the winding streets long enough, the din can dissipate suddenly. You find yourself in a quiet *hara*, a lonely alley, where the sound of children playing gives way to moments of stillness so complete that you catch the occasional flutter of pigeons' wings.

Aziz parked in front of Bab Al-Amud, the Damascus Gate, one of the seven main entrances to the Old City. Jerusalem is less than half of one square mile in total, the most contested land in the world. It's the ultimate proof size does not matter.

"Who built the walls of the Old City?" I asked Aziz. "Us or them?"

"Us or Them?" is what I call a game many Palestinians and Israelis play, oftentimes without knowing it. In it, we delineate which ancient monuments were built by us or them throughout the land, to use history to justify our laying claim to it. As if it mattered who had the stronger claim. All that mattered was who had the bigger guns. Our talk of history was a way to feel justified using them. I was no trivia buff and, therefore, exceedingly bad at the game. But Aziz could play.

"Us. It was built by Sultan Suleiman the Magnificent in the sixteenth century. They named him that to distinguish him from his father, Suleiman the Pretty Good."

"Are you kidding?"

"Yes and no. It's true that Suleiman the Magnificent built Jerusalem's iconic walls and gates. I have no idea what his father's name was."

"Funny," I said flatly, and I got out of the car. He followed me.

To enter the Old City, you have to descend one of the long rows of connecting stone steps that fan out in front of the Damascus Gate. So, if you glance backward before you cross the threshold, it feels like you're standing center stage in an ancient amphitheater. There is a deliberate regality that Brother Suleiman lent to the high stone walls by making their tops point to heaven in the pattern of a king's crown. The stairs, which are built of the same pale limestone as its walls, were awash in the morning sunlight as I began to tap my way down the steps with Aziz in tow.

Two young Israeli soldiers, sporting assault rifles slung over their shoulders, emerged from the entrance. They began making their way up the stairs toward me. One was olive-skinned and the other a red-head. Neither looked a day older than eighteen. Now that I was in my mid-thirties, when I saw teenagers, I couldn't help but think I was old enough to have been their mother. I read a study somewhere that our brains are not fully formed until our mid-twenties, especially in boys. Their impulse control is still juvenile in nature, which is why they still do dumb things like drive too fast, killing other people and themselves at alarming rates. And why they make good soldiers. I hadn't seen the sight of teenagers toting guns since my last visit to Palestine when I was, incidentally, still a teenager myself. It jarred me then as it jarred me now. I willed myself to keep walking down the stairs. To stay on my trajectory.

In my haste or fear or clumsiness, I stumbled and twisted my ankle on the next step. I cried out, "Ay!"

Not ouch. Not damn. Not fuck. Not any of the English words I learned later, which never came out of my mouth when I unexpectedly felt pain. "Ay!" is how a Palestinian cries out when hurt. It was a sound the soldiers recognized.

"Wakif!" yelled the olive-skinned soldier. His Hebrew accent was so thick I almost didn't recognize the Arabic word for "stop." I froze. They scaled the stairs two at a time to reach us.

As they approached, Aziz stepped forward to put half of himself between them and me, a protective stance.

"Tusreeh!" the soldier commanded. Permission. At all times, Palestinians have to carry paperwork proving they have Israeli permission to be where they are. They have separate forms of ID whether they live in the West Bank, Gaza, or Jerusalem. Soldiers could pop up anywhere and ask you for that proof of permission. This policy tore families apart and made commerce between Palestinian cities impossible. It dictated where you could work, where you could study, where you could receive medical treatment, and where you decided to go on a first date with a person your grandmother wanted you to marry.

Unless you were lucky like Aziz and me. Born with a magic carpet, also known as an American passport, which allowed us to transcend the checkpoints and high walls designed to keep people—just like us—in place.

Aziz took his passport out of his back pocket as I fished mine out of my purse. We wordlessly offered them. The soldiers took them and glanced at each other, clearly surprised we were Americans.

I wondered how we appeared to them. I was wearing expensive jeans, caramel flats, and a fancy red blouse. Aziz looked like he belonged at a resort in Miami. Were we stopped because my yell alarmed them? Or because we appeared to be a stylish local Palestinian couple with money, looking to hit the Old City for a good time, unforgivable to them because they were young and on duty on a beautiful morning? Impossible to know.

"You're from California? I'm going to UC Berkeley next year!" said the redheaded soldier after glancing at my info. It was the first time he spoke in English. He had a thoroughly American accent. Queens, to be exact. He was sporting a painful-looking sunburn and his pale blue eyes were suddenly friendly, excited to share his college plans.

Really, kid? You think I'm in the mood for getting chatty while you're slinging a gun? I glared at him and he went silent.

I noticed that Aziz, unlike me, gave them zero attitude. He stood tall and looked them in the eye, but magically (impossibly!) without a trace of fear or animosity, as he was handed back both of our passports. A calmness radiated from him. Or was the right word "dignity"? He was here as a medical volunteer. He had seen what guns like the ones they carried could do. He had tried to heal the damage they caused. If he could show such grace, what did it say about me that I could not? At least not yet.

The soldiers moved on, leaving Aziz and me standing on the steps. I turned to him.

"I'm starting to think you're pretty cool."

"I was hoping you'd notice eventually," he said.

People always talk about the first kiss as if it's some kind of a test. But you can teach someone how you like to be kissed. A first kiss has nothing on a first touch.

He offered me his hand. I took it. And every part of my body felt alive.

Hand in hand, we crossed through the entrance into the Old City and took the shortest path to the church. He didn't need to lead me and I didn't need to follow. We both knew the way.

12

ZOYA

The Atlantic Ocean
1963

I recoiled as if burned when I saw that the strong hands helping me to my feet belonged to Aziz. Was anyone watching us? Would they say we were holding hands? No, we were completely alone. People hid in their cramped cabins at the first hint of rain. A storm felt like the ocean revealing its true nature. It was a sea monster, whose slumber we disturbed, trying to shake our vessel off its back. There was so little to keep us from drowning. A few strategic snaps of steel and we would sink.

"That looked like a bad fall, Zoya," Aziz said. He spoke my name as if it was something holy. The rain had long since soaked me. It began to turn his gray suit black as it trickled over every part of him, even his thick eyelashes, which framed his glowing onyx eyes.

"I'm fine," I whispered.

He gave me a smile I did not like. Or was it that I liked it too much? I was a married woman from a respectable house. He was to know it.

"Do you intend to court my daughter?"

"Why would you think that, Zoya?"

"Why else would a single man dine at a table with a young lady present?"

"Perhaps so he can talk to her beautiful mother."

"You're dirty." Leave now, Zoya. Now.

"And you're beautiful. What if I pretend to court her so I can see you?"

"And hurt my child's feelings?"

"Woman, your daughter has no interest in me. She was staring at the blond waiter. Making eyes at him."

"That's not true! My girl is virtuous!"

Is she? Is anyone?

"She's human," Aziz said. "We all are."

The boat lurched. But we both kept our balance. The rain fell hard. Torrential.

"You go! Now, Aziz! We can't be seen walking together."

He didn't move.

"No one is here, Zoya."

"Are you trying to get me killed?"

The thought sobered him right up. For a moment. Then he unfurled his devilish smile.

"We are alone," he said, and took a step toward me. I took a step back.

"Did you promise Golda you'd marry her?"

Why bring up Golda? To erect a barrier between us? To remind him he brought another woman to my house, the house I shared with my husband? Or to remind myself?

"I made her no promise. Nor did she ask for one."

What woman doesn't want a promise of marriage? What else could a woman want?

"Sit down, Zoya."

He gestured to a backless bench bolted down to the deck. It was strange that I had walked around it, this love seat of cold steel, every day and had never noticed it before.

"No. What if someone comes?"

The rain lightened a bit, yet the wind picked up again. Its howling sounded of secret curses. Indecipherable commands.

"We say you're seasick. I'm the kindly doctor trying to make you feel better. Sit down, Zoya."

I sat and he next to me. Our clothes were so saturated that the wetness of the seat didn't disturb us. As he tried to move closer, I edged away from him, so there were still several inches between us. The clouds in the sky had shifted. It was as if Aziz had turned the moon into mist. To give us the cover of darkness. He turned to me, but I kept staring straight out, though we both knew there was nothing to see. He inched toward me again.

"Stay back!" I commanded.

"Give me your hand, Zoya."

"No!" I gripped my fingers around my knees. What am I doing here? The rain grew in force, battering us again. Unthinking, I licked a drop off my top lip, then reddened at how he might read the gesture.

I had two different thoughts at the same time. Kamal will kill me if he finds out. And no one else was coming out here before morning.

"Zoya, your hand."

I flipped my hand over and laid it on the bench, facing upward, not daring to look at him. He slipped his hand under mine, encasing it, and began to stroke his thumb back and forth across the inside of my palm. I felt myself burst within the first few strokes. The release was so intense that it was painful. The sound I emitted could only be called a grunt. Wetness now soaked the one part of me that the rain could not touch. Six decades later, when I decided not to tell my family I was dying and to suffer alone, it would comfort me to remember pain could turn to bliss. I had Aziz to thank for that.

"Women are amazing," he whispered as he watched me catch my breath in greedy gulps, like a half-drowned creature that had caught hold of a raft. I felt spared, astonished, awash in relief. But the reprieve would be short-lived. I was still stranded in the middle of an ocean. Reality, like a whirlpool, would overpower me in the end. I was married to another man. The name of my country was being erased off maps. We were sailing toward an uncertain future in a foreign land. I would never have Aziz like this again.

He leaned in to kiss me, but I reared back. He tried to coax my hand toward his body. I wouldn't let him. My message was clear. I would not look at him. He could only touch my hand. I feared that if I met his gaze, I'd turn into a boa constrictor. Slither to him, coil tight, and squeeze. He began stroking my palm again, watching to see if he could make me climax again by only touching my hand with his. He could.

He did. Both of us were soaked and breathless now, our bodies rocking back and forth in our seats. The only part of us that ever connected was our hands. It was the most erotic experience of my life.

I felt a pair of eyes on me. Young eyes. It was Naya, standing in the rain and watching us.

"*Yema?*" she said.

Aziz jumped up.

"Your mother is seasick. I was helping her."

"*Yema* doesn't get seasick. She and I have stomachs of steel," she told him. How much had she seen? More important, what would she tell her father?

"Everyone gets seasick sometimes," Aziz snapped, and then disappeared down the stairs.

"Your face looked funny," she told me.

I felt an urge to throw myself over the steel railing and into the sea. Then, I looked at my daughter, so little, and had a worse urge.

"Get downstairs, Naya," I told her. "Now."

As we made our way to the cabin, I said, "You're not like your brother and sisters. You're strong like me. You're the most precious of all my children. I have always loved you best."

Anyone who claims that isn't exactly what every child longs to hear doesn't know children. Nor adults, for that matter. She beamed.

"Let's never tell *Yaba* I needed to see the doctor, Daughter. We'll say everyone else got sick as dogs on this journey, except for you and me. You and I are made of steel."

13

ARABELLA

Jerusalem

2012

Ah, what is more delicious than making love in a hotel room? It's like the power of your craven urges coalesce and conjure up walls that spring up around you, a borrowed space, a mirage in the desert made manifest. You rent privacy from peeking eyes. You are royalty retiring to your chamber. A god is coupling with a mortal. But, which of you gets to be divine? Who has to die? If you're lucky, you get to take turns. On that day, Aziz and I both got lucky. We had all the time in the world to explore each other in our makeshift home.

We believe we want sterile environments. Unsoiled surfaces. Clean slates. But, what of making love where love existed? What's more potent with possibility than doing the deed in the country where so many generations in your lineage once did it? Were most of their couplings happy ones? Did the arranged marriages between young strangers grow in passion and blossom into love? Would it be fair to wager more often than not? Perhaps such thoughts can only occur to the children of immigrants, whose families left under duress, who've returned to a country that was lost to them. Would our encounter have felt different, perhaps prosaic, had we met while in ensconced in our very American lives? It felt impossible not to feel that if we were fated to get together, Aziz and I would do it here.

With dizzying speed, Aziz and I zipped our way through Damascus Gate and the narrow streets of souks that led to the Christian Quarter.

We smiled silently but ignored the calls of merchants who, as if anticipating our rapid footsteps, would appear in the doors of their stores just as we were passing. We soon found ourselves in the quiet courtyard of the Church of the Holy Sepulchre, a station of the Via Dolorosa. Luckily, it was not Christmas or Easter time, when candle-wielding pilgrims can trample and push their way as if their souls' salvation depended upon it. The bell tower cast a shadow. It loomed above us, but not by much. The church is easy to miss as it melts unobtrusively into the Old City's walled world and arched double doorways. It must be said the churches where Arab Christians pray appear humbler than their European counterparts, until you consider the years that they are older are counted in millenniums rather than mere centuries. As soon as we stepped through the carved wooden door into the modest church, we were promptly accosted and cursed out by an Armenian priest. Though we didn't understand a word he was saying, it was clear we were being told off for holding hands and thereby desecrating the holiest of holy sites. His outrage echoed long after we guiltily let each other's hands go. We should have known better. When I attended the Arab church of St. Nicholas in San Francisco, I knew I was expected to act modestly, but what that meant seemed to be a moving target. I only learned the rules whenever my mother chastised me for unknowingly transgressing. She'd swat at me if I crossed my legs while seated in a pew (the only acceptable way to sit in church was with your legs primly jammed together), for taking off a sweater while wearing only a tank top underneath (no showing of a women's shoulders allowed), for falling asleep with my mouth open (wasn't sure what the rule was there but, instead of ordering me to wake up, she hissed, "Your mouth is open!" as if I were inviting someone to put a penis in it).

Aziz and I approached the Stone of the Anointing, a worn uneven cracked slab, where Jesus's crucified body was supposedly laid after being taken down from the cross. We genuflected before it. I cocked my head in the direction of the Rotunda, the site believed to be Jesus's tomb. It was my favorite chamber of the church, as it glowed from the light of a circular window cut out of the domed ceiling, which shone like an eye from heaven, alongside the huge candelabras and hanging lanterns that framed the entrance. On my last family trip, Teta Zoya pointed to the lanterns, explaining they belonged to different Christian denominations, naming each one for me. Had she sensed, as I had back then, she wasn't getting any younger and that the first time we visited this church together might be our last?

It felt right that I honor my grandmother's request of me in the Rotunda. I found a tabletop filled with sand, set up for visitors to burn candles. I made a donation in the adjoining lockbox and a mental note I had to convert currencies. There were several candles of various lengths already burning in the sand. I chose the shortest one to use to light mine. I never lost the feeling there was something wasteful, perhaps even wanton, about lighting a new candle, marring the perfection of a wick.

Aziz and I watched it burn. We waited, unsure, a beat too long, for the other to say a silent prayer. Both of us were watchful for the telltale sign of the cross that signaled that the prayer was over. I made the sign first. As soon as I did, he hastily did, too, and we were free. We rushed out of the church like bats out of hell, stopping only to grab a dozen *mutabbaq* dripping with sugar and butter from the famed confectionary Zalatimo's, aka Big Lips. We then checked into the Jerusalem Hotel, an Arabic mansion turned hotel. It was an elegant limestone affair that had the advantage of being a stone's throw from the Damascus Gate.

We had to enter the hotel separately and rent two rooms, as Palestinian hotels will not rent a room to a man and woman who are not married, fearing the infamy that would follow if it was found out that johns and prostitutes frequented their establishment. By the time I'd stepped into my small stone room and put down my bag, Aziz was at my door. His mouth tasted of butter. In the few moments we were apart, he had eaten some of our pastries. It was almost sexier that we had to stay quiet as we made love. We heard other guests walking outside our room to get to the buffet. It was still breakfast time. The earthy smell of falafel, fresh parsley, and fried oil wafted through our window.

I erupted before, during, and after he spent himself twice. He kept his eyes open the whole time. Except when he lost complete control.

Then, all the courtly dignity dropped, like a mask, in those few moments of abandon when he was all animal.

I dozed contentedly in his arms until I was jolted by the sound of Aziz's phone ringing. I noticed the light peeking through the window had changed. Time was passing. Aziz answered in Arabic. Like me, he spoke with a thick brogue that displayed he descended from peasants. My people.

"Thanks for letting me know," he said into the phone. He hung up.

"The Qalandia checkpoint is open now. I can take you to Ramallah."

I groaned. There was a life outside this room that I had to face. I had a show to create with actors and designers, none of whom I had ever met. His chocolate eyes seemed to darken with concern as he looked at me.

"What's wrong, Arabella?"

"Nothing," I said.

It's hard to make a show with strangers. If only I could get Yoav to fly in and do the sound design! We were on a microbudget, but Yoav could be counted on to work for cheap if he thought the project was interesting. Should I ask him? Now that I was at the start of a rather promising new love affair, there could be no harm in having a Tony-nominated designer working with me. Right?

"Arabella, where did you go?" Aziz asked me. He kissed me. But a quick, almost uneasy peck on the cheek. "You look like you are a million miles away."

Not a million. Only as far as New York.

"Just thinking about my show," I lied. "It's got to be good. The Brits, bigwig folks who are paying for the production, are flying in from London for the opening."

"I'm sure it will be great. Did you always want to work in theatre?"

"Yes. It's the only thing I am any good at," I told him.

"I wanted to be a historian. Took as many history classes as I could in college. But I was groomed to be a doctor from birth. My grandmother blamed everything wrong in her life on the fact that Sido Aziz couldn't work in medicine after he immigrated. It was my duty to make sure there would eventually be a doctor named Aziz Habeeb practicing in America."

I imagined him as a young boy, burdened with the disappointments of family members long dead. In one way, I was lucky I had been born a girl. No one in my family expected anything from me professionally. So, I had been freer than he was and could choose my own path.

"Sounds like a lot of pressure. Is your family happy that you've come here?"

"Not at all. They think it's unsafe."

"And you clearly foiled all their hopes and dreams by not practicing in America."

"I will. Eventually. Can't be a volunteer medic in Gaza forever," he said wistfully. "Maybe I'll consider doing my duty to Palestine in other ways."

"How so?"

"At some point, I should settle down and contribute to the demographic threat." He watched the words land on me. His meaning was as clear as if he'd asked me if I wanted to have his babies. Israeli politicians had labeled the Palestinian stubborn propensity for staying alive and having children as a threat to their demographics. You could not have a state that remained both democratic and Jewish unless the Palestinian population, including those who managed to stay in their homes during the war of 1948 and constituted a fifth of Israeli citizens, was curbed, and how best to do that was a surprisingly frank open debate among them.

A Palestinian man might catcall you in the streets of Ramallah by exclaiming, "Pretty lady, come and contribute to the demographic threat with me!" Shows you how deeply hunted and haunted we felt by Zionists and their policies toward us: we couldn't even catcall each other like regular folk. The act of fucking each other, and all the steps of the dance of courtship along the way, became politicized.

It was weirdly both way too soon and right on time to be talking about having a child with Aziz. In other words, I was confused. I was consumed with the urge to have a child. It wasn't a desire I wanted to have. But I was attracted to motherhood in the way I was drawn to theatre. Inexplicably. Irrationally. Obsessively. Whether I was with Aziz or on my own, I was going to be a mother. Soon.

He stared at me, tried to read my expression. Since I didn't know what I wanted to express, I avoided his searching gaze. Too shy to look him in the eye, I decided to take him in my mouth. It was only fair since, well, he had gone to town on me more than once. I kissed him as I lowered myself. His sweat smelled of ripe cantaloupe and freshly tilled earth.

My hands reached around his legs and then I felt it. A dimple, a curving inward an inch above his knee, an indentation where it should have been smooth.

"What's that?" I asked.

"I'll tell you later," he said, gasping for breath. He was very excited. I know he wanted me to keep on the track where I was heading but was too polite to insist. I felt a flash of devilishness. Could I make Aziz get rough with me? He was so saintly, controlled, dignified. Everyone has an ugly side. Could I get him to show me his?

No. He pulled me up so I was on top of him, trying to insert himself in me in the least obtrusive way possible.

"Wait," I told him, and he paused, smiling but impatient.

I climbed off him and looked down at his knee. I saw what could only be a bullet hole. Like a Doubting Thomas, I stuck my finger in it. Then, impossibly, I saw another hole, on his other leg. This one was a hair above the round, rough circle of his kneecap. He had been shot in both legs. The holes looked like the gouged eyes of Oedipus, angry red wounds, markers of the strength of men to endure all the suffering, blindness, lust, and shame that an unlucky life could inflict on an unsuspecting body.

"What happened?" I asked. But he shook his head. Clearly, he didn't want to talk about it.

"They're superficial wounds. Neither bullet hit the bone. Don't worry. Once the snipers started targeting medics, I stopped going to the front lines."

"What front lines?" We didn't have an army to have front lines.

"The front lines of the demonstrations the Gazans are doing at the border. They've been getting a lot of international attention and it's going to lead to the end of the blockade. I'll take you sometime. So you can see how we're building a peaceful protest movement. So you can bear witness to history."

"And so I can get shot up, too?"

"You're right. Stay in Ramallah, where it is safer." I smiled and breathed a sigh of relief. He cared about me in the way my parents did. When it came down to brass tacks, my parents didn't give two shits for anything in the world except my brothers and me. We, their children with our beloved bodies and precious blood, were not fodder for a revolution. That's the only kind of love I understood. I knew, if I had a child, I would give him or her the advice I always felt like whispering in the ear of soldiers in uniform. Any uniform, all uniforms.

Save yourself. There is no army worth joining, no country worth dying for. A community that expects you to kill on command is a cult. Nationalism, a fable. Religion, a ghost story. Powerful, terrifyingly convincing, but not real. Run!

"We have to keep you safe at all costs," he told me. "Our movement needs artists, too. That is your role."

My role is to stay alive. Easier to accomplish when one doesn't have bullet wounds in one's body, I wanted to tell him.

"Your concern is touching," I said instead.

"I'm glad," he replied, and kissed me. Did he not notice my sarcasm? Or was he not responding to it? As I drank in my wounded warrior with my eyes, I realized I didn't care. I wasn't going near any Right of Return march, even if he wanted me to. Not in this lifetime. He didn't have to keep my ass safe. It was my job to do that. We made love again. Then we stumbled out into the sunlight and he drove me in the direction of Ramallah. Our ancestral hometown, our vanquished village that had blossomed into a city in our absence, awaited.

14

ZOYA

Detroit
1967

Detroit was a city that knew how to riot. Detroit was a city that knew how to burn. If there was any place in America I belonged, it was Detroit.

By any standards, 1967 was a summer to remember.

In June, Ramallah—my hometown—was conquered in my absence in the Six-Day War. I found the name of the war irksome. How long did it take to eviscerate our forces completely? Months? Years? No. Six whole days. Kamal, the children, and I watched the war from America. How did people get their news before the age of television? I found it hard to breathe during those days, though I was a world away from the unstoppable tanks and the endless boots on the ground. The Israeli army swarmed into the two swathes of unconnected land, the West Bank and Gaza, where Palestinians were supposed to be allowed to subsist after our country was partitioned in 1948. Jewish-only settlements would begin to be erected around Palestinian cities and towns. Encircling us. Choking us off further from each other and the world. Millions of our people suddenly found themselves living as subjects under military occupation, allowed neither to become citizens of the country of Israel nor establish our own, existing in a perpetual state of statelessness.

My father was one of them. His twenty hilly acres of olive orchards were confiscated and turned into a military zone. His olive trees were immediately bulldozed. Though his insatiable hunger for more, more, and more land had compelled him to send my sisters to serve as maids in Jerusalem to expand his lot, *Yaba* ended up with only the one-room stone home he had started out with as a strapping young man.

In July, Detroit—my adopted American home—burst into a flame of riots. We huddled around our television in our makeshift apartment above our liquor store, watching the coverage of the rioting that was going on around us. The pretty blond news announcer's calmness affronted us, the way she spoke of civil unrest when what was happening was more like civil war. We were surrounded by sound, the only sense we could access to gather real information about the tornado of rage on the streets below. Smelling the smoke of fires blazing in our neighborhood, Kamal and I took turns staying awake at night, keeping vigil lest a burning bottle came crashing through our window. Yet, hiding at home still felt safer than venturing out amidst so many gunshots and sirens. Also, we had no place to go. What ignited the Detroit Riots of 1967, among the deadliest in American history? If you live in Detroit, you know the real question is what prevented them from erupting for so long. American politicians seemed flummoxed by how one case of police brutality could inflame a city. If you come from a war zone, you know what an army looks like. It was no less than an army of policemen, with their state-sanctioned violence and intimidation, that kept our adopted city segregated. Forever separate, forever unequal in terms of food insecurity, education, and opportunity. My family came here to escape oppression. You can imagine my shock when I learned Black Americans were not allowed to live wherever they could afford to buy homes, that their movements would be monitored and restricted, that they'd be confined by actual borders like the Birwood Wall. I never fancied myself an idealist. I don't believe justice wins out in the end or that people are fair-minded, generous, or kind. But, being my father's daughter, I believed in the power of money. The Blacks of Detroit, like the Palestinians of Ramallah, would be taught that the power of the gun would trump even that. You could never earn your way into equality. What is the point of money if it cannot buy you freedom? Or cleverness? What is the point of anything?

In August, Kamal beat me for the first time. Is it fair to call it a beating? Technically I put my hands on him first. Soon after the National Guard stamped out the rioting, Kamal informed me that we were moving. When I understood he was serious, that he had put our life savings down on a house in an all-white suburb of Detroit without consulting me, I shoved him. Perhaps it's more accurate to say we fought and I lost.

Start a fight that you have no chance of winning, and maybe you deserve what you get. But, more often than not, you fight not because you expect to prevail, but because you cannot help it. To call it self-destructive is to misunderstand what it means to have a self.

I got in two good blows before Kamal knocked me down. I lay on the floor and our eyes met. It was clear I was scared. It was also clear I was still defiant.

He lifted his foot and I realized he was going to kick me in the face.

As I braced for the blow, my mind was full of questions. Why move us now, Husband? Why now?

Hadn't our small liquor store, and the makeshift home we made above it, been spared the looting, fire, and brimstone? Not even a pane of glass had been broken. Was it not a sign we belonged here? The rest of our block—the check-cashing store, the minimart, and the electronics shop—had been torched during the riots along with much of downtown Detroit. Just the day before, Kamal had claimed it was an act of God that our home and business had been saved. He made a *nidir* to donate 20 percent of our earnings to the Church of the Holy Sepulchre this year. I found that excessive. Yet, the sight of our store left untouched on our otherwise obliterated street did appear Biblical in nature, even to me, who was not wont to buy into the idea of divine intervention. If there are guardian angels, they take the form of friends. Hadn't such a friend saved our home, our business, and quite possibly our lives? Had it not turned out to be a blessing, rather than a curse, that we were ostracized from the Palestinian community in Detroit?

Back in Ramallah, I had no idea it had been found out that Kamal and I hadn't shared with his cousins the blood money we received after his uncle was killed in the auto factory accident. Kamal didn't tell me until after I, along with our dirty and bleary-eyed children, were deposited on New York's West Side Highway, disembarking our boat with other Palestinian refugees. Finding myself on that outer strip of New York, with cars whizzing in either direction, I felt New York was not a larger version of cities I knew back home. We were caught in the belly of a machine with whirling parts. The looming skyscrapers didn't seem fixed in place. They were levers that could swing your way and give you no time to run. My first thought was of Aziz. What would he think once he heard the story of our family's perfidy and greed?

After Aziz and I had been caught holding hands on the deck by Naya, I stayed in my cabin, feigning a headache for the rest of the voyage. I ate only what my children could sneak from the table. I was afraid to look Aziz in the eyes. What would I find there? Love? Indifference? I was also afraid I might kill myself. I had no thoughts of inflicting harm on myself, except when I approached the thresholds of high spaces or—as I learned on our voyage—the deck of a ship at sea. But, as soon as I stepped out of my cabin when it was time for us to disembark, I could not stop my eyes from seeking out Aziz. I could not find him in the crush of bodies trying to make their way to the ones who came to meet us, the ones we belonged to.

Would Aziz assume I had tempted my husband to steal the blood money from his cousins? Whenever a man was a thief, whether he stole in a souk or cajoled a gold bracelet off his mother's arm as she slept, it was attributed to the greediness of his wife. The unspoken assumption was that the woman, Eve-like in her capacity to encourage evil, wouldn't give her favors to a man unless he did her bidding. I could almost hear tongues wagging about me. All her sisters worked as humble maids except Zoya! Zoya wore Chanel dresses! Zoya demanded a house by the sea! I watched the clerks exchange glances whenever I shopped in the souks of Dearborn, a suburb of Detroit where the street signs were in Arabic and most of our hometown in exile had settled. Haggling was a birthright among my people, but not for the maniacal woman whose greed—and possibly her refusal to open her legs to her husband—drove an otherwise respectable man to sin.

Is all social rejection agony? Or was it particularly gut-wrenching in our case because our village had been transplanted to America en masse? Our people clung to each other with perhaps more than the usual desperation of other rudderless American immigrants. For we were from a country that we had not only abandoned but was now lost to us. To our chagrin, we were excluded from the comforts such a cohesive community might provide. We were not invited to the monthly meetings of the Detroit chapter of the Ramallah Club, the organization designed to give our people the illusion we might live, socialize, and marry our children off to each other exactly as if we had never left. The one time we attended Sunday service at the Arab church of St. Mary's, the Lebanese priest gave a sermon about how it was easier for a camel to go through the eye of a needle than a rich man to enter the kingdom of God, even if that man got his riches by honest means. Though the priest's diatribe probably wasn't directed at us, the congregation took it that way. Such smirks, such glares! Even my elder sister, Raghida, didn't greet me, lest it be believed she had benefited indirectly from the blood money we did not share. She briefly called me to explain, telling me her husband—a friend of an aggrieved cousin of Kamal—had forbade her to speak to me and hung up. When Kamal's feet began to swell from standing for fourteen hours at a time, it became clear we needed help in the store. In hindsight, could it not be seen as divine intervention that no one we knew wanted to be associated with us?

For had we been able to hire a fellow Palestinian, King Tut might never have entered into our lives. In a time of riots and rage, we were spared in part because we were recognized as the only Arab shopkeepers who employed someone from the Black community, the people whose patronage enabled us to begin to prosper, one bottle of Wild Irish Rose liquor at a time.

King Tut's real name was Jonah Jones Jr. We took to calling him King Tut because he wore a small gold pendant of the doomed young pharaoh around his neck, whom he resembled more than a little. Slender with a regal bearing, he had the same big, bemused eyes, delicate cheekbones, and full lips. But, instead of gold, his skin gleamed of black pearl. He was only eighteen but had the bearing of a much older man. When I learned enough English to converse with him, I observed he always spoke with a formality that gave his words weight, as if he were quoting the Bible, even when engaging in the most mundane of conversations. He overheard our son, Ghassan, use our nickname for him and decided he liked it. King Tut is how he introduced himself to our customers. In our store, they addressed him as such, even those who knew him as a pastor's effeminate son.

"I met him in a church and asked if he wanted work," Kamal explained to me in his characteristically laconic way when King Tut showed up for his first shift. I eventually got the real story from King Tut.

He and his father, Pastor Jonah, were the only ones in the church when Kamal walked in. Pastor Jonah was upbraiding his son about not adhering to the choir dress code. But mostly he was angry because it had become clear that his son was different. The reason why it became clear was that King Tut decided to make it so, to stop pretending to fancy the Supremes or the pretty girls in his father's congregation.

"What my father cannot forgive is not that I'm a homosexual," King Tut told me in his crisp and precise manner that belied his young age. "He cannot forgive that I am unwilling to hide it for the sake of appearances."

Pastor Jonah and King Tut were startled by the arrival of the stranger, whom they mistook for a light-skinned Black man, when Kamal wandered into the Second Baptist Church wordlessly, genuflected, and proceeded to collapse in a back pew.

They watched the stranger put his head in his hands and sob. Then, father and son approached Kamal, asking if he needed help. King Tut told me that Kamal didn't seem capable of responding right away, unwilling to lift his head until he was able to get ahold of himself enough to speak.

When Kamal finally did, he said in his heavily accented English, "I come from the Holy Land, but I am a sinner. I stole blood money from my family. I sell liquor to men who shouldn't be drinking. Do you know an honest man willing to do unclean work?"

The pastor was speechless, but King Tut was not.

"Me," he said. King Tut admitted he didn't know what Kamal was about to ask him to do. But, he was sure he would be willing to try it rather than stay for another moment in his father's house.

Thus, King Tut worked shifts for us in our liquor store and became our link to all things American. He introduced my children to the beats of Motown, high fives, trick-or-treating, and bell-bottoms. A student at Wayne State, he tutored them in the subjects Kamal and I did not understand. He made sure they weren't harassed too much in school for their accents. In return, they worshipped him. When the rioting reached the level of inferno, King Tut stood with a shotgun outside our shop to prevent our building from being torched with us in it. Before he saved our lives, King Tut saved my soul.

"Zoya should learn English," he said while perched at the cash register during lunchtime one day. I would descend at noon every day and bring them food, usually lentils and rice, which made up most of our meals, as we were parsimonious and intended to save every penny we could to buy the building where our store was leased. Gone were our days of elaborate dinner parties, meat sizzling on skewers, and fried pine nuts mixed with saffron rice.

"What did he say about me and English?" I asked Kamal, and he translated for us. For that, I would forever be grateful. Though he didn't approve of the conversation, he did not shut it down.

"I should learn everything," I told Kamal to tell King Tut as I handed them both bowls.

"I'm not speaking in jest," King Tut said with a smile.

"Neither am I," I told him.

"There are programs to teach adults to read at the library. They are free," King Tut said to me.

"Zoya is needed at home with the children," Kamal said, putting a sudden end to the banter for a moment.

"They must go with her. There exists no better place for children to be than a library," he responded after a beat. When Kamal had to admit he agreed it would be edifying for them, King Tut winked at me. It would be under those auspices that he would help me do as I should do and wished I could do, which was to have the chance to learn everything.

King Tut led me and my two youngest children, Naya and Ghassan, on a pilgrimage via bus to the magnificent Detroit Public Library. My elder daughters stayed at home with the Jackson 5 and the record player King Tut had secured for them. We entered the stately marbled walls with its serpentine trim just as the four o'clock afternoon sunlight infused it with warmth. When we left two hours later, it was like a switch had been flipped. The library itself became a source of light that emanated through its long, arched windows, brightening the way of those who were the last to leave it.

In that library, King Tut introduced me to Reginald, the first teacher I would have since my father forced me to leave school. He would show me how to pronounce a new alphabet. He taught me nouns and verbs. He gave me new names for things.

Aziz evaporated from my mind the moment I saw Reginald, a middle-aged coffee-colored man standing in the light, holding a satchel of workbooks. He had enormous dark eyes, an immaculately cropped short Afro dusted with gray, and the muscular frame of a man who had been an athlete as a youth. To be so easily eclipsed could mean only one thing. Whatever my feeling for Aziz had been, it clearly couldn't go by the name of love, since it was transferred wholesale to this man in a three-piece chestnut brown suit who offered me his hand when King Tut introduced us.

I know when Reginald initiated the idea of a literacy program for adults at the library, he didn't expect the likes of me, a mother of nine with hungry eyes that couldn't help but devour him. Though it was uncustomary for men to touch women in our culture, I shook his hand. I didn't let go right away, savoring the smooth feel of his skin. With a bemused glance at King Tut, he gently extracted himself from my grip.

Reginald was a high school English teacher and a cousin of Marjorie Blackistone, the first Black librarian hired in the Detroit Public Library, who had assembled a dazzling collection of the works of her people. This man would make it possible for me to learn to communicate in my adopted country, even as I sat with the knowledge—lesson after lesson—that the person I most wanted to communicate with was him.

"May she join your class?" King Tut asked Reginald. By then, Ghassan and Naya had wandered to the children's section, depositing themselves among the world of bright colors and magical stories of animals who could talk.

"Of course. If she doesn't mind being the only student," Reginald said. Or at least that is what I think they said. I didn't have enough English at the time to know what Reginald meant, so he pantomimed he would work with me alone as no one else had signed up. The literacy program was funded through the library, so the program would continue even with one student. His curriculum was designed for native speakers who knew how to speak the language but could not read it. I couldn't do either.

On Mondays and Wednesdays, I would clean the house until everything that could shine did. I'd take my time carefully in making the best meal I could with only lentils and fava beans, pack up Ghassan and Naya, and make our way to the library. I would sit next to Reginald at a round table. He began with the alphabet, encouraging me first to sing it like a song. The foreign letters seemed impossible to pronounce, particularly the explosive *p* that had no equivalent in Arabic. As we sat side by side, he showed me motions with his mouth that turned into sounds I couldn't make at first. But eventually I did.

Kamal was always agitated on those days that we went to the library. It was like he had a radar searching for signals of our family's faults, a litany of ways I was failing. I never made the caramelized onions crispy like his mother did. I was not monitoring how much time Ghassan, who had just turned nine, spent reading Superman comic books and in that way I was hindering our only son from becoming a doctor and achieving social mobility in America someday. Naya needed bigger clothes, as the hand-me-downs of her sisters flattered the contours of her prodigious curves, and as her mother, I should have been vigilant about protecting my eleven-year-old daughter from attention she didn't want or understand. It was like, by filling my mind with inanities, he wanted to leave no space for learning. Or maybe he was always exacting, but I found it especially enraging on the days I was infused with hope that I could master English and, by extension, anything.

I devoured page after page of our dictionary at home, hoping to delight Reginald with my diligence.

What did I know of him? He was meticulous. He wore a body oil that smelled of sandalwood and always, always, always was decked out in an impeccable three-piece suit. He seemed to have endless ensembles in various shades of dark and light brown. He was even-keeled, if that meant he was always patient, ever-smiling, and as mysterious as the Sphinx. The weeks I studied with him turned into months. Yet, I learned nothing substantial about him, and not through my lack of trying.

"Do you have a girlfriend?" I blurted out, not being able to help myself as he was explaining to me the grammar of the future perfect.

"No," he said, and went on with his lesson.

"How do you find Reginald?" King Tut whispered to me one afternoon while Kamal was busy haggling with our supplier of Hennessy. Kamal saw the supplier as his nemesis. He was sure he could give us a better deal, if only Kamal asked him enough times or in the right way.

"I love him," I whispered.

"I thought you would," he said.

"What are you talking about?" Kamal asked.

"We are speaking of how you are masterful in the art of negotiation!" King Tut lied deftly, because he understood that Kamal felt uneasy about my sojourns to the library. Was Kamal unenthused by the idea that I would learn English because I might eventually speak it better than he did?

It was on the holiday dedicated to lovers that I made my love known. I assumed my advances would be welcome. To be fair, Reginald did bring me chocolate.

"Happy Valentine's Day!" he told me. He brought three chocolate bars in the shape of hearts. Two for the children and one for me. I took it as a sign. I sat as close as it was decent to sit, taking in the scent of the sandalwood oil he wore.

His lesson was on conjunctions that day. He rested his writing hand on the table as he explained how to use words like "but" and "if." His other hand he kept cupped on his knee. I put my hand on his under the table. To my surprise, the temperature between us didn't change. He didn't push my hand away or respond to my touch. He simply stood still.

"Zoya, you know Jonah and I are together."

"King Tut?" I asked.

"I don't call him that silly name. But, yes."

"Please no tell him I be touching you." I found myself stumbling over words. Reginald was a fantasy. I could replace him, as cleanly as I had replaced Aziz. But King Tut was a friend. Friends were harder to replace.

"I hardly think Jonah would mind," he said. "We have an open relationship."

"What does that mean?" I asked.

"That's a lesson for a different day, Zoya," he said, but his wry smile gave me a grasp of what such a relationship might entail. Then, he turned his attention back to his tutorial on conjunctions. I stared at the words written in bold in the textbook in front of us. If. Until. Unless.

On the bus ride home, I took out my chocolate heart and ate it with a relish that was about more than cocoa and sugar.

As he continued to gift me with words in English—and gifts they did always feel like—we began to speak of ideas. An impenetrably private person, it was clear that access to his ideas was all he was willing to share of himself. He taught words like "resistance," "retribution," and "reparations." He explained to me the concept of "nonviolence," an idea defined only by what it is not. He taught me the vocabulary of revolution in its simplest form. There was a spectrum of ways to respond to injustice. On either end were two men who symbolized the two sides of that spectrum.

"Some of us believe in Martin. Some of us believe in Malcolm," he told me, emphasizing the latter's name in a way that gave no doubt in which direction he leaned. "Who do you believe in, Zoya?"

It was hard for me to articulate what I wanted to say.

"Both and neither," I told him. When he smiled, I knew I had nailed a way to express my meaning. It is the powerful who choose everything, including which forms of our resistance they find persuasive.

The powerful dictate whether nonviolent protest is effective—if not at making them stop hurting us entirely (for no one expects a more powerful side to do that), but to make them think twice before hurting us more than we can bear.

Ghassan told Kamal about the gift of candy.

"*Yema* wouldn't share the chocolate heart her teacher gave her," he complained, and I felt an urge to scream. Our family was addicted to Almond Joy, the American candy that most reminded us of the sweets of Palestine. I always gave him half of mine. Was it because he was my youngest? Or because I was taught to favor my only boy? Either way, the little pig got used to me giving him more than his share, so he expected it. It became normal that I would do so, and the one time I did not, it outraged him. He was telling on me to his father.

"Your teacher is giving you chocolates?" Kamal asked me.

"He's a man like our King Tut," I told him.

"Men are men," he said.

Could Kamal's jealousy of Reginald have provoked him to move us to an all-white enclave? The riots had literally cleared out all our competition in the neighborhood. People came from blocks away to buy liquor from us. The stack of money we kept in the freezer seemed to double overnight.

"It's too dangerous for you to take the bus to the library in these times," Kamal announced at dinner that night.

"It's no more dangerous than before," I disagreed under my breath.

"No more taking the bus!" he said.

So, we walked the hour it took to get to the library, three miles away. I stuffed my children with Almond Joy bars every time they complained. The humidity of summer hadn't yet given way, as if time was refusing to pass, as if the fateful summer of 1967 had no intention of ending.

We finally arrived, soaked in sweat and exhausted, and I learned about adverbs that day.

I should have known Kamal would not be bested. I could have waited a week before trying to make my return to the library. I might have asked again on another day, played it sweet rather than defiant, written him a love letter to show him how I intended to use my new-found language. He was moving me into an all-white enclave where foreigners like us would be tolerated, but barely. We'd be sneered at by unfriendly neighbors, though not firebombed and hounded out like Black Americans who tried to move into "their" spaces. King Tut and Reginald were not likely to visit. I wanted no part of a world that wanted no part of them.

But I was to lose the fight to stay in our home and to suffer for daring to start it in the first place.

The body anticipates pain, because our brains predict it. It knows when it is coming. After I got knocked to the floor, I saw Kamal's foot coming toward my face and braced myself.

At the last possible second, Kamal instead stamped his foot inches from my nose. I flinched and then I saw it. A flicker, gone as quick as it came. He made me flinch and, for a moment, it made him smile.

Because I saw that smile, nothing ever could be the same between us. The stranger I had married always possessed the potential to blossom into my true love. That is what I was told. That is what I had believed. Life was long. Who's to say he wouldn't have woken up one morning and said the right words? Touched me in the right ways? Held me in the exact manner I needed after I bore our family another child or, God forbid, if we lost one? Could he transform into a man I was glad had his fate irrevocably intertwined with mine?

No. The kernel of hope I had for us, the seed of the capacity for understanding between him and me, had been crushed. By him.

"Get up. Start packing," he ordered.

I did.

15

ARABELLA

Ramallah
2012

Enter the villain. Recycled, reborn, reincarnated in every generation. Long ago, he was Pharaoh So-and-So, watching the whirlwind of whips striking the backs of his subjects, a torrent of strings, an orchestra punctuated by screams. What does he feel? Nothing. What does he know? The pyramid built for him is not high enough. Centuries later, he returns as Sultan What's-His-Face, surveying the breasts and buttocks of his newest wives and pondering the age-old question of whom he will bless by bestowing his dick upon them for the day. In his current incarnation, he is Ramez, founding artistic director of Dar Al-Masrah. The House of Theater. Its very house. When you're a founder, you tap into a natural resource, a reservoir of energy. Harness the fuck out of it and exploit, exploit, exploit. What resource did Ramez find in a military occupied zone known as the West Bank? An entire population under siege with stories to tell.

The House of Theater was his dream. He built it so he could stand center stage.

Woe to us peasants, mere mortals, who do not know it.

Woe to us ruffians, groundlings all, who know not our place. Sallow-brained and lily-livered, we glean not the true meaning of the Shakespearean phrase "all the world's a stage," which is that most of us motherfuckers belong in the audience. His audience.

Woe to the pompous Palestinian and/or American Woman who

arrives unaware. Pretentious and presumptuous, she calls herself a theatre director. Even more astounding, some believe her! What's to be done with this weird sister? She, who is both exactly like and nothing like every woman he has ever met on the streets of Ramallah. Familiar and strange. A girl you might look at twice, but not three times, whose looks would be much improved if she went easier on the hummus. Someone should tell her. Hiring her to direct a show at the House of Theater is not Ramez's idea, of course, meaning it is a terrible one. She has been thrust upon his theatre troupe by the British funders who are sponsoring the cost of the production and, therefore, must be endured. Rarely do women directors work in high places in their illustrious European theatres, yet they inflict this bitch whom no one has ever met upon Dar Al-Masrah to pretend they give a rat's ass about female empowerment in the arts. They task her with directing an Arabic-language production of *Hamlet*, a recipe for failure. She apparently wants to have a female play the starring role and change the title to *Hamleta*. She will soon be dispelled of the illusion that she decides upon such matters. She, who speaks Arabic with the accent of a native but has the vocabulary of a simpleton!

Ah, now we have stepped in it! We have stumbled upon the subject of our villain's fatal flaw. His Achilles heel. His curse! Clearly, his Arabic accent was the only thing that had kept Ramez from the international stardom he deserved. Without it, Hollywood surely would have come calling. Clark Gable had nothing on him. Nothing! In fact, Ramez was his doppelganger. Even his wife agreed. He possessed blue eyes. This made the European artists and intellectuals who visited the House of Theater sometimes blurt out, "You don't look like an Arab at all!" which—of course—is meant as a high compliment. With his eyes of sapphire, he believed himself a god among mortals.

Or maybe he was just an actor who really wanted to play a part. A man who had devoted his professional life to creating a theatre company despite living under military occupation, where the key ingredient necessary to theatre—the right to assembly—was routinely curtailed. Obsessed with movies, he had aspired to something more than pretending to do combat by throwing rocks at the heavily armed soldiers who controlled his life and the lives of everyone he loved. In the midst of so much ugliness, to devote oneself to beauty is an act of defiance. When Ramez was young, there were no formal theatre training centers in Palestinian cities and, being the son of refugees, he had no means to travel. The only acting school he had access to was an Israeli one. So, impressively, he learned Hebrew in order to study theatre at a college in Tel Aviv. This was before the first intifada, the uprising, an earlier time in which such endeavors were possible. At age eighteen, he was the youngest in his class and the only Palestinian. Military service is mandatory for Israelis so they enter college later. How strange it was to be learning among peers who had all served in an army designed to protect themselves from your kind. He tried not to think about how acting was one such means they used to protect themselves. Since its founding, Israeli special forces has had a unit of spies who are trained in the "Arab Department" to infiltrate and live within Palestinian communities, especially easy to do because swarthy Sephardic Jews often cannot be told apart from Palestinians. Ramez reminded himself daily he was only there to learn Shakespeare, who belonged neither to his people nor theirs. He and his classmates practiced how to breathe together, hold their posture, enunciate. He was distant, polite, and avoided talk of politics. For his thesis production, his professors cast him as Shylock in *The Merchant of Venice*. Though all his classmates were Jewish, his teachers apparently wanted to watch him step into the shoes of Shakespeare's most famous Jewish character. His daughter was born the week before rehearsals began. He didn't tell his classmates about the birth. He didn't tell them anything about his life. As he stood onstage as Shylock, he imagined what it would mean if his little Karima—named to honor his long-dead father—grew up to betray him and his people. The very idea hollowed him. Real, hot tears would roll down his cheek every show as he recited the lines, "If you prick us, do we not bleed? If you tickle us, do we not laugh? If you poison us, do we not die? And if you wrong us, shall we not revenge?" And he was not the only one. The eyes of the actors playing Solanio and Salarino would go wet, too. When Ramez got a standing ovation for every performance of *The Merchant of Venice*, he knew he'd earned it.

Hamlet was his favorite play. While his widowed mother didn't marry his uncle, she did enough. She wedded an odious man when Ramez was twelve. It is not customary in Palestinian circles for widows, especially with children, to marry again. Thus, Ramez understood Hamlet's rage and shame, recognized it as an articulation of the defining story of his childhood and possibly his life. It had always been his dream to play the title role in the play that explained him to himself. And I got to be the person who arrived and told him that he couldn't. At least not in my production. He felt that his entire life's possibilities had been diminished because of his race and here I was telling him he was now the wrong gender. It was an integral component of my interpretation of the show that the title role be played by a female.

Who could blame him for hating me? For doing everything in his power, utilizing every tool in his surprisingly extensive arsenal, to plot my downfall, defame my name, and undermine my work? Wouldn't we all do the same if someone vastly more privileged came along and dashed our very specific and personal dreams?

I know myself enough to know that answer. Mess with my dream and it feels like you're choking me. I react as such. I might do all that Ramez did to me in his place. I might do worse.

In no universe would the likes of Ramez and I have hit it off. Yet, perhaps the shock of emerging straight from a steaming love nest with Aziz made my next encounter with any other man, especially a traditional and conceited one, seem jarring. I couldn't stop myself from beaming as Aziz and I left the Jerusalem Hotel. Aziz had treated my body as a thing of wonderment, a source of joy, a universe of surprises. He had let me sleep when jet lag overtook me and was there when I awoke, plying me with fresh sesame bread, savory hummus drizzled with olive oil and paprika, apricots, and mango juice he had magically made manifest. I ate with abandon, relishing the random assortment of foods he could buy within a few steps of our hotel. I glowed as if every inch of my body had been touched (nay, polished!) by him. In short, I was riding high as he drove me to Ramallah for my first meeting with Ramez and the cast and crew of the House of Theater.

In the passenger seat, with one hand resting lazily outside the open window and my other held firmly in his, I was lost in the kind of reverie that only a person who has been completely spent by lovemaking can feel. As it did the first time I visited, the dusty desert landscape reminded me of the Hollywood set for *Ben-Hur*, since I had watched that movie before I had seen my parents' homeland. One half of me expected to see an army of actors dressed like Roman soldiers come storming over a hill. Everything felt a bit unreal, including the watchtowers looming along the road and border-like military checkpoint of Qalandia that now separated Jerusalem from Ramallah, as if it were all a part of a movie set. The Qalandia checkpoint was new to me. It had sprung up since the time I had visited Palestine a decade earlier, when it had been possible to slip into a cab and move easily between the two cities, which were only eight miles apart.

"Do we have to go through the checkpoint?" I asked Aziz.

"No, there's a mountain road," he answered.

"Why don't we take it and not deal with soldiers?"

"It takes longer if we aren't stopped."

We were stopped. But the bored teenage Israeli soldiers, in their uniforms, felt like actors, too. Even as they pulled our car randomly out of line, detained us, and then summarily dismissed us after an hour wait, they barely registered in my mind. Nor did the impossibly high separation wall, also new, which snaked alongside our road. What can be said of art that is created to embellish what is unendurable? There were attempts to bring beauty to that wall that separated our people from ourselves: colorful graffiti of calls to action (Silence Is Complicity!); a Banksy mural of a shadow of a girl flying over the wall carried by a cheerfully abundant bunch of balloons. The colorful murals of Palestinian faces and the quotes ("Love wins" in Arabic and English) were there! The painfully young soldiers with menacing assault rifles were there, too. Why had their presence ceased to jar me as it had on the steps to Jerusalem just yesterday? The warmth of the connection between my left hand and Aziz's right hand had been the only sensory observation I could absorb, the only one that mattered in that moment.

Within the space of a day, I had already begun to live as a Palestinian, meaning I was accustomed to life under military occupation. It had become a backdrop, separate from my inner journey. At the helm of my consciousness was that my mind, body, and spirit—which were often at odds—were on the same page, basking in the joy of what had been—so far—an immeasurably satisfying love affair where I was cast as a leading lady riding astride her leading man. Everyone else was a bit player. When we finally crossed the checkpoint, I held my breath as we drove toward Ramallah's hilly terrain. Ramallah means Hill of God. It is situated on the crest of mountains where our forefathers had founded the village over four hundred years ago (obviously bringing our foremothers along for the ride). With each wave of refugees from each war, Ramallah had blossomed into the center of Palestinian culture, commerce, and art that was so enormous it was unrecognizable to my parents, who left as children, when the city was just a seed of itself.

"*Hathihe Ramallah?*" my parents asked each other in shock as they stood in Tahta, the district known as the downtown. Is this Ramallah? It was a question they repeated so often it became a refrain every time we seemed to turn a corner. They recognized Bouza Rukab, the ice cream parlor and the epicenter of their worldly desires as children, but apparently little else. Our trip to Palestine had been an afterthought for my bourgeois parents, hardly some spiritual sojourn to learn about my history. During the summer between high school and college, we made a stop there as a part of a highlights of the world tour that included Paris, London, Cairo, and—on a whim—their hometown. Is this Ramallah? It was a question I asked myself now as we drove in. I eyed scantily clad girls in heels and fully veiled ladies, weaving their way through the crowded streets. Is this Ramallah? A *cahway*, a coffee-house and traditionally all-male space, down the valley from Snobar, the open-air, co-ed poolside bar. Is this Ramallah? The five-star hotel Mövenpick hovering in sight of the souk, resplendent with wares of the latest fashions alongside rows of restaurants displaying skewers of shawarma meat spinning like planets on their axes. The whiff of hot, fresh meat made you dizzy with desire, no matter how full you thought you were. Is this Ramallah? I glanced at Al-Muntazah, the garden restaurant and only spot of greenery nestled at the foot of the hilly terrain for centuries. Four enormous stately stone lions had been erected, each representing a founding father of a clan of Ramallah. From their perch, the statues overlooked the boisterous epicenter, a circle of honking cars and screeching microbuses that dodge the undaunted pedestrians who wouldn't have waited their turns to cut across the dizzyingly busy thoroughfare even if there were actually pedestrian signals to suggest that they consider the idea. Could those founding fathers, humble farmers, ever have predicted such monuments to them would be built? What would they think of the fact that the vast majority of their descendants ended up in another world, a land that would be called America, another former British colony? Or that two of their progeny, Aziz and I, would have very different paths that led us to return and find each other here? Is this Ramallah? Aside from the chatter in Arabic, I caught snippets of French spoken among a gaggle of young foreigners milling about the cosmopolitan restaurants, open for business, that lined the newly paved streets. I figured most were students, young idealistic activist-types living in Ramallah while doing a year of study abroad at the nearby Birzeit University, the Harvard of Palestine, a place I surely would have attended had my family never left. As we stopped in the bumper-to-bumper traffic, I studied these teenagers who chose to sojourn to the place my family fled. Is this Ramallah? The answer, invariably, was yes.

The House of Theater ironically did not have a theatre space to call its own. Their office was located in a nondescript space in one of the newly built high-rises that transformed Ramallah's skyline. Screeching to a halt when he found a parking spot, Aziz dropped me at its entrance. He promised to wait for me at Sangria, an incongruously named outdoor garden café down the block, until my meeting was over. Before opening the car door, I turned to him, hungry for a kiss. He didn't lean in to give me one but squeezed my hand instead. It would attract attention to kiss. Even married couples weren't making out in cars.

"I'm going to miss you," he said.

"Me too. But the meeting should only take an hour or so."

"I know, but I should try to head back to Gaza tonight."

"Tonight? Why?" I whined.

"One of my patients was shot in the eye during the last demonstration. He's lost vision in the eye already, but it looks like we may need to remove more of the socket. I don't know how long the Israelis will keep me detained at the border, but the checkpoints are open now. I should check on him."

What could I say? Stay because if I don't feel you do that thing you did with your tongue again, I'm not sure I can convince myself life is worth living?

I looked into Aziz's earnest eyes and thankfully heard myself give the only acceptable response.

"Of course you should. But promise you won't leave me without saying a proper good-bye, Aziz."

"I promise," he said.

I felt warmed from my head to my toes in that moment and stepped out. From the curb, I watched him swing back into the flow of traffic, narrowly avoiding being sideswiped in the process.

I was alone on a busy street. Men, women, and children rushed past me. There must have been a school or two nearby, as boys and girls were coming from different directions. They marched in little blue uniforms, looking like officious miniature bureaucrats. I stepped under the awning of the white high-rise and stood there, feeling apprehensive. What if the theatre troupe didn't like me? Why had I made no effort to connect with them beforehand, relying on Lisa-Turned-Layla to handle all our communication? What if they thought my interpretation of *Hamlet* was stupid? What if it was stupid?

I picked up my cell phone and almost called my grandmother but thought better of it. She would undoubtedly grill me about Aziz. I was the loose thread, the unmarried granddaughter. She was desperate to knit me into the family tapestry of marriage and motherhood. My mother got married when she was fifteen. In a borrowed frilly white lace dress that is too large for her, she looks bewildered in all the wedding pictures save one. We have a tradition called the candle dance. The lights go dim. All the unmarried girls at a wedding reception form a line, each carrying a tiny white candle, in a procession. We make a circle around the bride, the light from the candles reflecting in our excited eyes like a thousand mirrors. In the center, the bride carries two large candles, embellished with white bedazzled ribbons, as she sways in time to the drumming. The traditional song that is played is slow, a violin-filled and almost mournful incantation, praising the beauty of the bride with its refrain of *"Ism Allah! Ism Allah!"* Name of God! Name of God! Invoking the divine powers, that which is responsible for bestowing beauty in unequal portions, is meant to ward off the eye evil of jealous onlookers. One by one, the bride gets to invite a few girls from the circle to come to the center with her, usually sisters or close friends, to hold the candles she is carrying with her. It's an honor to be chosen, to stare into the bemused eyes of a bride, both of you swaying together as you grasp the candles for a stanza or two. At the end of the song, the groom comes into the center of the circle and blows out the candles. I used to love the dance as a child, the chance to be ushered onto center stage and the excitement of carrying candles with fifty of my closest cousins, until I realized the point of it seemed to be to give an opportunity for old men to ogle "virgins" and mothers to scope out potential brides for their sons, since it was easier to tell which of us was decidedly the most beautiful when we danced side by side. In my twenties, I began to see the tradition as creepy, marking the transition from girlhood into wifehood with the extinguishing of light. In my thirties, I would hide in the bathroom, lest I be forced to stand with prepubescent girls in honor of a bride who was usually younger than I was, which bothered me more than I cared to admit to myself.

In a snapshot of this ceremony, my mother is looking at her mother—my beloved Teta Zoya—with utter loathing as my grandmother lights her candles. Something had happened between them on that day, something my mother would never reveal, something that told me my grandmother couldn't be trusted.

"Why do you look so angry in this picture, Mom?" I asked her more than once. Her eyes seemed to deaden and she would shrug.

"I don't remember," she said, but I knew she was lying. She considered it sacrilegious to criticize one's mother, especially unclever to do in front of a child who might grow up to do the same to her. Her silence meant there could be no real communion between us. It's a requirement of intimacy to be able to explain exactly why and how you hate your mother.

The most chilling part of the picture in my parents' wedding album is not my mother's look of loathing. It's my grandmother's expression. Eye to eye with her furious daughter, aware that they were being photographed, she wears a grim but triumphant smile. It's the look of the vanquisher facing off with the vanquished. I knew I could get turned off to Aziz for no other reason than Teta Zoya would push me hard to *ilcutey*, catch him. I wanted to figure out my feelings for him on my own. I called a different number.

"Hi," I said when Lisa-Turned-Layla picked up. "Look, I'm an asshole, okay? I should never have spoken to you like that."

"I don't need an apology, Arabella," she said. Her voice sounded sleepy. I had forgotten about the time difference. "But I could use a thank-you. I did recommend you for a cover story in *American Theatre*. And chose you to direct my translation of *Hamlet* at the best theatre in Palestine."

There was silence on the phone. She was waiting for me to say it. This is why I prefer working with playwrights who are already dead. The living ones think there is a certain script that everyone else needs to follow.

"Thank you," I told her, and discovered I meant it.

"You're welcome. How's it going so far?"

"It hasn't started yet. I'm supposed to go in right now and meet the theatre troupe. I'm feeling a little freaked out. Are they cool with the idea of having a woman play the lead?"

"I emailed Ramez about it. He didn't say anything, so I'm sure he's on board. You're going to do great, Arabella, and you can always call me if you need anything."

"That's kind of you to say."

"It's nothing. You know I've always considered you a friend, Arabella."

"Me too," I said automatically.

"Are you sure?"

Lie and say yes, I told myself. Fucking say yes! But I couldn't and I realized why. We were not friends. We were two women connected by tribal bonds we could ignore but never entirely break.

"We're not friends. We're sisters."

If you could hear the sound of someone smiling over a phone line, I did.

"But, can I ask a favor? When I met you, you went by Lisa. I know you as Lisa. Can I still call you Lisa?"

"No, Sis. You can't," she said.

"Come on."

"And we were getting along so well."

"Who in the fuck changes their name?"

"Lots of people, Arabella. You should get going to your meeting. You're going to love Ramez."

I believed her. It was with that belief that I launched myself into that room where the theatre troupe was waiting to meet me.

When I found the right office room on the fifth floor, I saw five men and two women seated in chairs arranged in a circle, except for Ramez, who was standing when I walked in. I was struck by the elegance of his features—the chiseled chin, high cheekbones sharp enough to cut diamonds, and eyes the color of water, especially striking because they were set off by his tanned skin. I was not physically attracted to him—it was more like looking at a natural wonder, as if Mother Nature was showing off. There are canyons and there is the Grand Canyon. There are men and there is Ramez.

"*Marhaba. Ana Arabella,*" I introduced myself thickly. I was entering a world where my facility with English was going to do me zero good, where half the words in my head would be unintelligible. When I worked in Europe, I was given a translator. Directing Shakespeare in Arabic was going to be a feat not just artistically but linguistically. I would have to learn new words—like setting, plot, pace, and climax—in Arabic, to expand my vocabulary beyond what I learned from my family. I should have recognized that earlier, but I hadn't.

Ramez stepped toward me and began clapping. The rest of the troupe, with their bright, dark eyes, got to their feet and approached me, applauding, as I smiled sheepishly. Ramez flicked his slightly long-ish dark, glossy bangs out of his eyes. There's a special kind of smile an actor gives you when he is sure you're about to cast him in a part he wants to play. It's akin to how a man looks when he realizes you are about to open your legs to him.

"Welcome home, Arabella," he said.

16

ZOYA

Detroit
1967–2012

Our home looked like every other on our block. Tract houses seem designed to defy the human desire to distinguish ourselves, to thwart any attempt to flaunt one's superior sense of style or access to excess resources. I'd be lying if I said I didn't find it comforting that all the two-story, four-bedroom houses of brick facade on our block were planted on identical plots of land. No need for neighbors to fight over fence lines. No cause for envy or enmity. You could pretend it was utopian if you ignored the fact that there wasn't a single black face in our subdivision.

"Are you a nigger?" a little towheaded boy asked my son on the first day we moved in when Ghassan went out to explore the neighborhood.

Having only heard that word used within the Black community and understanding it to mean "friend," my son replied yes. They played soccer all afternoon.

The next day, the same boy, whose name was Luke and who would become Ghassan's best friend, told him, "My mom says you're not a nigger. You're a Greek."

My son didn't correct him. They proceeded to play again all day.

"Tell him you are not Greek. Tell him you're Palestinian," I told Ghassan at dinner that night.

"Say nothing," Kamal snapped, and I went silent.

Before we moved in, Kamal had apparently knocked on each of our neighbors' doors, wearing a huge crucifix, and introduced himself. He gave them a tray of baklava, knowing we would likely be mistaken for Greeks. He hadn't asked me to go because he knew I wouldn't. The Greek community of Detroit were seen as closer to achieving whiteness than Arabs by far, especially in 1967. Within a year's time, a skinny Palestinian kid living in California named Sirhan Sirhan—who looked so like our brothers and sons—would assassinate Bobby Kennedy. Allegedly, Sirhan had felt personally betrayed that this liberal presidential candidate and icon of the left had pledged to arm Israel with fighter-jet bombers. The Second Kennedy, as we called him, would linger for a day and end up dying on the first anniversary of the Six-Day War. Many would say the killing had changed the destiny of America, that had the Second Kennedy lived and become president, America might have been put on an entirely different path. The Vietnam War might have ended much sooner. The Civil Rights Movement might have achieved greater gains toward true racial equality. The middle class might have grown into a powerful political force rather than continue to shrink. For me, the assassination was the first time that the violence of the conflict over our homeland had blasted its way into our lives in America, enveloping even a shining star of the country's most powerful family. No one was safe.

As I watched Kamal carrying the boxes I had brought from Palestine into the garage, I felt we would never move again. There is something ceremonial, a finality, about moving into a home you have a sense will be your last. You arrange the objects with care, imagining how they will weather the decades, which is colored by your premonitions of how you might weather those years, too. We furnished every room immediately. Kamal took me to a discount store and told me, "Buy whatever you want, Zoya." He watched to see if his freehandedness made me smile, clearly a touch contrite about making me move into a house I did not choose. At first, nothing appealed to me. But when you stay in a store long enough, the world of possibilities seems to shrink to what's inside. You don't have to love the choices being offered to develop preferences among the options you have.

I found myself gravitating to knockoffs of the Versailles style of ornate gold furniture I had in Jaffa, and big mirrors that gave almost the same effect of the mirrored walls of our lost home. Kamal didn't haggle hard and everything was delivered that day. I was surprised by how quickly I adjusted to my new life. It helped that we were soon welcomed back into the fold of the Palestinian community, many of whom had also settled in our subdivision, making us not the first family on our block where the smell of cooking with cumin was so strong that you could catch whiffs of it from the sidewalk.

When an affront against others involves money, it can easily be resolved with money. Kamal would pay back all his cousins their portions of the blood money with interest. They'd be overjoyed, and all would be forgiven. The story would be rewritten in everyone's minds that Kamal had been "protecting" the settlement money until his cousins all made it safely to America.

My sister, Raghida, called me up soon after and invited me to her home, which was three short blocks from mine.

"Why don't you come over on Monday, Zoya?" Monday was when the men were at work and the children were at school, a woman's first chance to breathe after a weekend full of their competing needs.

Like all our neighbors' homes, my sister's house was identical to mine from the outside. When I stepped in, I saw that the similarities didn't end there. She had bought the exact gold couches I now had, the style of which she had first seen in my home in Jaffa. We both had hung an oversized mother-of-pearl crucifix in the entrance of our homes, a replica of the one our mother had polished and prized above all her possessions, which gleamed in the eyes of anyone who entered our childhood home.

Raghida made me coffee. She didn't have to ask if I wanted sugar. We both liked it bitter. We drank together in her kitchen. She had straightened and dyed her coarse curls into a stiff platinum pageboy, which looked terribly false against her deep olive complexion.

"I like your hair," I told her, and she smiled. She thought she looked like Marilyn Monroe. Poor fool.

"You should think about going blond too, Zoya. With your light skin, it would look so good," she told me. "They are nicer in the stores to me now. They even greet me."

She meant white Americans, who ignored us when we walked into their department stores and made faces when they caught us speaking Arabic in the street. I didn't doubt that salespeople were more pleasant to her now. Though the dye didn't make my sister look any less of an Arab woman, white Americans seemed to appreciate it when one of us tried. To be polished meant to ape them. It cemented their sense of superiority. They were kinder to those of us who clearly despised our hair as much as they did.

"I'll think about it," I told her.

"I hear your husband is opening up a third liquor store?"

"Why do you ask?" I snapped.

"I'm just making conversation, Zoya."

Hardly. Clearly, she had invited me over to fish for information about our business dealings. She had six sons and only two were necessary to run their family gas station. But I wasn't about to tell Kamal that they were looking for work. College wasn't in the cards for them. Unlike my boy, Raghida's sons were in high school when they immigrated. They had come too late to catch up academically and, upon arrival, were drafted into helping to support the family. I felt for my nephews, especially Imad, her youngest, who had my mother's eyes. Nevertheless, I didn't want them in my family's business. Nor did I intend to give my husband an opportunity to consider replacing King Tut. Kamal had been complaining that King Tut was suggesting our store institute a policy where we would not sell liquor to someone who was clearly already drunk.

"This is a business. Sell to everyone with money," Kamal had replied. He repeated the conversation to me that night, expecting me to approve. We were lying in bed together at the close of one of those many married days where you're not sure whether the desire for love-making or sleep is going to overpower you first. I turned away before Kamal could read my expression, lest I betray that I agreed with my husband or how ashamed it made me feel that I did.

"Want me to read your fortune?" Raghida asked after we had drunk our coffee. Our eyes met. Suddenly, we were girls again, back in Ramallah, listening to our mother and her sisters talk of prophecy around our carved wood table. Had we grown into women like our meek mother, who believed clues about your fate could be read in coffee cups? Or did we favor our mother's sister, her opposite?

"No. I know the future," I began, quoting saucy, dear, and long-dead Aunt Miriam.

"We're all going to die!" we finished her infamous saying together, and laughed. She more heartily than I. For I could never be totally un-guarded with my sister again. She had cut me dead in public. She had not spoken to me when one kind word from her might have made this move to America slightly more bearable. She blamed it on her hus-band's orders, but Malik was thirty years her senior. Elderly and frail; if he had ever been a tyrant, he was not now. She did not want to be tainted by association with me. What's the point of having a sister when she abandons you when you need her most?

Would it have been better if Raghida had apologized during that first coffee we had together? I could have called her a *kelba*. She could have admitted to being the bitch she was, and acknowledged she didn't have to make a big display of refusing to speak to me at church. Or that she should have called me at least to check on my children. We could have worked through it together. But, alas, she did not and we would not.

Give rage a home in your body and lend it your voice, and it wears itself out. Otherwise, it turns into resentment, a ghost of itself, and you can never kill a ghost.

Though I never again fully trusted my sister, I was happy to have coffee with her every Monday for decades. She was a terrific gossip. Who better to keep me in the loop about the rise and fall of our peers' fortunes or the fate of their children? How else to learn which women had ascended to the annals of mothers of sons who were doctors, which was the only profession worth pursuing? Or to admire who had managed to marry their daughters (even the ugly ones!) to well-off men? These had been the concerns of the matriarchs in our family for generations. Yet in America, our worth as women was now tied up in how successfully we kept our children from completely assimilating into the culture of the country we had deposited them in. My sister helped me know how I was doing in the pecking order, by providing me the metrics to keep score.

By those standards, I would do swimmingly. Ghassan would figure out our love for him was dependent on his getting into medical school, and study hard. Kamal would become president of the Detroit chapter of the American Federation of Ramallah and a deacon at St. Mary's Church, both of which required hosting lavish dinners and dressing the part. I would soon deem the feeding and clothing of daughters as a waste of family resources, depleting that which was supposed to go to our son. I arranged to marry my seven elder daughters off and they were as happy to leave our home as we were to see them go. But with Naya, it would be different. Soon after we arranged for her to be engaged to a young man from California, I would get an unexpected call.

"You are missed, Zoya," I heard in a crisp voice I would forever recognize.

"I miss you, too, King Tut. How are you?"

"I am well. I intend to apply to law school in the coming year. There exists a chance I could do good work as a lawyer."

"That's wonderful!" I said. I wanted to express how proud I was of him, that I pitied anyone forced to tangle with him in a battle of wits in a courtroom, but I was not able to find the words in English. I had stopped studying English altogether when I had left downtown Detroit. I found no need for it, as my world was made up only of fellow Arabs.

"Reginald and I speak fondly of you often. We do hope you will visit us. Perhaps we can meet at the store."

He told me he planned to continue working nights for Kamal while attending law school. Now that Kamal had opened several more stores in "better" neighborhoods, I no longer went downtown.

"Naya has told me she would like to finish high school before getting married. She is not going to be able to do anything in life without a high school education. Will you let her stay in school?"

"*In sha Allah*," I told him. God willing.

"You forget I know what that phrase means and how you use it. You are essentially saying you will make me no promises. But I desire one of you. Promise me you will not force Naya into this marriage."

"We are from a different culture, King Tut."

"No, we are not, Zoya. There exist only two kinds of people in this world: those who love books and those who do not. When it comes to what matters, you and I are the same."

I should have known better than to tell King Tut the real reason I was pushing Naya into this marriage. My children handled their baptism by fire into American culture differently. Ghassan, who would call himself Gus, still went around pretending he was Greek. My four eldest daughters were once mistaken for Italians at a store. By how they spoke of it, you could tell they were dripping in joy that they were not immediately pegged as Arabs. My older girls aspired to whiteness.

Naya was different. She, of course, didn't tell anyone she was a Palestinian, either. Who in America in the sixties expected a child to own up to being that? My youngest daughter, instead, wanted to be Black. Even with my limited grasp of English, it was evident to me that she refused to adopt the Midwestern twang of the white kids, preferring the slight Southern drawl of the Black English she first learned in downtown Detroit. With her body that browned deeply with a touch of sun, along with her springy black hair that she refused to straighten and teased into an Afro she wore as proudly as a halo around her head, she scandalized our Palestinian community desperate to fit into white Detroit. I had tasted social death once. I did not wish to die a second time.

Naya also started coming home later and later from school. When she wouldn't come home on time, no matter how much I pleaded, I brought in Kamal, thinking he'd corral her.

"Why are you coming home late after school?" he asked her, tired from his long hours at our fourth liquor store.

She shrugged.

"We are Palestinians. You will marry a boy from Ramallah and are not to associate with American boys," I told her.

"I know that," she said.

"She knows that," Kamal said, bored already with our fight.

"What are you worried I'm going to do, Mom?" Her eyes were fixed on me. Devilish. I panicked. She had witnessed me holding hands with Aziz on the deck of the boat as a child. Had she grown to understand the meaning of what she saw? Or had she known all along? Fearing what she might tell Kamal, I let the matter drop. Naya continued to come home whenever she pleased until I found something I could use against her. An avid snooper, I found a Black Panthers pamphlet in her backpack.

"You will come home right after school tomorrow and every day after," I told her, "or I'll show your father this!"

Naya's eyes widened. She knew she had been defeated. The killing of Kennedy had made the Palestinian community terrified of being perceived as dissident in any way. Kamal was even afraid to let us vote, fearing we would be tracked and targeted if we aligned ourselves with the wrong side. Like the Palestinians who eventually became second-class citizens of Israel, we Palestinians in America believed we would be tolerated as long as we made no attempt for real equality, never tested the limits of freedom of speech by speaking from our hearts, and focused on making a living. We counted ourselves lucky to be able to do so, knowing too well the suffering of those Palestinians who languished in refugee camps. Kamal would have thrashed Naya if he knew she was cavorting with Black Panthers, the only group of Americans deemed more dangerous than we were.

On the phone, I should have told King Tut I was worried about her mixing with a fast crowd, that she might cross a line from which she couldn't return, and that if she got pregnant, I didn't know what Kamal would do to her. Such lies would have been easy to tell, though I knew my daughter to seize up in shy fear if a boy at Ramallah Club meetings or church tried to strike up a conversation with her. I should have told him anything but the truth.

"Naya is dark-skinned," I blurted out. Then, I thought of his ebony skin, how it gleamed like a black pearl in the sun, and a shock of shame went through me. "For a Palestinian girl, I mean."

"And?" King Tut asked curtly.

"Dark girls don't get many offers in our community," I tried to explain.

There was silence on the line.

"Kamal thinks this boy from California is the best that Naya can do," I stammered, wishing to shift blame onto Kamal along with the mortification I felt in talking with King Tut about colorism within the Palestinian community—how Naya being closer to copper made her less marriageable than her wheat-colored sisters. "He thinks—"

"Zoya, remember, I know you. You don't give a fig for what Kamal thinks. There exists no reasonable justification for taking Naya out of high school and forcing her to marry a stranger. Promise me you will at least think about what I am telling you, Zoya. School is where your child wants to be and where she ought to be allowed to stay."

There was a silence again. He was waiting for me to respond, to give him the answer he demanded of me.

"I promise," I whispered, and he hung up. I kept the phone to my ear long after the line went dead. I sensed it would be the last time we would speak. A friendship is a living thing. When it dies, a light goes out. King Tut's disagreements with Kamal would reach a crescendo when Kamal called the police on a teenage shoplifter. The officers beat the child within an inch of his life in front of our store. King Tut would leave our liquor store for good on that night.

I had promised King Tut that I'd think about what he had said and I did. Yet, when Naya dared to protest, I would lash out at her, including the morning of her wedding day.

"Stop the wedding or I'll tell *Yaba* what I saw you doing with that dirty doctor on the boat," she hissed at me as I held her wedding dress up for her to put on.

Dirty?! Who was she calling dirty? My memory of the feel of my hand in his would not be sullied by the world's insistence upon ugliness. Not by the girl who interrupted us. Not by anyone.

"We won't be blackmailed by you, you ugly dark thing! You want to go tell your father. Tell him! Tell him and see what happens to you."

I shoved Naya hard. She kept on her feet, surprise in her eyes. Was I going to slap her and send her down the aisle with my fingerprints on her face? I grabbed an ounce of flesh from her belly, pinched, and twisted.

"*Yema*, stop!" she moaned, and I let her go.

Shaking, Naya put on the wedding dress, a hand-me-down from her older sister. I zipped her up. Then, I opened the door to Kamal, looking stout and stately in his tuxedo, and to the photographer the groom had hired. Kamal had left the matter of marrying off our daughters to me, but I could tell he approved. Kamal was beaming, drunk with being congratulated over and over on the auspicious achievement of settling the matter of his last *sabeya*, unmarried girl. Everyone agreed Naya should be delighted with the match. The boy from California was poor, but smart. He had been the first in his class in Jerusalem. He would be taking her to live in a land with no snow, without unendurable winters. Behind our backs, people whispered that they didn't understand how my dark-skinned daughter had bewitched him, this boy who was clearly going places, who got one glance at her and asked for her hand the next day. Naya must have made eyes at him, gave him a look that spoke of sex, a promise of wildness. Naya's husband would indeed grow rich as a pharaoh, but Naya never seemed able to enjoy the money. Or her husband's adoration. Or motherhood. Or anything for that matter. Naya took pills for sadness, which Americans treat like a disease. Had we never left downtown Detroit, Naya's life might have turned out differently. Had she continued to come to the library with me twice a week, to breathe the rare air only rooms full of books can provide in regular doses, my daughter might have graduated high school and gone on to college. She might not have been the only one.

Of course, I always knew I was no better than my father for taking Naya out of school. Now that I was dying, I understood that being a woman and doing it to another woman, one I had brought forth into the world, made me worse. How to acknowledge my mistakes? How to apologize? Strangely, Naya had become obsessed with marrying off her daughter. When she bothered herself to call me, it was only to complain: "Don't you care that my child will die childless? I know Arabella likes this Israeli boy she met in college. She is always on the phone with him, pretending she is talking about work. He's nice enough but, if he was serious about her, something would have happened between them already. I won't have her waste her life waiting for him. You have matched up all your other granddaughters. Why don't you help Arabella the way you have helped them?"

Do to her what you did to me. Find her a match and make her agree.

Upon her arrival in Palestine, Arabella had gone silent. For my Arabella—the girl who most favored me—I pushed the hand of fate. Why? For what? In the vain hope the young man might resemble his grandfather?

I made up skits in my schoolyard—my granddaughter was directing Shakespeare! More important, she was rich and her father had made it clear he had adopted American ways. He wouldn't disinherit her in favor of her brothers, as is our custom in Ramallah. She lived like a queen in a castle in the sky. That's what I told her when I visited her in her New York apartment. She would never need a husband to support her.

What is the value in having children? Zero. All my life, I was told there was no fate more tragic than dying childless. But it is a lie. It's infinitely harder to deteriorate with children who barely bother to visit you or make it painfully obvious you're a burden if they do. It makes you wish you were already dead, because you know some part of them wishes that, too. Why was I so eager to push my Arabella into marriage and the physical servitude of carrying children? What if just one of the women in my line were allowed to be free?

The agony in my body started as a stab in my chest. It knocked the breath out of me. The pain pills weren't working anymore. Should I take more of them? All of them?

The phone rang. A loud, piercing shriek, like the cry of a child. The shock of it helped me find the energy to make my way to my feet. Whoever was calling was not giving up. It rang and rang until I managed to take the several steps I needed to get to the phone. It must be Raghida! She, the last sibling I had left, was the person I should tell I was dying. She would banish these troubling thoughts in my head. Explain to me that I was not a bad mother, a failure, a fool. No longer would I feel that everything I had learned and taught about how to be a woman in the world was wrong.

But it wasn't my sister calling me.

"Zoya, we did it!" Aziz's widow crowed in my ear. "Our grandchildren have met in Palestine. We will have a wedding soon. *In sha Allah.*"

"*In sha Allah*," I automatically responded. God willing. But my mind was screaming, "No! No! No!"

"Baby Aziz called me and said he liked her."

No mention of whether Arabella liked this Baby Aziz. Why hadn't she called me?

"But do tell your granddaughter to go easy on the hummus."

Was this woman implying my granddaughter was a fat slob? To me?

"*Shou?*" I asked her, giving her a moment to recognize her rudeness and correct herself.

"Baby Aziz told me that she is not thin," this woman continued to my astonishment. "He's a handsome doctor. Many European girls are after him. Palestine is apparently chock full of them now. Advise her to watch her figure at least until the wedding."

"There will be no wedding. Over my dead body will my granddaughter marry a grandson of the likes of you," I found myself hissing at her, an oath without teeth when you know you are dying.

17

ARABELLA

Ramallah

2012

"Can I get a side of hummus please?" I asked the waiter in Arabic. Aziz smiled at me from across the table. He had ordered us a rainbow of seafood kebabs and rice laced with roasted pine nuts, but I was longing for the simple and heavy peasant foods that my family favored.

I was glad he suggested we eat at Al-Muntazah, the lush garden restaurant and oldest in Ramallah, after my first meeting with Ramez and his troupe. My grandparents had held their wedding reception here. I tried to imagine Teta Zoya, barely a teenager and beautiful, alongside my Sido Kamal, probably pissed about the prices. My grandfather died when I was seven and my memories of him are mostly his incessant complaining about money. Every restaurant bill was a personal affront. The hired hand, a Polish immigrant who dug out a path in their driveway when it snowed, made millions off honest folks. As a child, I lived in fear of the tirades he'd inflict upon anyone who didn't shut off the lights when they left the room, having tasted his ire myself for that crime. As we waited for the food, I discovered I was ravenous. Since being detained in Tel Aviv and spending a night with Aziz, I hadn't had time for a proper meal.

"So, how did your meeting go?" Aziz asked after our food was served.

"Let me eat first. I don't know how much of what I'm feeling is because I'm hangry," I said.

Aziz smiled. He delicately slid a row of shrimp off a silver skewer with his knife and fork as I plowed rivers through the deep plate of savory hummus with pita bread, which was obviously fresh because they arrived as pita is supposed to be eaten, just out of a fire oven and puffy with air.

"Casting is going to be a bitch," I told him.

"How so?" Aziz asked. I watched him neatly dab his lips with his cloth napkin and decided I wasn't going to allow myself to complain about Ramez just yet. After I mentioned I wanted to hold auditions for the role of Hamleta, he coldly told me, "We will talk." I bristled at the memory. He then ended the meeting abruptly by saying he had another appointment and left me with the rest of the troupe, who made small talk with me until I decided to leave, too. He didn't offer to show me the theatre space at the newly built A. M. Qattan Foundation arts center, where we would start our tour. If I gave voice to my fears about working with Ramez, they'd feel more real. I'd have to act on them. Better not to whip myself into a frenzy just yet. Maybe he assumed I had already seen the space.

"Nothing I can't handle," I heard myself say with more confidence than I felt. "There is an actress who is perfect for Ophelia."

I described Sanaa, the pretty, delicate, dark-eyed flower of a girl, who was the youngest of the troupe. Sanaa had a bit of trouble maintaining eye contact with me but she spoke in a voice so resonant it felt as if her body were a taut drum made to make melodies. Amateur directors cast actors by how they look. Like painters who don't have access to a full palette of colors, they don't understand the power of costumes and lights. Stick a blond wig on almost any woman in a light with a red tint and voilà! You signal to your audience that she is an object of desire and they believe you. A play is more like its sister, opera, than either is to their distant cousin, film. You can add images to plays and operas, but—at their heart—they are stories of sound. So, I cast my plays based on the voices of actors. I cast my plays as if I were blind.

As Ophelia, Sanaa would have to carry the weakest storyline in the play, a character who starts out sane and is driven mad. In Shakespeare's masterpiece, it was the only journey I didn't believe fully. Every play has one, a minor (usually female) character who moves the plot along, whose life isn't as important as the effect she has on the main (usually male) character. Ophelia's trajectory would make more sense if she took her life out of rage rather than despair. I believed a woman writer would never have given us such a character. In our show, Sanaa's Ophelia would be bereft and broken, but also bold. The male characters would describe her as having gone insane, but the audience would instead see a sanguine woman choosing to exit a mad world on her own terms. I sensed Sanaa was up to the task and steelier than she appeared, even before I learned she spent a year in an Israeli prison for distributing revolutionary pamphlets.

"I've definitely got my Gertrude," I told Aziz after the meal was over and we lingered lazily over our glass cups of mint tea with a shocking yet delightful amount of sugar mixed in. I re-created for him my impression of Amina, the sexy, rail-thin woman in her fifties with her throaty smoker Mrs. Robinson voice, who was known as the godmother of Palestinian theatre. He had heard of her. She traveled to Gaza to teach acting workshops for children in the refugee camps. Her family was one of the wealthiest in Haifa before they fled. As if privilege were baked into her DNA, she retained an air of regality and watched me—a person she knew to be the product of several generations of illiterate peasant farmers from Ramallah—with a touch of judgment in her heavy-lidded eyes.

Amina's husband would be our Claudius. Bald and spry for sixty, it was good that Khalid looked a touch effeminate. His eyes wandered to his wife—our Gertrude—when he spoke. He was forever watching for the impression he made upon her. He also refused to address me in anything but painfully slow, broken English no matter how many times I answered him in Arabic. It was a point of pride he could make himself understood in English, which some of the younger actors didn't understand. In my production, it would not be Claudius's idea to off his brother. He was a soldier who killed on orders without malice. Gertrude was the general. She needed a male placeholder in power while she ruled the roost, which was in this case the kingdom of Denmark.

She would say she was sorry, but we would know she was not. Gertrude orchestrated the demise of her first husband because she believed her second would be more malleable.

The pair Rosencrantz and Guildenstern would be the two youngest men in the troupe, cousins named Mohammad and Mohannad. Both were brawny men with neat goatees, whom I had a hard time telling apart. They stared at my breasts while I spoke and, therefore, would be cast as clowns who get killed. That was a no-brainer.

"The work you artists are doing is so important for our people," Aziz said, and drained his teacup. It felt like a blanket statement. The kind of thing you say to end a discussion. Maybe it was unfair of me to expect him to say what every artist needs to hear, at every stage of every process, in every stage of their life. You'll find your way. You will make mistakes. Just make sure they are yours. You can only learn how to tell when your instincts are right or wrong when you follow them doggedly. Uncompromisingly.

I needed to talk about Ramez to someone who understood the intricacies of theatre dynamics, what it might mean to not cast the artistic director in a role he clearly wanted to play. I had a sense that Lisa-Turned-Layla couldn't be helpful from afar, so it was best I handled the situation alone. Worse still, she might tell me I should bend over and give Ramez the part. Would it be a terrible thing if I called Yoav? Maybe not. It would actually be nice to be able to lean on Yoav as a friend and fellow theatre rat. Now that I had embarked on a love affair with Aziz, enjoying the fruits of mere friendship with Yoav seemed more feasible. I took Aziz in as he counted out shekels and paid the bill. His build was perfect, masculine without being bullish, clearly a man who had been slender as a boy. The hot midday sunlight had turned the tips of his dark, wavy hair golden. I wished I could leap into his lap and that the fecundity of this garden restaurant, this little spot of Eden, would close in tightly around our table and give us cover.

I remembered he was waiting for me to answer him. What did he say again? Oh, yeah. That the work of artists was important to our people.

"*B'il ax*" I told him, which means the opposite. It's a way to answer a compliment you receive to indicate the person who gives it to you deserves the praise more. "I direct plays. You save lives."

"You tell the real story of Palestine."

"I beg to differ. I work on plays by old dead white guys."

"Your life, not the plays you put on, is our story. You're a daughter of a people who are demonized for the crime of refusing to be erased, who show the world there is a difference between a defenseless people and a defeated one. When the story of Palestine is told, it's the artists that history will remember. We've been flung to every corner of the globe. Wherever we find ourselves, we thrive. Call us animals? Go ahead. Depict us as monsters? Irrational? Uncivilized? No matter. History will remember the truth. Wherever we go, people like you prove we contribute. We make beauty. We make art."

"Well, shit. I better get to work," I joked, but felt uneasy.

"Damn straight, *Habibtey*," he said. My love. Did he just mean to introduce that word into the conversation?

I got my answer when he pursed his full lips ever so slightly and made the sound of a kiss, an almost imperceptible pop. I sent a quiet kiss back, but remained uncertain about his assessment of me. At the end of the day I was still someone who put on plays by dead white men. Why? Because I liked their plays and some part of me felt I had the right to do with this life exactly what I liked. How many decades would I get to make theatre? Three? Four? It hit me I didn't share his sense of mission. I didn't share his worldview. What kind of artist would I be if I did? Of course! I'd be Sister Lisa-Turned-Layla.

"You've got to meet my friend Layla. She's a hard-core Palestinian activist like you. She writes, thinks, and dreams about Palestine all day every day. I kinda want to set you up with her."

He raised an eyebrow. What in the fuck was I doing? And, more important, why?

"Where is this Layla from?" he asked me. Don't answer that.

"She grew up in Jersey. But her family is from Jerusalem," I heard myself say. I realized some part of me was trying to protect myself. Some part of me was testing him.

"Forget it then. I like girls from Ramallah," he said. "If I could be lucky enough to get one to have me. Do you think I might?"

"Maybe," I flirted. "Feel like coming to my grandfather's house?"

"I feel like going anywhere with you, Arabella. I'll drive you, but I don't think it's a great thing for you if the neighbors see you bring a man into the house. If people start gossiping about you, you're going to deal with a lot of . . ." He stopped, searching for the right word.

"Shit?"

"Yes."

I knew exactly what he was talking about. Men giving you the knowing eye everywhere you go. Assuming because you're doing someone that it meant you're obviously open to doing them. Women not wanting to be too closely associated with you.

I had an urge to reach out and take Aziz's hands. I knew I shouldn't.

The four young waiters were watching, curious about us, a pair who were clearly connected to this place but foreigners. Familiar, yet strange.

"And I have to get back to Gaza, Arabella," he reminded me.

The idea of his leaving me alone distressed me. I hadn't taken down the phone numbers of any of the theatre troupe. My great-grandfather had been my last relative left in Ramallah and he was long gone. I had no other friends to call. Our next meeting at the theatre wasn't until tomorrow. How was I going to fill my hours until then?

"You told me. Duty calls," I said to Aziz, and he smiled, signaling for the check.

When we stepped outside of the quiet garden restaurant and found ourselves on the busy modern street, it was like stepping into a different time and space. Folks whizzed past us. Growing up in San Francisco and living in New York makes your mind continuously register that the world is a varied place and humans come in a rainbow of shades. Here, the shades of the rainbow seemed to narrow. Everyone looked like they were related to me. For fuck's sake, on some level, they were. Aziz and I swerved to avoid a tall, tan trio of boys in their late teens, dressed in low-slung jeans like rappers and jostling each other. Hitting each other was the only acceptable form of touch now that their days of playing tag were over. I fixed my eyes on an elderly heavy woman crossing the street. She leaned upon the hand of a teenager, a young and slender copy of her, sporting a large yellow Walkman in her hand and headphones on her ears. What was she listening to? Though physically present, she seemed mentally absent exactly in the way I tried to be whenever I was with my family for too long. My particular form of escape was listening to recordings of plays. Drama. Comedy. Witty repartee. Ancient stories of heroes and monsters that always ended the same way.

There were no Israeli soldiers in sight. Though they surrounded Ramallah, they stayed out of its center, as the possibility for skirmishes were high in the midst of this dense place. It was easy to forget that their unseen hands held the keys to the city. They controlled the exits and entrances. The imports, the exports. There were settlements encroaching on it from every side. Ramallah's people are routinely arrested, tried in military courts, imprisoned, and killed. They are subjected to curfews, closures, and incursions.

It is a city under siege in a country that the world didn't fully recognize, but it felt like a country just the same, with its hospitals and universities and girls who needed to experience more than the din around them.

I watched the girl and the elderly woman, who leaned on her, until they got swallowed up in the crowd.

Aziz led me to his car. He had me sit in the backseat as if he were a hired driver, to avoid making me a subject of gossip among the people who would be my neighbors for the month I planned to work on the show.

"Do you know the way to your grandmother's house?"

"Yes," I told him. "Keep driving up."

The tiny one-room limestone structure was easy to spot. It was the only of its kind on the slope of the highest hill of Ramallah, surrounded by a confetti of bright white ostentatious villas and sleek apartment buildings. As we climbed higher and higher, I thought of the first time I stayed with my grandmother there.

"Look down," my grandmother had told me. She pointed to the

dusty valley below, the sand like a sea of skin, and the Israeli settlements and military outposts that looked like ships in the distance heading our way.

"All that land was once an olive orchard that belonged to my father. The trees I harvested are now uprooted. But my sweat is in that soil. Tell your children."

"What if I don't have children, Teta Zoya?" I asked her. I was seventeen and hardly popular with boys. Whenever a guy tried to strike up a conversation, I felt like I had stumbled into a play where everyone knew the lines but me. Early on, I had eschewed the glamour of acting for the power of directing. I liked being in charge. Few boys, whether Arab or American, seemed to prefer that quality in a girl. I could more easily picture a future where a family wouldn't happen for me than a life where it might.

"You will. You must! The worst thing in the world is dying alone," Teta Zoya told me with grim determination.

I stared at the back of Aziz as he drove. He looked commanding, a warrior at the helm of his chariot, with his hands resting on the steering wheel. Could we not find a place out in the desert where we could be alone again? Should I suggest it?

"That's my spot, sir," I told him instead, pointing to the dwelling that looked more like a cave shaped out of the earth's pressure than something human hands had made. He parked in front.

"Wow, Arabella. That's an original structure. How old is it?"

Our eyes met in the rearview mirror.

"No one knows for sure. Not even my grandmother. All she could tell me was that her father was born in that house."

Was he really not coming in? Would it be it gauche for me to ask again? To beg?

"Thanks for the ride," I forced myself to say.

"Thanks for everything, Arabella. Is it too soon to say something corny? Like maybe you and I are meant to be?" he asked.

"Yes," I told him, dropping my gaze for a moment. When I looked up, he was still staring at me, intent on reading my expression.

"Yes, it's too soon? Or yes, it's corny?" he asked.

"Both," I said, and I got out of the car. But the truth is it's never too soon to hear what you want to believe.

Before driving off, he waited for me to unlock the iron door with its huge old-fashioned key that Teta Zoya had mailed to me. I watched him drive away, the loud engine fading until the street was quiet again. I took in the scent of the jasmine flowers, which were planted on both sides of the doorway. Had my grandmother planted these flowers? Or her grandmother?

Then, I turned again and faced the open door. A flood of memories overpowered me, my vivid imaginings of my grandmother's stories about what she had endured within those walls. Gone was the voluptuous neighbor and ex-wife of my great-grandfather, but I could feel the shame that had seized my Teta Zoya when she caught her father at that circular window by the door, hungry for a glimpse of her. Gone was the newspaper that had printed a letter by Einstein that she had read out aloud for her parents, hoping her father would praise her for her acumen, only to fall into his trap by demonstrating she had learned enough to leave school. She would work in his olive orchard instead up until the day her marriage to my grandfather would be arranged. The house was hundreds of years old, a remnant of the past. As I closed the door behind me, I spotted a young couple on a balcony of the pristine white villa across the street eyeing me. No doubt they were surprised to see someone, a stranger, at the door of the little house that was always empty.

Alone, in a musty house heavy with the weight of ghosts, I found myself face-to-face with my great-grandmother's oversized mother-of-pearl crucifix that hung in the entrance. There was a double bed with a *tatriz* red quilt and a large wooden wardrobe. They looked out of place alongside a compact modern stainless-steel kitchenette and bathroom with a tiny shower. The house had otherwise been emptied. I was the first to visit since my great-grandfather died. My grandmother paid for someone to air out and clean the space. Thankfully, the four-poster bed my great-grandfather expired alone in was now gone. I regretted my decision not to rent a room in Ramallah's city center.

To call the house claustrophobic was an understatement. My

grandmother had been one of ten. And my mother was one of nine. All nine had lived here together after they first fled the fighting in Jaffa. How was that possible? It didn't feel like that many people could fit inside even when standing up. I put my suitcase down, collapsed on the bed, and fell asleep. I was so dead to the world that I didn't hear my phone ring, though my grandmother kept calling and calling.

18

ZOYA

Detroit
2012

"Sematey min al'bint?" Have you heard from the girl? I demanded to know when Naya answered the phone. Ragged and slightly crazed, my voice betrayed my panic that I was in the process of expiring at a time when my granddaughter needed me most. I had only reached out to my daughter after Arabella clearly wouldn't (perhaps couldn't?) answer my incessant calling.

With each breath, it felt like I was dissipating a little more of my life energy. A fact that had always been true but felt more so after you got a diagnosis like mine. My son had sent me to the hospital alone with a detestable young Syrian woman, a student from Halab whom my son hired as a driver and translator to take me shopping and to my checkups. I raised nine children. Could none of them be bothered to accompany me when I visited a doctor? Not even Ghassan, a doctor himself? I couldn't help but feel my son had hired this particular girl because he didn't mind having a pretty, green-eyed girl around. After we left the doctor's office, I told the Syrian, whom I always referred to by her nationality and never her name, she would be fired on the spot and have to find a new way to afford food for herself if she breathed a word about my diagnosis. She narrowed her cat eyes at me and I could see her swallowing what she wanted to say. It is easy to say nothing about you, *ya Agouza*, because no one bothers to ask.

She had done her job. She had translated. But she had to be punished for breaking the news with a touch of glee, so proud of herself for her astonishing fluency in both languages, she was unaware of the heartless way she blurted out my death sentence, "You have congestive heart failure. The walls of your heart are weak. Beyond repair."

"Yes, Arabella texted me when she arrived in Ramallah. She's fine," Naya demurred, answering in English. Was it deliberate? To speak in a language she was stronger in than I was as a way to hurry me off the phone?

Regardless, I would not be deterred today. Because I could not tell her I was dying, I told my daughter everything else.

"*Ana mitessif eny talatik min el-madrasa wa gasubtik tetjowizi.*" Even as I apologized for forcing her out of school and into an arranged marriage, I knew I had much more than that to be sorry for. I was sorry for regretting she had been born.

"You don't need to apologize for anything, *Yema*. You did well by me," Naya said. Did my daughter really believe that? Had her voice always been so calm? So distant?

"What I did—what I said—on your wedding day . . ."

"What did you say?" she asked.

"You don't remember?"

"Only how silly I was, *Yema*. I had convinced myself I was destined to marry one of the Jackson 5. Not Michael, of course, but one of them."

She hiccupped. Or was that the sound of forced laughter?

"*Bint*, I said ugly things to you on that day. I pushed and pinched you."

"No!" she protested.

Could Naya have forgotten? Had her brain, addled with the drugs she took to make her happy, flattened the sting of her worst memories? It might be the last time I ever spoke to Naya. Or anyone. I stared at my ruby-red rotary phone, my lifeline now that Ghassan took my car away and no one ever seemed to visit. I never allowed Ghassan to replace the phone with a newer one. My fingers knew the circular patterns of numbers I needed to dial to reach my children, my sister, and Arabella—the only granddaughter of mine who always answered my call. Until now.

"Anyway, I should go, *Yema*," she told me.

There was more than distance between Naya and me. I could no longer step outside my home, board a plane, and see her. We weren't inhabiting the same earth. I was in the past and she in the present. Or was it a future I would never see? Maybe that's how death happened. It wasn't your spirit leaving your body. It was a space you inhabit receding into a different realm, as the world spun on.

In the case of old women who live alone, the last cord to be cut was a telephone line. I half expected that an enormous hand holding a golden pair of scissors was going to appear and snip the curling cord, and that was how the end would come. Me, forever alone in this house, with no way to reach or be reached.

"I'll call you later," Naya promised. A promise she made every time I called her, and one she never kept. "I have a meeting with my book group."

"*Shou hada?*" I asked. What's that?

She sighed, impatient that she had to stay on the phone long enough to explain.

"A book group is people getting together to discuss a book they've all read."

"Is it a class? A college course?" I knew Daoud had encouraged her to go back to school and get her college degree, which some of the girls of her generation had done after they married and raised their children. Naya, who had so loved school, had refused to do so for reasons I never understood.

"No. It's just a group of friends who like discussing their impressions of books together."

What piece of heaven on earth was that? Time to read? To discuss impressions? Friends? How had I never known such a thing existed? I felt a stab of rage and—like all negative emotions—it gave me a surge of newfound strength that my sadness could not. I remembered why I called.

"Envy is the ugliest of emotions. I am your mother. I brought you into this world, but—once I did—you became another woman. I was taken out of school and married young. I did the same to you. I should have been the kind of mother who fought for you to have a better life than I did."

"I did have a better life than you, *Yema*. In every possible way. Me, the ugly dark thing."

So, of course, she remembered everything! Her way of punishing me was to close herself off. Never give me the space to apologize, so she would never have to face the fact that some sins are unforgivable. They go with you to the grave. Those sins always involve children.

"I really must go, *Yema*."

"Wait! I need to speak with you about Arabella. Arabella must not marry Aziz's grandson."

"The doctor? Have they met yet?"

So, Arabella hadn't told her either. To my shame, I was not sorry. I liked that Arabella had been closer to me than to her mother. How petty I had been all my life! How pathetic! I had made so many mistakes. I was determined not to allow one more while I was alive to prevent it.

"His cow of a grandmother dared to call me. She said the boy liked Arabella, but he thinks she needs to watch her weight."

"He likes her?!"

She was clearly missing my point. He should love Arabella. He should appreciate her. Is that what he called to tell his grandmother after meeting her? No! He wants her to take up less space. Already. I would not allow that for her. The girl was free. She must stay free.

"You are not hearing me, *Bint*."

"I'm no girl, *Yema*!"

"We must stop their courtship now!"

"Why?"

"His grandmother wants me to tell her to watch her weight! Don't you understand?"

"You tell her to watch her weight. Or you tell me to tell her. What in the fuck is your problem?" she howled at me in English.

"His grandmother said—" I began again.

"I don't care what she said. Did the boy complain to Arabella about her weight? Did he hurt her feelings?"

"I don't know," I admitted.

"Let the two of them work it out together!" Naya said. "My daughter is thirty-five. She's alone in the world! Stay out of it!"

"She's free, Naya! Can't we let one of us be free?"

"*Yema*, I hated you for forcing me to marry. Not because Daoud is a bad man. He's my perfect match because he's, well, perfect."

I knew otherwise. And so did she. Naya had confided in me once about a problem in her marriage. A big problem. We had never spoken of it again. Had she forgotten? Was she hoping I had?

"*Akeed*?" I asked as gently as I could. Really?

"*Akeed*!" she snapped. "I thought all men were like *Yaba*, a tyrant who wouldn't let you even learn English."

Naya was being unfair to her father. He was a creature of his time and upbringing, as I had been, as we all were. In some ways, he was better than he was raised to be. I wished I could have told Naya that he rejoiced in having her in a way I had not after her unwelcome birth. He had not minded she was a girl. He had not minded she was dark.

"Do I wish I had had ten more years to study and grow up before I married Daoud? Yes, of course. But life sometimes gives what you need before you want it. It is still something you need and—for that—you must be thankful. Yes, I got married ten years too early. But if Arabella marries, it will be ten years too late. She is unhappy, *Yema*. She has been lonely for a long time. She thinks she is an American, but she is not. How could she be? We don't have it in us to raise a girl to know how to survive by herself in the world. Not you, not I. I won't leave her alone in this world. I can't have her be a *hazeena* after I'm gone."

"Arabella is not a *hazeena*. There is nothing pathetic about her."

"*Yema*, I have cancer. I've had it for some time. It's not getting better."

My first thought was, "No, Daughter! Don't you dare!"

You don't get to die before me.

19

ARABELLA

Ramallah

2012

I was startled awake by the call for the morning prayer and found my-self enclosed in a small stone tomb. Then, consciousness washed over me and, to my relief, I recognized my surroundings. I was alone in my great-grandfather's house. In Ramallah, there are two mosques within earshot and the muezzins' voices seem to melt into and echo each other. To summon worshippers, Jews blow a trumpet and Christians ring bells. Muslims use the human voice. Which is most effective? My bet would be on voice.

I checked my phone. I had multiple missed calls from Teta Zoya. Was I in the mood for her usual lecture about my impending doom, the horrors of a life of perpetual singledom and irreversible childlessness?

Nope, not right then. But I didn't want her fretting about me. I texted my mom to tell Teta Zoya that I arrived safely in Ramallah but was too busy to call her.

My mother immediately texted back: I'll tell her. Have fun!

Though it was early, I called Aziz.

"*Sabah el-khair*, Arabella!" he said, not only wide-awake but cheer-ful. One got the sense that cheerful was his default mode.

"How is the kid?" I asked.

"It's definitely leukemia," he said. "We're applying for a visa to get him to Jordan for treatment."

"I thought his eye was shot out."

"Oh, that's a different boy," Aziz said. "That one is fine. He's almost adjusted to seeing out of one eye."

Well, that's not heavy.

"Anyway, how are you, Arabella?"

"Okay. I've got lots to do, though. I have to set up auditions. Check out the theatre space. When are you coming back to Ramallah?"

"As soon as I can," he promised. "I miss you. I can't stop thinking about you."

A shyness crept over me.

"Me too. I should go," I said, and hung up quickly.

I took a shower, which was not easy to do in the tiny upright glass, coffin-like contraption that had been installed in the bathroom. Then, I headed to the theatre office. I should have called a car. The winding road down the dusty hill to the crowded city center had seemed shorter when Aziz dropped me off yesterday. I arrived sweaty, dirty, thirsty, and famished.

When I walked in, the troupe was assembled except for Ramez. They had laid out refreshments. I found myself eating more than my share of the figs, falafel, and sesame bread. I made a mental note that I had to bring snacks at the break. Foreigners think Arabs are generous. But if an act of hospitality is not reciprocated, in equal or greater value, the transgressor is looked upon with disdain, if not loathing. In that way, we are the opposite of freehanded. Always keeping tabs. Always keeping score.

"How was your night?" Rosencrantz asked me. Or was it Guildenstern?

I shrugged. He stepped closer than necessary to me.

"Are you staying at a hotel?" he asked. Though he was irritating, who hasn't been socially awkward when trying for sex? Visiting artists are fresh meat in a place where meat—fresh or otherwise—is patently unavailable for most men until they marry. Then, he glanced down my shirt and my empathy evaporated.

"I am staying in the house of my great-grandfather!" I snapped, deliberately making it sound as if hordes of my burly brothers, uncles, and cousins might be there with me. It was like I could see his hot blood freeze. The grin on his face was gone and he stepped back as I knew he would.

I saw Sanaa standing alone in a corner and approached her.

"Is Ramez here?" I asked. Her skittish doe eyes dropped to the floor. Amina heard my question and stepped toward me. The others in the group did, too. I felt a bit surrounded.

"We need to talk," Amina declared. I felt my back arch at her tone.

"Layla mentioned to Ramez that you want to cast the part of Hamlet with a woman."

I nodded.

"Ramez wants to play that part. He is a great actor," Khaled said. "Possibly the greatest actor Palestine will ever know. He has been classically trained."

"Ramez played Shylock and he made Israelis cry," Sanaa murmured.

"He was born to play Hamlet," said Amina. "He knows how it feels to be haunted by a father."

"His mother has blue eyes," Guildenstern—the less aggressive of the Neanderthal cousins—told me knowingly. As if that explained why a widow saddled with a child would get an offer of marriage to a powerful man. Both Arab and American cultures are rife with colorism, unapologetic in their worship of Western standards of beauty. But Arabs often are less politically correct about acknowledging it aloud. I was to understand a man would throw convention to the wind when it came to a woman with blue eyes. A man would do what it took to have her, to put himself inside her.

"Ramez agreed to do this project at our theatre so he could play Hamlet," Khaled told me, glancing at Amina, who nodded her assent.

"So you're basically telling me that I'm supposed to change the entire conception of my production and cast the lead without auditioning anyone except him?"

"Oh! He won't audition for you!" Khaled exclaimed, scandalized by the thought.

"Are you kidding me?" I asked.

"You can do what you like," Sanaa said in that way that implied that what you *can* do isn't necessarily something that is recommended.

"We told the British folks who are funding the project that I would cast the part with a female lead. They're expecting a woman in that role. We can't disappoint them," I found myself telling them. It wasn't technically true. Nothing of the sort had been mentioned when we applied for the grant. Still, deception and subterfuge felt in order. The merits of my artistic vision held no water with men like Ramez. I could go fuck myself as far as he was concerned. There was only one way to intimidate him. He cared about the opinions of men. Especially white European men.

"What am I supposed to say to the British funders?" I asked, hating how I was making my voice sound whiny. Hating how I felt like I had to feign that I'd love to oblige Ramez, if I weren't beholden to promises I'd made to those who held the purse strings.

Ramez had anticipated my move.

"Ramez says you should tell the British that you couldn't find a Palestinian woman strong enough to carry the role," Amina informed me.

"In all of Palestine? Do you think they'll believe that? Do you?" I asked. "Where is he?"

Khaled took an infuriating full minute to tell me in English, "Of course, Ramez wants to give you the space you need to make your own artistic decisions."

"Can you call him for me?" I asked, impatient. They exchanged glances. Amina nodded to Khaled. Khaled called and, though he wasn't on speaker, I heard Ramez pick up.

"Hello!" Ramez boomed in a triumphant voice. Clearly, the shithead was expecting news that I'd kowtowed to reason and he was—of course—going to play Hamlet.

Khaled explained to Ramez that they were all assembled at the theatre with me.

"And?" Ramez asked curtly, waiting for confirmation I'd been convinced of the error of my ways.

"Arabella would like to speak with you."

There was silence on the other end of the line. I heard Ramez tell him, "I am too busy for talk."

Then he hung up.

"So, he won't speak to me? Or show me the theatre space where I'm supposed to put on a show? And you're all going to act like that's okay?" I could hear the rage in my voice.

No one could look me in the eye.

"*Killet gowab gowab!*" I snapped at them. No answer is an answer. People don't have to speak to give you all the information you need.

I stormed out of the theatre office and headed to the elevator. Sanaa followed me.

"Arabella, wait!"

The door of the elevator opened.

"You have to understand our perspective. You get to leave when the show opens," she said, her voice thick with emotion. "We live here. Ramez's stepfather is a bigwig in the Palestinian Authority."

Now I got why everyone, even queenly Amina, was tiptoeing around Ramez. Since the Oslo Accords, where the Palestinian Authority had been established, life had gotten worse for ordinary Palestinian citizens. Not only do they need to deal with even more settlements filled with armed Zionist zealots (who believed God specified the exact location and amount of acreage that He promised them) encroaching upon them from every direction, they now had a class of Palestinian bureaucrats who could make life difficult for them, too. Just having arrived, I didn't know the parameters, the specifics of their powers. But it was clear they were feared. Something told me what everyday Palestinians had to deal with when crossing the bureaucrats of the Palestinian Authority was worse than my experience at the DMV.

"The show must go on," she said. It was the first time she'd spoken to me in English. I found her accent adorable. She sounded like my grandmother, the way she pronounced *o* with the throaty deepness of an Arabic vowel.

I smiled in spite of myself. Sanaa smiled back.

"I spent a year in prison for handing out leaflets at Birzeit University. Do you know what those leaflets said? We women have to resist the military occupation alongside the men. Sitting in that cell, rereading over and over the few books I had access to, was a waste, perhaps a necessary one, as there is no struggle without suffering. But it meant some of my life had been squandered. Since I've gotten out, if there is one thing I cannot tolerate, it is waste. Don't throw away this chance to make a show, even without a woman in the lead. We have funds to tour it. Hundreds of boys and girls will see it! I was one of those kids who saw a show that foreign money paid for. It was a puppet show about *Aladdin*. Hardly *Hamlet*. It wasn't half the show we can make together. I've read all about you, Arabella. Or actually I've seen the articles on your website about your shows. I don't really read English well."

"You read it better than I read Arabic," I said, and she smiled gratefully.

"We can tour the show we will make together to all the Palestinian cities that the Israelis allow us to enter. Thousands of our children will see it. Maybe one or two of them, like me, will see that show and decide to devote their lives to theatre. Me, a girl who was too shy to speak in school. I knew I needed to stand onstage someday. I knew I'd be brilliant at acting. I am," she said, and I believed her.

"When I perform, I feel like I'm doing more than I ever did for Palestine than by passing out leaflets or protesting. I feel like I'm more powerful than a thousand armies. When I saw *Aladdin*, it wasn't the princess I wanted to play. No! I wanted to be the one who found the magic lamp and got to make the wishes, the one who had all the choices. So, I understand what you want to do by letting women play men's roles, Arabella. I want you to do that! I expect it of you. Eventually. But not yet. Not with this project. Opposing Ramez is not an option for us. Even if you can't direct this particular production exactly as you envisioned, don't abandon . . ." Her voice trailed off.

There were questions in her eyes. Was she going to say what she wanted to say? Reveal herself entirely?

"Me," she said. I found I couldn't meet her gaze. When had I been that vulnerable?

"I don't want to, Sanaa. But I can't go back on my promise to the funders. I told them I'd give the opportunity to a Palestinian woman to perform that part, to empower the women in the audience to see themselves in roles that weren't written for them."

Why did I continue to lie? Because I felt I must put on a dazzling avant-garde postmodern cross-dressing take on a classic for the artistic staff of the Royal Court, who'd seen tired-out traditional productions of *Hamlet* a million times. I was itching for this show to get me international press coverage and visibility, which might mean viability and a chance to create more work. It had to be risqué for that to happen. I fought dirty for what I needed to stay alive as an artist. I was no better than Ramez in that regard.

"You want to empower the women of Palestine? Come with me," Sanaa said, and took me by the hand. "I will show you how we are empowering ourselves."

PART II

20

NAYA

I had never heard a story of an honor killing happening back in our village. Was it because none of our people had the heart to murder a daughter? Or had no Ramallah girl dared to defy her family in the way I would?

"I'm a minor. I'm a minor. I'm a minor," I found myself muttering under my breath until I noticed Reginald and King Tut exchange glances.

They had invited me to their home in Virginia Park. Decorated entirely in shades of purple, their one-bedroom apartment was a whirlwind of violet drapes, eggplant carpeting, and lavender framed pictures of the two of them laughing, which was all they had hanging on their lilac walls. Even the toilet was purple, which made me smile the first time I saw it. While inside their home, I felt like I was turning purple, especially the bruises on my belly, the fresh ones darker than the markings my mother gave me years ago. I had bused my way there. I was not old enough to drive. But it seemed I was old enough to emancipate myself.

King Tut and Reginald were trying to prep me to meet with a lawyer, Ned. Ned knew how to navigate the family division of the Detroit circuit court and had helped other minors legally separate themselves from their parents.

He also apparently worked for free.

If we were back home, I could have said that I intended to become a nun to avoid being forced into marriage. I knew of women in my clan who had done that, joining the Deir Rafat convent and living out their days within its walls, rather than marry against their will. It wasn't that I disliked the boy who asked for my hand. I didn't remember him. Apparently, he saw me at a banquet dinner for the Ramallah Club held in the basement of our church, where sweaty young boys stood in groups wearing ill-fitting hand-me-down suits and stared at us girls.

None of those boys stood out for me, possibly because I refused to look in their direction. There was clearly no Randy Jackson among them. In the album-cover photos of the Jackson 5, I spotted pain in Randy's eyes. Everyone in Detroit knew he, not Michael, was the youngest brother. I sensed it was Randy who must've felt most deeply what it meant to always play a supporting role, to never be allowed to take center stage, in a family or a band. I thought of him as I tossed and turned at night, sleeping alone in a bedroom that I once shared with several sisters who—one by one—were married off. I imagined how Randy might spot me on a downtown street and find me fetching in my bell-bottom jeans that hugged me in a way that made men stare.

The boys at the banquet weren't afraid of being gauche as they gawked at us. They were clearly looking for wives. They had driven from all the corners of the United States to do so and had been instructed to identify girls they liked and to report back to their parents. Though their fathers would ask our fathers for our hands, it was generally the mothers who wielded more influence behind the scenes during the process of matchmaking. Because we tended to live with multiple generations in the same home, mothers were selecting not only wives for their sons but also roommates for life for themselves.

We girls weren't people who possessed eyes that could watch the boys watching us. We were portals to their manhood. The thing about selecting a portal is that it sets you on a path. There is no return. You only get to choose once. You have to choose wisely.

I wanted to stay in their purple world forever. I imagined that if there was just one more room, they'd invite me to live with them. Or—at least—King Tut would.

"You will like Cleo, Naya."

King Tut frowned when Reginald brought up Cleo, his friend who ran a women's shelter. She had recommended emancipation and put us in touch with Ned.

"A shelter is no place for Naya," King Tut told him rather sharply. It was Reginald's turn to frown. He didn't like that King Tut had given me a key, or that I hung out there and listened to their records after school.

"Don't you have these records at home?" Reginald asked, though he knew the answer. I did, because King Tut bought several of my favorites for me with money he made at my father's liquor store over the years. My father trusted King Tut with his store and his cash as well as the shotgun he kept under his counter. But he paid him minimum wage and had never given him a raise. Not even after King Tut stood in front of our liquor store with that gun and saved our lives. My father paid him his hourly rate for his time when he did that. Nothing more. Why had King Tut worked so long for so little? Jobs were hard to come by in Detroit. But why he would be so generous toward me was harder to explain. My parents gave me no money. I could never give him anything in return.

When Reginald and King Tut were both home, I knew I was in the way. It felt like they always wanted to make love. Or maybe they were just pleasant with each other all the time and I equated politeness with a desire for sex. My father was cordial only on the nights there was hunger in his eyes for my mother. In response, she grew short with him. It was one of the few times in their marriage where it seemed she had a modicum of power.

Someone desired me like that. A nineteen-year-old scion of Ramallah, who had managed to continue to study engineering at San Francisco State while working full-time in a corner store, a catch who had been first in his class in Palestine.

It seemed impossible. Because I was born dark-skinned in a community that worshipped whiteness, I half believed no one would ever ask to marry me. Where had I gotten that idea? Everyone I knew of in my extended family, light and dark, had married except for the nuns.

Reginald pulled an official-looking form out of his leather satchel. It was the emancipation application he got from Cleo.

"Cleo said to call her if you have any questions," he told me.

I took the paper but didn't read it. I had gotten the gist of the steps I needed to take. Demonize my parents. Cut off all ties with my community. Find a different way to have a family. I was ready. I would emancipate myself and stay within the Black community I grew up in. I wanted to marry a Black man and raise my children to call themselves Panthers.

Later, I realized that it never occurred to me I could live alone. Not bear children. Not have to pick a community in which a new generation might be allowed to belong.

King Tut handed me a purple mug of mint tea. I put it to my lips. Too hot.

"Can we tell Ned that I'm Egyptian?" I asked.

"Why?" said King Tut.

"Egypt is in Africa. If people think I'm from Africa, they will be nicer to me."

They exchanged glances. It was Reginald who spoke first.

"I have a great-aunt, Rosette, who passed as white. She moved to Buffalo and did not speak to my grandmother or any of her family, lest we intrude upon her little world and reveal who she really was. Nor did she have children because she feared they might be born brown. She moved back to Detroit when her white husband died. Other than her sister, my grandmother, no one wanted anything to do with her. It's not that we didn't forgive her. No one cared what a little old lady did at the turn of the century. We didn't know her. She'd come to church and sit alone."

He meant it as a cautionary tale, but it had the opposite effect upon me. The idea that the woman came back to her people at the end of her life, when she still had a sister to take her in, was comforting. Maybe that would be possible for me? But let me live the defining years of my life around the Black people of Detroit, the people I admired and understood, the only people who seemed truly vivid. They articulated their rage in a way we immigrants did not. America was theirs. They had built it. Black people knew they deserved the forty acres and a mule they were promised when slavery ended, even if they would never get it. Black people acted, sang, wrote poetry, mastered sports, created comedy, and ran for public office like a people who knew they were deserving. My people were so frightened that we'd be thrown out of here as we had been our homeland. No matter how many generations we would stay, that fear would never fully dissipate. It would always be under the surface.

"I used to pretend to be Egyptian, too. I would tell myself I was a descendant of a pharaoh. It was comforting to assume my ancestors were royalty," King Tut added, fingering the gold pendant of the doomed young pharaoh he always wore around his neck.

"Maybe they were!" I ventured.

"Perhaps. There exists that possibility. But some of my ancestors were also slaves. The people who want me to feel shame about that fact are not allowed to win. Do you understand what I'm trying to tell you, Naya?"

I couldn't meet his eyes, because I disagreed. Didn't those kinds of people always manage to find a way to win? Somehow?

"Nothing in your life can go right if you don't tell the truth about who you are," King Tut continued.

"That's the type of statement that sounds true, but isn't," Reginald told him. "Not everything will go right, but plenty can. We should go. We want to be early for our meeting with Ned."

Every comment Reginald made was in some way trying to get me further out the door. Face an American judge. Get emancipated. Find another place to be. Get out of my purple world!

"Can't I just run away?" I asked. But they knew what I was really asking was if I could stay with them. They exchanged glances. Reginald had a hard expression in his eyes. I got my answer. No.

To spare them the embarrassment of having to say it, I quickly added, "I wouldn't mind staying in a shelter."

"You can't until you are emancipated. Cleo would have to refer you to child protective services since you're not legally an adult," Reginald explained.

"What if the court doesn't emancipate me? What if they put me in a foster home?"

I would not say to an American judge that my mother beat me. I couldn't. King Tut saw the horror in my eyes. He saw I was not cut out for that kind of emancipation.

"You don't have to speak ill of your parents. From my understanding, it's best if you don't. All you must prove is that you can take care of yourself on your own," King Tut reassured me as Reginald ushered us out the door. They drove me to the courthouse in their enormous blue Lincoln Continental, big as a submarine. We circled the downtown Detroit streets slowly, looking for a place to park. Grimly, I followed King Tut and Reginald through the stone entrance. It felt like a mausoleum with bustling ghosts who didn't seem to notice they were dead. King Tut knew his way around. He led us to a quiet corner, a chamber. On the way over, they had filled me in on Ned, who worked for the court and did his pro bono work during his lunch break. I was surprised to learn he was white. One of Ned's uncles was a famed white civil rights worker who was killed by a KKK mob for registering Black voters in Mississippi.

I don't know if everything would have been different if Ned had been a woman. With a woman, even a white one, I'm almost sure I somehow would have managed to speak.

Ned, tall like a Viking, was sitting when we arrived. With hair so blond it looked white, he appeared not to have eyelashes. When Ned stood to greet us, he seemed larger than any human should be, as if he belonged to a different species. There was a half-eaten homemade ham sandwich in front of him, the white bread oozing mayonnaise and outlined with bite marks where his teeth had been.

"Hello, Naya!" Ned boomed at me, and put out an enormous pink hand to shake mine. I found myself staring at him. Men in our culture, strangers, don't offer women their hands. I had gotten used to the American custom. Hadn't I?

We sat down.

"Cleo told me a bit about your situation, but it would be helpful to have a few more details," Ned said.

Do you have proof of employment? Your ability to manage your personal affairs? Evidence that you can take responsibility for your own education? A place you can afford on your own?

To each of his questions, I simply shook my head. They were

questions to which I always assumed that the answer, now and forever, would always be no.

He should have just started with the most basic question of all.

"How old are you, Naya?"

I couldn't make myself answer.

"Does she understand English?" Ned asked finally.

"Of course she does. Tell him your age!" Reginald commanded, exasperated.

Was I afraid that if I opened my mouth, I'd start screaming? No. I was afraid I'd find my ability to speak Arabic magically replaced with perfect English. I'd answer all his questions politely with no trace of an accent, take the steps required, and cut all ties with my parents. I was a girl when they wanted a boy. Though they wished I was born in a different body, they still took care of me. They ensured I stayed alive. Would I know how to do that without them?

"She's fifteen," King Tut said finally in my place.

We learned the youngest age one can apply to be emancipated is sixteen. My birthday wasn't for another six months. My wedding was scheduled for Sunday. Ned informed us he couldn't help me.

He said it was too soon for me to try to be free.

"I'm sorry," I told Reginald and King Tut when we were back in their purple apartment and I'd found my voice again.

"For what?" Reginald asked.

For almost hating you for not offering to be my new parents. For half believing that if I were Black and gay you might be more inclined to let me stay.

"For not looking at the application you gave me, Reginald. It says you need to be sixteen," I said instead. "Let's just lie and say I'm older. I wasn't born here. I don't have a birth certificate."

It seemed impossible to me that the long arm of a government could have its fingers on the pulse of every citizen, even those who landed as children on its shores.

"That's an idea!" Reginald crowed. But King Tut would have none of it.

"No. Once you start lying, you can never stop," King Tut told him.

"I will call your mother tomorrow while you are at school. Perhaps I can get through to her."

I felt a glimmer of hope. My mother loved King Tut. She would not want him to think poorly of her. He noticed me brighten and smiled.

"Deep down, I know your mother has a good heart."

"And a pair of hands she can't keep to herself," Reginald added under his breath.

"Enough!" King Tut protested.

"What? Zoya is no angel. The woman was always edging up close to me when I was trying to teach her in that library. Too close for comfort. Mine, anyways."

"Reginald, stop it!"

But he wouldn't. Instead he leaned in, making sure each word he said landed on me.

"When she grabbed my hand and tried to hold it, I had to explain she wasn't my type."

What would my father do if he knew? He fancied every man was after his light-skinned wife and was insanely jealous, but I had never considered *Yema* had hungers herself.

An image of my young mother gripping the hand of a doctor on the deck of the boat that brought us to America came into focus and I finally understood what I had seen. It was like encountering a song you once sang as a child and being jarred by the innuendos—the blatant bawdiness—of the lyrics you can only now comprehend. My mother had told me she felt sick. But that hadn't quite made sense to me, even then. I had never seen her looking so happy, so free. Until she saw me.

I left their apartment in a bit of a daze. Outside the bus window, snow began to fall. As I watched those first flakes of winter turn into a deluge, I decided upon a plan of action. I would threaten to tell my dad about my mother holding hands with that doctor if she didn't put a stop to my wedding.

When I walked in our door, my mother frowned. She wordlessly watched me take off my wet tennis shoes. Since she thought I was getting married off soon, she had given up on grilling me about why I came home so late. My brother didn't greet me either. Each of my sisters had been surly in the weeks before their weddings. They took liberties like snapping at my parents and talking back. My parents seemed determined to leave them alone. Was it out of a sense of indulgence? Or because we were about to become someone else's problem?

Ghassan was doing his homework at the gaudy gold dining room table, a biology textbook spread out before him. Instead of studying at his desk in his room, he commanded the central space and demanded we keep quiet. He was turning into quite the tyrant. Just like my dad. Or maybe it was his only way of avenging himself upon my mother for hounding him into spending every waking hour studying, telling him what a disappointment he would be to her and the entire Palestinian nation if he didn't become a doctor. To say it was easy to be a boy in my family would be a lie.

"Make tabouleh!" she hissed under her breath. A punishment because she knew I found it to be the most tedious of kitchen tasks.

"Hi to you, too!" I told her before she shushed me, cocking her head toward Ghassan, who didn't bother to look up to greet me. Then she disappeared into her bedroom.

I beheaded the parsley. Mixed it with barley. Doused it with olive oil and laced it with salt.

It was now time to attack the tomatoes.

Picking up the smallest one, I placed it on the chopping block, remembering how I learned the word for tomato in English. It was my first week of school in America. Fifth grade. My elderly white teacher who, with her white bun and round gold glasses, reminded me of Mrs. Claus, pulled out a flash card with a tomato on it and called on me. She was trying to teach a bunch of Black and brown kids about classifications.

"Is this a fruit or a vegetable?" she asked me. I didn't dare tell her I didn't know what either word meant, terrified I would be held back a grade because of my poor English.

"Vegetable," I ventured in my thick accent. The English *v* is especially hard on native Arabic speakers. We have no equivalent sound in our language. The class tittered. I had not been popular back home. More than once, an older sister of mine had to step in and threaten violence to stop classmates from teasing me, usually about my skin color. But never had an entire room erupted in mirth to mock me for how I spoke. The terrifying part of entering a new world is not that you will suffer. It's that you'll suffer in a set of ways you can't anticipate.

"A tomato has seeds. That makes it a fruit!" Mrs. Claus reprimanded. I had no idea what the word "seeds" meant either or why I should memorize which foods possessed them. You could as easily group the same items by color or size instead. Classifications are arbitrary. Meaningless. But I, of course, had no words to express all that.

So, instead, I exclaimed, "Who cares?"

Delighted, the class turned their snide laughter onto the teacher. Miguel, the most popular boy in our class, turned to give me a high five. I didn't recognize the gesture and only stared at this smiling boy who had his hand held up, as if he had an answer to a question I hadn't asked. No matter. For a moment, there was a new world order and, for once, I found myself on the winning side.

I would be made to suffer for it. Mrs. Claus would surely rap me hard on the inside of my hand with a ruler as teachers did to unruly kids back home. I expected to be flogged. I wished for it. Anything would have been better than the guilt and shame that flooded me when I saw the hurt in her eyes. I realized she hadn't singled me out to put me on the spot. No one else in the class was paying attention. She had sensed my hunger to learn, my need for her approval. She hadn't believed I was capable of turning on her. No one did.

If my mother called me on my bluff, was I ruthless enough to go through with my threat to betray her to my father? Could I use everything in my power to destroy someone who was trying to destroy me?

In short, was I my mother's daughter?

I touched my knife to the tip of the tomato. Rather than slice it, I found myself sinking my teeth into its skin, half hoping it would scream.

21

ARABELLA

Ramallah

2012

People had heard rumors of the existence of this underground group of women. When and where they met was supposed to be secret. But there are no real secrets among an occupied people. The only way an occupier can sustain control is by infiltrating the ranks of those they've conquered, by inspiring the cooperation of collaborators and spies.

It makes everyone suspicious of everything. No unexpected blessings go unnoticed. You got a visa to visit your relatives in Qatar? How? A scholarship to Cambridge? Why you? Funding from a foreign theatre company to pay for your production of *Hamlet*? Oh, really?

The group called themselves Al-Sittat Al-Hazana, the pitiful women—a tongue-in-cheek name. Sanaa was transgressing by bringing me into the fold before getting their permission.

We had a few hours to kill before the meeting began. Sanaa took me to a café on the outskirts of the city center, a tiny three-table affair overlooking the dry hilly landscape. She explained all about Al-Sittat Al-Hazana over our lamb shawarma sandwiches, dripping in tahini and onions purple with saffron spice. She demanded to pay for my meal and I reluctantly let her. I hated the usual pantomime of fighting over the check, which every Arab is taught is the only way to end a meal. The rage in her eyes when I pulled out my money stopped me from exclaiming "For God's sake, let's each just pay for ourselves!" as I was wont to do in such situations, to the chagrin of my mother. Now, according to the social contract I had unwillingly signed, I owed Sanaa a meal or a present, a debt I'd have to make good soon, preferably the next time I saw her. One more tab I had to keep running in my head.

Over tiny cups of coffee, our talk turned to theatre, as it inevitably does when you get two theatre rats anywhere together for more than a minute. She asked me to describe in detail all the theatre productions I'd directed. She seemed to listen with her whole body as I spoke. I realized she was imagining the sights, sets, and sounds. It made me slightly sad I had devoted my life to theatre, rather than film or painting, this ephemeral art that you could never experience in its totality after the run was done. I found myself speaking about Yoav, how his sound design had shaped so much of my work, and then it dawned on me: yesterday was the Tony Awards. He had been nominated. I had been so far removed from my life in New York that I hadn't remembered.

I checked my phone and—yes! Yoav was now a Tony Award–winning sound designer for his work on the Broadway production of *All My Sons*. He'd gotten theatre's top prize before he was forty, a prediction anyone would have made if they saw his early work. A prediction I had made.

"What's happening?" Sanaa asked me.

"My friend just won the biggest design award in American theatre."

"That's great news!" she said.

"Absolutely," I muttered.

"Then, why do you look so upset?"

"I'm not upset," I said. In terms of our profession, Yoav and I were now in different galaxies. He'd get offers to work on big Broadway shows and splashy musicals. Even if I managed to land an off-Broadway gig in New York again, he'd probably be too busy to work with me on it. I'd have to learn to work with others. I missed him already.

Get ahold of yourself, Arabella. You're mourning not having Yoav available to work on gigs you haven't even been offered. Relax. But I couldn't. Why was it suddenly hard to breathe? Oh, because if I did, I might burst out crying.

Yoav wasn't the only one I'd thought would win a Tony before age forty. It hadn't occurred to me, when I was young and unafraid and making predictions about the careers of my peers and myself, that women artists rarely win Tonys. The one or two who do are hardly ever young. We had to have done twice or thrice the amount of work on Broadway that men did. Those few women who were begrudgingly granted the accolade counted themselves lucky that the world had changed enough for them to be acknowledged at all.

Yoav clearly deserved his award. The dude worked like a madman for little or no money for almost two decades. I'd often tease him in rehearsals, telling him everything he touched turned to gold because it was fun to see him blush. But it was true. You could trust him to underscore any awkward entrance or exit with finesse, to use music to highlight the work of the best actors in a cast while adding cadence and depth to the worst. How could I not feel anything other than unadulterated happiness for him?

"I have to make a phone call," I told Sanaa, and stepped away from the café. I found myself at the edge of an olive orchard.

"Congratulations, Winner!" I said when Yoav answered the phone.

"Thanks. You're next, Arabella," he said.

"No, I'm not," I said reflexively. I noticed Sanaa watching me with an intensity that felt invasive. To hide from her sight, I walked around a large, gnarled tree and stood in its shade.

"You deserve to be."

I felt a warm glow come over me and leaned against the tree's thick trunk. I wanted to close my eyes. Beam myself back to Veselka, where we often seemed to end up together because it was next to all the downtown theatres that we loved. And where I always suggested we go because I knew it was his favorite restaurant and I wanted him to associate getting what he most wanted to eat with being with me.

"Did you hear my speech?"

"Not yet."

"Check it out. I thanked you in it."

Waitamotherfuckingminute! What?! He had invoked my name at the Tony Awards! Every person who mattered in our world watched him do it. Except me. What I would have given to have been there in person! Who had gone with him? Who had been his date?

"Arabella, are you there?"

"That's really nice of you, Yoav. You didn't have to do that."

"And you didn't have to give me my first real gigs, Arabella. You had your pick of designers when we got out of school, but you always hired me. How is the melody working for you over there?"

While I was overjoyed to hear him suddenly switch into using our shorthand, I felt shy with him. The weight of an award of that scope made me feel he was suddenly a stranger to me. He had been acknowledged as being at the very top of his game. It's like he traveled to a different planet and had experiences he couldn't convey from that new world, which I wouldn't be able to understand. I glanced back at Sanaa. She pointed to her watch. It was time to go. I turned my back on her.

"It's a melody," I answered Yoav, sounding our alarm.

"What's up?"

"I want to cast my production with a female lead and the very male head of the theatre wants that role," I began.

On the phone line, I heard a voice in the background. A woman's voice. He had, of course, partied after winning the Tony and clearly hadn't partied alone.

"Anyway, I'll let you go. Congrats again! Bye!" I told him.

"Arabella, wait!" I heard him say before I hung up. I didn't need to blab the whole sordid story of how Ramez had cowed his entire company into trying to get me to cast him as Hamlet. I knew what Yoav would tell me to do. Fuck him. You direct the play exactly the way you want or you walk. He had dropped out of productions where he felt someone was artistically stepping on anyone's toes, not just his. Things were black-and-white to him. He was uncompromising. Once upon a time, so was I.

Who was the woman with Yoav? A fellow artist? Would their night of jubilation after his Tony win cement them together forever? Would they marry?

Though Aziz and I had agreed to talk in the evening after he had done his rounds, I felt compelled to call him next. To confirm that I had heard loud and clear when Yoav told me that we were just friends, that the world I left behind in New York was not my only world now. In this new world, there was someone who wanted to be more than friends with me.

"Hey," I said in my sexiest voice when he answered.

"Is everything okay, Arabella?" Aziz demanded. He sounded panicked.

"Not really. I'm casting my play." There was silence on the phone. "That means picking actors for roles and—"

"Can I call you later? I'm getting ready to operate. Two kids just got shot multiple times in the legs. They play for the Palestinian national soccer league. Arabella, we think they were targeted."

"Yes, of course," I said, and hung up without giving either of us a chance to say goodbye. It was as if my hand had a life of its own and—having heard enough horrific news for one call—deemed it time to shut it down. But I couldn't unhear him, couldn't expel the image of blood and bullets being dug out of the bodies of boys as they screamed for their mothers. Always their mothers.

Taking a deep breath, I walked back to Sanaa. She searched my eyes and could see something had transpired. I had returned to her, changed. Heavier. She seemed to understand I didn't want to talk.

We walked back into Ramallah's city center. She led me to a tiny freestanding stone house and knocked twice on the door. It opened a crack from the inside.

I would learn later that knocking twice means two members are coming in.

"Let me do the talking!" she whispered. I nodded vigorously to indicate "Worry not. I ain't saying shit." She pushed it fully open and we entered, me a half step behind her.

Thirty pairs of big, dark eyes turned on me, the stranger. There was not enough space for everyone in the small, cramped living room. Some women were sitting, some stood. A few younger ones lounged on the floor. They looked like a tableau of *Les Demoiselles D'Avignon*, the way their dark eyes accosted me with their challenging glare.

Or had I only connected them to Picasso's famous painting because an enormous replica of it hung on the wall? In this irreverent rendering, the five staring women were no longer naked but decked out in the Palestinian embroidered traditional dresses known at *thobes.* Similar replicas covered every inch of the walls. There was Mona Lisa in a *thobe.* Venus de Milo rising from the sea in a *thobe.* Girl with a Pearl Earring and a *thobe.* The renderings were masterful. Whoever made them was no amateur painter.

It made me smile to see the most iconic images of women created throughout the ages sporting Palestinian dresses, a style that would be considered old-fashioned, even in my grandmother's day. She donned them only for ceremonies. In America, so did we. We wore the embroidered dress for *sahara* parties, the pre-wedding celebration where the family of a groom gets together for a last hoorah to celebrate his being shorn, i.e., get his final haircut as a single man to the tune of drumming and reveling. Traditionally, the bride-to-be is not invited. Nor is her family. She has her own henna party, where her palms, hands, and feet are adorned and painted while she is among her own people. Each clan eats, drinks, and dances alone. It's as if both families need a way to connect one last time, as they once were and will never be again, before being transformed by the unknowable force of its newest member. Before they can be sure if it will be for better or for worse.

The replica artist seemed to have decided that since Palestinians cannot travel to visit art in the different museums of the world, we would re-create that art in our image. Though perhaps it is more accurate to say we can travel anywhere anytime—it's our return that isn't assured. Given that allowing Palestinians to get back to their homes was not high on Israel's list of priorities, many of us living in the West Bank or Gaza who had the means to travel would rather stay put.

"This is Arabella," Sanaa explained to the staring eyes who regarded me with mistrust. "She's a Palestinian who has lived her entire life in America."

"Has she been jailed, Sister?" someone asked. Challenging.

Sanaa smiled. She had explained to me over lunch that the group only allowed women who had been imprisoned to attend their clandestine meetings. When I told her that I clearly didn't qualify, she told me she would handle it.

"As I said, she's a Palestinian who has lived her whole life in

America," Sanaa announced. "That means she has been imprisoned all her life!"

They took that in. As did I. I thought it was a stretch. By their sardonic expressions, so did they. I found it hard to meet any of the penetrating gazes fixed on me. Since I was not looking up, the voices strangely seemed to emanate from the paintings on the wall.

"She's probably an Israeli spy," I heard someone mutter.

The accusation against me hung in the air.

"Doesn't matter. We're not doing anything wrong. We are committed to nonviolence."

As if in a chorus, they said in a singsong tone that dripped with sarcasm, "*Ah-na bes Al-Sittat Al-Hazana.*" We are only the Pitiful Women.

I understood it was a refrain and it wouldn't be the only one I heard that afternoon. It was a way for a contentious group to come together, to remind one another that they shared a common experience. No matter how far apart they seemed, more often than not they would circle back to speaking with one voice.

It defused the tension in the room. Banter struck up. Tiny cups of coffee on a huge silver tray were passed around. Sanaa didn't take a cup, so I followed her lead. I was glad when I saw there weren't enough cups in that round for everyone. I felt invisible enough to take a closer peek at the panoply of women. They were young and old. Veiled and unveiled. Pretty and plain. What were their supposed crimes? I assumed, as in Sanaa's case, they had been jailed for nonviolent political activity—Palestinian women who attempted to carry out acts of political violence would likely never be freed. I pushed out unwelcome images of these women being shackled, accused, judged, and jailed. Were any of them tortured? Raped? Who awaited them at home after their release?

"Are they mostly unmarried?" I whispered to Sanaa. Are they fruitless fruit, which is the lovely nomer by which my grandmother—and increasingly my mother—called childless women?

"No," Sanaa told me. "We meet during the day because the children are at school."

I glanced down at Sanaa's hand. She was wearing a gold ring I hadn't noticed before, because I hadn't thought to look. We spoke only of theatre at the café. Correction . . . I only spoke of theatre and only of shows I had made. Sure, I had an agenda, describing my former triumphs in detail. I was trying to impress upon her the importance of my work, so she'd buy into my vision of casting a woman as Hamlet. So eager to get her on my side in my fight against Ramez, I hadn't thought to ask her about herself. Not about the work she had created nor where in Palestine her family was from. Nothing. Had the stress of being out of my element consumed me? Or was I always so completely self-absorbed?

"How long have you been married, Sanaa?" I asked. She looked eighteen, but I realized she was older. Had I observed her more closely, I would have seen her forehead was not unlined and the beginning of crow's-feet had formed at the edges of her black eyes.

"Five years," she whispered.

"Do you have kids?" I asked. She put out three fingers to indicate three. There was more to this woman, with her strange embodiment of boldness and skittishness, than I had previously imagined. In New York, it would be almost inconceivable for a serious devotee of the theatre to also be a young mom of three. Our idea of how an American female artist moves through the world rarely makes room for that narrative. Then again, there are so few women artists throughout history in any culture. With such a minuscule sampling, is it any surprise there's so little variation in the types of lives we lead—or can even imagine trying to lead?

I spotted a copper-colored chick with a small, neat Afro lounging on the floor and watched as she downed her hot coffee like a shot. I liked her immediately. She was the same coloring as my mother, who as a young girl had also sported an Afro, which apparently my dad dug so much he immediately asked for her hand. He liked to tell that story. I'd seen pictures or otherwise I wouldn't have believed him. There are no Afros in Atherton, California. My mother had straightened her hair for as long as I could remember.

"Let's get to the problem at hand!" the woman who looked like my mother demanded. Suddenly, it was on.

"The problem at hand is that you're not in touch with reality!"

another young woman screamed. Literally at the top of her lungs. I couldn't help but notice she was *bayda*, a white-skinned woman like my grandmother. It felt weird to watch women who looked like young versions of your mother and grandmother, suddenly the same age and vigor, going at it. Especially since my mom and her mom were always studiously formal and polite with each other in a way that could only mean that they knew if they let down their guard, it would be a fight. Quite possibly to the death.

"Don't scream at me. Ever."

They stared each other down, daring each other to break eye contact first.

"We all know you are brilliant!" the woman like my mother started in.

"I am!" the girl with my grandmother's skin asserted, her eyes wary. What's your game here, sister?

"At being a bullshitter!"

"No name-calling!" several women admonished. That was another refrain I'd hear a lot that day. Attack ideas. Not people. But thoughts are like children. They belonged to you. They might be ugly and stupid, but woe to the motherlover who dared call them so.

"Okay," the woman like my mother modulated, swallowing hard, but judging from the fire in her eyes she was clearly going in for the kill. "Your idea is bullshit. Everyone keeps their mouths shut. We endure what we endure and go to our classes. They don't get to take that away from us, too!"

"What's going on?" I whispered to Sanaa.

"There's an Israeli soldier who is stationed at the checkpoint in front of Birzeit University. He stops college girls on their way, makes them get out of their cars, and feels them up. The girls from the camps don't want us to tell anyone."

Even my American-born ass knows why. The people of the refugee camps are our poorest. When they fled their homes, they lost everything. They are often the most radicalized among us, the least likely to take it lightly that their girls were unsafe. A sizable number of suicide bombers came from camps.

"If we complain to the Palestinian Authority, they *might* alert their contacts in the Israeli army who aren't trying to get more rocks thrown their way. The Israelis *might* station that particular shithead elsewhere. But the girls from the camps are afraid that if their families find out, some will insist their girls stay inside the camps to keep them safe. They won't be able to get to their classes."

"We take a vote!" announced the woman who looked like my mother.

"Vote on what? Whether or not I get to go to college? Only girls from the camps get to vote!" the woman with my grandmother's skin screamed. Then she stepped forward, ready to charge.

Some people have to shout to halt a fight or silence a room.

Others simply stand up. That was all Manal did and everyone froze, waiting for her to speak. To say she was statuesque was an understatement. Tall and possessing such symmetrical features that she seemed crafted out of clay, like a statue of a Greek goddess that had sprung to life, she was the unofficial founder of Al-Sittat Al-Hazana, I would find out later. This was her house. Manal came from a Druze family, a religious minority in a land wracked by religious strife, and had devoted her life and her not insignificant resources to the solidarity of women. Her sister lived in Lebanon and had apparently married exceedingly well. With the money her sister sent her, Manal commissioned artists and supplemented the college tuition of many of the young girls who made it out of Israeli jails.

"We will vote," Manal said. "But, first, we will listen. Women of the camps, each of your voices will be heard. You will have your say."

Chaos erupted again.

"If my brother hears about this shit, he's not letting me cross the checkpoint."

"I'm a few months shy of getting my engineering degree! Can't we wait a few months?"

"I just got out of jail. I can't be confined to my house. I won't!"

Manal raised a finger. Again, there was silence.

I glanced at Sanaa. Her eyes were shining as she returned my gaze. "See!" she seemed to convey. "Who cares who we cast in our little show as the lead, Arabella? The real fight for women's rights is being played out in this arena."

I was inclined to believe her until a voice rang out.

"To tell or not to tell?!"

A gamine girl, lithe and lean with short, dark hair, stepped into the center of the room. She looked wired, as if she had been up for days, but seemed more likely to combust than lay her head down and rest. A teenage face with dark circles under her shimmering almond eyes. Already too full of too much light and too much shadow. She addressed us all with her penetrating gaze.

"Will it cost us more to suffer in silence? Or speak out? To tell a truth means you first have to face it. We have no army. Our men can't protect us. We despise ourselves for despising them for it. Our brothers cross those checkpoints, too. Our brothers get more than an occasional finger in the asshole when they do. But some of you will argue: isn't there power to be gained by speaking out? Yes! There's power in everything. But if we speak out for its own sake, should we not speak of everything? Should we not also question how much safer we girls really are at home? Among our own men? None of us bitches have the stomach for that. So, I counsel we do what we always do. We rage and mourn behind closed doors, then stay quiet. We recruit girls from our camps to cross the checkpoint I do every day to go to college, face the same soldier or a thousand like him, and learn what knowledge can be taught."

I stared, transfixed by this child, this ethereal being. I wanted to know what she knew and how she learned it. I wanted to bring her back to my world so I could question her about all my choices.

So I could beg her to tell me, "How do you face the world with such surety? How do you understand your own mind? How have you figured out how to live, which is another way of saying how do you know which ideals are worth compromising and why?"

Theatres were built so that women like her could stand on stages and speak. So that we in the audience, we mere mortals, might watch her do it.

Sanaa turned to me. When our eyes met, she frowned. She had brought me here to demonstrate to me there was a political feminist movement well underway in Palestine, to show me that casting a man in the lead of our little show—instead of a woman—was no travesty.

Instead, she had led me to my star.

22

NAYA

Daly City
1975

How was it that I was more worldly than the man I married? For our wedding night, Daoud booked a hotel he had found in the Yellow Pages. When we arrived at the Hotel Ivory and the receptionist asked him whether he wanted to rent a room for four or eight hours, he didn't understand it was a place for johns and prostitutes. But I got it right away as I looked at the elderly Black woman sporting enormous diamond earrings no hourly worker could afford.

"We need the hotel all night," Daoud told the madam, confused. I looked at Daoud through her eyes, a caramel-colored teenager in a tuxedo too big for his slight frame. By her bemused expression, it was clear she saw what I did in him. Innocence.

"I'll book you for twelve hours, but only charge you for eight. Consider the extra hours my wedding gift," she told Daoud, handing him a key.

When we got out of the elevator, Daoud and I ended up walking behind a couple, a slender blond woman in a skintight red leather catsuit and a stooped elderly Black man, down the dimly lit hall to our room. Music and moaning could be heard emanating from the doors as we passed them. When the woman glanced back to see who was making the footsteps behind her, she winked at me before they disappeared inside a room.

Daoud and I stopped outside our room. He insisted on carrying me across the threshold in my ill-fitting white dress, his hands rough and his feet unsteady below us. The room had mirrors on the ceilings and a round bed with a bloodred velvet comforter. I stood where he planted me in the middle of the room. The pageantry of the wedding with its *dabke* circle and candle dance was over. Now was the first time we had ever been truly alone.

"Are you hungry? Or thirsty?" Daoud asked.

"Why did you marry me?" I blurted out.

"What?"

"Why did you marry me?"

Daoud was taken aback. My eyes bored into his.

"You looked so sad. I thought I could make you happy. I wanted to."

"Why?"

"Ashan intey ahla bint ena shuft fe hayati."

Beautiful? Me? In the space of a day, I had been told I was ugly by my mother and the opposite by my husband. Only one could be true. Which was it?

Maybe there was no truth, only what you could fool people into believing.

Which of them had been the fool?

Daoud reached out his hand, but he made no other move toward me. This was a man who would not subject a woman to his will. If I refused him, Daoud might divorce me, but he would do it quietly. He would do it in the compassionate way Joseph had intended to break off his betrothal to the Virgin Mary, after he learned she was carrying a child that could not be his, until God intervened. When I last heard our priest recount that story from the pulpit during Advent, my parents were sitting in the pew in front of me. I glanced at my father's broad back, which took up twice the space of my mother. I couldn't imagine God Himself and all His angels convincing him to take an already pregnant woman as his bride. He would sooner see the woman stoned. My husband was different from my father.

I gave Daoud my hand. Relieved, he lifted it to his lips and kissed the middle of my palm. We stared at each other. Then, he kissed my wrist. He kissed his way up the length of my arm until he reached my neck. Our bodies knew what to do next.

When his mouth found mine, I was not completely sorry I was leaving my world to join him in his. In fact, I was the one who pulled him to the bed and unbuckled his belt. Still, I closed my eyes and pretended he was Randy Jackson our first time together.

"Baby! Baby!" I imagined Randy was whispering in my ears as Daoud caressed me after the shock and pain of it was over. "With a sexy mama like you on my side, I know I could have a solo career. I could make it bigger than Michael."

If Daoud could sense I wasn't completely present, he didn't seem to mind. Was he pretending to be with someone else, too? Who was he, this boy I'd married who was not yet twenty?

The next morning, Daoud refused to show our bedsheets, the proof of the virginal blood that every bride was supposed to have after her wedding night, to the men in his clan. But, to my relief, it was there, looking like a spot of spilled pomegranate juice. Brides who didn't leave their blood on the sheets after the wedding night were shamed and sent home.

When we learned I had gotten pregnant on our honeymoon, he said he didn't care whether I was carrying a boy or a girl. He was determined to keep only the best parts of Arab culture alive in this new world we found ourselves in.

Daoud didn't make me live with his widowed mother. I never addressed her as anything other than *Hamaty*. Mother-in-law. A squat and shifty-eyed woman, she religiously dyed the few strands of hair she had left on her head a henna red so bright it seemed they were burning embers. Since Daoud's father was long dead, my husband had asked for my hand from my father directly and did so without consulting with her. Even if my father hadn't been present to reinforce her will over our fates, my brother wouldn't dare choose a bride without my mother's consent. How had she made her grip upon us so strong? What makes one mother more powerful than another?

The first thing *Hamaty* said to me when I returned from our honeymoon was that I would have to lose my Afro, my last link to Detroit, the life that I had not wanted to leave behind.

Her favorite phrase was *lazum*. One must. It made her requests sound like demands, which I ignored.

Lazum or no, she wouldn't prevail upon me to cut my hair before I was ready. Even my mother, who could eat a mouse of a woman like *Hamaty* for breakfast and barely burp, had failed to do that. Too bad for her that when she brought it up to Daoud, he smilingly told his mother that my hairstyle made me look like Diana Ross, which was his way of informing her that he loved it. And me.

Daoud had rented us a tiny, refurbished basement apartment that we had all to ourselves. It was a considerable expense to shoulder two households and a grand gesture, which my elder sisters envied mightily as they found themselves stuck in cramped homes with multiple generations of in-laws. But it meant I was isolated in a new place, a land of no seasons. A land of perpetual fog. Daly City is the armpit of the San Francisco Bay Area, where the thick sea air settled in a way that made it so you could barely see a few steps in front of you. When Arabella was born, my husband worked at our corner store in the Tenderloin during the day and attended college at night. I, on the other hand, was left with little to do except observe other mothers.

An only son, Daoud had hordes of female cousins who doted on him, especially on his mother's side. The women in Daoud's extended family only had older children. Getting them outside to brave the fog and watch their kids at a playground was no easy task. If these women dressed and drove anywhere, instead of chattering endlessly on the phone in their robes, they'd rather smoke around each other's kitchen tables and let their children play in the streets. They lived for gossip, the rise and fall of the fortunes of families of Ramallah who had settled in California. I didn't know the people they discussed, so it was hard to care if strangers made a killing at a Reno casino or were caught selling hot goods in Emeryville. *Hamaty* informed me they spoke disparagingly of my Afro behind my back and were embarrassed to sit with me at church. Daoud's cousins were never unkind, but any chance for connection I might have made with the womenfolk of his clan felt tainted by *Hamaty*. They were her creatures.

Upon Daoud's urging, I began to venture to the local playground with my daughter. It was on that playground that my girl took her first steps. The majority of other mothers were Filipino. Daly City is called Little Manila, because of the huge Filipino population who have settled there. I found them surprisingly friendly to me, a stranger who did not speak their tongue.

They made an effort to speak in English or translate from Tagalog when they could for my sake. I felt like a bother. My presence a disruption to the flow of their banter. I didn't mean to cling to their circle. I would rather have been alone, but my daughter gravitated toward their children. I felt compelled to stay half a step behind her.

Daoud cherished the girl I bore him with a ferocity that was only matched by the love he strangely and unexpectedly showed me. It must be admitted I grew to adore the skinny boy with big dreams who was my husband. What I felt for our firstborn, on the other hand, was anxiety. Death was always beckoning her and my days were daily battles to keep her from Him. To snatch away a dime that Death has handed her before she tried to swallow it. To grab her before Death coaxed her to crawl toward the long stairwell outside our apartment. To long for nightfall, my sleep a respite from staring Death in the face all day and insisting not yet. Not yet. Not on my watch.

It wasn't only concern for my child that made me so anxious. I was frightened of what Daoud would do if I let something happen to her. The only time I'd ever seen him visibly angry was when I once shook her when she wouldn't stop screaming. He took her from me wordlessly, but the flash of wild rage in his eyes made it clear he wanted to shake me. To show me how it felt.

"You are very young," the Filipino women often would say at the playground. It was a way to coax me into conversation.

I smiled silently. Would they be shocked if they knew I was sixteen?

One day, they had a picnic. They offered to share the food they'd brought with me and my daughter. Well, actually, Arabella demanded it. She pointed to the basket of lumpias from which their children took. To make a demand, she would point to the desired object and cry, "Me! Me! Me!" She did not yet know the word "mine." When would she learn how to distinguish between what she wants and what she is? There was no separation in her one-year-old mind.

"No thank you!" I told them firmly. I had nothing to offer in return. "We just ate. No, Arabella! Don't take."

Giving me the sly side-eye of a child who understood a command she had no plans to heed, Arabella followed the lead of the other children who went for the lumpias. They each took one. My daughter grabbed two in each hand, then proceeded to drop them. Four perfectly shaped deep-fried rolls, wafting steam and a smell so heady it made one dizzy with desire, now lay in the dirt.

It was a terrible moment. Would they think badly of me if I allowed their food to go to waste? Or worse if I let my daughter eat off the ground of a public playground?

"You care so much about what other people think," my husband told me. It was the closest Daoud ever came to openly criticizing me.

To that I answered, "I grew up very differently from you."

The thing that annoyed me most about my husband was that he was so determined to believe in people's good intentions that his sense of righteous indignation was not easily roused. It was hard to tell Daoud about all the things my mother did and said to me, but I tried. I understood that my rage toward my mother was the key to unlocking why I felt so disconnected from my own little girl.

"That generation didn't know any better," Daoud told me when I described how she beat us.

When I told him she called me ugly, his dark eyes clouded with concern. Of course, I omitted the fact she did so to better force me into marrying him, to make me believe no one else would want me. That's the key to coaxing a woman into submitting to a marriage she might not otherwise want. It's a way to coax yourself. You are unlovable. Take what you can get.

There! I would get him to condemn her! But, instead, he smiled and the cloud lifted.

"Your mother loves you," he said with finality. A truly infuriating response, but also not untrue.

Daoud moved to San Francisco in the sixties, the era of free love. Though he never was a recipient of any love (free or otherwise) as a young man and had been a virgin until our wedding night, he would never stop being a hippy at heart. The fact that he excused bad behavior in others more easily than most would turn out to be a blessing. He would eventually have to excuse it in me when I began telling lies.

Arabella reached for the fried rolls she had dropped. Incensed, I raised my hand to strike her and the universe screamed, "No!"

It was Rita, the mother who spoke the most English and was the friendliest to me. She had terrible acne scars. Does suffering make a person kinder? Anyone who has picked at their own skin that much— so deeply that it never heals—has to have suffered.

"Don't hit her. Please. I made plenty. We have plenty."

Rita swooped up the fallen food and handed Arabella a fresh roll. She offered me one, insisting I take it, folding it tightly into my hand when I refused. The thought of eating it made my stomach turn. The squeezing of the roll had altered the shape. It suddenly looked like a tiny corpse in a death shroud. When Arabella tottered over, I handed it to her and she smiled up at me. I recognized she was adorable, all red cheeks and tiny teeth and bright black eyes. Why did I not adore her? I would never slap a one-year-old child, any child. It seemed impossible that I had raised my hand to strike my own flesh and blood. I didn't. I couldn't have. Death did it.

Who stopped Death? Another mother who saw what He was trying to make me do and screamed.

I never returned to that playground.

"Why aren't you leaving the apartment anymore?" Daoud asked after a few days.

"How do you know?" I asked. Was he spying on me? Turning into my father?

"You haven't been brushing Arabella's hair," he told me. My mother would never let me leave the house without arranging my hair in tight symmetrical braids when I was a child. I did the same with Arabella.

"I think it's good for the baby to get fresh air," Daoud ventured. "And for you, Naya."

"I hate the fog," I told him. This made him sad. He hated that we couldn't afford a sunnier suburb.

"Drive to Burlingame," he said. "It's only fifteen minutes away."

The San Francisco Bay Area was the strangest landscape I'd ever encountered. Unlike in the Midwest, change was quick and easy in California. Every fifteen minutes you drove away from the shore brought different weather. Fifteen minutes and you escaped the fog. Fifteen more and you might find yourself burdened by the heat of the sun.

I told Daoud I would try the parks in Burlingame. But instead, I braided my daughter's hair to make it look like I went out instead of actually doing so. Then, I discussed it with King Tut.

"You must get outside. You require friends," King Tut told me.

"I have you."

"Besides me, Naya."

"Tell me again about your new job."

In the era shaped by the impact of white flight, the exodus of whites from downtown Detroit to nearby suburbs in which my father eagerly took part, King Tut graduated law school from Wayne State at the top of his class. He had his pick of firms recruiting him but decided to clerk for an organization that was working on the desegregation of the Detroit school system. Rather than focus on busing black kids into all-white schools, which we both felt was a nightmare for those children, he aimed to change the discriminatory lending and housing policies that led to segregation in the first place. I admired his fervor but didn't see how it would help solve the essential problem of racism. How to face hatred and not absorb it, to not allow unrelenting derision to infect some part of how one saw oneself? Yes, we could force integration. But how would it make it easier to deal with white people who were willing to grow proverbial wings to not have to live next to a Black family?

"What's the name of the organization you work for again?" For some reason, it never seemed to stick in my head.

"The National Association for the Advancement of Colored People," he said, not without a touch of pride.

"It must be admitted that Black Panthers is catchier," I told him.

"You are not the only one who finds it so," he said with a sigh. Reginald was much fierier in temperament and radical in politics than King Tut, especially after the Black Panthers were targeted by the FBI. When we spoke, Reginald often started ranting about how no one cared that an arm of the US government executed American citizens in their sleep and tried to frame it as if their forces had been fired upon first.

"All they have to do is say our people are violent, not even prove it, and they can do anything they want to us. The horrors they have systemically inflicted upon us beggar the imagination and yet we're supposedly the violent ones! Must be nice. To act like demons and demonize anyone who gives you a taste of your own medicine. You know what I'm talking about. You're a Palestinian!"

I remained silent. I had been infected by my family's fear that the government was tapping the phones of all Palestinian Americans after Sirhan Sirhan was convicted of killing Bobby Kennedy. Also, talk of injustices overwhelmed me. Maybe because I was married off and became a mother before I had developed the mental tools I needed to fight for liberation, including my own. Or maybe I just couldn't make myself care as much as I knew I should. Either way, I was always relieved when Reginald wasn't home when I called, as he was not that day.

"You must get outside, Naya. Do it for me. Learn your new world well, if only so you can show it to Reginald and me when we sojourn your way. I have always wanted to visit California."

There seemed to be only white women in Burlingame. After a few weeks, I noticed the mothers usually came and stayed in pairs. I liked their park better than the one in Daly City because there were swings. I could deposit Arabella in a swing for an hour without having to interact with the other women because my curious child had toddled over to one of theirs.

My cloak of invisibility did not last. One day, I noticed a painfully thin and artificially blond woman watching me intently as I fed Arabella a hummus sandwich. It was as if she felt entitled to observe me, as if she were a queen in her kingdom and I was there only due to her largesse. The sad thing was, on some level, I must have agreed with her. Rather than assume she was a strange bird, I became self-conscious. Imperious and placid, she watched me distracting Arabella with toys while shoving morsels into her mouth. The child never ate enough. But I usually did my song and dance of getting Arabella to eat against her will without an audience.

The woman eventually approached me as I was coaxing my daughter's legs into the torturous-looking leather contraption that is the seat of a toddler swing.

"Are you looking for more hours? Perhaps in the evening?"

I realized she had mistaken me for Arabella's nanny because I was darker than my daughter. I observed how the color of my newborn nieces and nephews seemed to deepen after infancy. Arabella's had not. Having inherited my mother's *bayda* skin color, she was already being mistaken for white. She would have the choice to distance herself from her people, even me. Would she want to?

"I belong to a book group and Adam apparently can't handle the twins for a night."

She turned and pointed to her two fat cherub blond babies in the sandbox. The boy struck his sister with a toy shovel. I noticed the woman had a nose job. It looked like it was done by the same surgeon who knifed several of my sisters, giving them a ski jump of a nose with incongruously large nostrils. I had slowed down on pushing Arabella on the swing. She didn't have words to complain but pitched herself forward and back. The message was clear. Get back to work.

"No, I am not looking for more hours," I told the woman, and gave Arabella a big push.

"That's a shame. I wouldn't trust half the nannies I see here. You care for that girl as if she's your own."

"Maybe because the girl is her own. Haven't you noticed she calls her mama?" a big-boned woman with lively blue eyes and a halo of cop-per hair said as she deposited a child—a miniature version of her whom no one could mistake for anyone but her daughter—in the swing next to mine. When the woman smiled, she revealed a tiny gap between her front teeth that gave her an insouciance, a sensuality. "Hi! I'm Esther."

That's how I made my first Jewish friend. I'd like to say her religion didn't matter to me. To pretend I didn't closely clock how she moved in the world, perceiving all her choices as indicative of her tribe, forever watchful for clues about how and why they had so soundly beaten mine time and time again. But I would be lying. Throughout our friendship, I'd watch myself for how I might reveal, if only to myself, how be-longing to the tribe that never seemed able to triumph had scarred and shaped me. Because I knew there was no way in heaven or on earth that it could not have done so. Yet, despite all that being true, it was also true that she was a good friend to me and I believe I was to her, too. When I would look back on my life, I would find that the hours I shared with her felt like my richest.

"Want to grab a bite? There's a great brunch place on Primrose," Esther asked me on that first day we met after we were forced to relin-quish our swings, to give other mothers and their waiting children a turn.

"Okay," I said. But when we strolled our daughters down the street and stopped in front of the restaurant, I recognized the old woman standing behind the counter.

"I know the family that owns that place," I told Esther.

"You don't like them?"

"No, they are nice," I said, and went silent. *Hamaty* was friendly with that woman at church. If we ate there, I'd feel observed. It would feel like *Hamaty* was sitting at the table with us. Esther seemed to un-derstand.

"There's another good place around the corner."

When I was a child, I liked to imagine I was alive in Jesus's time. I knew the only way I'd truly believe a tenet of our faith, that an ordinary man could be the Son of God, was if I myself were a leper whom He personally had healed with His touch. The power of miracles can best be appreciated by those who suffer most acutely in their absence. Some things only a leper can understand.

On that first day, we fed our daughters pancakes and they both promptly fell asleep in their strollers. Our girls were safely in view and we could eat a full meal in peace. We could think and talk in complete sentences. Only a mother of a young child can know the fullness of that relief.

"It's a godsend we got them both to nap," Esther said as we lingered over our second cups of coffee.

"I know. Arabella never falls asleep at this time," I told her.

"I don't think Yael ever sleeps," she said. We laughed together and suddenly hushed ourselves, afraid we'd wake the sleeping tyrants.

"Parenting in little units of nuclear families is unnatural. We are supposed to live and raise our kids in flocks. Did you know flamingos have a daycare system? The baby birds in a flock are left on the shore with one adult, who watches for predators. The rest go forage for food. Isn't that great?"

"For everyone except that one adult flamingo stuck at the shore," I said.

"Never thought about it that way," she mused. "I wonder how they roped that poor bird into that job."

"Is it always a female?"

"Not quite sure, but probably."

We shared a smile. I felt my body, full of warm eggs and sweet coffee, relax. Never before had I been able to even hint that motherhood was anything but a blessing. To complain felt like asking for trouble. Begging for it.

"My mother had nine children. Can you imagine?"

"No," Esther said.

"Me neither. Becoming a mother almost makes me have sympathy for her."

"Almost? Is your mother a pill?"

A pill? I had only heard that word used to mean medicine. I stared into my coffee cup, flustered as I always was when I encountered yet another American idiom I didn't understand. Furious at my lack of fluency. However, when I looked up and found sympathy in her eyes, it was like she unleashed a dam in me.

"My mother is not human. She used to beat all of us violently. With objects. She called me ugly on my wedding day."

As our coffees went cold, I confided a litany of injustices I endured at my mother's hands. Not everything, but almost. Unlike Daoud, Esther didn't try to justify my mother's behavior or excuse it. She simply took it in.

When I was spent and went silent, she dropped her gaze. Why had I revealed so much of myself to this woman? Was I that hungry for pity? How pathetic. I vowed I'd never return to that park in Burlingame. I'd hide. This stranger would return to being a stranger.

But then she lifted her head and told me a family secret of her own. When our daughters woke up, we strolled them back to the park together, knowing more about each other than seemed possible with a person you only broke bread with once.

"I come to this park in the morning and stay here all day," Esther informed me.

"All day?"

"All day. I go stir-crazy at home."

"What time do you come in the morning?" I asked.

"By nine," she said.

The next day, when I arrived at quarter to nine, she and her daughter were waiting.

What is a best friend? How do you know you have found one? How to form a tribe of two? You worship the same gods. Not the God with a capital G, the One your parents speak of that belongs to the legacy that you inherit from them. Not that God that requires no imagination. No, you share your adoration for the lesser deities you find and follow all on your own.

As we met almost every day in that park for years to watch our children play, Esther and I would discover we both worshipped at the altar of the god of Despising Hypocrites. Paid homage to the goddess of Self-Deprecation, who wards off the jealousy of the envious. Bowed down before the deity of Academic Achievement. We prayed to the patron saint of Survivors of Narcissistic Parents, a term we would discover together. We followed the flutes of the satyrs from the Land of Mocking Pretentious Women, who believed in the illusion of beauty's power so strongly they starved, plucked, and primped with the fervor of self-flagellating zealots. Her thought patterns were more like mine than those of any other person I had or would ever meet.

On the surface, we made an odd pair. I was a Palestinian teenage bride who didn't finish high school. She was a Jewish medical doctor and twice my age. Nevertheless, we preferred each other.

Soon after we met, she invited me to attend a feminist book club for mothers. I didn't feel comfortable in the room full of white women, dressed with the Jordache look to discuss Betty Friedan. Esther seemed right at home, though she stuck out in the soft cotton sweat suits and white tennis shoes she favored. In my outdated bell-bottoms, I felt I had more in common with the two Mexican maids hired to occupy our children in the next room and do the dishes than with any of those women. If Esther and I were to return for the next meeting, I vowed I would ask Daoud, who denied me nothing, to buy me exorbitant designer jeans. Was it time for me to finally lose my Afro, to lighten and straighten my hair? The women in Daoud's family would be delighted, but their opinions held no weight with me. Why did it matter more to me to fit into an American world, either Black or white, than with my own kind? What was it about a circle of wealthy white women that made it so important for me to show I could afford everything that they could, that I belonged among the people being served rather than those who did the serving?

"What'd you think?" Esther asked me after we left the book group meeting and strolled back to our park with our daughters.

"Did you see how the hostess stared at your shoes, Esther?" I blurted out. I didn't mention how she also patted my Afro and said that she liked my hair, but not in a way that seemed like she meant it.

"Renee?"

I nodded. I wanted to poison Esther against them.

"She's a snotty one, isn't she? They sort of all are, aren't they?"

I shrugged. The poison worked. We never went back. Some of the women in that group were probably nice enough, but we had no use for them. We began reading books together, lending each other the ones we liked best. Self-help was all the rage in those years and we devoured those tomes together. My favorite was *How to Win Friends and Influence People*. I liked how it articulated a truth about life that is easy to forget, which was you are always either influencing or being influenced. With every word you said or swallowed.

She preferred *I'm OK—You're OK*.

"Is everyone really okay, Esther?" I asked her skeptically. "Everyone?"

"Either we all are or none of us are!" By the way her eyes shone as she cracked open the book and began reading a passage aloud, it was clear in which direction she leaned. I remembered the family secret she told me and almost brought it up, but I couldn't bear to remind her that evil exists in the world. To dim the glow in her eyes.

Only when I borrowed Esther's copy of *One Thousand and One Nights* did I realize my mother, for all her faults, was an unusually good storyteller. As I read the clunky English translations of the tales that she had told us in Arabic, I understood how revolutionary it was for a mother of mostly daughters to change the genders of main characters so we could see ourselves as primary in the adventures of Aladdina, Alia Baba, and Sinbada. The only time I hadn't lived in fear of being caught in the vortex of one of her rages was when she was lost in the act of telling a tale. Conjuring. Dreaming. Escaping.

Were Esther and I kind to other mothers, the women who arrived friendless to the park with their children in tow and tried to make small talk with us over the years? No. If they greeted us, we were forced to greet them back, then we'd fall silent until they got the hint and moved away. We felt overstretched as mothers, daughters, and wives. Was it so wrong for us to decide we didn't owe anyone else an ounce of our energy in the hours we were together?

"Do you want more kids, Naya?" Esther asked me after we dropped our girls off together at Burlingame's toniest preschool and, for the first time, went to eat together without them.

"Absolutely not."

"Neither do I. But will we have more?"

"Probably," I said. "It's expected. I always do what is expected of me. Eventually."

"So do I, Naya."

"You?" I asked, incredulous.

"Yes. Everything I've ever done was part of my parents' plan. Everything. I became a doctor because they convinced me that I'd be admired if I did. Not because I have an affinity for science. Or listening to people talk about their ailments. Unless, of course, it's Burt Reynolds. I could listen to him talk about anything he wanted all day long."

She smiled, but the smile didn't quite reach her eyes. In fact, tears were welling up. I had never seen Esther cry. How to comfort her?

"Esther, your parents might have influenced what career you chose, but at least they didn't arrange your marriage for you."

Esther swallowed hard before speaking.

"In some ways, my marriage feels like it was arranged as yours, Naya. When I turned thirty-five, I was made to feel like a weirdo for being single. For never really wanting to have children. My mother and aunts kept telling me not to miss the boat, that I'd regret it if I was never a mother. I couldn't be sure I wouldn't. So, I married a Jewish doctor in my circle who I thought would annoy me the least. I picked out exactly who they would have picked out for me. As expected."

The young waitress stepped up to our table. She was new and snapped gum as she took our order. We disliked her because, even though we tipped well and the place was almost empty, she was always rushing us out.

"Can I get you anything else?" she asked. Snap. Snap. Snap.

"Freedom!" Esther told her.

Confused, the waitress frowned.

"If that isn't on the menu, we'll take refills of our coffee instead," I told her.

When she was gone, Esther asked, "So, are we having more children, even though neither of us really wants to?"

"It is expected."

"Let's do it together."

We smiled the knowing smiles of women who were going to return to their homes and seduce their husbands. We gave birth to sons within weeks of each other. The cycle began again. As soon as we were up and running, we took our children to the park, where we met as often as we could.

Though she was passionate on the subject of abortion rights, Esther was not especially worldly or knowledgeable about international politics. She had never left America nor did she yearn for distant shores. The farthest she had ever traveled from California was Hawaii. The fact that I was a Palestinian didn't seem to register deeply with her. To her, I could have just as easily been Indian or Chinese, existing in that amorphous category of American that is neither white nor Black. Or maybe I simply I told myself that because I wanted to believe it. It felt safer to guess at her worldview, to assume it was limited, rather than delve into difficult conversations and discover it was diametrically opposed to mine.

One time, the news was playing loudly on the radio in our café and the two guest speakers were hotly debating whether what had happened to Palestinians constituted ethnic cleansing.

Esther frowned and said, "I hate war."

I said nothing. I never spoke to her of how my family came to be here. Maybe our friendship would have survived if I had, if I'd known how to be completely honest with her. Or anyone.

If I hadn't felt so ashamed of how little I had accomplished in life and what that implied about the people I came from. If the first thing I'd said to her had not been such a blatant lie!

"I never thought I'd miss going to work, but anything is easier than full-time motherhood. I'm a radiologist on staff at UCSF. Or I was,"

Esther told me as we pushed our daughters on swings in tandem together that very first time. "I feel like my brain is turning to mush."

She turned to me and smiled. It was then that I noticed the pendant on her necklace. It was a Jewish star.

"Me too. I'm a lawyer on staff at the National Association for Advanced Colored People. Or I was."

23

ARABELLA

Ramallah

2012

The door to Aziz's hotel room was left ajar. The front desk clerk at Mövenpick Hotel, seeing me arrive and check in with no luggage, had put me in the room next to his. A skinny boy with watery blue eyes and an unappealingly prominent Adam's apple, he must have been accustomed to pairs of lovers illicitly renting two rooms, the assigned watchdog instructed to enforce the rule that an unmarried man and woman couldn't stay together in one. He gave me a knowing smile that I did not like. Glaring at him, I pasted a big stupid fake smile on my face. Only when he looked down, cowed, did I smile for real.

Yes, I'm about to make love. No, you're not going to make me ashamed. Give me my damn key. When he did, I snatched it from him. I skipped through the lobby, generically ornate, like a theatre set, with cheap Oriental rugs and teardrop chandeliers meant to convey elegance but not built to last. I hummed my way to the elevator that shot me up six flights to the door that my lover kept open for me.

"Hello!" I sang as I burst into the room. I couldn't wait to tell Aziz all about my first rehearsal. *Hamleta* had the makings of a truly good show, perhaps the best I'd ever made. My brain was abuzz with possibilities. For a theatremaker, there is only one question to ask, one dream to dream, one plan to make. How to get as many people as possible to see your show when it can still be seen? Before you lose your actors. Before you lose your space. Before the magical thing you made together disappears completely except in the minds of those who were—too soon—themselves to disappear. Our show had funding to tour Palestinian cities. How to find a way to take it to London? To the world?!

I found Aziz collapsed on a cream love seat. He was staring straight ahead with his arms folded in front of him. I stepped in and closed the door behind me.

I sat next to Aziz and took his hand in mine. He gave off the same sweet masculine smell but mixed with a chemical scent I didn't recognize. An antiseptic? Something doctors used when they operated?

"Are you okay?" I asked him.

He shook his head, still staring straight ahead.

"I am okay. Those boys won't play soccer again. It'll be a miracle if they can walk. I've been in Gaza for a long time. I've seen kids younger than them shot to death in front of me. I've gotten used to it. But the cruelty of shooting soccer players in the feet on their way home from their practice, I can't understand it. Then, the Israeli border patrol claimed the boys were trying to throw a bomb, these kids who were training for the World Cup. They don't want us to have a Palestinian national soccer league because they don't want us to have a nation. They shot Adam once in each foot. They put ten bullets in Jawhar's feet. Ten!"

He choked back a sob. I stood up and led him to the bed. I sat him down. He still didn't lift his head. It was like he was doing everything he could to stay compact, to keep himself together.

I began to undress him, kissing his lean, muscular chest as I did so. The sounds of the street, horns honking and the occasional screeching of brakes, filled the room, magnifying the silence between us. He did not help me undress him, but he let me. Slowly, patiently, I did what so many women have done for men when they suffer wounds that leave no mark, when they feel powerless because they are. I kissed him alive. We began to make love tentatively, mournfully. We made the kind of love that only survivors make and only with each other, feeling the intactness of each other's bodies while knowing so many of our people are not so lucky.

"I'm sorry. I didn't remember to bring condoms," he said at the moment one has to reveal such things.

"I don't care," I told him.

"Are you sure?" he asked me.

"Yes. Are you sure?"

"Absolutely. Let's make a thousand Palestinian babies together, Arabella."

"Why don't we start with one?" I said, and let him enter me. It was my first time having sex without a condom. So, it felt a little like an out-of-body experience. I was observing how it felt to have unprotected sex more than I was feeling it, surprised by how little difference it seemed to make, at least to me. I had never had a relationship long enough to warrant going on the pill. Also, I was a bit of a hypochondriac, or whatever you call someone who is excessively anxious about taking any kind of medicine. Instead of his sunny disposition, that was apparently what I inherited from my dad.

"Never take medicine if you can help it," my dad used to tell me. "Nobody knows all the effects of drugs that doctors say are safe."

"Old Hippy," I once said, which was my mother's nickname for him. My father grimaced. Was it her way of calling him a fool?

It occurred to me that maybe I got the order of things wrong all along.

Did I never go on birth control because I never had a relationship that lasted long enough to warrant it? Or did I always unconsciously fixate on men who clearly wanted no real relationship with me, to save myself from doing things I didn't want to do—like taking a pill that altered my hormones daily rather than requiring a man to occasionally slip on a piece of plastic, which was emblematic to me of all the ways women normalized bearing the bulk of the burdens in a relationship. It's what girls did, at least those who wanted to keep their men. Make things as pleasurable for them as possible or lose them to girls who would.

Aziz began to move quicker inside me. His breathing became short, tense. I felt myself clench when he climaxed, both terrified and thrilled by the prospect of pregnancy.

When he pulled out, he collapsed next to me and stared at the ceiling. Tears streamed down his cheeks. I wiped them as they fell.

He took a deep breath and turned to me.

"I told myself I'd leave Palestine if I started becoming bitter. I can feel myself becoming bitter."

"Feel like living in New York?" I asked, and he smiled softly.

"I feel like making a family," he said, and twirled a lock of my hair around his forefinger. "Where I do that doesn't matter."

"Well, that's a relief. Because wild horses couldn't make me leave New York."

He laughed.

"What's so funny?"

"I imagined a bunch of wild horses heading your way. You'd give them one of your Looks of Death and they'd stop in their tracks and turn around, whimpering with their tails between their legs."

My Looks of Death? Sure, I knew how to glare at a fool, but what New Yorker didn't? I decided to roll with it, but his words smarted because I could feel Ramez calling me a bitch to anyone who would listen, like when I ran into male actors around town after they had auditioned for me and I hadn't cast them. Men were not used to women being in charge of the roles they got to play. Maybe being called a bitch was a rite of passage for any woman artist who aimed to execute her vision. Maybe that's what I was, or—at least—it was the word the world used to describe women like me. Maybe it was time to embrace it.

"Damn straight, especially if those wild horses caught me on a day when rehearsals weren't going well. They might get more than a Look of Death from me then."

I thought it might be a moment when I could turn the conversation to the triumph that was my first rehearsal, but it was not to be.

"Can you imagine the children we'll have?" he told me. "With our education, we could raise them to be Super Palestinians."

"Super Palestinians? Will they fly around with keffiyeh capes?"

"Maybe," Aziz said, and laughed. "Let's hope they have your looks. I want our two girls to have your pretty face."

How sweet, I thought. Until he continued.

"And our two boys will grow up to be soccer players."

"You mean 'or,' right?"

"What?" Aziz looked at me, confused.

"I'm thirty-five," I said. "Even if we started today . . ."

"*In sha Allah*," he said. God willing.

"*In sha Allah*," I parroted automatically. Really? Did I really just say that? Even if He was willing, was I? I had a show to direct.

"At my age, I probably couldn't even have four kids."

"Nonsense," he said. "Think of our grandmas, having babies until they were practically fifty."

He reached for me. I recoiled.

"Okay. Maybe I'm not being clear. I don't want four kids, Aziz."

"How many kids do you want, Arabella?"

"One," I said.

"One?" he gasped.

"Yes. One. And then, I'll see how I feel. What I can handle."

He sat next to me and pulled me into his lap. I pulled up the sheet to cover my breasts. I had been proud of my prodigious breasts all my life. I wore them like a diamond necklace. Suddenly, it occurred to me that, at thirty-five, they might have changed. They might look more like what they were. Not the stuff of boyhood fantasies anymore but repositories of fat.

Then, he held me tight against him and all my insecurities flew from me, exorcised by the feel of his skin against mine and the tender look in his enormous chocolate eyes. I was beautiful again. An object of desire. Lovable and loved. Nothing the world did to me could touch me if I could come home to this feeling every night. Some part of me wanted to give in to him. To keep him, by any means necessary.

"Imagine how intelligent our children will be," he whispered. "Think of the advantages we could give them, what they might be able to accomplish. At the very least, they'll have a leg up when they apply to Harvard and Stanford, because their parents will have went there. We must make up for the losses our people have suffered."

"I can only handle having one kid with my kind of career," I found myself saying.

He let go of me and stood up.

"We wouldn't even be replacing ourselves with one kid, Arabella. If we don't do that, what's the point?"

"The point of what, Aziz?" I asked.

"Life!" he snapped. Then, he turned from me and began to get dressed, his expression hard. I had never seen him looking so angry. In fact, it was the first time I'd ever seen him angry at all. He headed toward the door.

"Where are you going?" I asked.

"To get food. I'm hungry," he said, and left, shutting the door hard behind him.

As I listened to his footsteps echo down the hall, I calculated how long it would take for him to return. At least half an hour. Long enough for me to call Layla and tell her all about my first rehearsal.

Without hope, I had posted the cast list on the door of the theatre with the names of the people I wanted in each role, expecting no one but Cherifa—my Hamleta—to show up. Getting her to agree to perform in the show had been a feat. Layla would love to hear how I traveled to Cherifa's camp. In that place that had seen so much despair, I spoke to the elders of her community of poetry, of power, of giving their girl—who had spent nine months in jail for slapping a soldier—a spotlight. I managed to convince them to let her star.

In the end, the rest of the troupe chose to join the show. They chose integrity. They chose art.

Or at least they chose to side with me against Ramez.

It was electrifying. That's the only word I had to describe my elation as, one by one, the rest of the troupe minus Ramez slipped into the rehearsal space and sat down in the circle of chairs I put out for them. My Ophelia, my Gertrude, my Claudius had appeared, rounding out my cast. They joined in the first reading of the play as if nothing had happened between us and they had not collectively threatened to quit if I didn't cast Ramez in the lead. As if they were no longer fearful of his inevitable retaliations against them. As if fear no longer existed. For that moment, we were magnetic beings beyond such limitations, drawn together to do what we were put on this earth to do, and could only do together.

We were going to make a show.

Unlike Aziz, I wasn't searching for a point to life. I was looking to feel enthralled by it.

I dialed the number of the person I wanted to speak to the most right then. Yoav answered on the first ring.

24

NAYA

Entering the purple apartment was like stepping back into my fifteen-year-old skin.

"How is he?" I mouthed to Reginald when he opened the door. His hair was now completely white, but his face was barely wrinkled and he stood as upright as a general.

Reginald simply shook his head and pointed to the bedroom. I headed toward it, but paused.

I had felt honored when King Tut called and asked me to visit. Honored, but afraid.

"I cannot get to San Francisco at the moment. Come and bring San Francisco to me."

"Of course," I promised him before I knew if I had the courage to do so.

No one fully understood this new plague at the time, which emerged from nowhere and had everyone terrorized. People were frightened to send their children to school with kids who had it. A mob of Florida residents recently torched the house of a family with two hemophiliac sons, who sued the district to keep their boys in school. Were those parents right to try to protect their children at all costs? Could I catch it? Bring it back to my family? All I knew was my friend was sick. He had asked me to visit. I would. Come what may.

Did it make me brave that I was willing to put my family at risk to see King Tut one last time? Or did it just mean I never loved—or felt I owed—any of them as much as I did him?

"Can I go to Detroit to visit a friend?" I asked Daoud at breakfast the next morning, a little nervous he would refuse. Of the fact that he had AIDS, I—of course—said nothing. I had made Daoud his favorite morning meal, my homemade *labneh* spread on sourdough bread, a fusion of Ramallah and San Francisco flavors. My request felt strange, even to me. I had not spent one night away from my husband since our wedding.

"But I'm not telling my parents I'll be there. If my mother calls, don't tell her where I am."

"What else is new?" Arabella sauntered in with her Walkman on her ears, catching only the last bit of our conversation. She was listening to her favorite cassette, so loud I could hear it. "Control!" Janet Jackson crooned. The idea of a song called "Control" befuddled me. If you are really in control, you don't have to sing about it.

"I'm not talking to you," I snapped at her, and her eyes narrowed.

"Well, you're going to have to, if you expect me to lie to Teta Zoya for you," she said, and walked out in a huff. Why was it that she and I were always at odds? She was off to college in September. In a matter of months, she'd be living on another coast. As I watched her stomp away, I wondered how I'd feel if she visited San Francisco and chose not to tell me. Relieved. With Arabella gone, it felt less likely my Atherton friends would find out I was younger than the age I pretended to be or that I never attended college.

Of all the people most likely to out your lies, your children are at the top of the list.

Recently, Arabella had asked me why I always lied about my age.

"None of your business," I told her. "And, if you tell your brothers or anyone else, I'll kill you."

I told my children with regularity that I would kill them. This was strange because my biggest anxiety was that one of them would die before me. What is motherhood except wrestling with the fear you might have to encounter the corpse of your child, to see the spark of life that you once carried within the folds of your body snuffed out? It's not only tragic but also embarrassing to outlive a child. How can you continue to walk and talk and breathe and laugh? Why would you want to? Even if you wish you could exchange your life for theirs, there is something shameless about the fact that you're still standing.

It's akin to the guilt one must feel when immune to a sexually transmitted virus that is painfully and pitilessly destroying one's lover, as with Reginald.

"Has Naya arrived?" I heard King Tut ask from inside the bedroom. He must have heard me come in. Or could he sense my presence as I stood, hesitant, outside his bedroom door? What I dreaded most was seeing Death's approach rob King Tut of his dignity. Then, I realized nothing could. Even if he screamed, writhed, cursed, and soiled himself, he would always be the man who once saw my family and me not as we were, but as we wanted to be.

"Yes," I said, and entered the bedroom. I tried not to convey my horror at how he looked. He was skeletal, his skin sticking to his bones, and his large red sores looked like leprosy. Tubes extended from both his arms and up his nose. The light seemed to already have gone from his eyes.

He sat up. Not an easy move as he was fettered by the tubes.

"I am in need, Naya. You can help me," he said, and winced.

"Me?"

"Yes. I will never visit San Francisco."

"Yes, you will!" I cried out. "You're going to get better and visit me."

In Palestine, we don't tell people they are dying. We hide it from them. Not for the sake of the dying, but for our own, so we can avoid conversations like this one.

"No. I will not. Will you take me there?"

I nodded, but did not understand.

"Describe your home!" he commanded.

Disoriented by his sharp tone, I almost blurted out, "Ramallah has a lot of hills." But I remembered he was speaking of San Francisco and stopped myself.

Home had always referred to Palestine in our family, the paradise from which we were barred, the place where my ancestors had lived for as many generations back as we could count. But if you stay in a new place long enough, apparently a day comes where an act of alchemy occurs. Enough of your sweat hits its soil, and suddenly you belong to it. It's your home, whether you acknowledge it or not. California was where I had spent my entire adult life, where I bore my children, and where I would likely die. The only way King Tut could ever visit would be if I took him there.

"The streets of San Francisco are steep. You're always either on your way up or your way down," I told him. "It is not an island, but you feel as if it is. At the edges of the city, there are long bridges leading to other shores. Our beaches are not tropical. They are designed to bring out the intellectual in you, to lull you into deep contemplation, as you walk alongside them. There is nothing inviting about the cold waves. You know your place is not among them as you watch them crash and dissolve. We might have emerged from the sea, but we lost our gills long ago. We adapted. We can't return to its depths safely or for long. In the avenues, the houses share walls. They are literally stuck together and painted different colors. So walking down those streets feels like skimming along the edge of a rainbow. The city's skyscrapers are an afterthought, confined to a pocket here or there, which are frankly dwarfed by the dizzying heights and depths of the roller-coaster hills. Even when it is crowded, it is congenial. It's not unheard-of for strangers on the street to greet. The faces of the people come in black, white, yellow, and red. Every shape of eye stares back at you. There is an ivory tower perched on a hill where visitors from every continent congregate. From that tower of Babel, you can see the lights of the entire city, which stretch out to infinity. There is a square named after a Union, of what I am not sure, but it's a welcome spot of green. In winter, you can ice-skate in this place where no snow ever falls, making it a world where there is no danger of thin ice. There is a street with a Spanish name. There are many streets with Spanish names, a reminder that no amount of erasure can wipe out every trace of the people who came before. On Castro Street, you can be who you want to be and love who you wish to love in public. You can't always tell men from women, and you soon stop trying. Since you can't tell a difference, there seems to be no difference. Or rather, none that matters. On that street, you can hold anyone's hand. If anyone sneers at you for doing so, it is they who are in danger. It is they who might get jumped, beaten to death. It is they, who don't mind their own business, who are made to feel afraid."

Or rather, I tried to say all that. But I had not the words. Instead, I picked up a tourist guide of San Francisco I bought on a whim in the airport along with a gift basket of sourdough bread from my husband's company. I had seen the huge, life-sized advertisement of the 49ers quarterback catching one of our loaves, which was featured at the airport's food court. It was still strange, to see your own product in a store and watch customers flock to it. I would never get used to the fact that my husband's choice to buy a bread company, an unusual career path for a Middle Eastern immigrant who studied engineering, had turned out to be such a success. People said everything he touched turned to gold. When they said it, I tried not to think of the story of the Greek king whose golden touch turned out to be a curse.

I showed King Tut pictures of the places I could not describe and he stared at them. My heart ached that my friend was dying, especially because I had killed the friendship I had with Esther.

"Want to try some sourdough bread?" I asked.

"No, but I would like to smell it," he said. I broke the bread in half, so the scent could escape, and held it to his nose.

"What have you been doing in San Francisco for all these years?" It had been at least a decade since I had called him. It was I, lonely and desperate, who had always called King Tut. So, when I stopped reaching out, we lost contact.

"Hanging out with white people," I told him.

"How are your children?" he rasped.

"Fine," I said. Why did I not want to speak of them? Aren't mothers supposed to always want to talk about their children? It was like they had no place in this world where I had belonged before I became their mother.

"Do you remember I stopped wanting to leave my apartment and you talked me into going out again? Well, I met a friend. A Jewish friend. She was a doctor. She still is. A doctor, but we are not friends anymore."

I heard Reginald moving in the next room. I wished he would join us. He wasn't dying. His presence would make me feel less guilty that I wasn't either.

"Why are you no longer friends?"

"Lots of reasons. She has never been to the Middle East. But any Jew anywhere can get citizenship and live in the place where I was born, but I cannot because I was apparently born the wrong religion. She can take a flight anytime and declare herself a citizen. Bang! She is one! Must be nice! To never have seen a place, but have it decided that it's yours. My grandfather still lives in our family home and I'm not allowed to even visit without her people's permission."

"Is that her fault?"

Reginald walked in, bearing me a cup of tea. I was glad to see they still had the same purple teacups that I had drank from countless times before.

"No, but it's her fault she doesn't know more. Ignorance is a privilege. It's a choice. Once, on the radio, folks were talking about what was happening to my people back home. What does she do? She turns to me and says, 'I hate war.' War? What war? What in the world are you talking about? War requires both sides having an army. War requires it being a question of who is going to win."

"Is it not always a question of who will win?" King Tut asked.

"Not when it comes to Palestinians and Israelis."

"How can you say that?" Reginald asked me, aghast.

"Because it's true! And we all know it!" I wanted to say but stopped myself.

"It got too exhausting to be her friend," I told them instead. "I was always trying to outmatch her. She lived in Burlingame. I moved to Atherton. That's the most expensive zip code in California."

I saw Reginald and King Tut exchange glances. I had deliberately never let on how rich we had become. Part of it was because I would never feel truly wealthy or the security that money might bring. Yes, my name was on the deed to a palatial home. But my father's deed to his home and business in Jaffa did him no good. We had been expelled from our country, our place in the world where our roots were much deeper than the fresh, weak ones we had sprouted in America. This was a country that had rounded up its Japanese American citizens, who lost whatever homes and businesses they once had, and none of their kind had even done anything close to killing a Kennedy. Unlike my husband, I believed there would be more political violence on the horizon between Arabs and Americans. I could feel it coming. It was only a matter of time.

I would never trust that my world wouldn't be turned upside down, that racism wouldn't make it so that every generation in my family would have to start over from the bottom and claw our way back to the top. But I also felt the unshakable confidence that comes from living through that experience. We might have to start over, penniless, but we were of the ilk that knew we could.

"I told her I was you, King Tut. I mean, I pretended that I lived your life. I said I graduated as a lawyer from Wayne State. That I worked for the National Association of Advanced Colored People."

"You mean the National Association for the Advancement of Colored People?" Reginald corrected me.

"No. I wish. I got it wrong when I lied to Esther. That's her name. I don't know what's funnier, that I said the name incorrectly or that a highly educated doctor didn't know enough about the Civil Rights Movement to catch my mistake. She once invited me to be a part of a feminist book club. You should have seen these women. Oh, they could quote *The Feminine Mystique*, but they were frightened by Angela Davis. Feminism to them means getting to act like men, to reach their full potential by finding women with less resources to do the grunt work of cooking, cleaning, and childcare. Basically, they are hypocrites. They are so nice to their Mexican maids, and so aware they are being nice. With my daughter, I could compete. Both our girls got into North Star Academy. That's the magnet school for gifted kids in our area. We have sons the same age, too. We decided to get pregnant together again, because what saved our lives in those early years of motherhood was that we could go to the park together on a schedule as if it were a job. My move to California wasn't easy. Before I met her, I had a hard time getting out of the house."

"I remember," King Tut said.

"Her Aaron got into North Star and my Amir didn't. And you know why? At the Jewish community center, they have free tutoring for the admission tests you have to take to get into North Star. And she didn't tell me." I could feel my rambling thoughts coalesce into a rant, but I couldn't stop myself.

"She had been prepping her son for that test for a year. She told me she thought I knew that there were ways you could prepare, books you could buy to help them do it. It was no oversight on her part. We talked about everything. We shared the most intimate details of our marriage, our dreams, our hopes. But the best way to prepare children to take tests that decide their academic futures? The best tutors to hire? The best books to buy for them? This, she keeps to herself. I've stopped returning her calls. I bet she decided to stack the odds against my son, so it might help her son's chances of getting in. 'I thought you knew you could tutor kids for the test,' she says to me! How was I going to know if my supposed friend didn't tell me? If I was a part of her community, she would have. Why? Because it would have been easy to invite me to her community center, a place designed so that people like me and my son are not welcome."

"This seems like an opportunity for you," King Tut told me.

"To make better friends?" I asked.

"No. Do you have a community center?"

"Yes," I said. The Ramallah Club of San Francisco was thriving. We had just bought a banquet hall downtown on Ocean Street.

"Help set up a program to tutor kids there, so Palestinians also have access to the information they need to help their children succeed. So no one in your community will feel like you do now."

To my shame, I knew I didn't give a fig about anyone else in my community. In fact, it would be hard to stomach seeing other Palestinian boys get into North Star if my eldest son could not.

"I will. What a great idea! I'm so glad I came up with it. That's just the kind of idea that someone like me, who worked for an association for Advanced Colored People, might envision."

We laughed.

"I'm sorry. I'm supposed to be here helping you and all I'm doing is talking your ear off."

"I love it," King Tut told me. "Talk my ears off. Please."

I looked him in the eye. He appeared to have more life in him now. The old gleam was back.

Keep me here in the world, his eyes seemed to say. Talk my ears off while I still have access to ears that can listen.

"Why not give this Esther the benefit of the doubt?" Reginald said, to my surprise.

"Fuck that honky!" was more of the response I thought I'd get from him.

"It's too exhausting to be around her, Reginald."

"What is?" King Tut asked me.

"I'm sick to death of competing! Proving she is no better or smarter or more deserving in any way than me and mine!" I wanted to yell, but that was too humiliating. Not that I needed to compete with her, that was a given when it came to a Palestinian and a Jew. I was grieving that when it came to my son in an academic arena against hers, mine had not been able to keep up.

"It's not like either of you have white friends," I said instead.

"No, but we have Arab ones," King Tut said, and I saw the gleam in his eye grow. "Can you imagine what it is like to live in a neighborhood all your life and never be allowed to thrive? To watch your people be blocked from getting home loans or leases to start businesses? Then, you witness others, strangers, waltz in. They are not born here. There is no blood of their ancestors in this soil. They don't even speak the language. But they find loans and leases. They prove what you always knew to be true. There is money to be made here, this neighborhood in which we are confined, but never by us. The only job available to you is to work for them, they who are allowed a full citizenship you are always somehow being denied. The minute those people can afford it, they leave, happily absconding to places that only retain their value if no one who looks like you is ever allowed in. Could you befriend a daughter of those people? Ask her to visit you when you are dying, because you loved her like a sister?"

"I don't know what to say," I said.

King Tut put out his hand. Though it was free of sores, I felt a twinge of fear. I overcame it. His grip was comforting, strong. Then, I reached out and took Reginald's hand.

"Say you'll give this woman the benefit of the doubt. She sounds like she is your friend," King Tut told me quietly, and to my surprise, Reginald nodded. He seemed softer, more uncertain. Reginald was going to be very alone in the world soon. I would have to check in on him from time to time. I could no longer call this apartment as a child—full of problems and concerns—might reach out to their parents for solace and advice. I would have to be an adult, which meant I'd have to take care of the people who had tried to take care of me.

"Hold on to your friends," King Tut told me. He winced and let go of my hand to shakily reach for a bottle of painkillers.

Hold on to your friends. They'll be taken from you soon enough. One way or another.

25

ARABELLA

Ramallah
2012

"It's me!" I sang into the phone when Yoav answered.

"I know!" he sang back. "Thanks to the wonders of caller ID. How's the melody?"

"Fantastic. Everything is fantastic. Yoav, I have so much to tell you. I decided I wanted to have a woman play the role of Hamlet. Not just because all roles—male and female—in Shakespeare's time were played by men. It's about more than me thumbing my nose at patriarchy, though—of course—some audience members will take it that way."

"Of course."

"And we will let them. But is that the only way to interpret it?"

"When Arabella is at the helm? I think not," he said.

God, I missed him. Because I was still smarting from his telling me we were just friends, I never would have dared to reach out to him if I wasn't dripping another man's seed from me, a man who actually wanted me. Yes, primarily so I could bear and raise uber-Palestinian children with him. But it was something. It was a shit ton more than I had back in New York.

"I've always had a lingering question about *Hamlet*, Yoav. If Hamlet's father is king and Hamlet a young prince, why doesn't he inherit the throne immediately upon the king's death? It's never fully explained in the play."

"Good point," Yoav said.

"Throughout history, plenty of young women passed as boys. Presenting as male is a way to be safe. Cross-dressing is at the heart of *Twelfth Night*. It's all over the tales of *One Thousand and One Nights*. In England in the time of Shakespeare, it might have been a way to stay alive. Failing to procure a male heir is what got Queen Elizabeth's mother beheaded. It must have been tempting for a royal mother, the possibility of pretending a princess she bore was a prince. If a girl was secretly raised as a boy in a royal household, who would know it?"

"Only the family's inner circle, including Uncle Claudius, who takes advantage and crowns himself king?" Yoav answered.

I let out a sigh. It felt like a breath I had been holding for a long time. Oh, the joy of being understood!

Yoav got that I wasn't just casting a woman in a man's role. I was suggesting it might never have been a man's role in the first place.

"Is the idea so far-fetched, Yoav?"

"Yes and no. For fuck's sake, there were female popes in Rome that people didn't even realize weren't men."

"Exactly. And I found this amazing chick to play the lead. She's never been onstage before, but she's electric. Her name is Cherifa. She's from Jenin."

"Jenin? What's that?" he asked.

With those words, the gulf between us seemed to widen. We were no longer separated by an ocean. We were on different planets.

The Jenin refugee camp was the site of some of the most intense fighting during the second intifada. To not have heard of Jenin or what happened there meant you must not have followed international news during the entire popular uprising. He didn't know what had been done in the name of protecting his people, in his name. He had not been inclined to learn. In all the years I had known him, I had never probed Yoav about his politics regarding the Israeli-Palestinian conflict. I knew it would be too easy for one of us to say something that the other found unforgivable. My relationship with Yoav meant the world to me, professionally as well as personally, and I had been too cowardly to risk losing it. I had assumed our opinions about the conflict between our peoples would differ. But it had never occurred to me that Yoav wasn't closely clocking what took place in the land our parents left behind. I wished I had that wondrous privilege, which comes with being born on the winning side.

What had Yoav been doing during those days of the siege on Jenin when I was dodging emails requesting donations for the injured and orphaned, too frightened I would be accused of supporting terrorism to donate a dollar? Reading Rilke? Voltaire? I envied him.

My joy at being able to talk through a show concept with him evaporated. I didn't want to take him with me on the trip I made to the camp, to conjure up the children playing in the squalor of streets ravaged by war. When Palestinians speak of the steadfastness and tough character of the refugees who settled in Jenin, we often say it took less than a week for the Israeli Defense Forces to destroy the armies of Egypt, Syria, and Jordan in the Six-Day War in '67, but it took them a whole ten days to be able to fully infiltrate and gain control of this one refugee camp in 2002. Jenin was forever being bombed, bulldozed, rebuilt. You could feel it as you passed walls full of bullet holes, the remnants of incursions past and present, and the skeletons of destroyed homes in the process of being reconstructed. Again. The streets were teeming with children in every alley and square. They wore Western clothes faded from too many washings. The hair of the girls, too young to wear hijabs, were tightly braided in the way my mother had done to mine for years.

They had mothers determined to show the world that their girls were groomed, cared for, loved. Like me.

"Arabella, are you there?" Yoav asked.

"Yeah, sorry. Jenin is a city in the West Bank. There is a refugee camp in it."

It suddenly felt weird that I was naked while talking to Yoav. I began to slip on my clothes.

"I went there because Cherifa asked me to meet with her father."

I decided not to explain that, though Jenin had a wonderful theatre company in the heart of the camp, it was still frowned upon in some refugee circles for women to be onstage. I wanted to pretend every Palestinian woman had come from a family as sophisticated as mine, every one of us had as liberal a father. Should I tell him of the demand Cherifa had made of me when I approached her after the meeting of Al-Sittat Al-Hazana, babbling about how much star quality she exuded and offering her a part in my show?

"I'll only act in your play if you get *Yaba*'s approval. He had a heart attack after I went to jail and I don't want to add stress into his life right now," Cherifa had told me "It shouldn't be hard to convince him. Just tell him probably no one from the camp will marry me now anyway."

"Why not?" I asked her.

"It is assumed I've been used, because I've been in prison. So, I hardly see how performing Shakespeare could damage my marital opportunities more than they already are. Everyone admires a woman activist, but few men want to marry her."

Her young, dark eyes bored into mine. Defiant, but also hurt. She offered to meet me at the main Ramallah taxi stand the next day and accompany me through the checkpoints that led to Jenin.

"So, I went to visit Cherifa's family," I told Yoav. "Waiting for me there were her father and six elders of her clan. They were in their sixties and seventies. One was in his eighties. They reminded me so much of my dead great-grandfather. Maybe it's because I am staying in his house now, but I missed him terribly when I saw those men. My eyes teared up at the sight of them, which is weird. It's not like I even knew my great-grandfather well."

"I get it," Yoav said.

But I wasn't sure he did. Or could. None of the women in my family had anything good to say about the man. It was said he mourned the birth of each daughter, refusing to be congratulated. I was the daughter of his daughter's daughter, the member of his clan he probably valued least. He was obsessed with having sons and did more than most men might dare to have them.

"By all accounts, my great-grandfather was a dick. My grandmother told me people back in our village used to call him Henry the Eighth to mock him because he changed Christian sects in order to divorce his first wife and marry my great-grandmother, because the first wife couldn't bear him a son."

"Damn," Yoav said. "I didn't know you came from royalty."

"I'm full of surprises, Yoav. Meeting those men was like coming face-to-face not with one ghost, but with the ghosts of my great-grandfather at different stages of his life. I thought if Shakespeare wants the audience to buy that a character is being haunted by a dead parent, let me show how a real haunting feels. The ghost of the father isn't going to be played by one actor. It's going to be played by seven village elders!"

"Fuck yeah, it is!"

And then we were on the same planet again. Or rather we were meeting somewhere in between, where stars twinkle and comets streak by, in the vast and glorious space where people from different worlds come together when they speak about art.

"In this show, they're going to hound Hamleta's ass. They're going to appear everywhere. Onstage. In the audience. They're going to show up as dear ole Dad at various ages, different stages of vigor. They're going to speak in a chorus. They're going to drive her fucking insane."

"I love it, Arabella. How did you get them all to agree to be in the cast?"

"I have my ways," I wanted to play the coquette and say. But I thankfully stopped myself.

"I flattered them," I told him instead. "When I asked them to be in the play, to stand onstage alongside their brave and beautiful girl, I told them they were embodying a patriarch who was wronged. That didn't work. Then, I told them they reminded me of Omar Sharif. Every one of them, even an ugly one with bug eyes and a face not even a mother could love, believed me."

"Of course they did. We men are very easy."

No, you're not. Or maybe you are. Maybe Yoav had always made it easy to figure out he only saw me as a friend, but I chose not to believe it. I refused to accept it.

"It's fucking fantastic that all seven said yes to you!" he said.

I recalled the vulnerability in the eyes of those men when they nodded in unison. It felt as if they had been waiting all their lives to be asked to stand center stage, like they were expecting a strange woman from afar to show up at their door and ask them to play her ghosts.

"Yes, it's pretty fucking fantastic."

"I want in. Need a sound designer?"

No, no, no! I need a whole lot more, Buddy. I'd like a lover. I require a baby daddy. I have to create a life with more in it than theatre and men who make it clear we are only friends.

"The pay is shit, Yoav."

"Did I ask about the pay? I want to work on your show. I'm a little done with New York right now."

"One can never be done with New York."

"Yeah, you can. My mom reached out to me recently, by the way. She has cancer."

What a relief she had told him! I would be furious if someone knew my mother was dying and didn't tell me. But how could I have said anything to him without revealing that I had stalked her? And pretended to be—of all things—a Jewish girl?

"I'm so sorry, Yoav."

"Yeah, it sucks. I took her as my date to the Tonys. She liked that. I was very happy to have been able to give her that. She always wanted a life of glamour. She expected it."

I know, I wanted to say. She told me.

"Shouldn't you stay in New York at the moment? To, you know, help take care of her?"

"We've kind of said our goodbyes."

"Really?" I asked. What kind of guy says "peace out" to his dying mom and heads off into the sunset? This was not a Yoav I recognized. Or one I was sure I particularly liked. It felt lawless to be so free. There is a reason why humans need duties, affiliations, obligations. Isn't there?

"Arabella, I'm her great disappointment. I used to like to compose music as a kid and won a few awards. She was sure I was going to become the next Mozart. She stopped speaking to me for a year when I gave it up. I was fourteen. She thinks being a sound designer is beneath me. She said that if I had to work in the theatre, I should be an actor since they get more money and more attention. She tells me this on the night I win the Tony."

Ouch. Nevertheless, the woman didn't deserve to die alone.

"My mom is a pill, too. And a compulsive liar. But I'd drop everything if she needed me."

I could barely stand to visit San Francisco for the required trilogy of pilgrimages I took for Easter, Thanksgiving, and Christmas every year. But I dragged my ass there nevertheless. I did what was expected of me. Yoav was the most unfettered person I knew. He didn't feel compelled to give out the obligatory thank-you cards to the cast or stay for toasts at the end of a run. So, why was I freaking the fuck out about Yoav being footloose and fancy-free when it came to his mother? Outraged by his "abandonment" of her as if it had anything to do with me?

I couldn't forget the oft-quoted Arabic saying I heard all my life, uttered mainly to console unhappy women who ended up married to mama's boys, but still with a ring of truth to it.

Al-zalamey b'amel mara'tey zay b'amel oum'ay.

How a man treats his mother is how he'll treat his wife. Our lovers become our children and parents in turn. A man's relationship with his mother will be the model for how he will relate to you, when he inevitably transfers the same feelings of attachment and responsibility—along with the resentment of the inescapable obligations that come with them—onto you.

"We are not the kind of family who hold each other's hands. I was planning to take a year off, do a bit of traveling," Yoav said.

"Right after you win the Tony? Aren't the job offers pouring in?"

"Yeah, but nothing of interest. A couple of musical revivals with reality stars. Brock offered me a gig on his next show, too."

Brock, my old friend who had been invited to direct *Footprints in the Promised Land* at the Public probably without ever having stepped foot here. Instead of me.

"Not the one about Mexicans with no Mexicans on the creative team?" I could hear the sneer in my voice.

I had read on Playbill.com that Brock was directing a play about Mexicans in detention who had been caught trying to cross the border. Brock went from directing plays about the plight of Palestinians to plays about Mexicans trying to find a better life on the land that had once been part of their country, that some might say had been stolen from them. More misery porn written and directed by white men for white audiences. In it, never are we characters who are brilliant, sophisticated, or even particularly complex. Never did we ever have even a semblance of a sense of humor.

"The very same. Yep. It's the same old Broadway bullshit," Yoav scoffed.

"Take one of those gigs, Yoav. Any of them. I'd give my eyeteeth to work on Broadway. Even after I find out what eyeteeth actually means."

"You won't when you do. It's the teeth in your upper jaw. You'll want to hang on to those, Arabella. Working on Broadway means you have a slightly bigger stage on a particular street. It's not Olympus. You'll see."

But I didn't believe I would. Barring a miracle, I would never get to Broadway and I was at the stage in my career where I had to reckon with that reality. Yoav didn't care about working on the Great White Way and he ended up there. I cared more than I should and I found myself a world away.

Did my naked need for more career opportunities, my laser-like focus and intensity, make it somehow harder for me to get them? Or did it make sense that a Jewish man would have an easier time making inroads in American theatre than a Palestinian woman? Was Yoav really the most talented sound designer in America? Did he deserve the success he so easily acquired, that he waltzed in and took, as if it were his birthright?

For fuck's sake, Arabella, I cajoled myself. How can you resent his success? He's your friend. Plus, we weren't even in competition for the same jobs. The boy is a designer. You're a director. Sure, he made it clear he had only wanted to be friends and that had hurt my pride, but a true friend he was. A true friend he had always been.

"Anyway, I was planning to visit Vietnam, but Vietnam will still be there," Yoav said.

"Will it, though? How can we be sure any country will always be there?"

He took that question in characteristic stride.

"We can't. But, if it is, I can head there later this year. Your show sounds incredible. I want in."

You want in? Really, dude?

"But Broadway is calling."

"Fuck Broadway! I would be excited to work on your show. And I'm only taking work I'm excited to do."

"That ain't no way to build a career in the theatre. Or any field."

"You sound like my mom."

I thought of his mother, sitting in a department store café. Beautiful, elegant, dying. And telling me that people should stick to their own kind when she thought I was one of hers.

"Sorry," I muttered. "Anyway, who am I to give advice? My career is in the shithole."

"You're doing just fine, Arabella. Better than fine."

I realized it was true. I was about to make a show that stretched me as an artist, that required all my imaginative powers to be firing on all cylinders. Sure, the show would be performed as far away from the bright lights of Times Square as could be, but I wasn't sorry I was making it. And I only could make it because all my choices as an artist and a person—conscious and unconscious—had led me here.

For the first time in a long time, I felt I was exactly in the right place.

"So, do you need a sound designer?"

Damn, he was relentless. I toyed with pretending I was worried about his safety as a Jewish hipster from Brooklyn in the heart of the most Palestinian of cities, though I wasn't. I knew there was always a sizable smattering of young liberal Jewish American activists volunteering all over Ramallah, particularly from a group called Jewish Voice for Peace. If I knew it, chances were he did, too.

The truth was I was worried for me.

Working side by side with Yoav again, close enough to touch each other though we never did, was the last thing I needed. It would confuse me and I had spent my entire adult life being confused about whether we might have a future together. I was trying to move on. Move forward. Move.

"Yoav, you've got to capitalize on this moment. You need to take another gig on Broadway."

"No, I don't."

His petulant tone made my back arch. I felt like smacking him upside the head. If he disappeared from the Broadway scene now, it would make the Tony win of a downtown designer seem like a fluke. Why was he insisting upon shooting himself in the foot? Didn't he understand that he had to seize this moment?

"Do it. For me."

His silence on the line made it clear he did not want to. Nor would he. At least, not for me.

"Um, Arabella? My mom thinks she ran into you, um, in Bloomingdale's. She's mistaken, right?"

The sudden knock on the door startled me.

"*Meen?*" I asked.

"It's me," Aziz answered from behind the door. "I forgot my key."

26

NAYA

Atherton

2000

I was my most attractive the year I turned forty. A woman that age is a rose in full bloom with all her layers unfurled and the once-hidden folds within her shamelessly on display. For the first time, she is nourished enough to stretch out, open, expand.

I went to Kepler's Books to pick up a cookbook. I expected to leave unchanged. I was wrong. I met Duong.

I had recently joined a new book group. I liked my new book group. Perhaps a better way to say it is that I lived for it. The white women of Silicon Valley and I, who had somehow landed in their midst, aimed to be worldly in our book choices. We read novels in translation from other countries. Each brought a dish from that region's cuisine. None of those women would become dear friends like King Tut, who had slipped from this world soon after I visited. Nor did they approximate Esther in warmth or intelligence, the woman I had ejected from my life whose calls I ignored until she stopped making them.

The white women of Silicon Valley welcomed me into their fold. My neighbor Marie invited me to my first meeting.

"Her husband owns Dough!" Marie announced about me.

"I love your bread!" they exclaimed.

"I'll bring you all some," I told them, and they brightened as if they'd won the lottery. These obscenely wealthy women seemed overjoyed to receive a free loaf. Several of them presented me with jams they had made or vegetables from their gardens at our next meeting. It touched me deeply, these gestures of reciprocity. Why had I expected they would only want to take from me?

Just as I had adopted the Afro during the sixties in Detroit, I found myself straightening and lightening my locks at the Palo Alto salon these women frequented. Wearing the wildly expensive designers they did felt like a form of camouflage. I might blend in if I dressed like the rest. So, if the American government tried to round up Arabs as they once had their Japanese citizens, might one of my neighbors come to our defense? To proclaim Naya and her family are just like us?

Sometimes, when we sat for a meal around their dining tables, they appeared as if they were one monster with many heads. I watched their gestures, the way they smiled and sipped and swallowed. It was fascinating to see them smudge their lipstick on coffee cups and dirty the linen with their used forks, shiny with spit.

Eating was as much a part of our book group as reading. The women searched for recipes on the internet. I liked actual cookbooks. Browsing the web seemed like no way to discover a cuisine. You can't seek a recipe for something you don't know exists.

When it was my turn to suggest a novel, I would always call Arabella and ask her what to pick. I was not confident enough to recommend a book, or speak my thoughts about the ones they chose, lest I reveal I did not finish high school.

"I'm in rehearsal. I don't know why you make this my job?! Pick a book from the bestseller list!" she always seemed to snap, then hang up rudely. But within an hour, she texted me a book to recommend and what I should say about why I wanted to read it.

When one lady lazily asked me, "Why don't you ever suggest a book from the Arab world, Naya?" I excused myself and called Arabella, frantic, from her palatial bathroom.

"They want me to recommend Arabic books."

"Okay. Whatever. How about *The Cairo Trilogy* by Naguib Mahfouz, Mom?"

"Who is that?"

"An Egyptian writer. I was asked to adapt it into a play."

"How lovely!"

"Not! I didn't take the job. The only reason the white producers asked me is because they were looking for an Arab to work on it."

"Who cares why they asked you? The important thing is that they asked you. You always complain no one hires you."

"I don't adapt novels into plays," Arabella snapped. "I direct postmodern interpretations of Shakespeare."

It was no wonder the girl had few friends. I became aware I was taking too long in the bathroom and so tried to hurry the call.

"And why should I tell them we must read this Naguib?"

"He's a Nobel Prize winner, Mom. Gotta go!" Arabella said, and hung up.

They looked at me funny when I emerged from the bathroom and recommended it. I did not know at the time that a trilogy meant three books. But they agreed to read it for our next meeting.

They all brought *ful medames*, the dish you'll find first if you ask Google the most popular Egyptian food. They didn't know it was street food for poor people, the cultural equivalent of bringing Spam as a representative of American cuisine. As we had nothing but their fava beans to eat alongside my *macarona bechamel*, I realized how little effort they put into selecting which dish to make. They blindly bought into whatever came up first on their search engines, especially about other cultures. Why was I so judgmental? These were women who were looking for windows into other worlds. They read three Egyptian books because I suggested them. Maybe their lives were fuller than mine. I had nothing to do most days except read the assigned book, and plan my dish and my outfit for our next meeting. So, I had time to go to bookstores.

"Hello, Beautiful!" the young Asian man behind the counter at Kepler's Books greeted me. He was more lanky than tall, but with such symmetrical features, gleaming dark hair, and shining ebony eyes that I was knocked breathless when our eyes met.

"*Itkuneesh hebla!*" I heard my mother hiss. Don't be a fool.

There were a thousand ways to be a fool but the surest one was to believe a compliment. No one wished you well. No one said anything nice for free. Everyone is a salesman, even if all they want you to buy is a worldview in which they are nice people whom it would behoove you to keep around.

When people complimented her, my mother would scoff.

"Never believe praise, especially from pretty people," she told me. "Because they receive adulation for their looks, they believe that's the way everyone speaks to everyone. They think it's normal."

I smiled, regarded the young man closely, and chose not to believe him. Nor did I speak to him. I was no *hebla*. I turned and walked out of the bookstore.

But I was glad for every exorbitantly priced face cream I bought and that I went to bed hungry every night. Atherton was a hothouse of delicate flowery women trying to keep their wealthy husbands. Though I had no doubts about Daoud's loyalty, I had not let myself go.

I went back to the bookstore the next day. I wore a monochrome red pantsuit that hugged my slim frame well and got my hair done for the occasion. In fact, I went to the bookstore straight from the salon. My black and gray roots were barely peeking out, but I dyed them back into oblivion with the honey-blond color that had been my signature style for years. Esther was the only woman I knew who wore her hair natural, her curly halo had gone prematurely gray but turned a white so pure it looked platinum.

"Hello, Beautiful!" the young man greeted me again, but this time I was ready for him.

"Hello, Handsome!" I forced my lips to form my much-rehearsed answer. Now it was his turn to be taken aback. Did he assume I was the type of woman who would never respond to him because I hadn't the first time?

"I'm on the hunt," I said. "For a cookbook."

"What kind of cuisine?"

"Chinese," I told him, because that was what I believed him to be.

"Follow me," he said, and led me to the cookbook section.

"Where are you from?"

He stiffened.

"San Jose," he said evenly.

He was annoyed by my question, the kind I only found invasive when white people asked me. Had he mistaken me for a white woman with a tan? That was the look I was usually going for. If so, I had to signal I was not what I seemed.

"I'm from Palestine," I told him. "I came on a refugee boat."

The cloud lifted, as I suspected it would. He smiled, revealing glorious strong, white teeth.

"I'm from Vietnam," he said. "My family are refugees, too. We came when I was four."

"What's your name?" I asked.

"Duong."

"Does it have a meaning?"

He paused a moment before answering. God, he was lovely.

"It means virility," he said.

Of course it did. Again, I was treated to the sight of his smile. He slipped out a Chinese cookbook from the shelf and gave it to me. We headed to the register. As I handed him my credit card, I noticed him glance at my huge diamond ring, flashing lasers of fractured light.

"Chinese food is great. But, if you ever want to try Vietnamese food, maybe you should come to my place."

I blushed, kept my eyes down, and left the bookstore.

I initiated sex with my husband that night. Daoud was pleased. When I wanted sex, I would put on a pretty nightgown. That's as far as I'd go. If he ignored that signal, I went to sleep. That night, he took me in a new position, a surprise. If it weren't for a Harrison Ford movie we once rented from Blockbuster, I wouldn't have known beforehand that a man and woman could have sex without facing each other. Or that one might enjoy it that way as much as I did. Our house was empty. Our daughter was a world away in New York. Our boys were gone, too, married off to young women we introduced to them. They lived in nearby houses, and they worked in the business Daoud built for them. I allowed myself to be loud, unrestrained. We both slept soundly and woke up cheerful. It had been several weeks since Daoud and I had made love. Or was it months?

At the next book group meeting, I made my first suggestion without Arabella's input. I didn't need it because since I had met Duong, I'd been reading everything I could about Vietnamese culture on the web. You could say I considered myself a bit of an expert.

"We need to read Bao Ninh's *The Sorrow of War*," I announced.

"I haven't heard of it," said Jill. She was the wife of a retired general. The elder in our group at sixty, she had the feline eyes of a woman who has had too many facelifts, on a head that was too big for her skeletally thin frame.

To say you haven't heard of a book in our group was not to admit ignorance, but to dismiss it as something not worth knowing. Gritting my teeth, I forced a smile. The other women were married to men who made computers or software of some sort. I was slightly uncomfortable around all those women, but I actively disliked the general's wife. Her husband sat on the board of an arms manufacturer. He had served in the war in Iraq. How much blood of innocents was on his hands? Did the blood transfer to the wife who held that hand? Or to me, who broke bread with her?

"*The Sorrow of War* is considered one of the greatest war novels of all time, Jill. Given the disastrous role America played in Vietnam, I think the least we can do is read a story of how our destructive and shortsighted foreign policy impacted the people of that country."

I had never spoken so much to them at one time. I was quoting what I'd read on the web word for word, but saying the sentiments out loud made me feel like they were mine.

The mouths of the many-headed monster were shocked into silence. I was triumphant. We would read *The Sorrow of War* next.

I now had an excuse to return to Kepler's Books. Maybe I would tell that beautiful man I wanted to go to his place, to try Vietnamese food. Maybe I was ready to accept his invitation. It was not because I was a lascivious, immoral, disloyal creature that I would go. I was simply learning to make a dish for my next book group meeting. Who could fault me for that?

When I got home from the book group meeting, Daoud was sitting on the couch, his hands folded in his lap, his head bowed. He didn't look up when I approached him.

"What's wrong?" I asked.

When I saw he couldn't speak, my mind jumped to my worst fear. Which of my children had died? If it was Arabella, all alone in New York, had she been raped first?

"What happened?!" I cried out.

"Nothing. Nothing," he said. "I had an affair."

The relief made me start to laugh uncontrollably.

The whole sordid story came out. He had slept with an auditor who had been assigned to our company. She had opened our books, and seeing how much his company was worth undoubtedly inspired her to open her legs to my aging husband with a tiny pot belly and thinning hair. They had been carrying on an affair for two years. Now she was pregnant. I understood he was confessing because he wanted her out of his life. Our life. I married a man who didn't know how to make that happen. I married a man who wanted me to clean up his mess. And I would.

"Tell her to meet you at your office tonight."

When she arrived, I was there, too. Daoud sat in his office chair and didn't say a word. She was a pretty young Dolly Parton, all hair and makeup, the theatrics of femininity that are easy to strip away. All you need is a hose. I introduced myself. She tried to leave. I told her she'd want to hear what I had to say.

"You will not destroy our family," I began.

"I'm pregnant. What about my child? I'm part of Day-oud's family, too."

I laughed in her face. She couldn't even pronounce his name. I glanced at Daoud, who seemed to shrink into himself. This was going to be easier than I thought. It's too bad I never actually practiced law. I would have been a force to reckon with. I would never have known that about myself had I not been tested.

"My husband will pay you child support, but not as much as you think. You're an accountant, aren't you? Why don't you tally up how much you'll make in child support if we decide to expand our business?

If we pay for an entire new factory to be opened in the Midwest? Or blow all our profits on advertising? We can reinvest every dime of profit back in the business. You'll get practically nothing."

"I don't care about money," she said, but she wasn't convincing.

"Give me a number. My husband will never speak to you again. He will never speak to your child. Add up how much we'll pay you in minimal child support for eighteen years. We'll pay you that to get an abortion and go away. Name your price."

She looked at Daoud. He still said nothing.

"Two hundred thousand," she finally told me. "Cash."

We would have paid thrice that. Maybe more. I was lucky the young woman believed me, but I had been bluffing. If she had borne a child, there was no way Daoud would ignore its existence. He was too good a man. Fool.

When we returned home, I made Daoud take out the bricks of cash we kept on hand in the freezer, as many Palestinians do. I would replace the bricks as soon as I could just in case. It was only a matter of time before we'd have to be on the run again. When that day came, I didn't want to be wishing I still had the cold, hard cash I gave to my husband's mistress to abort their child. I made him count and pack the money in a suitcase I dropped at his feet.

"Now you know there is no such thing as free love," I told him. "Old Hippy."

He winced.

That night, I reached out and called my mother in the wing of our house where Daoud wouldn't hear me. I had never called her before with problems or seeking advice. I deliberately only dialed her number to relay news like "my mother-in-law died" and "this is the date of the graduation party we are planning in case you'd like to attend."

That night, I needed to speak to her as a fellow woman. There were very few I knew who wouldn't sneer at me. I couldn't even trust my sisters to not secretly rejoice my marriage wasn't as perfect as it seemed or to not spread gossip that would ruin the respectability of our family. I still had Arabella to marry off.

If Esther were in my life, I would have called her instead. Long after we stopped speaking, she still swam in the undercurrents of my every thought. I was always imagining Esther might say this. She might recommend I do that. She would help me understand myself.

In the end, the woman I had relied on first was the only one I had left.

"Daoud has faltered," I told my mother. She immediately understood what I meant.

"Is she gone?"

"Yes," I said.

"Do you think it will happen again?"

"No."

"Then you have no problem. Marriage is like driving on a long road. When one falters, it is as if they soil themselves on that road. What do you do if someone soils themselves, *ya Bint*?"

My girl.

"I don't know, *Yema*."

"Yes, you do. You give them a chance to clean up."

"Why are men allowed such things?"

"It's not only men, *ya Bint*."

She left it at that, and I did not probe further. But something about our exchange freed me. I decided I would accept that young man's invitation and not lie to myself about why I did so, what I wanted. I was going to soil myself and I was going to love it.

I arrived at the bookstore in a white summer dress and tan sandals with heels too high for anything but seduction. I remembered how Duong stared at my ring, so I decided to go to him dripping in my diamonds, their sparkle encircling my neck and snaking around both of my wrists. Vulgar. Shining. Expensive. He was behind the counter.

"Hello, Beautiful!"

"Hello, Handsome! I'm in the mood for Vietnamese food. Is the invitation to come to your place still open?"

"Of course!" he said. He smiled, but his eyes were calculating.

"How about tonight?"

"Tonight? Sure. I'll call my mother. She's an amazing cook. She is hoping to get into catering. We had a restaurant in San Jose, but lost our lease. I'll have her make some dishes. If you like them, maybe you can order from her when you have a party. Or recommend her to your friends."

It took him a moment to register the expression on my face, the shock I could not fully hide.

"She really is a good cook."

"I'll take your word for it." I pulled out a hundred-dollar bill. Then I pulled out two more. "Have her make her favorite dish for my book group. It's this Friday."

I put the money in his hand roughly. If I could've taken off my diamonds and flung them in his face, I would have. I wanted to.

"That's a lot of money," he said.

"It's nothing."

"How should I get the food to you?"

"I can pick it up from here."

"On Friday? Maybe before my ten a.m. shift?"

"Right. Before your shift," I said. I needed to escape from him. A sob was bubbling within me. The door was too far away. It would erupt before I made it out. I ducked behind a shelf, bit my fist to keep from making a sound. Where were our famous California earthquakes when you needed one? I wanted the shelves to fold in on me, the books to strike me like stones. I needed the ceiling to collapse. I needed to call Esther.

"You were right to think what you did. He was absolutely flirting. He called you beautiful," she'd say.

"Maybe he was just being pleasant," I would protest.

"No one is that pleasant. That young buck knew exactly what he was doing."

Esther would have helped me process this experience in a way that would transform it from tragic to comic. We would have been able to laugh about it together. But I could not call her. Not yet.

No, I endured that humiliation without laughter. I endured it alone.

While I was still hidden behind the shelf, the door opened and someone else walked in.

"Hello, Beautiful!" Duong greeted the new customer. I forced myself not to peek at whom else he had addressed that way. If it was an old lady, I would scream.

A woman of forty is a flower fully unfurled. It's also the instant before she starts to wilt.

27

ARABELLA

Ramallah

2012

They say that the distinction between a human and our closest cousin, the chimpanzee, is that we know how to lie. I needed to give an answer to Yoav that sounded probable. I also needed to unlock the door and let Aziz in.

"I don't shop at Bloomingdale's. I'm a Barneys kind of girl," I told Yoav as I opened the door.

I heard Yoav chuckle, but it sounded forced.

Aziz stood in the doorway carrying plastic bags full of food. I pointed to the phone on my ear and mouthed the word "work." He nodded and entered silently, carrying containers of seafood kebab and tabouleh. The unwelcome smell of fish made my stomach turn.

"I told my mother she was mistaken," Yoav said. "Apparently, she has learned the wonders of Google and was sure she recognized you from photos on *Playbill*."

I thought of the many Obie Awards and opening-night industry photos of us that were on the *Playbill* site. She had probably landed on my favorite. Yoav and I had posed for a picture with his arm around me, both of us wearing shit-eating grins. We'd just opened a show that was going to go down in theatrical history. Or so we clearly believed that night.

"That's funny," I said. Aziz placed the food on the table and settled into a chair. I sat in his lap. Perhaps it was more accurate to say I collapsed. He slid his long arms around me.

I was being held. I was safe. It felt like every cell of my body rejoiced. I was not someone who could plan for a lifetime, but I decided I would venture into my future one step at a time. He wanted children. I wanted a child. We would have at least one together. This man was real in a way that the man on the phone had never been to me. The man on the phone never wanted me.

With one ear pressed against Aziz's chest, close enough to hear his heartbeat, I said into the phone I had pressed to the other, "It's very generous of you to offer to work on my show. But it's kind of a Palestinian thing. I wouldn't feel right giving the opportunity to someone outside our community."

There is a moment of silence when one person hears an unexpected answer to a question. The brain is startled and the time it normally takes to process a response is extended. It's usually a crossroads, a moment of choice. Engage or withdraw. Fight or yield. Bring forth life or kill it. In theatre, we call that moment a pregnant pause.

The pause between Yoav and me in that moment was as pregnant as they come.

"I get that," he said finally. "Break a leg, Arabella."

"Thank you. Enjoy your trip to Thailand."

"It's Vietnam," I caught him saying before I hung up the phone.

"Hi," I said to Aziz, still resting in his embrace.

"Hi," he said with a smile, and tightened his grip around me. We fell silent. We'd had our first fight. But we'd also made love for the first time without protection. We were feeling the weight of both things.

Aziz's stomach growled and we laughed.

"You really are hungry," I said.

"I really am."

I picked up a skewer of shrimp, slid one off its stick, and held it up by the tail, offering it to him. Pleased, he bit in.

"Very fancy. No shawarma sandwiches from the corner shop for us."

"I'm a pescatarian," he said.

"Really?" Guess we weren't going to steakhouses together. That was a shame.

"Yes. You might give up meat if you saw how it was processed, Arabella."

Or I might not, I wanted to say.

Instead, I spooned out tabouleh into two plates and felt annoyed with myself. Why was I serving him? I grabbed a plate and dug in. The tang of lemon juice was welcome in my mouth. It was clearly freshly chopped, the diced tomatoes shining like rubies in a sea of minced parsley.

"Would you mind chewing with your mouth closed?" Aziz asked me.

I looked at him. Was this motherlover serious? Yes, he was. And was he the slightest bit embarrassed to make such a request of a lady? No, he was not.

My tongue itched to utter the worst Arabic curse I knew. It was worse than all the lesser curses, like damn the woman who bore you. Damn the man who spurted the sperm that made you. Damn your religion. Damn your God!

Kus oumuck trumped them all. Cunt of your mother. Not "May the cunt of your mother be stricken with a terrible itch" or "I hope the cunt of your mother becomes riddled with sores," which might have made sense. Nope. Just the words themselves. Merely mentioning it was the ultimate insult.

"Sure," I said instead, and pushed my plate away. Had I really been chewing with my mouth open? Had I always done so? Some comments, even innocent ones, embed in your consciousness. Some criticism sticks and gives you newfound ways, shorthand language, to question your-self. Early in my career, a self-appointed critic wrote in his blog that my work was "convoluted and overwrought." I never produced another play without, at some point, asking myself, "Is this show I'm making convoluted and overwrought? Am I?"

Was I uncouth? Did I have bad table manners? Had I never known it, because no one cared enough to tell me? Is that why no one in New York would hire me anymore? Why I couldn't keep a boyfriend? Why Yoav wanted to be nothing more than friends?

As if he could read my thoughts, as if on cue, Aziz finally asked the question I'd been dreading since he knocked on the door.

"Who was that guy on the phone?" he asked. Our eyes met.

Who was Yoav to me?

"Just some Jew," I said in as dismissive a voice as I could muster. If you can feel your humanity shrink, your life span shorten, or the arteries of your heart start to harden, I felt all three in that moment.

Aziz raised an eyebrow, an admonishment on his lips. Sophisticated Palestinians never spoke disparagingly of Jews, not even in private, not even among ourselves. We prided ourselves on being better than that. We were not the ones who had a problem with people of different religions. Our struggle was for equality for ourselves, not the degradation of others. All we had was the moral high ground, and, if we lost it, we would have nothing. Aziz, the man whom I had wanted to impress by distancing myself from the man I yearned for, was disgusted with me.

I felt a wave of nausea overcome me.

"Are you okay?" Aziz asked as I ran to the bathroom and lifted the toilet seat. My hands felt the unwelcome moisture that could only mean one thing when you touched a toilet you shared with a man. Repulsed, I retched and retched. Nothing came forward. Whatever was inside would stay. No relief.

I stumbled to the sink, scrubbing my hands over and over with the sense that, when you touch filth, you absorb it. You can't ever get clean again.

28

NAYA

San Mateo
2012

Esther held my forehead up as I vomited in a Starbucks bathroom at the Hillsdale Shopping Center, where we had agreed to meet for coffee. She'd followed me into the bathroom when she saw I was going to be sick. It was good she did so. I felt myself go faint with the last convulsion, like I was about to pass out from the pain. She then helped me stand. Seeing I was still unsteady on my feet, she put soap in her own hands and washed mine, one at a time, between hers.

"Sorry," I said when I noticed a speck of my filth had landed on her New Balance sneakers.

"For what? For having cancer?"

"No, Esther. I'm sorry for refusing to talk to you until I did."

Our eyes met. It was the first time we had seen each other in nearly twenty years. She had aged beautifully. I got a flash of foresight, an image of her at age ninety with pronounced laugh lines around her blue eyes, surrounded by her children and her grandchildren. She was going to live a long life. Though I knew I was not, I was glad for her. I was proud of myself for being able to feel happy for someone else for having something I didn't.

There were no paper towels so I wet a bit of toilet paper and dabbed at her shoe.

"Don't worry about it. I'll throw them in the wash when I get home."

"Can I take you shopping?" I offered. Let me make the story of our reuniting end happily, with something new I gave you, rather than my soiling what you already had.

"No. You know I don't care about shoes."

She had always been so unlike other women in that way. Is that what happens when you make it in a profession like medicine? You don't feel the need to be ornamental. We sat down, not bothering to order anything.

"So, you want your second opinion now or later?"

That had been the pretext under which I phoned her after decades of silence. She still had the same landline. We had been friends before people had cell phones. I had moved from Daly City to Atherton in that time. I'd first heard of Atherton through her. She said the schools there were stellar and lamented the fact that her family couldn't afford to move there from the house she inherited from her mother in Burlingame. The Bay Area had blossomed into Silicon Valley in the years we were raising children, so only giants of industries—not a family living on the salary of a mere doctor—could afford to live in its toniest suburb. Even though I wasn't speaking to her when we moved to our new house, I chose it partially because I believed she would envy me for it. I had modeled myself on impressing her, a woman whom I was too competitive with to keep in my life, except as someone I was always able to best. You can only maintain the illusion you can best someone else at everything if you never allow yourself to see their strengths for all that they are. Or you simply choose to never see them.

"Hi, Esther," I had said when she answered my call. "It's Naya."

"I know."

She waited for me to speak. I didn't. I couldn't.

"How are you?" she asked.

"I'm dying. Well, at least that's what one doctor told me. I need a second opinion."

I offered to take her to lunch. She suggested we do coffee and picked a chain coffee shop the white women of Silicon Valley convinced me was gauche, in a mall that didn't have "real" stores.

I opened my Louis Vuitton bag to take out my medical records, then snapped it shut.

"I didn't call you to look at my scans, Esther."

"Good. So, I don't have to tell you that I'm not legally qualified to give you an opinion. I stopped renewing my radiology license."

"You never went back to work?"

"Nope. It felt like a torment to keep taking the tests if I knew I never would. I never wanted to be a doctor. Do you know which professional women are least likely to go back to work after having kids?"

I shook my head.

"Doctors and lawyers," she said.

At the mention of the word "lawyers," she looked at me, giving me a chance to speak. But she quickly looked down, unnerved. I had sprung a lot on her, calling her out of the blue and announcing I was dying.

"Most doctors and lawyers don't go into their fields because they are passionate about them," she said. "They do it because they don't know what else to do. At the first excuse we find, like the supposed need for a mother to be with her children every waking moment or else they'll turn into serial killers, we jump at the chance to stop working."

"I never went to law school. I lied to you about that," I blurted out.

"I know, Naya. We don't have to talk about it."

"How long have you known?"

She sighed and looked ashamed.

"It's embarrassing."

"I'm the one who lied. What do you have to be embarrassed about?"

"You disappeared from my life, Naya. You wouldn't even tell me what I did to upset you. I started to think we were never friends at all, that you were someone I met once in a while in a park and that—in my loneliness—I exaggerated how close we were. We were real friends, weren't we?"

Were we? We never celebrated holidays, even secular ones like the Fourth of July, with each other.

"Of course we were real friends, but to a point. I mean, it's not like we tried to get our families together."

"I thought that was because they would have gotten in our way," she said, and I recognized the truth in it. Back then we spent so much of our lives being our husbands' wives and children's mothers. We couldn't wait to dump our kids in music and swim lessons so we could talk. The time we spent with each other was the only time we lived for ourselves.

"I told you something I hadn't ever been able to talk about, not before and not since," she whispered.

"What?" I said, genuinely curious. She glanced around before speaking. She wanted to make sure that the smattering of people surrounding us, college kids on their laptops or couples seated together but staring at their phones, were paying no mind. Then she leaned in toward me.

"About my uncle," she whispered.

Oh, that. I hadn't recognized it was such an important revelation, so inconsequential to me that I almost didn't register it as something hard for her to confess at the time. Was it because I had been taught, as an Arab woman, that girls had to be protected, that how our family loved us was to shield us from men? Because we assumed they were bastards, and the proof was that there was hardly one woman alive who could not point to a time when some man had tried to interfere with her when she was a girl?

"I've known for a long time that you were younger than you let on, probably too young to have finished law school, because I peeked at your driver's license. I borrowed a diaper from your bag and your wallet was open."

I found myself unable to meet her gaze. She was always forgetting diapers. I used to tease her that she seemed surprised every time her children soiled themselves.

"I'm sorry I snooped. I couldn't help myself. But why did you lie to me?"

Why would a woman who wasn't allowed to finish high school lie about her education, Esther? Ask a better question.

"No, don't answer that. I don't care. Why did you disappear, Naya?"

Our eyes met.

"Your eldest son got into a gifted program and mine didn't. I was envious of you."

"That's it?"

"That's it. I felt you had an unfair advantage because your community center had resources for kids, free tutoring, and special classes to prepare them for the required tests that mine didn't. If I was Jewish, you would have told me about those resources. We enrolled our kids in everything together, except in a place where they couldn't be together, because the point of that place is that they are separated."

"Is that really all? That's the reason you stopped talking to me?"

"Yes. Stupid, isn't it?"

"It's not stupid. It's sad."

"Let it be noted that the Palestinian and the Jew must agree to disagree. Surprise, surprise!" I said, and again we laughed, hard and loud and involuntary. It was not unlike a sort of vomiting, a removing of bile, an expulsion of poison.

"It would all have been fine if Amir had aced the test like his older sister. Or if one of my younger two boys got in. We could've been friends for the last twenty years. I wouldn't have wasted so much time missing out on being with the person who makes me feel the most alive."

Then together we did the most taboo thing that mothers could do. We mocked our adult children, these creatures we poured all our attention into helping to thrive, at the expense of everything else, including questioning how and if we were managing to do so ourselves.

"Does it make you feel better to know that Aaron is a ski bum who works the lifts at Tahoe and chases college girls that are too young for him?"

"Slightly. But what really would have helped was realizing all three of my boys were just going to end up working in our family business, where no one asks if the boss's sons are gifted."

Next, I confessed to her that I had only told Daoud and my mother about the diagnosis, swearing them both to secrecy. My sons were infantile. I would have to comfort them, to reassure them they'd survive my death. It was the final act of mothering for most of us, a duty I had no desire to prolong. Arabella, my loveless and prickly girl, had a chance at landing a boyfriend. My mother had set her up with a man who didn't bow out immediately after meeting her. I could not pull her away at the moment of true possibility for her. I would not.

"You have to tell Arabella."

"Not now. She is very busy. She is working on a theatre project. She is a director."

"I know. I've kept tabs on her trajectory, which is easy to do in the age of Google. Very impressive. She lives in New York, right?"

"Yes. She has just met a boy. A doctor."

"A doctor? Tell her to run."

"He went to Stanford."

"Fancy."

"Fancy."

I didn't tell her that the boy was volunteering as a medic at the front lines of the protests in Gaza. If she said the wrong thing, it would hurt me. I couldn't afford to lose her again.

"It's not the time to make her play nurse to me. I need Arabella settled before I die."

"By settled, do you mean 'married'?"

"Yes."

"We have husbands. Have we been settled?"

"Not at all. But, what else would we have done with our lives if we hadn't married?"

"Who knows?" she asked. I loved the life I had enough to feel bereft that I was being wrenched from it so young. What would have happened to me if I had made entirely different choices? If I had run away? Not submitted to marrying a stranger? Actually gone to college instead of pretending to do so? Who knows? No one did and no one ever would.

"We have children," I said. "That's important, right?"

"Says who? What good have they done us?" Esther asked, and smiled.

I smiled back.

"Not much apparently when it comes down to brass tacks. When

I need support when I'm dying, it's a poor old friend from my past I reach out to. She's the person I want holding my hand."

Esther reached out her hand and took mine. "I'm here for you, of course, but you have to tell Arabella what's going on."

"My daughter is the most selfish person I've ever known. We pay all her bills. She manages to make me feel small if I call and ask her for a book recommendation. It's too taxing on her precious time. If I ask her to come here and nurse me, she will make me miserable."

If I'm miserable, I might make an end of it sooner than later. The effort it takes to try to eat might become too much. I was afraid my daughter might unwittingly kill me faster.

"Your daughter might surprise you. I bet Arabella is more mature than you give her credit for."

29

ARABELLA

Ramallah

2012

"Motherfucker!" I screamed, and kicked the door of the theatre. "Fuck you! Fuck everyone who looks like you!"

Ramez must have changed the lock. He had waited until the day of the dress rehearsal, the most precarious point in the process, the last time we would perform the show in its entirety before we faced an audience. My cast stared at me spewing curse words in English as if I were insane.

Aware of their eyes on me, the impression I was making, I still couldn't stop myself from punching the door. Bang! It represented every threshold I faced that I couldn't manage to cross.

Bang! Bang! My hands were not my own. They hit the door again and again.

In that vortex of impotent rage, I wished the worst thing a bitch can wish. I wished I had cried "Uncle!" or rather *"Amo!"* Why couldn't I have just let Ramez do the fucking role that His Royal Shittiness wanted so badly? What would it have cost me? I was a New York artist. I could have taken my lofty female-centric postmodern interpretation of *Hamlet* back with me to my world. This was one buttfucking production in the middle of Nowhere (aka Anyplace Not New York), in Arabic to boot. Why did I care? Would it have killed me to have submitted?

As I banged over and over on a locked door with a crowd of people—strangers, really—gawking at me, I noticed it was Cherifa who stared at me with the most uncertainty in her eyes.

Ramez had been like a ghost, an unseen malevolence haunting our production. I tried calling him when he delayed payment to the actors, until I gave up and emailed a "friendly" reminder to a staff member of the English theatre that my cast—artists of the Third World creating theatre—needed their shekels. It felt so slimy to do so, to admit that we Palestinian artists were clearly squabbling at worst, or not communicating at best. In the stories of the British occupation that my grandmother told me, she always reserved her greatest ire for those of us who snitched, the collaborators, who looked for favors from Europeans when we couldn't settle our differences among ourselves. But it cowed Ramez into releasing the funds. He sent his daughter, a thirteen-year-old ice queen. She wore her blue eyes the way I had worn my light skin as a girl, aware it made me rare. As she had been instructed, she counted out the money to pay everyone in the cast and crew except me. But she smiled at me as she pranced out the door, an open and happy child who either didn't understand or didn't care that her father detested me, and I found myself smitten with her.

Ramez then cajoled our costume designer, a matronly widow and retired actress who as a girl had studied theatre in Cairo, into quitting our show. Apparently, he went around saying it was evil to dress a girl as a boy, and our production had the hint of sin to it. When I told her that was nonsense, reminding her that the best of Egyptian cinema—Arab Hollywood—was rife with cross-dressing, she simply said, "I agree. I'm sorry. But my sons want no issue with Ramez's clan." So I spent my nights sewing black tunics for the living characters and white ones for the ghosts, refining and rehearsing the day's staging in my head. It was relaxing, this women's work that I always avoided. It wasn't like I had any plans. No one from the cast or crew was rushing to have me over for dinner or invite me out after rehearsal for a cup of tea.

But, seeing Cherifa glance at me with such uncertainty forced me to admit that the Assholeness Personified that was Ramez was not the only problem our production was facing.

As our lead, Cherifa had to carry the entire play and she had no prior theatre experience. We were opening the show tomorrow. She was still tripping up her lines, sometimes jumping several pages ahead at a time. The other actors had to scramble to figure out into what point in the storyline she'd propelled them. I needed this last rehearsal with her today. I'd planned to do a speed-through of the text twice with her until she'd gotten it in her bones, before we did a run with lights and sound. That usually did the trick, but I usually worked with trained actors. Maybe it was a mistake to cast someone who had never stepped onstage in a title role. Cherifa was nervous. Nervous people are always looking to turn on someone.

Bang! Bang! I felt pain in my knuckles, but I couldn't stop myself from striking that door.

I should have known it was a bad omen when you have a perfect first rehearsal, when the actors read through the text for the first time and their impulses are exactly right. The world is new and they are re-acting to the flow of the story as it comes. When the first reading is so good, there is nowhere to go but down. The rest of the rehearsal period is about keeping them fresh, alive in the moment, as if they hadn't al-ready said the same words a million times before.

Memorization remaps the brain's neural networks. It reorganizes your master muscle. The human attempt to harness our minds is why we have mantras, why we say prayers, why we make plays. Memoriz-ing the text of a tragedy in its entirety, as I had done in Arabic, by listening to it over and over, does a number on you. You carry the useless deaths and the maddening sorrows within your folds until you forget.

Aziz braved the daunting checkpoints to visit me often during those weeks of rehearsal. Our lovemaking took on a perfunctory, al-most grim quality. Without discussing it, we both decided we wanted to make a baby together. Would we have more children? Set up a shot-gun wedding if he knocked me up? Those were questions we didn't ask each other or ourselves.

Bang! Bang! Now the look in Cherifa's eyes changed from uncertainty to revulsion. She glanced at her grandfather. Are you seeing what I'm seeing, a woman becoming unhinged? I could not read her grandfather's expression.

Recently, a few of the male neighbors in white villas that surrounded my great-grandfather's cave-like house started giving me ugly smiles. Gossipy and lewd, they had watched for proof I was no nun and they had found it. Again, Ramez was to blame. I had no idea what was in store for me the next time I tried to meet Aziz at the Mövenpick Hotel.

The same skinny clerk at the front desk curtly informed me, "We have no rooms to rent you."

"*Kazab!*" I snapped. "You have plenty of rooms and you know it."

"I have plenty of rooms. None for you. Maybe if you have a friend who can vouch for your character, we can find you one."

"My dollars vouch for my character!"

Really, Arabella? Who are you? If there is a string of words that should never be uttered, it's these. You can't take them back. You can't unknow you're the kind of tool who says such things when it comes down to brass tacks.

"Who is the manager here?"

"I am. By the way, I should inform you that you won't get a room at any of the other hotels here. You're on a list of names not to rent to in Ramallah."

Names? What kind of names? Ah, of course. The ones of women you wouldn't want associated with your place of business. In my rage, I picked up my phone to call Aziz. He didn't answer. It went to voicemail. Fuck!

"You work in the theatre, do you not? Have someone from the theatre vouch for your character and you can rent a room."

"Excuse me?"

"Have Ramez call and vouch for you."

I stared into his eyes. His blue eyes.

"Are you related to Ramez?"

"*Oulad al-am*," he said with a proud smirk, excited to tell me he and Ramez were cousins. Great.

Glaring at the clerk, I called Aziz again and he thankfully picked up.

"Sorry, Arabella. I was in the shower."

In Arabic, I loudly explained the *haywan* at the front desk wasn't letting me rent a room. With his hair wet, Aziz came down to try to deal with him.

"I'm sorry, Doctor," the clerk said, deferential. He had recognized Aziz, the American-born doctor who volunteered in Gaza. It was all over the news when he got shot in both legs while wearing his medic uniform. "It's an honor to have you, but I have my instructions."

Aziz sighed and checked out of the hotel.

"You're famous," I told him as we walked out.

"Yeah, I'm right up there with P. Diddy," he said. We jumped into his car.

"Want to go to Jerusalem?" I asked. I could hear the reluctance in my voice. The thought of crossing the checkpoint didn't appeal to me. I had taken to never leaving Ramallah. It was only in its very center that you weren't accosted by the Israeli-only roads, military outposts with their ominous sniper towers, teenage soldiers slinging assault rifles, or the shadow of the monstrously high separation wall. Thankfully, the idea didn't appeal to Aziz either.

"Not really, Arabella." He stared at me, clean and handsome. We wanted to be in bed with each other. We should have been in bed with each other.

"Fuck it! Let's go to my place, Aziz."

"But what will the neighbors say?" Aziz said, teasing me.

"That you're a stud." And that I was a whore. In the coming days, that's exactly how my male neighbors made me feel with their knowing looks, after they spied that I'd brought a young man into my place who left the next morning. Why did their gleefully intrusive glances fill me with rage? Not at them. At myself. Why was it that any man in any place, with a mere look, could make me feel ashamed?

Bang! Bang!

Rosencrantz and Guildenstern stepped forward, approaching me like a wild animal.

"Arabella," one of them said. "Can we try?"

I nodded and stepped away from the door.

The other pulled out a small wire he inexplicably had on him. They proceeded to jimmy the lock. It popped open and we all cheered. We were going to have our dress rehearsal and our opening night. The show would go on.

As the designers rushed past me, eager to get the light and sound systems up and running, my cell rang. It was my mother.

"Hi, Mom."

"Hello," she said, sounding surprised, as if she hadn't expected me to answer.

A loud clanging came from the light booth. Someone had dropped something heavy. I clicked mute on the phone and yelled, *"Kul'she tamam?"*

"Tamam!" came the answer.

Tamam, my ass. I headed toward the light booth to see what was broken.

"How are you, Arabella?" my mother's voice asked me over the line.

"Fine," I said.

"Arabella, are you there? Are you okay?" she asked, sounding worried. I realized I hadn't unmuted myself.

"I'm fine. Just busy, Mom."

Click. I got a call on my other line. I saw it was a European number.

"Someone busted something backstage and I'm getting another call. Do you need me, Mom?"

"No. Have fun, my daughter. Always, no matter what, have fun," she said softly, and hung up.

Okay, that was odd. She usually responded with rage when I was short with her. Shaking off a sense of uneasiness, I answered the other call.

"Hello. May I speak with Arabella?" a British male voice purred.

"Speaking," I said.

"It's John Tilbury. I'm the Associate Artistic Director at the Royal Court. We've exchanged emails."

"Yes, hi!"

John was the guy I wrote to who got the cast and crew paid when

Ramez was holding the funding hostage. He was basically the number two man to *the* Philip Gladwell.

The Philip Gladwell was, well, only one of the most powerful artistic directors in the theatrical circles of Europe. His career had not been hurt by the fact that he was quite pretty and quite promiscuous. He had been discovered as a director by Kevin Spacey when he worked as a mere intern at a theatre where Spacey starred in an O'Neill play. They were believed to have been lovers.

What did we theatre people think of those of our ilk who sleep their way to the top, in our heart of hearts? That at least they managed to get somewhere for their pains unlike the rest of us?

"Philip and I just arrived in Tel Aviv," he told me. "We'll be here for two nights. Philip is quite taken with what he knows about your work. He's looking forward to seeing your show."

"Red Rover, Red Rover. Send *the* Philip Gladwell right over," I thought.

"We're going to watch *Othello* at the Habima tonight and plan to head to Ramallah for your opening tomorrow."

The Philip Gladwell was going to see a Shakespeare production at the national Israeli theatre and our show back-to-back. Habima had cast an Ethiopian Jewish rising star in the lead. Cherifa would be able to rival him. She was magnetic. How to remind her of that? I decided I wouldn't force her to submit to a speed-through of the text with me, that grueling process of speaking the words at twice the speed you need to in order to cement them in your mind. That would only terrify her if she stumbled over a section or two. Instead, I would tell her that she should relax, even if she jumped a few pages ahead in the text while onstage. Everyone knows how the story ends, just like we know the ends of all our stories. They were there to watch her live through it in the way only she could.

"Lovely! I know it's quite a journey to make it to Ramallah. I so hope Philip and you won't be disappointed," I said, squelching the urge to speak in a British accent.

"I can't imagine we will, Arabella. Will you have time for a late supper with Philip and me after the show?" he asked.

"Of course."

"Smashing. See you tomorrow night."

Smashing it was. And smashing it would be. I would charm John. I would charm *the* Philip Gladwell. If Jesus Christ felt like making a reappearance on Earth in time to see our show, I bet I would charm Him, too. I felt as I hadn't since my heady early days of making theatre, when I didn't doubt that a daughter of Arab immigrants with talent could become a titan of American theatre if she had enough charisma.

There is a reason charisma is also called charm. It is magic. It makes people believe in your vision. It makes people bet on your brilliance. It makes people give you money. I would get them to find funds to bring my *Hamleta* to England, and when it was a hit in England, then I would be hired to direct in the Public Theater's Shakespeare in the Park season. From there, it was only a matter of time before I made it to Broadway. I had taken a detour to my dreams, but I was finally back on track.

The cast had assembled onstage, waiting for instruction, except for Cherifa.

"Where's our star?" I asked. Then I spotted her.

She was standing by the door. Why wasn't she in costume yet?

"I'm so sorry," she told me. "I can't do this, Arabella."

30

NAYA

Atherton
2012

I needed a pill. A painkiller. A bridge to jump off. A way out.

Does the body know better than we do? Does it understand when we are done with life? A part of me wanted to believe I was choosing my exit. A part of me was still in control. That is what I tried to think, when I could think, when the pain was not mind-numbing. The medicine brought a relief so intense it was almost sexual. Who was going to help me die? Who was going to give me my last bit of fun?

Daoud was not a likely candidate. The man was always blubbering.

"I want to go first," he sobbed. It didn't make it less annoying that he meant it.

I knew I should be gracious and give my blessing for him to go on with his life, which meant to marry again. I intended to do so. Eventually.

When the pain swelled, I'd scream.

On the hills of Ramallah, I once saw a rabbit in the mouth of a wild dog.

"Why doesn't the rabbit make a sound?" I asked my mother. "Why doesn't it cry out?"

"God gave them no voice," she said as we watched it be devoured. "What good would it do them?"

"How can I help?" Daoud asked over and over.

"Shut up!"

There was one good hour between the time my medicine made my brain foggy and the pain returned. I liked to spend that hour talking on the phone with my mother. She told me her secrets and I told her mine. What would I have been doing with that time if I hadn't gotten sick? I'd be trying to fit in with the white women of Silicon Valley, whom I didn't want near me now.

How I had longed to impress them. Had I believed, if they allowed me to belong, it would somehow make up for all the times and places that I hadn't? Why else would they and their opinions have felt so important? So life-or-death?

I insisted my mother not travel to see me. Something about the way her breath grew short told me that she, too, needed care, which I could not give her now. She would suffer alone. If I was still healthy, would it have been any different? Would I have blossomed into the kind of daughter who would put her life on hold to care for a parent?

We talked openly of our resentments for each other. We didn't call each other *Bint* and *Yema* anymore. We took to calling each other *ya Mara*. O Woman.

"It was cruel of you to marry me off at fifteen, *ya Mara*."

"Forgive me, *ya Mara*. If I'd had your money, I would have sent you to college like you did with your daughter."

We rarely spoke of my children. They felt like newcomers, who belonged to the future. My mother and I wanted to mine our past. Mothers are expected to die first, but having one around when you are dying is a source of comfort.

"The husband I forced on you is rich and kind and only had one affair, *ya Mara*."

"True. I'm sorry I interrupted you on the boat when you were holding hands with that handsome doctor, *ya Mara*."

"I'm sorry I was so afraid you'd tell your father that I considered tossing you overboard."

"*Akeed?*" Really?

"*Akeed.* But I didn't do it."

"Obviously."

We laughed.

I told her the story of how I tried to throw myself at a very young man in a bookshop, who was only interested in me as someone who might help his family's finances.

"You should have offered to pay the boy to make love to you, *ya Mara*."

"I should have," I said.

We laughed again.

Daoud refused to hire a nurse. He took on my caregiving entirely by himself, even the ugliest parts.

Esther visited every day. Daoud greeted her like an angel descending on our doorstep. It gave him time to shower and answer a few emails while we talked. Against my advice, he stopped going into work. Our sons could not manage our business. Our sons could not manage anything.

"That husband of yours is a good egg," Esther told me more than once. I didn't have the heart to confide in her about Daoud's affair and, more important, how I handled it. It's the one secret I would forever keep from her. I sensed she would not approve, and I needed her on my side.

"When the time comes, will you help me kick the bucket, Esther?" I would ask her. "Maybe show me how many painkillers I'll need to take?"

"Stop that talk. You have to tell Arabella you are sick," she would always answer, her soft blue eyes frantic. I could feel she wanted to run from this room, run from me, to flee from what I was asking of her.

"Not now. If I need you, will you help me die, Esther?" I asked.

"Probably," she finally said.

It was only then that I could make the phone call I'd been dreading. Later that day, when Daoud collapsed from exhaustion on the couch, I took just the right amount of OxyContin so I was still in pain, but functional.

Clutching the handrail, I made it up the spiral staircase to his home office. I looked for a phone number in his Rolodex and I found it. Jennifer Burr, the accountant who seduced my husband. I wanted to tell her she won in the end. I was dying. I had a beloved friend who would help me do it before things got even uglier. I could afford to be magnanimous. I could afford to let this woman take my place. You can have my husband. Please take care of him. No hard feelings.

When I called, a young girl answered.

"Can I speak to Jennifer?" I asked.

"My mom isn't here."

"I'm an old friend. Who is this?"

"It's Arabiyya," she said. Arabiyya was the given name of *Hamaty*, Daoud's mother. The name I had refused to saddle my daughter with and had instead anglicized to Arabella.

"We can't raise an Arabiyya in California. Either we move back to Palestine or we give the girl a break," I had insisted from my hospital bed, clutching my newborn in my arms. Daoud had reluctantly agreed, though it was considered a slight to not name your eldest daughter after the grandmother on her father's side. My mother-in-law never forgave Daoud.

Jennifer gave him a daughter with the name he wanted. They must have discussed my refusal to do that. They must have discussed everything.

"How old are you, Arabiyya?"

"Twelve," she said. She seemed an obedient girl, who must have been taught it was polite to unthinkingly answer the questions of adults. If there is an injustice done to girls everywhere, it is teaching them to err on the side of politeness. It costs them. It would cost this child.

"Is your dad home?" I asked.

"My dad is dead," she told me. "Do you want to leave my mom a message?"

"No. Thank you, Arabiyya."

I hung up, feeling confused. Did Daoud know of the girl's existence? Had Jennifer raised their daughter on her own? I decided it didn't matter. There was only one thing left to do.

When Daoud woke up and came in the room to check on me, I told him that I wanted to make arrangements with our lawyer.

"Why?" Daoud asked.

"I want you to move on after I'm gone."

"Don't talk that way," he said, but his eyes brightened. With hope? Relief? Was it this conversation he would remember, repeating it to himself and reminding our children of it, on the day he married for the second time? He was not yet sixty. If he lived to be a hundred, he would have only just passed the midpoint of his life.

"I give you my blessing to marry again."

"I don't want to."

You wanted other women while I was alive—don't act like you won't when I'm dead, I wanted to snap. But what I needed to do was find a way to win in the end somehow. Staying calm was almost always the best way to do so.

"You have my blessing to live your life, but I want our children to have our money. Our children only. Not any other children you might have with another woman in the future."

"I won't marry again," he insisted.

"Or any children you might have had in the past," I said pointedly. He looked down. He knew about the girl. He had let the child believe he was dead. Out of love for me? Fear of what I might do? Are those two always intertwined?

"Call our lawyer. Tell her to come here and that we want to give most of our money to our children while we are both alive," I said. "Tell her we need to change their trusts. We need to make them irrevocable."

He made the call, stuttering.

"You understand that this will be set in stone?" the lawyer told us when she arrived with the paperwork. She was a slender young Asian woman wearing sandals and ill-fitting white chino pants that had seen better days. We had hired her initially because we wanted to ensure our wealth didn't go to our daughters-in-law if they ever divorced our sons. I had chosen her. I liked that she seemed tough and spoke with such a thick Bostonian accent that she sounded like a Kennedy. I loved to observe female lawyers. I was fascinated by these women who lived my phantom life. She really should have dressed more professionally given how much we were paying per hour. Someone should tell her. Had I been a lawyer, you would not have caught me dead looking like that.

Daoud hesitated, frowning as she handed him the paperwork that would leave him relatively penniless and give our children control of his company. Then he glanced at me. I smiled, the grim grin of a future fury prepared to hound and haunt someone who crossed her forever. He signed on the dotted lines. Then, so did I.

My final act would be disinheriting his illegitimate child. I kept what I could for me and mine, saving it for the grandchildren I would not see. It was my mother's suggestion.

In the end, I was my mother's daughter. We had never been angels, nor did we aspire to be. Being an angel is overrated.

31

ARABELLA

Ramallah

2012

I was a monster. Worse still, I was a fool. I rode Cherifa too hard. I fucked up my only real job as a director, which is to figure out my actors' capabilities. To get them to trust their own instincts. Meeting them where they're at is the first step to getting them where I need them to be. I failed. I was a shitty director and, if my condomless assignations with Aziz proved fruitful, I was going to make a shittier mother.

Stunned by Cherifa's pronouncement that she could not perform, the cast and I watched wordlessly as she ran out the door. By the time she began descending the stairwell, I was on her heels, catching glimpses of her as she circled her way below me. I called her name over and over. She didn't look up or back.

When I reached the lobby and raced to the double glass doors, I collided with a man in the doorway of the building. Ramez, in costume. He had someone sew him the same tunic that Cherifa was supposed to wear onstage in his size?!

"Arabella, I can step in," he said. I caught a glimpse of Cherifa turning a corner on the crowded Ramallah street.

"Over my dead body!" I said as I ran past him.

"*Asif! Asif!*" I apologized over and over, pushing my way against the people I couldn't weave around as I followed Cherifa through the serpentine streets.

"*Mugnoona!*" a voice hissed at me. It was not an inaccurate assessment. I felt crazy.

She was younger. More slender and fleet-footed. But, by sheer force of maniacal will, I kept up with her, following her pristine white T-shirt that seemed to wave like a flag of surrender. I finally caught up with her in a deserted alley, grabbing her by the shirt.

"*Mugnoona!*" she gasped.

"You are going to be wonderful, Cherifa. You can do this!" I panted.

"I know. You always made me feel like I could. For that, I'll always be grateful," she panted back.

So, I hadn't terrified the living daylights out of her? Why else would she quit?

She raised her hand—a flash of gold. She was sporting a *khatim*, an engagement ring.

"A man asked for my hand. And he said he won't marry me if I go onstage."

"What's his objection? Your costume covers you completely. Your precious skin will be safe from the eyes of men. You're playing a boy." These were the thoughts I was trying to convey. Emotion and stress made expressing myself in Arabic, my first language that I found my fluency in again on that trip, a struggle. I began shouting the broken equivalent of "You be boy! You safe from eyes! You be pretend boy!"

Did I really have to tell the Artistic Director of the Royal Court that I couldn't deliver, that I wasted all their grant money? Sorry, Sir. There's no show. Our lead's fiancé decided he doesn't think women should be onstage. Apparently, we're living in the Elizabethan times up in Ramallah. In lieu of seeing a show, want to try our falafel? I know a place.

Fuck, fuck, fuck. I couldn't do that, not if he and his second-in-command would be seeing an Israeli show the night before. Did I really want to reinforce the idea that Israeli artists had it together in ways we Palestinians did not?

Should I just let that bitch-ass Ramez play the role? From all accounts, he was brilliant. Sure, it wouldn't be a groundbreaking feminist interpretation, but it would be a show worth watching, right?

How I detested the thought! For fuck's sake, he had showed up in costume, so cocksure that I would cast him. How could he have known she wouldn't go on?

On a whim, I asked Cherifa, "Is your fiancé related to Ramez?"

She lowered her eyes and said, *"Oulad el-am."*

First cousins on the father's side.

"He has a great job. He works in a hotel." Fuck, fuck, fuck. Cherifa was marrying the piece of shit who threw me out of the Mövenpick.

"It's not like he's the goddamn Prince of Monaco," I told her.

Then I realized that to Cherifa—a daughter of refugees—he was the equivalent of a prince. It was a stroke of luck to be able to work in a hotel. To escape the backbreaking labor of building Jewish-only settlements, the primary job available to the young men in her camp, whose parents had been dispossessed when they fled in 1948. They lived squeezed together in teeming houses. As did she. The home she would have with him would feel like a palace in comparison.

Incidentally, the mousey Prince of Monaco made the same demand of Grace Kelly, that she give up her acting career for the honor of being his wife. Grace Kelly did and probably counted herself lucky. How did I expect a girl who never had access to the kind of power, independence, and money of a motherloving Hollywood movie star (or even a homeland to call her own) to choose differently?

There seemed to be no limit to Ramez's ability to fuck with my show. Had he really managed to orchestrate a marriage to get himself cast as Hamlet? Yes, the hell he did. Getting that skinny nothing of a boy to agree to have the gorgeously gamine Cherifa as his wife was no hard sell.

"Your grandfather and all your clan's elders are standing on that stage with you, Cherifa. There can be no shame in it."

"I agree. There is no shame in it. My grandfather and all my clan want me to perform with them. They don't think it is right of him to ask me to step down before opening night. But they cannot deliver me a husband who has a job and an apartment outside our camp."

Nor can you, American-born girl who was soon going back to her world full of so many choices. She didn't say that and she didn't have to. I thought of the way I had clung to Aziz as if he were a life raft, as if I would drown in my particular whirlpool of anxiety, loneliness, and despair without him. As if I would die.

I asked her the question I had been afraid to ask myself about Aziz. Because I already knew the answer.

"Do you love him?"

"I will," she said.

She did not right then. Nor was it absolutely clear that she ever would. I knew she could read the anguish on my face. She probably couldn't have guessed I was as sad for myself as I was for her.

But her eyes gleamed with the glow of a girl who yearned for a salvation of some sort and believed she had found a way to have it.

I sighed and knew my pleading was hopeless.

I walked back to the theatre, trying to reimagine my staging with Ramez in the role. I couldn't. The production hinged on the idea that the main character was female. The point of my adaptation was that a dead king had wanted a son so badly that he pretended his daughter was a boy.

It had to be a girl playing the role. She had to know the entire text and my staging. How to make that happen in the next twenty-four hours?

Because there was no fucking way I was putting Ramez on that stage, to reward him for bullying me.

"I'd rather die," I thought.

At once, I had an idea for a solution—a stroke of brilliance. But, like all strokes of brilliance, it would cost me. Stubbornness always comes with a price.

I would rather die than put Ramez on my stage, but the best alternative made death seem, well, rather manageable in comparison.

When I got back to the theatre, I walked in to find Ramez holding court. He was perched on the edge of the stage. The rest of the cast sat in the audience, waiting to find out what I would say.

"What are you doing here?" I asked him.

"I know the part. I can play it," Ramez said.

"You know the text, Ramez. Not any of my staging."

"I can figure it out by tonight. This is bigger than you and me, Arabella. The Europeans are coming. We can't have nothing to show them."

"You're right. We can't," I said.

He smiled. I couldn't help but think the expression on his face was that of a rapist who had just finished tying up his victim, who could take his time now.

"I'll do you a favor and play the part," he told me.

"You're not playing the part. I am," I said. I had spent so much time working on the play that I had inadvertently memorized the text in Arabic. I, who had gravitated to the kind of career in theatre where I was forever safe from the eyes of men, was going onstage.

When the cast broke out in a cheer, I saw they were as done with Ramez as I was. It was my turn to smile.

The best way to vanquish a villain is to turn him into a fool. The show would go on.

EPILOGUE

I enter the plane with my newborn strapped to my chest. Little Naya, whom I named after my mother, is asleep.

I think of all the steps that got me here. Or rather, I should say, us.

I stepped out onstage for the first time as Hamleta on quaking legs. My body was not my own. Up until right before I had to go on, I had been in the bathroom. Petrified by stage fright, I gained a deeper, more visceral understanding of what it meant to lose one's shit. On the toilet, I called Cherifa over and over, hoping she would pick up and tell me she was on her way to play the role, to save me from having to do it for her. She never did. When Sanaa began banging on the door to make me leave in time for my cue, I finally gave up and turned off my phone.

The lights were blinding.

"A little more than kin and less than kind," I began. With my first line about Claudius, the detested usurper who had stolen my father's kingdom, I finally found my footing. What did I call him? Not an animal, monster, or devil. No. I said he was "less than kind," which encompasses all those things. Thus, I began the journey where I would kill and kill until I was killed.

There are moments from that performance I will always keep with me. The delight I felt as I found myself speaking every line from memory with precision. The roller-coaster thrill of slipping between who I was (a woman standing on a stage with about two hundred people watching her) and who I was playing (a haunted youth who had endured too many injustices to avenge in a thousand lifetimes). That split second of terror when I fumbled and forgot where my light would be and had to start the "To be or not to be" monologue in the dark.

Onstage, I felt myself growing physically attracted to Sanaa, my delicate Ophelia, who played with me like the pro she was. I grew hot when she cocked her head back ever so slightly and fluttered her eyelashes during our scene together. I wanted to possess her in unnatural, impossible ways. My revulsion with the violence of my desires made my snapping of the line "Get thee to the nunnery" more like a bellow. I needed to protect her from the me who wanted to choke and fuck her at the same time.

To act onstage is to revel in the slipperiness of life, to be yourself and not yourself at the same time. It's the one time you can take two journeys at once.

As Hamleta, I enjoyed the act of thrusting a stage knife, the simulating of killing bringing me a gritty satisfaction.

As Arabella, I realized killing is the closest to death you could come while still staying alive. To destroy is to fleetingly harness the power of the element that would soon enough destroy you.

On that stage, I finally understood Shakespeare had been right. Grief can turn a person mad. When I drove Sanaa's Ophelia to lose her sanity, I cried real tears, barely stifling my sobs enough to make out my last lines.

During the show, I killed. I died. In between I did a lot of talking, mostly to myself.

But the play wasn't over until the kingdom my uncle usurped from my father's line was taken over by a foreign king. Our infighting led to us losing our much-contested land forever. He who gets the kingdom also gets the last line.

My legs started shaking again when I took my final bow, the relief so intense that my knees almost buckled beneath me. I remember thinking I gave a good performance. As we say in the theatre, I killed it.

As the applause followed us long after we stepped off the stage, I felt overcome with melancholy that Aziz hadn't been there to see our show. He had backed out of coming to the opening at the last minute. A fellow medic, a comely young woman who was a well-known figure in her white coat and famous in Gaza for claiming she was stronger than any man, had been shot and killed that morning while attempting to evacuate a wounded protester at a rally. Aziz knew her fiancé and wanted to attend the funeral to support him. The distance from Gaza to Ramallah is fifty-one miles, but the uncertain time it would take to get through the checkpoints—even with our American passports—would have made it impossible for him to attend both.

He had to choose.

"I have to stay, Arabella," he told me.

I knew it was true. He had to stay. He wasn't moving to Manhattan to start a family with me. He belonged to Gaza. He couldn't understand what he was doing in the world if he wasn't continuing the struggle there. Healing the most beleaguered of our people, who suffered more intensely and unceasingly than any of us for insisting upon our rights as a nation, was his calling.

"I know, Aziz."

"Good luck with your show, Arabella."

I didn't think I was superstitious, but hearing those words filled me with dread. You're supposed to say "break a leg"—to pretend to wish bodily harm on a performer. You wish for the opposite of what you actually want.

"Goodbye, Aziz," I told him.

I knew he'd picked up on the finality in my voice because I heard it echoed in his when he said, "Goodbye, Arabella."

We wouldn't make a big deal of things. We just wished each other well with all our hearts and stopped speaking. He didn't even ask if I was pregnant, and I didn't tell him I wasn't. I had gotten my period that morning.

As I showered, rubbing an olive oil bar of soap around the contours of the belly that still belonged only to me, I felt the twin emotions of grief and relief do battle. Relief eventually bested grief. Maybe the universe had been looking out for me. If I wanted to be a mother, I would have to find another, possibly better, way.

After the applause died down, I rushed backstage to change out of my costume and meet the artists from the Royal Court Theatre. I caught sight of John, a white man standing alone and looking lost among the Palestinian crowd waiting to congratulate their friends in the cast. I recognized him from his photo on the Royal Court's website. He looked barely old enough to be out of college, a pudgy, sweet-eyed chap with an egg-shaped head so enormous that he might be easily cast as Humpty Dumpty. I introduced myself.

"Wait! You're Arabella?"

I nodded.

"No one told me you were playing the title role!" John said.

"I wasn't supposed to be. Our main actress dropped out yesterday," I explained.

"That's incredible. The show was incredible. Truly."

"Thanks, John. Where's Philip?" I couldn't help but ask.

John informed me that apparently *the* Philip Gladwell, esteemed Artistic Director of the Royal Court (aka a Godhead of International Theatre), had a "change of plans." He had not been able to attend, but he sent me his regards. John could read the deflation in my eyes.

I had fantasized that the Artistic Director of the Royal Court would be so floored by our performance that he would make it his life's mission to take the show to England, that I would soon be the toast of London. Fat chance. The man didn't think it was worth his time to even see my show, much less transfer it to his theatre.

I was surprisingly thankful that Ramez somehow invited himself to my supper with John, which I wished I could have gotten out of. I felt too spent to schmooze. We ended up going to Al-Muntazah, the outdoor garden restaurant where my grandparents had married. They had been living under British occupation at that time. If a British man like John had come to Ramallah back then, it would most likely be in the guise of a colonial soldier.

Managing to come across as both arrogant and sycophantic at the same time, Ramez babbled on and on about himself to John, particularly about the Israeli reception of his performance of Shylock. No matter how despicably he had treated me, I could never bring myself to truly hate Ramez. I understood him and his hungers too deeply to do that.

I smiled silently when John told me he admired my work and intended to stay in touch. It was polite to say such things. I remember thinking I'd never see him again.

Those memories all feel like a prologue. They belong to a past life now.

That life ended when I turned on my cell phone during dessert. Warm and cheesy *kinafa* doused in rose water, my mother's specialty, was being served. I saw dozens of missed calls from my dad.

"What's wrong, *Yaba?*" I said when I called back.

He was crying. It was hard to make out the words.

"Your mother is sick. The doctors gave her six months. They were wrong. Come home," he said. I was in the land of his birth, but he meant the land of mine. I got on the next flight to San Francisco.

She was on life support by the time I arrived. She had named me her health proxy. In theatre, when one actor plays two different characters in the same play, we say they are double-cast. You only ask it of those you think can handle the challenge of contrasting roles. My mother had double-cast me as both her liberator and an agent of death.

From the hospital lobby, I called my grandmother.

"Teta Zoya, why did my mom choose me? And not my dad?"

"She didn't trust your father would have the stomach to set her free," she told me. "That's what she wants, Arabella. Set her free."

The hardest steps I hope I ever have to take were to walk into the cold, sterile hospital room where my mother would be unhooked from machines. I knew I would exit it motherless. The room was filled with the men in my family—my father and brothers—sobbing so hard I would not be able to catch when exactly she took her last breath.

I decide not to return to New York right away and to stay with my father at our sprawling family home instead. I lost one parent without taking the time to fully know her. I am determined not to make the same mistake with him. He doesn't seem able to function. I volunteer to go to work in his bread company, mostly as a way to force him out of the house. I find there is a rhythm to accounting. There is a satisfaction in reconciliation, which is the word I am delighted to learn is used for when you've balanced your books, when you can account for every charge and who in your company made it.

I'm not surprised when I get a call from Layla. She gives her condolences and tells me Ramez stepped into the role of Hamlet the day after I left Palestine. I suspected that's what he'd do.

"That's fine, Sister," I say. "As long as he takes my name off the project."

"He already has," she tells me sheepishly. "And apparently mine, too. He reworded a few monologues and listed himself as the translator."

We could only laugh.

I make overtures to the folks from my Yale Drama days who are now connected to San Francisco theatres, looking for work as a director. I propose projects. My emails are uniformly ignored. Had I somehow slighted the entire San Francisco theatre clique and that's why I can't get work now? No. I'm not significant enough to actively dislike. I'm one more nuisance, one more grasper looking for work in an industry where there isn't enough to go around. These people run theatres I would have scoffed at working with in my "New York years," which I realize is going to be a phrase I use to describe that time in my life—to delineate it as a period that has passed. I find myself settling in San Francisco, a place that always felt like it wasn't a big enough city for me.

The only thing that feels real to me is that my mother is gone.

In some ways, this year after I lost my mom has been a time of excavation. I spend it trying to discover who she was. At her funeral, I reconnect with her old friend Esther, a woman I knew as a child. Esther tells me amazing stories of my mother (who apparently had a thing for young Vietnamese men) and of her childhood friendship with a pair of Black gay men in Detroit. I am able to locate Reginald. An elderly man with long, white dreads and the best posture I've ever seen, he visits me. Together we fulfill a promise he made to his long-dead partner, which was to scatter some of his ashes on Castro Street in San Francisco.

I now talk to my grandmother every day, even this morning, despite the fact that it felt overwhelming to get myself and little Naya to the airport on time. She knows I cannot fathom why my mother kept her illness from me, nor can I fully forgive her for it.

Teta Zoya relates to me differently after we lose my mom, now that the link between us has been obliterated. She comes clean with me about the details of her heart condition. I am prepared that she, too, might go soon. She no longer addresses me as *Bint*, as she does her other granddaughters. I am now *ya Mara*. O Woman. She tells me ribald stories, like how she was hot for Aziz the Grandfather to the point it made her panties wet and she didn't understand enough about her body to recognize that sexual desire was the cause. She speaks of how she cussed his widow out when the *haywana* dared to tell her I was too porky for Aziz the Grandson's taste, a fact I probably didn't need to know, especially after pregnancy did a number on my body.

Would you believe that talking with Teta Zoya helps me finally feel ready to have a child on my own? It's not her suggestion, of course. Having a kid out of wedlock is hardly in her wheelhouse of Middle Eastern matriarchal advice. But, when I casually posit a hypothetical scenario, she's more open than I expect.

"What would you say if I got married for a month to a man no one in our family ever met? And then divorced and had a baby nine months later?"

"It happens, *ya Mara*," she demurs.

Maybe she doesn't understand the particulars of artificial insemination. But she knows a story that won't shame future generations of our family forever when she sees one. It's not that she encourages me to have a kid on my own, but it's enough that she doesn't actively oppose it.

Time to find a donor. What do I do? The same thing I always do when I need anything. I call Yoav.

"How's the melody, Arabella?" he asks.

"Great. I'm ready to be a mom. Got any sperm you're looking to donate?"

I hear him let out a long sigh, a sort of whistle.

"Ask me for anything but that," he says.

"Anything?"

"Pretty much. You know I'm hot for you, Arabella. But I don't want children. I never have. Never will. I've known it since I was a kid myself."

He proceeds to tell me a story of a teenage boy who was working on a college production of *Macbeth* with a teenage girl. They share the same obsession. They are serious about theatre in a way that most kids, most people perhaps, are not serious about anything. The girl tells the boy that she sees herself in Lady Macbeth. She understands a woman willing to drown her humanity in ambition, to listen to dark forces and relish what they have to say, to kill for power.

"I think being childless unhinges Lady Macbeth in a way I am also easily unhinged. Maybe that's why I want to be a mother, Yoav. I aspire to be like those lady directors who scoff at having children, but I'm not," the girl admits to the boy. "I think having kids will make me more human. If I don't have something tethering me to life, something other than my career ambitions, I'm lost."

"Feeling lost is not a reason to have kids," the wise and prescient boy tells her. "It's not fair to them."

What neither says—but both know to be true—is that the girl is the kind of creature who has never seen the world as fair and, therefore, she was not required to be.

I don't recall that conversation, my telling him when were both nineteen that I wanted children badly and making a point to say it to a boy I adored from the first moment I met him. So, that's the reason we never drunkenly groped each other at some closing-night party and ended up in bed together. It was the reason he insisted we stay friends. Or so he says. Some part of me will always believe if I was a bit more charming, perhaps prettier, I could have coaxed him into having a kid with me. To bend his will to mine.

"Where are you now?" I ask him.

"Bali. Studying the flute music they use in their Gambuh performances."

"Of course you are, Yoav."

"You'd love this shit, Arabella, especially the wayang shadow plays. They're wild. Want to skip the baby-making and join me?"

Absolutely. If I were a man, I would. Spend another decade fucking about and traveling and learning and making art. But I'm a woman.

And I'm one who doesn't trust that any man, not even Yoav, could love me forever. He'd probably tell me to fuck off at some point, possibly at a time when I'm too old to have the child I have always wanted so desperately. Then, he might do that magical thing that men get to do, known as changing their mind about having kids at any age, a metamorphosis not available to me.

How badly would I feel if I gave up having a child to be with Yoav and he ditched me? And sired a baby with a younger woman? Why would it hurt me more if the phantom younger woman who has Yoav's baby after he leaves me happens also to be Jewish? I don't know. But I can't have that. I can't risk it.

So I don't answer Yoav's question. I doubt he knows the Arab saying "No answer is an answer." But he gets that if a woman doesn't immediately say "Hell yes!" when a man asks her to join him in Bali, she's probably not going to Bali.

After a moment of silence, I ask Yoav, "How's your mom?"

"Great! She's in remission. The doctors say she's officially cancer-free."

The news takes me by surprise. The woman who announced to me she was dying is alive and my mother who never breathed a word about her illness is gone.

"Mine died of cancer," I blurt out.

"What? I'm sorry, Arabella. That's terrible," he says. "I liked Naya. She was so sweet."

I had forgotten Yoav had met my mother a million times. She flew out from California to see all my shows. If I hadn't searched his mom out, I never would have met her.

"Do you know what her last words to me were? 'Have fun.' Not 'I love you' or 'You are the best daughter in the world' or any of that shit. 'Have fun.'"

"Huh. That's actually really cool, Arabella."

I recognize in that moment that it is. I also recognize, though he's too polite to bring it up again, Yoav probably has an inkling I did indeed stalk his mother in a Bloomingdale's café and lie to her about who I was. I will never in a million years admit to it. It was somehow easier to ask him to have a baby with me than to do that.

Was it because rejection is easier when you expect it?

As I had picked up the phone to call him, I sensed he'd say no and that I'd end up going to a sperm bank. When I do, I request that the kindly white female doctor select a random donor, a father for my child, for me.

"I don't care about the race of the donor," I tell her. "Race does not matter to me at all."

"That's admirable," she says, clearly taken aback. "And, I must say, rare."

Little Naya is born nine months later, a tawny beautiful baby. I feel the most whole I've ever felt when I have her strapped to my chest. I love that I can name her after my mom, not some mother-in-law or other matriarch of her father's clan, as is the tradition. I also love that when she enters school, a classroom full of American kids carrying their fathers' surnames, I have made it so I can give my daughter mine. By having her on my own and naming her as I do, I combat the different ways American and Arab cultures erase traces of a child's matriarchal line.

On the day little Naya gets her first set of shots, a series of events is set into motion. First, a movie director has a heart attack while directing his latest blockbuster, *Supergirl II*. The Actress du Jour (aka Supergirl II) demands a theatre director whom she knows from her early days on the boards be the one to finish the film. At her behest, he drops out of directing a production of *Antony and Cleopatra* at Shakespeare's Globe a day before rehearsals were set to start. Who can say no to Supergirl?

And who, my friends and fellow citizens of this world that we so uneasily share, do you think might recently have been appointed as the head of Shakespeare's Globe Theatre of London? None other than the former Associate Artistic Director of the Royal Court (aka Big Dick Almost in Charge) and my new best friend, John.

John called and offered me the job of directing *Antony and*

Cleopatra. I, who had spent a decade of summers watching the Public Theater's Shakespeare shows in Central Park while biting back tears, because I knew I was nowhere near being asked to direct there. Nor might I ever be.

Oh well. I was going to direct at a bigger and better venue in the Bard's old stomping ground. It wasn't that I had been dreaming the wrong dream. It was that I had made my dream too small, too provincial. Your fantasies can only be as worldly as you are.

I had been knocking on one gate rather than believing sometimes the universe makes you strong enough to fly over all of them. Or it makes you feel like you can, which is more important. It's what you feel you can do that gets you through the day.

I book the first flight out from San Francisco to London the next day. I'm on it now. An hour in, little Naya begins to shriek. My neighbors give me murderous glances.

"Who you looking at? Don't fuck with a New Yorker," I want to snap, but I'm not technically that anymore. I'm a theatre artist. I now know the only place artists really belong are cities where we are invited to make art, and only for as long as we are making it.

Eventually, little Naya nods off. I, like so many women who find themselves saying yes to sudden opportunities in faraway places, will have to figure out childcare after I get there. But I'm going to direct this show, even if I have to do it with an infant strapped to my chest.

I know it isn't going to change my world to work on that stage. I will eventually want a bigger one. I'll still suffer disappointment and despair. I've had several generations of bitterness baked into me. I would always believe some critics are harder on me because I'm a woman. Some won't want to root for a Palestinian chick wrestling with the best white culture has to offer, miffed that I dare to stage their tragedies as if they were comedies.

Throughout my lifetime, I'd always have to contend with people who try to convince themselves that my kind either do not exist or do not matter, and who become enraged when we prove we actually do. And probably so would my beloved little girl.

"I told my board we had to hire you," John said. "If you can make theatre like that on a microbudget under military occupation, you can do anything."

It's not true. I can't do anything. But I know how to put on a hell of a show.

No one makes a show on their own. I'll need someone to set the props, man the lights, and build the set. I'll need a sound designer. When we land, I'll call Yoav and ask if he'll be mine.

ACKNOWLEDGMENTS

I am deeply indebted to my brilliant editor, Carolyn Kelly, for lovingly bringing *Too Soon* to the world. Thanks to my fantastic agent, Mary Krienke, for her peerless advocacy and indispensable insights.

I am so appreciative of the all-star visionary team at Avid Reader Press. Rhina Garcia is a dynamite publicist in every way and Caroline McGregor made magic happen as a marketing manager. Thank you to fiction editorial director, Lauren Wein, whose advice was always spot-on and to managing editor, Allison Green, for your support. Our production editor, Jessica Chin, brought such meticulous dedication to the process. It was a pleasure to collaborate with the Art Department, Alison Forner and Clay Smith, and with Ruth Lee-Mui on the interior design. It was an incredibly lucky break to have Elizabeth Shreve, CEO of Shreve Williams Public Relations, come aboard to collaborate with our team.

I will always be grateful to the wonderful Geraldine Brooks for being my first reader and giving invaluable feedback on my initial drafts. Thanks to the Radcliffe Institute for bringing us together and enabling us to be fellows at the same time as well as to my other Radcliffe Sisters, including Eve Troutt Powell, Salem Mekuria, Tera Hunter, and Susan Terrio. I was fortunate to have Rachel Smith as my inspired teacher who cheered and coaxed me along as I brought this novel to completion. This book benefited greatly from having feedback from Charlotte Carter, Marina Johnson, Sarah Stone, Courtney Maum, and Malena Watrous at various stages.

Thanks to Francine Volpe for being the truest of friends in every way. I am grateful to Eisa Davis for showing me the meaning of solidarity. I deeply appreciate Marcus Gardley being my personal superhero and advocating for my work in so many different arenas. Thanks to Margo Jefferson for her unswerving support, and to Florencia Lozano for believing in this story and, by extension, me.

Colman and Raul Domingo are not only the most glamorous power couple I know but also the kindest. I will always cherish the drama and the magic of the New York nights we shared together, which I tried to capture and convey within these pages. Life is rarely fair and yet, when I see how the world has begun to give the pair of you some of the opportunities you deserve, I am reminded that sometimes it is.

Having a home is every artist's dream. Thank you to Ty Jones and the team at the Classical Theatre of Harlem for selecting me as their Mellon Foundation playwright-in-residence, ensuring I always have a place in New York, and producing my most wildly ambitious comedies as I developed this book. You are family.

I have had the unbelievably good fortune to have worked with some of the best theatre directors of my generation, oftentimes when they were early in their careers. As I am a writer who knows better than to dare to direct, I'm in awe of the cult-like leadership skills it takes to helm a play. I modeled the young antiheroine, Arabella, after the kind of uncompromising directors who were my collaborators, including: May Adrales, Ian Belknap, Annie Dorsen, Scott Elliott, Will Frears, Raeda Ghazaleh, the late Marion McClinton, Jessica Heidt, Ian Morgan, Matthijs Rumke, Damon Scranton, Karl Seldahl, Marisa Tomei, Takis Tzamargias, Gerhard Willert, and Tamilla Woodard. Thank you to Dr. Samer Al-Saber for both believing in the importance of Arab comedies and knowing how to make them work. Shout-out to Sam Gold, who directed my first professional production and inspired me to be a braver artist than I was ready to be. I cherished learning from all of you.

I am indebted to the esteemed artists of Al-Harah Theatre for hosting my residency at the Bethlehem Peace Center that enabled me to collaborate with several luminaries of Palestinian theatre, an endeavor that was made possible with support from the Doris Duke Foundation.

In 2002, I joined a delegation of American playwrights who traveled to the West Bank and Gaza to meet Palestinian playwrights, which was organized by the indefatigable Naomi Wallace and Connie Julian. Kia Corthron, Tony Kushner, Robert O'Hara, and Lisa Schlesinger were incredibly brave to take that journey with us and to return to America to write about what we saw together. Glimpsing my parents' homeland through their eyes changed me and I could not have written this book in the same way if I not done so.

I need to acknowledge the Palestinian American community for their early embrace of my work and my extended Ramallah family, especially Joseph Shamieh, Natalie Shamieh, Charles Shamieh, Sara Shamieh, and James Shamieh. I am indebted to Muna Hishmeh and the late Naimeh (Norma) Shami for sharing the story of their journey to America with me. Thank you to Tina Jaghab Harb and Carol Dughman, my dear cousins who made it so I never felt like I was without a sister.

All love to my incomparable parents. Thank you to my father for always making the improbable seem possible and for modeling how a gentleman of the highest order leads with kindness. My mother is the heart of our family and the best of storytellers. She brought to life the early stories of my beloved grandmothers, Badia Shamieh and Najla Ghannam, who we lost too soon. It is through her tales that I learned not only where the women of my family came from but also where we might aspire to go. Finally, I must acknowledge my husband for being my foundation and our son for being my greatest source of inspiration.

ABOUT THE AUTHOR

BETTY SHAMIEH is a Palestinian American writer and the author of fifteen plays. Her six New York play premieres include the sold-out off-Broadway runs of *Roar* and *Malvolio*, a sequel to *Twelfth Night,* which were both *New York Times* Critic's Picks. Shamieh was awarded a Guggenheim Fellowship and named a UNESCO Young Artist for Intercultural Dialogue. She is a founding artistic director of the Semitic Root, a collective that supports innovative theatre cocreated by Arab and Jewish Americans. A graduate of Harvard College and the Yale School of Drama, she divides her time between San Francisco and New York.